Moscow Moles

MOSCOW MOLES

BOOK 4 OF THE MOSCOW NIGHTS SERIES

BY BETH H. MACY

EDITED BY DORI HARRELL

Moscow Moles eBook ISBN: 979-8-9896791-9-5

Moscow Moles paperback ISBN: 979-8-9908250-0-0

Moscow Moles hardback ISBN: 979-8-9908250-1-7

Book Cover Design by ebooklaunch.com

Edited by Dori Harrell, of Breakout Editing

Interior Design by Colleen Jones, of Breakout Editing

Acknowledgments

I want to thank my partner, Chris,
who enthusiastically encouraged me
to send her daily writing snippets
and listened to me read the book out loud.
I am thankful to have back my wonderful editor,
Dori Harrell, who continues to teach me
how to be a better writer.

Chapter One

THE BUILDING SHUDDERED FROM THE NEARBY IMPACT. Charlie Burlamachi could hear the air-raid sirens warning everyone to take shelter. She blew the dust off her wristwatch and moved closer to the exit so she could scram, if necessary. Charlie knew she could run fast. She jogged and worked out daily, and at five feet eight inches tall, possessed a thirty-two-inch inseam and powerful leg muscles, so she had long strides. On top of that, being more of a sprinter than a marathoner served her well in dangerous situations such as these.

Charlie thought back to her last discussion in DC with her boss, Ed Wilson. It seemed a lifetime ago. "You're on your own in this. Yes, the United States would love to have this man eliminated. He betrayed the United States and the United Kingdom, and he helped set up Tosh's and Elda's teams for the assassins in Operation Bittman. And now he's working with the Russians against Ukraine. Having said that, we're *not* sanctioned to assassinate him, especially with the oversight we're receiving from Congress in our Ukrainian involvement. But . . . should he die accidentally while being politely questioned for intelligence . . ."

Had it been only a half hour since she'd eliminated the traitor? The ground beneath her feet shook. Another bomb, nearer this time. She brushed the dust out of her short hair. She should probably should wear a helmet. Not standard issue for a spy though. Some days she missed the military.

Charlie hoped her contact would arrive before the drones blew the building up. She tapped her watch. Where was he, and could she trust him?

The engine coughed and sputtered. In her dark confines of the trunk, Charlie felt the car decelerate. She shifted and was rewarded with a hamstring cramp. Damn, she couldn't reach it. The cramp traveled upward, grabbing her butt muscle in a vise. She gritted her teeth against the pain and breathed as deeply as she could, inhaling the road dust seeping into the trunk. She stifled a cough, not knowing where she was and who might be around.

The trunk opened and light streamed in, temporarily blinding her. After nearly seven hours in the dark, her eyes struggled to adjust. She sensed, more than saw, a tobacco-scented hand reach in, and she grasped it, praying the person it belonged to was friend and not foe. His grip was warm and firm. She perched on the edge of the trunk, rubbing her legs, pushing blood into them so she could stand. The hand materialized in front of her eyes again, holding a pair of plastic sunglasses. She stood, put them on, and squinted up at a tall, bearded stranger.

"Who are you?" she asked, dizzy and disorientated.

"It's best we don't exchange names," he countered, his voice gruff. He held out a soiled packet containing identification papers and money.

Charlie shook her head to orient herself and took the offerings.

He gestured up the road. "You are not far from Lviv. You can catch a train from Lviv into Poland. In your packet is a letter to expedite your crossing. We're grateful you removed the traitor. He sold both Ukrainian and American secrets to the Russians. But if the Russians catch you, we will disavow any knowledge of you. Understand?"

Charlie gave a curt nod.

He offered her a well-worn canvas backpack. "We cannot supply you with weapons. Inside is a change of clothing and a toiletry case, including a razor and a single-edge razor blade. If captured, you can always cut your wrists. Good luck." The man climbed into the passenger side of the car and drove back toward Kyiv.

Glancing right and left to make certain no one was around, she ran to the side of the road and bent over the ditch. She pawed through the backpack and located the razor, which she used to shave the back and sides of her head. She used the single-edge blade to shorten the top. Short hair was much easier to care for. Not to mention that her mentor, Elda, had stressed long hair was a liability for an operative. A buzz cut made disguises much easier. Just add a wig or a cap. Charlie forced herself to stop musing and focus on the immediate need to get out of that area.

To guarantee there would be no trace of her, she buried the small amount of light-brown hair clippings in the dirt. She found an old dark-blue watch cap in the pack and pulled it down over her ears. Removing her jacket, she pulled on a bulky sweatshirt over her T-shirt. Finding a spare pair of socks, she doubled them up and inserted them in her boots, under her heels, to give her more height. She hoped all the changes would fool anyone who might be looking for her. Muscular with broad shoulders, Charlie *could* pass for a small man.

She squatted and leafed through the papers. She inserted the money into the left front pocket of her jeans and the letter into the right. She opened her European passport and impressed on her memory the details. She read a small piece of paper and memorized the number and address of her next contact and then popped the paper into her mouth. *Pretend it's a steak, Charlie.*

Charlie stared into the compact muzzle of a Russian-made SR2-Versk submachine gun. She clinically noted the weapon had the larger magazine inserted, which could mean up to thirty rounds, and the stock was folded up. Lightweight and small, weighing in empty at about three and a half pounds, it could be easily carried or stashed into a backpack.

She observed the scene as if a third person and noted she was more curious than afraid. The man holding the firearm casually cradled it with one hand. Good. These were not professionals. And from the sour smell wafting her way in the breeze, the man holding the SR2 had not been near soap and water for a long time.

"*Kto ty!*" he barked.

That's Russian. Think. What was her identity? She cleared her throat and lowered her voice. "Jack Williams, from Canada. I'm reporting on the war." She held out her papers, the card with PRESS on top. She scanned past him to inspect two men in camouflage leaning against a dusty, battered Jeep that had seen better days. Three against one and her without a weapon. Not good odds.

The first man signaled for Charlie to wait and took her papers to confer with the other two. While his back was turned and the other two men distracted, Charlie moved the majority of the money from her from her front pocket to her rear one and palmed a note.

He returned and snatched the pack from Charlie.

She prayed he wouldn't search her and discover she wasn't a man. She held out a hundred-dollar bill. She hoped he didn't notice her eyelid twitching. To calm herself, she inhaled into her abdominals and practiced the Relaxation Response technique Elda had taught her.

He grabbed the money and stashed it in a packet, then performed a cursory search of the backpack. Grunting, he tossed it to her and motioned for her to move on. She pointed at the papers in his hand. He didn't move. She reached into her left pocket and took out the remaining money, pulling the empty pocket inside out as she did. He took and counted the money and shook his head.

Sigh. Here goes nothing.

Charlie seized him by his beard and head butted his nose, resulting in a satisfying snap. As he cupped his nose, she snatched his weapon. Using him as a shield, she shot the other two, who'd raised their weapons to fire. She cracked the man with the broken nose on the side of his head with his weapon. He went down hard. Charlie searched for a pulse and found none.

Cautiously approaching the others, she confirmed they were dead too. She searched all three bodies and pocketed their IDs and car keys. She examined the surrounding territory to verify it was deserted and sprang into the retrofitted Jeep. It was a long way to Poland, and this vehicle could be put to good use by the Ukrainians.

She left a cloud of dust behind her as she sped up the road to freedom.

A loud explosion shook the building. Pieces of ceiling bounced off Anatoly Petrov's solidly built back. A shard caught his cheek and drew blood. He rubbed it off on the back of his sleeve. He kicked his boot through the wreckage on the floor, his blue eyes scanning the room. Dead bodies in various stages of decomposition lay scattered about outside the building. He had applied Vicks VapoRub to the inside of his nose to mute the smell of death.

Aga! There's something. He spotted part of a hand through the debris on the floor.

Anatoly cleared the rubble to one side and dispassionately considered the body. He kicked it and got no response. Someone had put a bullet hole in the traitor's forehead. Anatoly squatted and examined the wound more closely. Definitely the work of a professional. But who'd gotten here before he'd arrived?

The Ukrainian air sirens sounded loudly. Dust and building bits sprinkled onto his head, a few pieces sticking in his blond buzz cut. He shook it off impatiently. Anatoly searched the body, finding only Russian money, which he pocketed. He clicked a photo of the man's face and took a fingerprint kit out of his pocket and copied the victim's prints. The corpse's hands felt cold and clammy, but rigor mortis had not yet set in. The kill was recent.

Anatoly surveyed for evidence of another person having been here. The wreckage remains were too neatly arranged over the body, but he didn't detect any footsteps in the dust. He scanned inch by inch. *Vot!* A partial tread! He measured the impression with his hand. Standing, he rubbed the top of his head, the familiar feeling of his buzz cut somehow stimulating his thinking. A small man or a woman. Combat boots.

Satisfied he'd discovered all the evidence he could, Anatoly erased all traces of his own visit and the partial footprint of the other assassin. He disappeared into the night, his way illuminated by drones being blown up in the sky.

After clearing away the wreckage, Nyoka Morozov evaluated the corpse and the single bullet hole in his forehead. A bomb rattled the building and deposited dust in her long black hair. Removing her black gloves, she brushed the dust out, her red-polished, pointed nails separating the strands of her hair. She breathed in the nectar of fresh death.

Inspecting the area, Nyoka saw no traces of anyone having been in the room, but the debris seemed strewn too orderly. She searched the body, but the pockets were empty. She whirled around as a Ukrainian soldier entered. She drew her Makarov pistol and blasted the man. He fell over, gagging and gushing blood from his throat. With a blank expression, she watched him thrash and become still. With gloved hands, she took his Makarov PM pistol. Good choice of pistol. She positioned the barrel against the bullet hole in the corpse and fired. Returning to the soldier, she wrapped his fingers around the metal trigger and mahogany plastic grip. She knelt by him. "You died a hero. This man betrayed your country."

She smiled, displaying sharply tapered canines, as she inspected the scene once more. She needed to find the assassin who'd been here before her, find out what he knew, and slay him.

Chapter Two

I T WAS A DANK AND BLUSTERY DAY along the Thames. The nine-story green-and-cream MI6 complex stood out against the cloudy sky. The moats around the building lent a sinister feeling to the area.

An older gentleman with a cane stumbled on the sidewalk near the building and fell into an employee leaving MI6. "So sorry." The old gent held on to the other man to steady himself.

The younger man wrinkled his forehead and scowled. "You all right, g'vnor?"

The man with the cane licked his lips and replied in a quivering voice, "Not to worry. Just a tad wobbly at this age. Please excuse me." He patted the man on his arm and stumbled on, turning to watch the MI6 employee walk away. Ensuring no one saw him, he glanced down at the badge in his cupped hand. TREACHER WALKER. Same security access level as Sophia. Perfect.

Treacher strode off to the Underground, and a well-disguised Tosh Chelovek carried on into the building, swiping himself into the elevator and down to a restricted sector. Tosh paraded through the zone to a cubicle displaying the name tag Sophia Brown. He slipped into the cubicle and photographed all in it, including the mug shot under her keyboard. Her laptop was gone. Knowing Sophia, probably it was locked away for the night. As he departed without leaving a trace, he texted, Leaving now. Erase video.

Stepping out the door, he dropped the badge from his gloved hand and disappeared into the night.

The custodian wheeled his cart through the silent halls of the building in DC, unlocking and entering offices. With swift, practiced moves, he emptied the trash cans. His keys jingled from his waistband, and his beige coveralls were stained at the knees and cuffs. He wore a cap low on his forehead and blue rubber gloves. He guided his cart into a storeroom and closed and locked the door. He walked to the back wall of the closet and unscrewed a large vent. He pulled his cart in front of it, leaving enough room to enter the duct and pull the vent grate up, loosely securing it behind him. He snaked himself up and over the poorly built fire wall between the two buildings and found himself staring through another grate into a room similar to the one he'd left.

Reaching into his side pocket, he pulled out a flexible ratcheting screwdriver, extracted the four screws holding the vent in place, and settled it to one side. Jumping out, he secured the vent with one screw and padded to the door. He held a cup-like device against the door and inserted two earbuds into his ears.

No sounds.

Satisfied, he exited and jogged down the hallway, stopping at a door with a plaque identifying the office: Ed Wilson. He rapidly picked the lock and slipped inside. He noted it the room was tidy, except for some crumpled papers lying around the wastebasket, which had a basketball hoop on its top.

He still misses the basket. A wave of nostalgia washed over the intruder. Shaking it away, he unscrewed the plate covering the outlet for the electricity and cable wires. He snapped a device onto the internet cable and replaced the cover. Next he stuck what appeared to be a chewed-up wad of gum under the front of Ed's desk. Hopefully, the Americans hadn't cracked this technology yet. Job done, he relocked the door and scooted back over the fire wall to the custodian room. He had just secured the vent, when the door opened. He froze, breathing with shallow, slow breaths.

Identified as the floor janitor by his name tag, the intruder entered, whistling a nameless tune. He hesitated, staring at his cart. "Did I leave that over there?" Shaking his head, he retrieved the cart. "Getting sloppy, old man." Humming, he exited the closet with his cart, locking the door behind.

The custodian took a long, full breath, backed into the duct, and cut a hole into the metal. Bending back a piece, he located the electrical wiring and, careful not to touch the live wires with bare skin, spliced an extension in. He connected the new wire to a small device, which he set at the bottom of the electrical conduit, to receive and transmit undetected. He bent the metal back into place and covered the cut edges with silver tape.

Cleaning up any stray bits of wire covering, Elda, the imposter janitor, finished her trek through and out the ducts. Back in the first closet, she retrieved a hidden sack of clothing and changed.

A short man in worn blue jeans, Red Sox baseball cap, black hoodie, and neon-orange running shoes left the building and jogged to the metro.

Exhausted from her trip, Charlie trudged into Ed Wilson's DC office. Each time she visited, she was struck by the stark neatness of it. The only discordant region was the wastebasket with a basketball hoop on top of it and crumpled papers scattered about.

"I wasn't expecting you so soon." Ed picked up some papers from around the trash can.

Charlie's denim jacket, hanging from one hand, hiking boots, casual T-shirt, and khaki pants contrasted with Ed's ironed white button-down shirt and blue tie. His suit coat hung neatly on a hanger on the back of his office door. His suit pants were crisply pressed, and his black Corfram shoes shone in the office overhead lights. Charlie rubbed her hand over the stubble growing out on her head and assumed the military at-rest position, waiting to give her report.

Ed set down the file folder he held and turned to Charlie. He gestured to the coffee urn in the corner. "Help yourself."

"Thank you, sir." Charlie strode to the coffee. "May I pour you one?"

"Yes, please. And it's Ed, Charlie."

Charlie poured two cups of coffee.

Ed put in his order. "Black, please."

Charlie passed him his cup and poured cream into hers. She shut her eyes and drank in the aroma. Opening them, she caught Ed smiling at her, and she blushed. "There weren't any opportunities to obtain a decent cup of coffee over there, sir." Damn. She hated blushing! She had to control that reaction. *Do not let anyone, friend or foe, see your feelings.*

"Please, *Ed*," he reminded her.

"Ed." Charlie chewed her bottom lip. This was not at all comfortable. He was her superior.

"Congratulations on a job well done, Charlie. I read

your handwritten report. Do you have anything to add?"

Ed's question seemed innocent, and his face was open and accepting, but Charlie's muscles tensed. She felt as if she'd fucked up by doing away with the guy before she'd had all the intel . . . Charlie braced herself for his criticism and shook her head. "No, sir. I searched the body and found only an ID, which I included with the report, and some Russian money, which I left. It was a clean kill, and I left the body under rubble. There should be no way to trace it back to us."

"Excellent. Did you extract any details from him?"

Charlie gazed down at her feet and scuffed one foot back and forth. Damn, there it was. The nub of the debrief. She took a sizable breath and exhaled loudly. She looked straight back at Ed. "Only a bit, sir. I'm afraid he wanted death by cop, and I obliged. I had him cornered, and he taunted me . . . 'You'll never find all of us. We are everywhere.'

"I laughed at him and told him, 'We know who you are and where you are.'

"He retorted, 'So you think because you got James and Alexei, you got the tree by its roots, but you're only raking up the leaves. Ask yourself, Who ran them?'

"He rushed at me with a dagger. I fired to kill. In hindsight I should have tried to wound and torture him for more information. But in reality, I didn't have any time for that, even if I had thought of it. I had to adhere to a fixed extraction place and time."

Ed held up his hand. "No regrets, Charlie. You did well. Finding him in the first place was a long shot. Eliminating him was of higher priority than obtaining the material. You got enough to prove our instincts right. There are more moles to be found in the United States and Russia."

Characteristically hard on herself, Charlie shook her head in disagreement. "*No*, I should have done more. Next time I will do better." Charlie paused. "Sir . . ."

"Ed."

"Ed. Calling you by your first name will take me a while, sir. You're my boss." She hesitated. "May I talk frankly?"

Ed tensed, frowned. "Of course. Always. What is it?"

Interesting. His facial expression, words, and tone didn't match. Charlie wished Elda were here. She'd be able to put a finger on it. "I'm aware everyone's moved on, but my gut says Elda is still alive somewhere. I would like to work on finding her. In my spare time, of course."

Ed scowled. His eyes narrowed. He put his hand on his chin and inspected Charlie. "I gave you *two* months off to try and find Elda and Tosh. You traveled throughout Europe and even made a unsanctioned foray into Russia and came up empty handed. What makes you think you would come up with different results now?"

Charlie fell out of her military position and gazed at her feet while scratching her head. She had no real evidence. She stood tall and bored her deep-blue eyes into Ed's dark-brown ones. "I just know, sir."

Ed shook his head a few times. His eyebrows knitted together. "Sorry, Charlie. Elda was a friend as well as my employee. I wish it were true, but we exhausted our efforts. It's time to leave the past behind. That last job was the final one of our off-books missions for now." Ed picked up Charlie's report, crumpled it page by page, tossing each one into his wastebasket. He lobbed a lit match in and turned on the air purifier to remove any traces of smoke. "There. The past is gone." He skipped by any protests. "I have a new assignment for you."

Feeling unheard, Charlie scowled at Ed. If he was truly Elda's friend, he would not be giving up. Charlie set her jaw.

Ed sighed. "You can work on your own projects, *if* you have any spare time, and use our resources to research any leads. Even so, you must keep me in the loop if you find anything. That's the best I can do."

Charlie nodded, acknowledging Ed's position. "What's my new assignment?"

"We have numerous new DOS attacks on hospitals and energy plants. We also discovered various identity-theft scams ongoing, targeting government personnel. I assigned Ashok Bhatt to ferret out where these are coming from, but I would like you to liaison to the CIA anti-cyberterrorists on an ongoing basis to retrieve what intelligence they have."

"Can't we just ask them for it?"

Ed lifted an eyebrow.

Charlie figured it out. "So they're not being forthcoming, hey? And you would like someone on the inside to attempt to suss out what they're not telling us. And it can't be Ashok because they'd view him with his technical knowledge and computer skills as a threat. But a dumb female grunt is less of one."

"Exactly."

———

Every bone in his body screamed for him to turn around and help Charlie. A short man in worn blue jeans, Red Sox baseball cap, black hoodie, and neon-orange running shoes jogged down the street in DC, Beats Studio Pro wireless headphones on his head. He had spotted Charlie walking into the building he had just left, so decided to test the bug in Ed's office before catching his plane to Italy. It was so clear Charlie needed additional mentoring.

Although he felt sure his disguise was good, every minute spent in the United States risked exposure. And he definitely had been captured by the building's exterior security cameras. He grabbed his red canvas pack from his back and popped into a stall in a nearby café rest room.

An older man with a pudgy pocked face, slightly hooked nose, gray scraggly hair, and a rumpled suit walked out of the bathroom. The man appeared taller than the previous one and walked with a noticeable limp. He was carrying a black canvas pack. He wore hearing aids, carried a wooden cane, and sported black leather shoes. His contact lenses changed the color of his eyes as well as his biometric reading. His fingertips were covered by a thin film that matched the fingerprints for the ID he was carrying.

He limped to the curb and held up his hand for a cab. "Where to, mister?"

"Dulles International, Alitalia departures."

***

Charlie braced herself for her first meeting with Frank Garcia. Frank headed up the CIA anti-terrorist information group. Chauvinistic, with an abrasive personality, Frank had worked hard to get to his present level of respective incompetence. He had been successful at his previous jobs, requiring less knowledge and skills, but was now over his head.

"Charlie . . . Is *that* your real name?" Frank Garcia sneered.

Charlie winced inside. She hoped she could finish this job quickly. Frank had intercepted her on the way to his office and now stood in an open area surrounded by gray cubicles. The gray wall-to-wall carpeting looked as if it had seen better days. A hum of voices on phone calls and clattering of keyboards emanated from the workspaces. The smell of coffee wafted over from the break room. One fluorescent light buzzed and flickered in preparation for burning out.

Silence. Not taking the bait, her face impassive, Charlie

waited for Frank to finish expressing his discontent.

Glowering, Frank eyeballed the paperwork Charlie provided him. "Jesus! They want you to work with me. What do you know about cyberterrorism?"

Charlie shrugged. She looked at him with dead eyes. Best not to give the man any ammo. He'd obviously disliked her on sight. Hopefully, she wouldn't have to work with him more than a few days.

Frank grunted and designated a small desk in the corner by the exit. "You can work there. Settle in and meet me in my office in ten minutes." He stormed away.

As Frank passed another employee, Charlie overheard his complaint. "Jesus, Joe. They sent some freak to work with me. I don't know what agency she's from or why she's here. She better be cautious though. There's a lot of flights to those stairs by her station."

Charlie marched to her desk with Joe's laughter echoing in her ears.

CHAPTER THREE

THE UNMISTAKABLE PURR OF A WELL-MAINTAINED VESPA approached the house and stopped in a cloud of dust in the driveway. The yellow-ocher plaster-and-stone Tuscan villa stood by itself on a hill overlooking the panoramic views of the rolling green and raw sienna-brown countryside, dotted with olive groves and Mediterranean cypress trees. The sun shone off the terra-cotta brick roof. The odors of olive, combined with rosemary, sage, and tarragon, wafted in on the dry, gentle breeze.

Olga Sokolov hopped off her dark-blue Vespa and bounced with joyful anticipation to the door. Her months of research and calling in favors for access to paper and online records were finally paying off.

Standing at the door, she held up her hands and turned 360 degrees to show she had no obvious weapons. Olga didn't need weapons. Although a gentle giant—squarely built with a wide freckled face and high cheekbones—she was strong enough to kill with her bare hands. Her dark-brown eyes mirrored her internal emotions, and right now they sparkled with happiness. She could not wait to see the look on the occupants' faces. She removed her helmet, and her short, unruly chestnut, with blond tips, hair stuck out at all angles.

She looked at the shoe mat to the side of the doorway and saw two pairs of well-worn, dusty jogging shoes, one pair a woman's 8.5 and the other, a man's 10.5. Olga knew her athletic gear well, and this sight helped verify she was in the right location.

An umber-brown eye peeped through the spyhole, and then a gray one. Olga detected the mumbling of a conversation within. She tapped her foot and rolled her eyes but otherwise stood still, with her arms out and away from her body.

The door flew open, and a short salt-and-pepper-haired woman smothered Olga in hugs. The hugger drew back. "Wait! How did you find us?"

* * *

"Who is this woman? And why is she here?" Tosh barked to Elda.

Although a slender man, at five foot ten inches, Tosh stood a half a foot taller than Elda. A deadly Russian spy, he'd played cat and mouse with Elda since the Cold War. His steely gray eyes bored into Elda's dark-brown ones.

Elda stood her ground calmly. She and Tosh had lived in the same villa together for months now. She understood he did not like surprises. And this was a big one. She had to help him see how good this was.

Her stomach clenched. *Is it good?*

Olga's eyes narrowed, and she moved on a line to intercept Tosh's path toward Elda.

Elda held up her hand and motioned for Olga to stand down. "Let's all go inside to talk."

Tosh reluctantly led the two women indoors. Once in, he turned to Elda. "Well? Are you back to not telling me things? We're a couple now, you realize? Two dead people stick together."

Her eyes watering with humor at his statement, Elda exhaled and ran her hand through her curly salt-and-pepper hair. "Hold on, Tosh. Stay with me." She chortled. "I'm sure this will all become clear." Her stomach relaxed. She knew she could rely on Tosh and Olga.

Tosh snorted and took a full breath. He snatched his cuff to check his blood pressure.

Elda waited.

He nodded that he was okay. "Did you invite her here without asking me?"

"*Of course* I didn't do that, Tosh."

Hands on hips, he glared at Elda.

Elda massaged her temples. Her head pounded.

Olga piped up in a thick Russian-accented voice. "My God, you two are like an old married couple. Stop the bickering. No one invited Olga. Although *someone* should have."

Elda stood in the dining room, staring at the stone walls, wondering how to defuse Tosh. She took three abdominal breaths before motioning the other two to sit at the long table.

Tosh set his jaw and shook his head.

Olga elevated an eyebrow, took a chair, turned it sideways, and sat. She ran her hand over the well-polished cherry table as she sat, eyes glued to the scene in front of her.

"All right, don't sit." Elda turned her head in both directions and rubbed her neck. She massaged her jaw before clarifying, "Olga is a loyal friend. She supported me off the grid for many years. Olga possesses many useful and unique skills. She's been part of my private army. I don't understand how she found us or why she's here, but I trust her implicitly."

Olga cleared her throat. "Olga is here, you know. You can talk to Olga."

Elda turned to Olga and inquired, "Why are you here, Olga?"

"You need Olga. And you need to be undead. Our Russian friends are up to no good."

Tosh raised his eyes to the arched terra-cotta ceiling and took a deep breath. Elda put her hand on his arm and was heartened he didn't shake it off. They turned to Olga and queried in unison, "How on earth did you find us?"

Olga tapped the side of her nose.

Elda rubbed her forehead and grimaced. "Olga, we are going to need to know. If one person can find us, others may be able to."

Tosh felt his pulse. "I can't concentrate. I need to clear my head. This is too much after being nonoperational and isolated for so long."

"I can wait." Olga put her feet up on the table.

"Then I'm going for a run," Tosh declared.

It might be a good idea if Elda went with him. "May I come with you?"

"I'll run your ass off," Tosh challenged.

Olga waved them on. "Go. Olga needs to shower. Can Olga use yours?"

"*Chert*," Tosh swore and ran out the door.

Elda dashed out after him.

———

Panting, they ran side by side up the hill. At the top, Tosh turned to Elda. "Does she work for you?"

Taken aback, Elda blurted, "Olga? No, no. You will

find, as you know her more, Olga is a free spirit."

The two faced each other, arms on hips, standing silhouetted against the backdrop of the rolling Tuscan hills.

"Who do *you* work for, Elda?"

"Myself." Elda grinned and shrugged. She brought her hand up to her chin and held her other arm across her waist, supporting the first. She felt amused that Tosh still sparred with her and delved for facts about her and her history.

Tosh stamped his foot. "Damn it, Elda. You know what I mean."

Trying not to anger him more, Elda kept her voice even. "I *do*, Tosh. There are some things that we just cannot share. You *know* that."

"What does it matter if we're both dead and no longer working for our agencies?"

"Our current situation and relationship may not always be the case. Answer me this—when we first met, what did you do?" Elda parried.

"I was a student at the university. And what did you do?"

"I taught mathematics," Elda deadpanned.

"Touché."

The two shook hands.

They ran back to the villa in silence. The only sounds were their shoes crunching on the dirt road and their lungs gasping for breath as one tried to outrun the other.

Thud. Olga smiled at Tosh's attempt to slam the heavy door.

Tosh slung the large wooden door again, which swung shut with a near-silent click. "How did you find us, Olga?" he demanded, nostrils flaring.

Olga, drinking a steaming cup of tea, her feet on the

hassock, enjoyed the puzzled looks on Elda's and Tosh's faces. Instead of replying, Olga lowered her cup to the coaster on the nearby side table, rose, and bounced to the wall on the opposite side of the room. Humming tunelessly, she studied the charts Elda and Tosh had posted. With her forefinger, she traced the strings connecting one picture to another in a giant relationship graph. She examined the timeline charts. She tapped on the causal graph and indicated her approval.

Finally, Olga turned to them. "Don't worry. Olga covered her tracks. And yours. No need to move. You did an excellent job hiding your identity when you bought this villa. I doubt anyone else could have recognized the meaning behind the names *Dean Roman* and *Turka Getup*. And if they could, the records of your sale have now been lost in a fire."

Olga reached into her backpack and presented Elda a manila folder with the sale records in it. "*Vot*. Now you have all the paperwork."

"Who *are* you?" Tosh asked, bewilderment written on his face.

Olga held out her hand to Tosh. "Olga."

Tosh flung his hands in the air. "Obviously a friend of Elda's."

Elda held her hand over her mouth, her eyes sparkling and body shaking with apparent laughter.

"*How* did you find us, Olga?" Tosh entreated.

"Olga knows everything." Olga sat back in her chair and sipped her tea.

Elda turned to Olga. "I'm sorry, Olga, that I didn't tell you I was alive or where I was. It was too big a risk. So please do tell me how you found us."

Olga shook her finger at Elda. "Yes, you should have told Olga. I can always help you. You did a brilliant job of faking your deaths. You left a lot of blood behind . . . How *did* you do that?"

Elda waved her hand in a dismissive gesture. "Oh, that was easy. Tosh and I had been secretly communicating over ways to find the moles without our governments intervening. We determined we couldn't find the plants while working for our agencies, but we couldn't see any graceful way to leave and not be monitored for the rest of our lives. So we had to die. Accordingly, we stashed a couple of liters of blood over time and hid the bags under our clothing for our final standoff."

Olga nodded. Her eyes brightened. "That was very good."

"And *now* you tell how you found us," Elda demanded in a stern schoolteacher's voice.

Olga grinned broadly. "Where would be the most obvious place you two would go, hey? Italy, of course. But since *that* was obvious, everyone decided you wouldn't go there. Except Charlie. Charlie scoured Tuscany for you. Olga listened to all going on in the searches. Olga has many eyes and ears, you know? It is said even Santa doesn't know as much as Olga."

Elda laughed at Olga's old joke. Tosh's eyes crinkled in amusement.

"So, Tosh, you *like* Olga," Olga ribbed.

Tosh scowled.

Olga beamed back at him. "So since Italy was obvious and you wouldn't go there, obviously Italy would be the place you'd go, and by the same logic, Tuscany. Charlie is capable, but there are things about Elda she doesn't know. Olga knows." She tapped the side of her nose.

Elda grinned at Olga's familiar line.

Tosh leaned forward in his chair. "And . . ."

"Everyone uses what they have knowledge of. Elda is a personal trainer. As am I," pronounced Olga, with pride. "I figured Elda would leave a . . . what do you call them?

Kroshki pechen'ya . . . Ah, cookie crumb?"

"Breadcrumb," Elda corrected.

Tosh lifted his eyebrow.

Olga stuck her finger in her mouth and pantomimed throwing up. "Ugh. Cookies are much better. Anyway, these crumbs would be for the right people to find her. Elda knew it would take a couple of months for the official search to be dropped and only her allies would continue searching for her after that time. The names she chose were ones that would resonate with a personal trainer, not a military person or a spy."

Elda's lips quivered, and her eyes filled with mirth.

"So, Elda, you left these tasty crumbs for Olga!" She plopped herself back in her chair and took a gulp of her now cooler tea. "Do we have cookies?" Humming, she popped up and stalked off to raid the kitchen.

CHAPTER FOUR

"**D**ON'T JUST STAND THERE, ANATOLY, COME IN."

"Have you swept the office today, Snezhana?"

Anatoly's muscular body filled Snezhana Chelovek's office doorway. A comforting smell of aged wood emanated from the old oak floors in the well-organized and clean office. Wooden file cabinets containing Tosh's papers, and now theirs, stood to one side.

Snezhana rolled her eyes. "Of course the office is bug-free, Anatoly. As the general director and senior partner, I handle all the administrative tasks for our business, while you go galivanting off into the field. Trust that I know what I'm doing. Now, come in. I need to hear more about what happened in Ukraine."

"*Da.*" He stepped over the threshold and scanned the room for danger.

"Who do you think got there first, Anatoly?" Snezhana motioned for Anatoly to shut the office door.

Snezhana smoothed her black slacks over her long muscular legs and checked to ensure her white silk button-up shirt was securely tucked in at her slender waist. Perched behind her shiny mahogany desk, she motioned for Anatoly to sit in front of the desk on the beige two-person sofa. He sat on the edge of his seat, his feet firmly planted at the ready.

The sign on the open office door broadcasted, in block letters, Toshchiy Chastnyye Detektivy. A dirty window behind Snezhana commanded a view of a parking lot surrounded by buildings that had seen better days. This was not the high-rent area of Moscow.

Anatoly pounded his leg with his fist and growled. "I don't know, Snezhana, but I was robbed of the joy of disposing of the man."

Snezhana picked up a mug shot from her desk and compared it to the picture Anatoly had taken of the corpse in the Ukraine. She was proud of her ability to identify and match faces. It equaled, if not surpassed, any software. Only her uncle, Tosh Chelovek, was better than she. *Identical.* She dropped both likenesses on her desk. "They are the same person. We will have to inform Sophia Brown her lead is dead." She blinked her blue eyes a few times while thinking of the next steps. "Let's upload the prints to Sophia, which will verify the death for her, and perhaps she can come up with more background from them."

Head hanging, with his large hands resting, fists clenched, on his thick thighs, Anatoly regarded the untouched *soknichi* on the table in front of him. "*Der'mo.* I don't have a clue where to look next, Snezhana. They betrayed us and caused us to lose our jobs. They are the reason Tosh and Elda are dead. This dead man was the only path we had to the remaining moles in the Kremlin, MI6, and America. Can we also ask Sophia if she discovered anything more for us to follow?"

"Have you thought through, Anatoly, that by following this trail, we may discover Tosh's body? It's rather comforting at times to believe he may be alive."

"Chert, Snezhana. Stop that. He's dead!" Anatoly slammed his fist into the table in front of him. His guns clattered on the wood. "If I can get my hands on a live one, I will squeeze out the scoop on how many are still remaining. I'm itching to kill someone." Anatoly reached into his well-traveled black leather weapons kit and laid out his pistols on the table in front of him. He placed his 9mm PYa beside his Makarov, flanked on the other side by his MP-412 REX .357 Magnum revolver. He fondly stroked the .357 Magnum, his favorite.

Snezhana played with her short tawny ponytail, tied up with an elastic. Her fingers repeatedly slipped off the end and downward, in memory of what was once there. "I appreciated Sophia sending us this. She gave us a free one. Of course, she does not have the same luxury we have, to drop everything and follow a lead. But we do owe her. Therefore, I want to give her some data in return." Snezhana twirled in her chair as she thought.

Anatoly ground his teeth. A vein popped out on the side of his neck. "*Der'mo*, Snezhana! Stop that! You're making me dizzy." He reached into his bag and added to the collection in front of him—an MSS Vul silent pistol and his NRS-2 survival knife, with a single-shot pistol round hidden in the hilt.

Snezhana stopped spinning. "Did you look under the corpse's nails or behind his ears to see if he had been injected with anything before they terminated him?"

Anatoly walloped his thigh with his fist. "*Der'mo*. I'm an assassin. I'm not a forensic scientist. The hole in his forehead seemed to be the obvious cause of death. And there were a lot of bombs going off." He grinned sheepishly. "I never thought of that."

Snezhana nodded. "Don't worry about it. Sophia told us he was ex-CIA turned mercenary and had spied for

James. As we are aware, James was a Kremlin mole. So perhaps this man may have possessed some intel on James's contacts. And if I'm thinking that, whoever went after him may also be thinking that way. Either they eliminated him because he was a potential leak or because they desired his intelligence."

Anatoly snorted. "What's next?" He reached into the bag again and drew out a collection of knives, from switchblades to skinny stilettos. He favored the one he could release from a firing mechanism strapped on the inside of his wrist. He held it up. "This one should have killed Aurelio."

He pulled out a push dagger and a scalpel, followed by a Karambit knife and knives for combat and throwing.

Snezhana watched him stroke each one "Are you thinking of the day that Elda gave you those weapons?"

"Da." Anatoly threw a knife at the wall behind Snezhana.

Snezhana swiveled, pulled the knife out of the wall, and tossed it, landing point first, in the floor by Anatoly's feet. "Don't make this dump any worse than it is."

Anatoly snorted again and put the knives away. "So what do we do now?"

Snezhana twirled in her chair again. "I'm not sure. I wish Tosh or Elda were here."

Anatoly slammed his fist into his thigh. "*Der'mo*, Snezhana. Stop that twirling. And Elda and Tosh are dead. We looked everywhere for them."

Snezhana examined her fingernails and sniffled. "I know."

⌣

Elda breathed in the familiar smell of Tuscany and let its comfort touch her heavy heart. The sun shone, illuminating the living room and reflecting warmth from the yellow walls. The embers from the fire Tosh had built earlier had taken the night's chill away. Elda, basking in the relaxing morning, turned to Tosh. "Did you learn to make fires in the Young Pioneers?" She took a large sip of her coffee.

"My father was a pyromaniac," Tosh deadpanned.

Elda sputtered in delight, and the coffee flew into her nose. Tosh handed her a napkin.

"Damn you, Tosh." It was a pure gold, but fleeting, moment. Her smile disappeared. She rarely laughed anymore. The sadness crept back in. She missed Vee. Tuscany was beautiful, but she longed for the sound of the ocean waves. She felt the need to get moving and be an operative again.

Olga jogged in from the kitchen. "I will go shopping. You need more food here." She stopped and touched Elda's face. "Elda, you are not happy? Why?"

Elda brushed Olga's hand away. The kindness threatened to open the floodgates of emotions. "It's nothing big, Olga. I miss Vee. She's the only thing I left behind that is so important to me." Elda exhaled and gave a weak smile. "But we must go on."

"You need to move. You are becoming complacent and weak. Motion is lotion for the emotions. It will cheer you up."

"You're right, Olga. We need to get going." Elda stood and stretched. It was time to sharpen mentally and physically.

Olga trotted over to Tosh and massaged his slender arm. "You need more muscles, *toshchiy muzhchina*. Olga build you up."

Elda grinned at the frown on Tosh's face and at Olga's familiar antics.

Tosh slapped at her hand. Olga guffawed and danced away. She stopped and traced the chart on the wall. Strings ran from one name to the next, with hubs and spokes radiating outward. She chuckled. "This is like Shane's chart from the *L Word*."

"Olga, how are you aware of that television series?" Elda asked. Olga's knowledge and connections always amazed her. She wouldn't be surprised if Olga knew the show's producers.

"Olga knows everything," Olga announced, beaming. "But we are off topic. Look at the chart. James Richardson at one hub, with Henry Davies, Arabella Johnson, Nigel Davies, Angelina Rodin, and various bit players, like that dude from the Russian Embassy in DC and the MI6 janitor. Alexei Alexeev off to one side, with a tie-in to Adrik Lebedev. There's a big card with *SENATORS?* on it."

Elda felt her very being wake up from the inactivity. Her brain cranked like an old Model T Ford as it struggled to get ahead of where Olga was leading them.

Olga referred to a picture off to one side. "Who is this man?"

Tosh shrugged. "We're not sure. I popped over to the UK and did a nighttime raid of Sophia Brown's office and found this photo under her keyboard. We think he had something to do with James, and if so, potentially with Operation Bittman."

Elda slammed her fist into the palm of her other hand. Damn that man. He was always taking risks. He could have been captured. "MI6? So that's where you went while I was in DC!" Elda burst out. "Damn it, Tosh! You could have been discovered." It struck her with surprise that she cared about him as a friend would.

Tosh stared at Elda with his steely gray eyes and lifted one eyebrow.

Elda chuckled. "Right. The gray ghost strikes again."

Tosh winked at her. "Like it wasn't risky for you to break into Ed's office and bug it?"

"Touché," Elda acknowledged, with a smile. They were two peas in a pod. She switched to frown at Tosh. "But that doesn't let you off the hook. You should at least tell me where you are going. I told you when I played janitor and broke into Ed's office."

Olga clapped her hands. "Hey. You two *stop*. Listen to Olga. You need to look differently at all this." She waved her hands at the wall. "These strings don't show us who is behind everything. Plus, you've listed a lot of dead people. They can't help us now. Who else is there? Where does this dead guy in the Ukraine fit in? Who is far undercover waiting to be activated, hey?"

"We need to remove those who were behind Operation Bittman and trying to sabotage our team," Tosh said. "We want vengeance, and we want to be undead and get our jobs back."

Elda stepped forward. It was time to take charge. "Although I'm mad as hell about what they did to us and to our people," Elda put forth, "it's less about vengeance, for me, and more about bringing things back to status quo. In the past we operated well, defending our countries, at times pitted against each other, but there were rules. These people didn't obey the rules and are traitors to our countries. We need to remove them. Olga, can you help us?"

Olga touched the photo from Sophia's office. "Olga can throw dead Romanians around, so she can handle this dead guy. I will find out for you who this man is. But you forget people." She took a card, wrote a name on it, and listed it under the Kremlin moles.

"No, it can't be!" Elda's eyes popped wide. "Kevin Ball? He's the new finance guy in charge of Ed's budget."

Olga touched the side of her nose. "Yes, he is. Kevin Ball laundered the funds for the Kremlin to finance Operation Bittman."

CHAPTER FIVE

THIS WOULD NOT BE FUN.

Charlie took a huge breath and squared her shoulders, before rapping on Frank Garcia's partially opened door. From inside he motioned her to enter his office. The smell of gym locker and fast food assailed her nostrils.

Charlie sized Frank up. Frank looked fit but had the ex-athlete's paunch. His football trophies took up the entire top shelf of his bookcase.

Frank stood about five foot ten, in his mid to late thirties, with a prematurely graying buzz cut. Stacks of soda cans teetered on his windowsill, and cheeseburger wrappers overflowed his trash can. His half-open gym bag in the corner gave his office the special aroma. It resembled a college dorm room rather than a business space. Great. Another full-of-himself ex-jock.

Charlie waited for Frank to begin the conversation.

"You may be hot stuff in whatever agency you work at, but *here* you work for *me* and you take orders from *me*. Understand?" Frank glared at her.

Charlie nodded. "Completely." In her assessment, this man did not deserve the respect of a "sir." "So what does your crew do, Frank?" Charlie, displaying a smile that did not reach her eyes, pumped him for background. She could feel the tension grow in the back of her neck.

"Good god, freak," he snapped back. "What do you fucking think we do? We're at war with cyberterrorists, and you're a thorn in my side. We're on the front line, and we need brains, not a female ex-grunt."

Charlie bit her lip and forced herself to stand in place and not slap the arrogant man. She entreated, with syrupy sweetness dripping from her voice, "So what type of cyberterrorists? Those who spread disinformation? Political? Those who attack the infrastructure? Those who go after our businesses?" She could hear Frank's teeth gnash together.

"The only important type is social media disinformation." He snarled. "The rest are decoys. Ignore them."

Charlie realized she could hate this man. She curled her toes tightly in her shoes and released them. Charlie gave him a radiant smile. "With your permission, I will be talking to each member of your organization to understand what they do and what they have information on, so I can be the most help to you."

"You're dead weight to me and my organization. Do what you have to do, but keep out of my way. Be gone by week's end." Frank clenched his fists, and anger oozed from him. He exhaled. "Do you spar?"

Do I spar? What an ass. "I can box, plus I do a smidgen of martial arts." Actually, in the service, Charlie had been trained in boxing, plus she learned from Elda a combination of many styles, as well as Elda's own invented moves. These techniques mixed in the Peruvian street-fighting style of Bakom with the Japanese martial art Aikido. From Elda, Charlie was also well versed in the Brazilian fighting style Capoeira and the American martial arts system Kajukenbo. Although not yet at the level Elda was, she was a formidable opponent.

Frank smiled thinly. "Great. Meet me in the gym at lunch. Bring a first-aid kit. You're going to need it."

***

"I tell you, I don't like the fact that this woman has been assigned to me. And I don't know what department she's working with." Frank Garcia paced the parking lot near his office in DC, his burner phone connected via Bluetooth to his earpiece. A dismal drizzle settled in around him. He hoped this phone call wouldn't take long.

"So can you remove her?" a soft voice on the other end suggested.

"I don't want to draw attention to my department by complaining." Frank spluttered.

"*Remove* has many meanings" came the response. "Accidents happen in the workplace more than are reported."

Frank shook his head. Realizing his gesture couldn't be seen, he voiced, "I'm in cyberterrorism on purpose. It's clean. No blood. I don't handle bodies."

"You may have to. You better ensure nothing lands in the way of our two groups working together," the other party retorted.

Frank blinked at his phone, listening to the dial tone. Suddenly the rain didn't feel bad anymore. He *just* realized what he signed up for when he consented to pass secrets to his Russian counterparts.

***

Okay, where was that asshole? Charlie had purposely fed his tendency to underestimate women. Now it was time to show him a lesson. Then she would switch back to the agreeable little woman. His head would be spinning from the two Charlies, causing him to make errors. Charlie had learned a lot from Elda about how to play games with another's head.

Wearing shorts, a T-shirt, and running shoes, Charlie stood in the door of the gym, scanning the room for Frank. The gym was small, equipped with a stair-stepper, tread-mill, punching bags, weights, and a wrestling mat. Full wall-sized mirrors made the gym appear larger.

She spotted Frank, standing in front of his reflection, performing bicep curls with twenty-five-pound weights. She strode over to him. "You don't want to wear yourself out before the match, do you?"

Frank sneered. "Don't worry, girl. I *am* well endowed in stamina."

Charlie let the air fill with expectation. His eyebrows furrowed. As he opened his mouth to speak, she retorted, "Not *that* well endowed."

His mouth hung open. Before he could respond, she reached out and took the weights from him, did an over-head press, and returned them to the rack.

On his way by her, Frank slammed her in the back with his shoulder. "Oops, my bad."

Charlie turned and gave him a huge smile, with nar-rowed eyes, which belayed her cheerfulness. "Shall we start?" She strolled to the black padded mat.

"It's your funeral."

While she was still moving into position, with her back turned, he moved to attach her.

Charlie felt the air of his rush toward her and side-stepped. *Thud.* He crashed to the floor off the side of the mat.

"Damn!" He rubbed his elbow as he rose.

"It's much softer on the mat." Charlie motioned for

him to join her. She rocked from side to side on the balls of her feet, her eyes glued to his movements.

Frank lunged at her in a second attempt to tackle her. Charlie did a forward summersault over him. Frank's face smacked the mat. "You know, Frank, you might want to view more boxing and less football."

He rose, blood dripping from his nose. He blotted it on his sleeve.

"Would you like to attend to that?" Charlie sauntered toward him.

"I've had worse," he snapped.

"I'm sure you have." Charlie kicked his legs out from under him. He landed with a thump on his back, his head bouncing on the mat. He lay prone for a moment.

"Uncle?" Charlie held out a gym towel.

He rose and shook his head like a wet dog. Blood scattered across the mat. He warily circled Charlie. She chucked the towel to one side and stood awaiting his next move.

"Do something, damn you," he screamed.

"Ladies before gentlemen."

He moved closer and was rewarded by a swift kick to his solar plexus. The air driven out of him, he gasped and doubled over. With joined fists, Charlie slammed her forearms down on his back, driving him to the ground. He lay facedown, breathing heavily.

Charlie bent and whispered in his ear. "I look forward to our rematch."

He grunted.

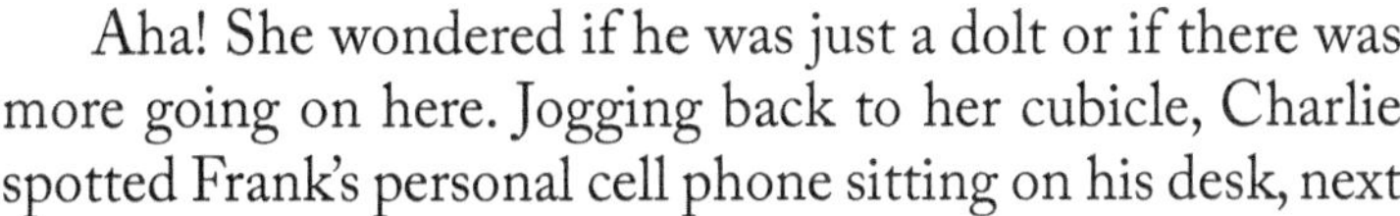

Aha! She wondered if he was just a dolt or if there was more going on here. Jogging back to her cubicle, Charlie spotted Frank's personal cell phone sitting on his desk, next to his issued work phone. She reached into her gym bag and pulled on a pair of touchscreen work-out gloves. She poked the dark screen, and it lit up. She typed in his first initial followed by his last name and the year of his birth. *My God! That worked. What a dolt.* Working quickly, she made note of the phone's number and airdropped his contact list to her phone. Replacing the phone exactly where she found it, she strode past her desk and slipped into the stairwell to make a phone call. She brought up the special application that Ashok had developed. Through this they could send and receive encrypted messages and untraceable phone calls, without resorting to burner phones.

Ashok answered her call on the first ring. Charlie could picture him in his Anacostia, DC, bachelor pad, with fast food and candy bar wrappers strewn on his desk, and empty caffeine-loaded soda cans piled up in a neighboring trash can. She envisioned him surrounded by multiple computer monitors, his fingers flying over his keyboard, teasing out the secrets within. His security with layers of multioperating-system firewalls surpassed anything they had at the office.

"Ashok? I need you to look up this number and pull any calls made on it over the past few days. Also, I'm transmitting to you a contact list. Screen it and see if anyone on that list has connections to our friends in Russia. There's something off about this man, and I suspect he may be blocking us from getting the information we need."

The click of Ashok's typing persisted. "Not a problem Miss Charlie, ma'am. I have started as you wish. I can have that data to you most directly. Will you be joining us at Ed's weekly meeting? It will be at Jackson's place."

Oh drat. She'd forgotten about that meeting. Suddenly the stairwell seemed confining. She longed to be in the field again. She sighed. "I appreciate the reminder. I will if I can make it. Ed put me on a project that I think is a dead-end street. But your findings will help me immensely and get me off the project, so please call me when you have *any* info."

"I will most certainly do that. It is my pleasure. It will be to you most promptly." Ashok's boyish charm blunted any hint of arrogance.

"Thanks, Ashok." Charlie knew from experience with Ashok, that, given enough time and the right equipment, could solve any problem she threw his way.

Charlie jogged down to the ground floor and back up the stairs to give her an excuse for being in the stairwell. She glowed with a layer of perspiration after four round trips. She opened the stairwell door and found a battered Frank searching through her desk.

Oh God, there's the asshole. "Looking for something, Frank?"

Frank slammed her desk drawer closed. "I needed a pad of paper. Thought you might have one."

Charlie's eyes narrowed. "*Really*, Frank? Look at the cabinet over there. You see it? The one with the enormous sign on it that says SUPPLIES?"

"Being a smart-ass won't get you anywhere in this department."

"Better a smart-ass than a thief. Just so you know, the only things of mine you'll find here are smelly work-out clothes."

Frank pulled back his arm to swing at Charlie.

Charlie eyed him scornfully. She held out her arms. "Seriously, Frank? Take your shot if you must, but remember how our gym bout ended. Are you aware of the definition of insanity?"

"I'll take you down a peg and show you what you're made for," Frank sputtered. "You better lock your doors, especially the bedroom." He dropped his arm and stamped away.

There was something seriously wrong with that man.

She'd better obtain Ed's info and be gone from here before she injured or did away with Frank.

———

Someone is following me . . . Charlie knelt on the damp pavement, untied and retied her shoes, and listened. The footsteps behind her also stopped. A novice. Anyone experienced would have walked past her and positioned themselves as a front tail. Whoever it was, she couldn't lead them to any of the off-site offices or her apartment. Damn. She'd be late for the meeting.

Walking faster, Charlie heard the faint sounds of the other matching her strides. The smell of ozone and rhythmic rumbling of engines clued her in that she was close to her exit. She dashed toward the metro and walked up the moving escalator. Breaking into a jog, she ran up the last few steps onto the platform of the McClean Metro stop. She glanced into a train window and, in the reflection, she recognized an out-of-breath Frank pop onto the platform and hide behind a map display.

"Ah, you fool," she muttered under her breath. Why was he following her? Was he looking to ambush her and get even for their gym match? Or was he attempting to gather more information on which agency she worked for? Whatever the reason, he definitely was not well skilled as an operative. She needed to find out who he was working for. Was he even working for American interests?

With a squeal, a train to Metro Center pulled up, and the passengers filed off. Charlie moved nearer to the door, turning in Frank's direction, effectively trapping him behind his pole. As the train's doors started to close, Charlie slipped inside and saw Frank dash and skid to a stop, failing to catch the train. Now to verify she'd lost him entirely. There would be nowhere for him to hide at the Metro

Center stop if he managed to make it that far.

Charlie hopped off the Silver Line train at Metro Center. She stopped for a moment to admire the view and to glance around for Frank. The lit intersecting lines and arcs forming the ceiling mesmerized her, but she forced herself to focus. People milled around her in a rush, heading off in many directions. Not detecting anyone suspicious, Charlie took off to the escalator to catch the Blue Line. The sounds of the trains made it impossible to detect any footsteps following her cadence.

Lucky! A train to Crystal City. Charlie ran for the car and darted in just as the doors were closing. That should have gotten rid of any tail.

Charlie's phone vibrated, indicating she had an encrypted message. She spun up the app and read from Ashok, PHONE NUMBER FG CALLED BELONGS TO ALEXEI ALEXEEV.

How could that be? Alexei Alexeev was dead.

CHAPTER SIX

ELDA PACED IN FRONT OF THE CHARTS on the wall. Who was the leak in Ed's organization? Kevin Ball had only been recently assigned to Ed. It definitely wasn't Charlie or Ashok. She lightly tapped her forehead. *Think Elda. Think.*

Thud. Tosh slammed his coffee cup down on the wooden kitchen table. "Elda, who the *blyad'* is Olga? How does she know so much? Can we trust her? And where is she now?" he spilled in rapid-fire questioning. Tosh's gray eyes flashed with anger, on the edge of losing his usually controlled demeanor.

Elda wondered why it was so hard to think. She rationalized that no one could think with all these interruptions. But was her brain just slow from lack of focus on these things, or was she getting old? It was time to attend to the present and put on her therapist hat. Hopefully, *that* part of her brain still worked.

Recognizing the warning signs of an irritated Tosh, Elda chose her words. "Tosh, I've been friends with Olga for years. I trust her implicitly and wouldn't hesitate to discuss this in front of her. In any case, Olga went out for a run, so you can feel free to speak frankly."

Elda paused to study Tosh, who raised an eyebrow. Since he looked calmer, she went on, "Olga started out as my personal trainer. She had just arrived from Russia and was looking to establish herself. As a personal trainer myself, I could pass her connections and clients. Olga is very talented as a trainer and soon required no additional help from me."

"*That* woman is not only a personal trainer," Tosh snorted.

Relieved Tosh was engaged in the conversation, Elda carried on. "You're right. She has lot more talents, connections, and resources. After carefully vetting her, I often used her to help me gather intel. She is extremely resourceful."

"Where are her allegiances?" Tosh's face relaxed. His voice was gentler.

Okay. I'm bringing him along. At least I haven't lost my therapist skills. Elda shrugged, and her forehead creased into a frown. "Olga follows her head and heart. She does what she feels is right. Her actions are rooted in a strong sense of ethics, but she does not act rashly. She researches matters thoroughly."

Tosh scowled. "How did she find us? Did you really leave her those clues?"

"Olga's instincts are unmatched." As Tosh's eyebrow moved upward, Elda held up her hand to stop the anticipated outburst. "But yes, I left clues I figured only she could decipher. I knew we must disappear and be considered dead by the rest of the world, but I also figured we would need some help in the future. Thus the breadcrumbs."

Tosh nodded. He took an extended breath and visibly calmed. "We do need help ferreting out the double agents. They're buried and well established."

Elda brought the disagreement to an end. "And the whole point of us getting declared dead was so we could freely move against these mutual enemies without our movements being tracked. *Vernyy?*"

"*Vernyy,*" Tosh acceded.

Whew. He's on board. Now to move him forward. "So let's build our private army, Tosh. We lost too many good agents in our past missions. We need to destroy this network."

Would more people find them? Was Olga really on their side? Tosh contemplated the tea leaves at the bottom of his cup. Did he have it within himself to be operational again after this respite? Yes. He wanted vengeance.

Tosh's teacup rattled in its saucer as the front door slammed open. Olga, wearing gym clothes and jogging shoes and breathing heavily, popped into the living room. "Olga be right back. Olga need to cool down and stretch." She ran back out the door.

Bozhe moy! Can't that woman do anything quietly? "Does she live here now?" Tosh offered in a sarcastic tone.

"Perhaps," Elda quipped, as she strolled into the kitchen. She called back into Tosh, "More tea?"

"*Da, pozhaluysta.*" He felt his wrist for his pulse. *Slow and steady. Good.* He shouted into the kitchen, "We need to talk about where Olga is staying."

Elda came out of the kitchen with a wooden tray, carrying a pot of English Breakfast tea, some bottles of water, a package of bourbon creams, and a pile of chocolate Quadratini cookies.

"She is buying a villa near here, but I felt it was important to have her here for a while."

"We're a team, Elda. But more importantly, I am living here too. And she is *loud.* Perhaps running a decision like that by me first would have been in order?" Tosh took a deep breath and rechecked his pulse.

Elda set the tray of goodies in front of Tosh. "You're right. Shall I send her away?"

She was serious. "No, no. You're right. We need to know more what she knows and get moving again. She's a good catalyst. I reserve the right to complain, however. You know I like peace and quiet."

Olga bounded in, grabbed a towel from her gym bag, and scrubbed off a layer of sweat and Tuscany dust. Placing the towel on her chair, she plunked down in front of the tray of goodies. "Now these are the right type of cookie crumbs," she purred. "Olga likes them."

"I thought you would." Elda looked at Tosh, who was on his second Bourbon cream, dipping it into his cup before taking a bite. Elda wheeled a whiteboard in front of them, and after swallowing her own cookie, wrote, TOSH AND ELDA'S ARMY.

Olga took a slug of water, swallowed, and blurted out, "Olga!"

Tosh rolled his eyes and took another biscuit to stifle a snarky retort.

Elda wrote OLGA SOKOLOV as the first one on the list.

"We'll need muscle," Tosh proposed.

Olga flexed.

Tosh shook his head. Thawed by Olga's enthusiasm, he chuckled. "We need you and Yuri for logistics, Olga. I want Anatoly. And I'd like Snezhana to help in the field, since we're technically dead and may need to operate in the background."

Elda listed them next and wrote, JIM MARTIN.

Tosh swallowed his cookie and took a sip of tea. "Is he the guy who got you that RV in Maine?"

Elda nodded. "Exactly. He's ex-military and can be useful as background logistics during an op. Plus, he's not known to anyone we've worked with in the past."

Tosh stood and paced. "We need technical expertise to wade through those files gathered from that tap you left on Ed's network, when you broke into his office."

Elda put one arm over her waist and the other under her chin. She frowned. "Who would that be? Ashok works for Ed. And although I would love to recruit him, and by the way, Charlie too, Ed's organization leaks like a sieve. I'm not sure how to grab either of them without raising suspicion. What's Stas's status?"

Tosh frowned. "Last I heard, Alexie's replacement, Adrik, shanghaied him as part of his cyberterrorist division. That would be deadening work for Stas. He's far more creative than that."

Elda scribbled Stas, Ashok, Who? on the whiteboard. She looked expectantly at the other two.

"I hear Yuri's out of work," Olga proffered. "We can easily recruit him. And as you mentioned, Tosh, Olga can use his help in gathering intel and performing necessary logistics."

Who was Olga? How did she know all this? Tosh shook his head. "How on earth . . ."

Olga tapped the side of her nose and winked.

Tosh narrowed his eyes. "I will figure you out, Olga."

Elda cleared her throat for attention and wrote, Yuri.

"What about Sophia?" Tosh proposed. "The mole network probably stems from Russia, but it goes deep into the US and also the UK. We need at least one person from each of these countries."

Elda added Sophia and Tom Williams.

"Tom? That Secret Service guy who worked in the president's protection team at the White House?" Tosh asked.

"He's the one," Elda verified. "His reach into the various intelligence agencies is long, and he's extremely trustworthy. He may be hard to obtain, since he's still an active

Secret Service member. But we might need him for intelligence now and again."

Olga clapped. "So there's the army!"

"We just have to gather them together," Elda murmured.

"Just . . ." Tosh shook his head. Could he operate as a handler still? He winced at his own negative thoughts about his abilities.

"You need to be happier, Tosh," Olga admonished. "We will have a second villa. Leave it up to Olga. That way you two won't be connected to it. So now we make the plan!"

Elda put down her marker and plopped down onto the couch. "The plan . . . damn, they always want a plan . . ."

CHAPTER SEVEN

FRANK PACED BACK AND FORTH IN THE stairwell. Doors opened and closed below him, and footsteps reverberated down the stairs. The air was stagnant. He found it hard to breathe out of his swollen nose.

He was pissed off that a woman had beaten him in a fight. First Elda, when he was in his last job, and now Charlie. He was used to winning his games. Give him a football and he'd show them all a thing or two. Women had thrown themselves at him in high school and college. He was angry the Kremlin had its talons in him. He felt powerless and couldn't punch his way out. That thought started the pounding in his head again. He realized his controller was waiting for an answer.

"No, I haven't figured out what to do yet," he snapped into his phone.

"We do not need strangers looking into your organization and finding the details you're hiding," Boris barked back. "You're in a city with a lot of traffic. Run her over. Wear a mask and gloves. We'll supply you with a car that you can ditch afterward."

Dumbfounded, Frank stopped and stuttered, "I-I-I can't do *that*." This was turning into a nightmare. He had signed up for a simple clean job of passing information, hiding data, and gathering money into his offshore accounts. A few years of working for the Russians and then he could quit and retire to some place that had beautiful women and lots of alcohol. He now suspected there was no path to retirement. He was getting deeper and deeper into a dangerous world.

"You can do it, if you know what's good for you," Boris. retorted

Beads of sweat ran down his forehead as Frank stared at his silent phone. Boris had terminated the connection.

What a beautiful day. Charlie hopped onto her bicycle to ride from Ed's downtown DC office, on Washington Ave, to &pizza at 1215 Connecticut Ave NW for lunch. She cut in and out of the heavy traffic, drafting on bumpers, being beeped at. A slight breeze mitigated the heavy exhaust smell.

Suddenly her "spidey sense," as Elda had called it, kicked in. She glanced in her rearview mirror and saw an old beat-up 2012 Mazda3 cutting in and out of the lanes behind her. Someone was in one heck of a hurry. It would not be worth it in the long run. The driver would gain perhaps a minute or two max, frustrating other drivers and potentially have caused an accident. She glanced again. He had not slowed. He was closing in on her. She had to move it fast to get out of the way.

She pulled into the right lane to let him pass her and saw him crank the steering wheel to the right. The driver wore a black N95 face mask and dark sunglasses.

He was coming right at her. Slamming on her brakes,

she popped a wheelie, pivoted the bike on its back tire, and pressed down hard on the pedal to move forward again. She jumped the curb. The front tire came down with a jolt, and she raced down the sidewalk in the opposite direction, to the satisfying crunch of a car accident behind her. She couldn't say for certain, but from estimating his height behind the wheel and seeing a gray buzz cut, she would swear that was Frank.

The wood reverberated under his fist. In the Kremlin, Boris Sidorov pounded on his large, brass-trimmed mahogany desk.

His network was not efficient. He had spent years building and cultivating his web of agents and moles, only to lose so many over the past few years, foiled by that American agent Elda and Adrik's spy handler Tosh.

James Richardson was one of his biggest losses. Also gone were Henry Davies and his son Nigel, Arabella Johnson, Anton Morozov, and many capable assassins in the US, Russia, and UK whom Boris used to readily tap. It was time to activate the sleepers and cultivate new agents. He needed to rebuild.

Boris marched over to his whiteboard to map out his organization. Adrik Lebedev headed up his cyber group, focused on disinformation. Adrik once also had a boots-on-the ground spy organization, headed by Tosh, but that was now mostly disbanded, the remnant scattered into other divisions under Boris. Perhaps he needed a new org, similar to Tosh's, with some updated skills?

Gorky Krovopuskov, whose expertise was poisons, headed the next team in Boris's organization. Boris calculated that he didn't need as many lab staff since Tosh's folks, with their Cold War techniques, were gone. Perhaps there was a requirement for this talent in the new division. He needed to own technical knowledge, as well as brute strength. He would tell Adrik he was taking that computer whizz. What was his name?. . . Boris went to his laptop and referenced an old organizational chart. Ah yes, Stas Garin.

He was angry at Adrik's lack of assurances that Tosh and Elda were dead and made a note to obtain his reassurance. In Boris's opinion Adrik was lazy and lacked follow-through. He vowed to rid himself of Adrik, create a new organization, and awaken a new army of sleeper moles to do his bidding. Now was the time to activate a long-hidden asset in the United States. He was vital for this next initiative, as well as for going around Adrik to gather the inside scoop on Elda and Tosh's death.

Boris picked up his phone and commanded Adrik to come to his office. Some things were best done in person, leaving no trace of the conversation, and Adrik would be on the hook if things went wrong. Nothing could be traced back to Boris.

***

"Ahem." Standing at the open door, Adrik cleared his throat, requesting to be allowed in. Boris motioned for him to enter the office. Adrik took a few slow steps into the office.

"You're late," Boris hurled at him. "It's been almost an hour since I called."

"I am sorry, *ser*. I had a nature call."

Svin'ya. The man is a pig. Boris rose from his desk. At a fit six foot one, he towered over Adrik's five foot eight bulky body. He leaned against the front of his desk to accentuate the differences between the two men.

Adrik gulped and took a step backward, tripping and

falling into a solid-wood chair positioned near the desk. He caught himself before falling over sideways.

"Please do take a seat." Boris slammed the door and noted that Adrik flinched.

"*Spasibo, ser.*"

Boris spotted beads of perspiration on Adrik's forehead. The man was disgustingly fat. He was bound to screw up, and Boris could then remove him from his job.

Boris let the silence grow until he couldn't stand the stink of Adrik's sweat anymore. He returned to his own desk chair. "You did a reasonable job with your cyberattacks. Of course, I expect you will be more efficient in the future. On that note, however, I'm going to need to take Stas Garin from your organization to do some work for me. But that's not why you're here."

Adrik swallowed and coughed. Tears welled up in his eyes.

Boris motioned to the glass of water sitting on a coaster on the table next to Adrik.

Adrik swigged half of it. He stopped and stared agog at the glass.

Boris chuckled. "Don't worry. If I wanted you dead, you would be so already. I would like you to do a mission for me."

Adrik exhaled and wiped his mouth on his sleeve.

Boris went on. "There is a sleeper agent in the United States whom I would like you to activate. I want him to find any traces of the American agent Elda or your agent Tosh. We must confirm they're gone before I activate more agents. *Ponimat'?*"

"You want me to go to America?" Adrik croaked.

"*Net, pridurok!*" Boris slammed his fist on his desk. "Send someone! There are people left over from Tosh's organization. Tell me which operative you choose, and I will give that man the US agent's identity. Now go." He shook his head and motioned Adrik to leave.

———✦———

Adrik waddled back into his office. He plopped his bulk behind his chair and pulled open the bottom drawer of his desk to grab a candy bar. Meeting with Boris always unnerved him. Adrik possessed no leverage to threaten Boris with and needed to win him over by doing a good job. That worried him. He shoved the entire bar into his mouth.

As he chomped, bits of bar spit out onto his desk. He licked his finger, picked the crumbs up, and put them in his mouth. While chewing, he speculated whether Tosh Chelovek and that American agent Elda Ainsworth had ended each other's life.

Tosh had been an irritant to him. Tosh's success with his old-school techniques belayed Adrik's push to succeed in the cyber world. With Tosh gone, Adrik had successfully dismantled Tosh's team and positioned his own organization as the wave of the future. The only member of Tosh's team Adrik retained was Stas Garin, whose computer skills were unmatched by anyone in Adrik's crew. Now he was losing Stas to Boris. Just as well. He would be free of any traces of Tosh's influence on these people.

Adrik was surprised Snezhana Chelovek, Tosh's niece, and Anatoly Petrov had left the organization so willingly, but he assumed their extreme grief had knocked the wind out of them. When he'd last inquired, the two of them had opened a private investigator company. He made note to send them some business. If they were any good, it would be an excellent off-book way to accomplish his personal objectives.

Adrik viewed the online daily report, pleased that his cyberattacks on the US infrastructure had temporarily disabled selected zones of electrical flow and took offline targeted hospitals and municipal buildings, but knew the attacks should ramp up, to outdo the GRU and FSB cyber units. Adrik was uninterested in the reconnaissance and clandestine surveillance that followed. He wanted immediate results.

Adrik was especially interested in outperforming GRU's Unit 54777, also known as the

72nd Special Service Center, responsible for the GRU's psychological warfare, including online disinformation and information operations. He knew the Kremlin used Yevgeniy Prighozin, a wealthy oligarch with troll farms, to back the Internet Research Agency. This group focused on disinformation by impersonating domestic activists and people, primarily through various social media channels. But Adrik wasn't satisfied with targeting individual's Facebook and Twitter accounts. He wanted to sow discord at a higher level.

Boris was right. Adrik needed to ensure Tosh and Elda were dead. Snezhana and Anatoly had been too close to them to be trusted to give Adrik truthful information. Adrik had given Yaromir Koslov to another division but was sure he could borrow him back. Yaromir was a dumb brute, but this job did not require finesse.

Adrik picked up his phone.

"Find Yaromir. I have a mission for him."

CHAPTER EIGHT

KATYA POUNCED ON THE RED DOT, only to find it moved. Yuri Kuznetsov blinked the laser pointer on and off and moved the dot along the black-and-white-checked linoleum of his Moscow apartment floor, laughing as his cat danced along chasing it. Pausing, he typed on his phone to check for messages.

Nothing.

Yuri was a sizable, solidly built, well-muscled man, often mistaken for Anatoly Petrov's twin. Until Tosh's death, Yuri had worked for Tosh as an operative focusing on logistics. His past experiences in arranging shipments for the Mafia had built him solid skills in that domain. Scratching his coffee-brown buzz cut, he puzzled over his financial situation. If he didn't land a gig soon, he would need to dig into his secret reserves. He drummed his fingers on the table.

If Elda were alive, she would have given Yuri something to do. He loved when she'd assigned him to babysit the Troodles. He'd played with two small dogs all day and been paid lots of money to do so. It was a good contract. He shook that thought away. Elda was dead.

He wondered if Anatoly and Snezhana had any jobs they could use him for. No. Last time he had spoken with them, they were struggling to start their private investigator business. Perhaps the Kremlin had some work for him? No. There was no one he trusted there. He was also sick of the lies and intrigue.

Well then, the Mafia was always good for something. In that organization the rules were clear.

Katya leapt up on his lap. Yuri absentmindedly scratched her behind her ears.

He startled as his phone rang. Katya hissed and flew off his lap. Yuri pressed Answer.

The voice on the other end boomed, "Privet, Yuri."

Yuri broke into a smile. "Privet, Olga!"

Vee's sharp bark rang out over the water in the Maine cove. Yuri recognized Vee's *A stranger is here* bark. He called her name, and hearing the familiar voice, she ran to him for a treat. She crawled up into his lap and licked his face.

Yuri watched as Jim Martin hobbled up to the house from the rocky beach. He set Vee down, stood, and held out his hand. "Yuri Kuznetsov," he presented, in a thick Russian accent.

Jim's eyes narrowed, but he stepped forward and shook Yuri's hand. "Jim Martin."

A dark sedan motored to a stop beside the house. "It's Eldah's lawyah," Jim observed. "Ah haven't seen this many visitahs in months. Something is up. Ah sure hope it's good news."

Elda's lawyer stepped out of the car. "Hello, Jim. And you must be Yuri. Is there somewhere the three of us can sit and talk?"

Jim motioned them inside to the small wooden kitchen table surrounded by four mismatched wooden chairs. Yuri noted that Jim sat with his back to the wall with a clear view of the doors and a cleaver within reach. Elda had said that Jim had been a Vietnam special forces veteran, so he had a few tricks up his sleeve. Elda had also taught him some additional techniques, and Yuri could see from the well-used targets set up in the yard that Jim practiced shooting on a regular basis.

"So, Yuri, how does Vee know you?" Jim inquired.

Yuri held Vee in his lap and submitted his hand to many doggy kisses.

"We've only met once through Eda, of course, but Vee knows I love animals." He reached into his pocket and slipped Vee a Cheerio. Yuri looked out through the kitchen window to the sparkling water in the receding tide, in the cove beyond. The hum of fishing boats heading in from a day's catch from the next cove over came through the open window. The thin screech of an eagle flying to its nest and indistinguishable voices of periwinkle gatherers starting their day's work floated in on the breeze. "Nice view."

"Ayuh," Jim allowed.

The lawyer flipped through some papers resting on the table. "I won't keep everyone long. As you both are aware, Elda's will has a number of clauses that are time-released actions."

"Ayuh."

The lawyer went on. "Elda specified in her will that four months after she was declared dead, this man, Yuri Kuznetsov, will take Vee."

Jim's face fell.

"Furthermore, Jim, Elda required you travel with Yuri to Vee's destination to ensure Vee is settled comfortably. There is money put aside for all of this," the lawyer concluded.

Jim's calm facade shattered. He rose. "What? Eldah wanted that? I haven't been out of Maine for yeahs. Where ah we going?"

CHAPTER NINE

KEVIN BALL TOUCHED HIS FINGER to his twitching eyelid and glanced over his shoulder. Dressed in a corduroy jacket with frayed cuffs thrown over a faded T-shirt, blue jeans, and sneakers, he shuffled nervously along the concrete path in Lincoln Park in DC. He could hear the faint sounds of children playing and dogs barking. He wiped his runny nose on his frayed sleeve. His feet hurt from his walk, through the park to the meeting spot.

He paused in front of the statue of President Lincoln, where his contact ordered they would meet. The statue depicted Lincoln holding the Emancipation Proclamation. He sneered. *Damn leftist liberals. If they had their way, this country would be run by Blacks and immigrants.* The irony that he himself originally came from another country didn't strike him.

Kevin had been waiting for years to be activated and finally serve the motherland. His parents had told him how they'd wanted a baby and couldn't conceive. That when he came, he was a *such* gift to them. They'd impressed on him his need to pay back that gift when the time came. He'd never realized as a child what they'd meant. He wasn't sure he did now. He stopped and spat on the walkway.

No one knew he was not his parents' biological child. His grandfather, Herbert Ball, once worked with Robert Clark at Boeing. Kevin was unclear about the details, but somehow Robert had arranged the trip to Moscow, where his parents had stayed for over nine months before returning to the US with Kevin as their own. They had faked a pregnancy, complete with increasing baby bumps and maternity clothes. When it came time for the delivery, a midwife was brought in and amply paid off to spread the good news of the baby boy for the American couple.

Kevin's parents had encouraged him to go into government work. In college, Kevin studied accounting, and through the help of John Clark, Robert's son, he now worked on the staff in charge of the US Intelligence budget. On paper, he listed a sizable amount of people reporting to him. In actuality, a skeleton staff reported to him and tracked the budgets. He funneled the excess money into a private offshore account.

He had done a favor a couple of years ago for Nigel Davies, a friend of Doug Clark, John Clark's son. Kevin had met Doug and Nigel when on vacation in the United Kingdom. They'd gone pub crawling together. After a lot of pubs, Nigel had asked if Kevin could help him out and transfer large sums of money to various accounts in the US, Canada, and the UK. At the time it seemed like an innocent favor, returning the goodness John had shown to him, but he now wondered if it was a prelude to today's meeting.

He nervously peered over his shoulder and checked his watch. *It's time.* He scanned his location. All the benches looked the same. What if he was at the wrong place?

He turned to pace the other way and spotted a large, squarely built man striding toward him. The man he supposed to meet?

The man motioned for Kevin to join him in his walk. As Kevin fell into step, the man said quietly, "My name is Yaromir. There is no need for you to know anything else, except I will be your contact. My instructions are to tell you to find out any facts you can on an operative called Elda Ainsworth. We were told she is deceased and would like to verify that. Understand?"

Surprised, Kevin protested. "What? I'm an accountant. I know nothing about operatives!"

Yaromir snarled. "Man up. *Vyrastit' shary.* You will be, and do, whatever we ask you to. We need information. As an accountant working on the intelligence budget, you're well positioned with contacts in the intelligence community. Just do it. I will be back in two weeks to hear what progress you made."

Kevin exhaled loudly the breath he had been holding. "Wait," he cried out. "How will I contact you?"

"You won't." Yaromir turned around and strode off.

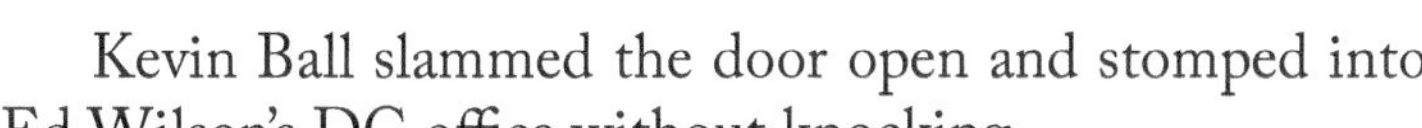

Kevin Ball slammed the door open and stomped into Ed Wilson's DC office without knocking.

Deep in thought, Ed sprang up from his desk, knocking his chair over, and fumbled to bring it upright and back into position. *Damn that man. Always sneaking around.* He kept his face impassive as he studied Kevin, waiting for an explanation for this rude interruption. Kevin had only been assigned to Ed a few months ago to handle the high-level budget, but he was quickly proving himself to be bothersome. Ed's last accountant just gave him a sum of money and left him alone. Kevin was always asking questions that didn't relate to his budgetary duties. Ed did not trust him.

Kevin smirked and stood with his pudgy hands on his waist, his belly protruding over his belt. The cuffs of his well-worn slacks fell onto the tops of his tennis shoes. His concession to being in a work environment appeared to be a blue corduroy jacket over a white T-shirt. His black chest hairs peeked over the neck of the shirt. Ed wrinkled his nose at a stale scent emanating from the man's clothing and evaluated when they had last been in a washer.

"Not much of a spook, hey, Ed, if I can sneak up on you." Kevin snickered.

Ed restrained from rolling his eyes and shrugged. Kevin had been trying to get Ed's goat all week. The best way to make him stand down would be to ignore him.

"Cat got your tongue, Ed?" Kevin taunted.

Ed ground his teeth together. "I'm not sure what you want, Kevin." His patience with this man was growing thin. He took a deep breath and composed his face.

Kevin wandered around Ed's office, looking at books, moving papers. "Well, you see, Ed, I'm supposed to be your financial boss, but no one gave me any intel about what you do, or who works with you, or who for you. They tell me to approve your budgets. But there's the rub too, Ed. Your budgets are only a total sum of money, without any breakdown. Now, how can I, a responsible government employee, give you blank checks?"

Ed clenched and unclenched his fists and filled his lungs with calming air. "Sorry, Kevin, but you're not cleared for that level. Your job is to give me the money and leave. Is that all?" Ed turned back to his desk. The papers out of order bothered him. There was nothing in this office that would give Kevin any lowdown on what he or his people did. It was merely a government front for Ed. Ed had not been able to find the source of the leaks from his office, so he worked around them by handling anything sensitive off site.

Kevin sneered. "No, Ed, that's not all. You're going to see my face in here every day until you give me something to go on. Tell me, does Elda Ainsworth work for you?"

Ed's heart skipped a beat. Why was Kevin asking about Elda? That line of questioning was different from Kevin's usual annoying neediness, blathering about male rights and white supremacy. He contemplated Kevin. "My personnel records are none of your business." What was this man up to?

"Well, perhaps *she* will be more forthcoming," Kevin rasped,

Ha! Apparently Kevin didn't know Elda was dead. "I sincerely doubt that," Ed bantered. "Are you done?" He examined his nails. He should stop biting the sides of his fingers. It was bad habit he'd picked up from Elda.

Kevin smirked. "Oh no. I may have to sign your budgets, but I don't have to make your life easy. You *will* answer my questions in the end. Anyways, you and I should have common interests."

Ed yawned. "Why's that, Kevin?" He studied his hands again. This was getting to be tiresome. What game was Kevin playing?

Kevin frowned. "We should be banding together to protect this country from those who don't belong. We're the class of men that need to be running things. I have made many connections to help me go far. Stick with me, and you can climb the ladder with me."

Ed shook his head and sighed. That same old story. "What if I'm happy where I am?"

For the first time in the conversation, Kevin came off as sincere. "Then help me up the ladder. I'll be gone and out of your hair. Win-win."

He'd had enough of this idiot. Ed faced Kevin and glared. He squinted his dark-brown eyes and set his square jaw. "And if I don't?"

Kevin sniggered. "You never know, Ed, my boy . . . I'm sure personnel has your home address . . ." He trailed off with an insinuating grin.

Ed narrowed his eyes. "Is that a threat, Kevin?"

"Could be. Could be a promise. Or could just be idle thoughts, as I start to understand the departments here. Have a nice day." He sauntered out, leaving the door open.

Ed slammed his door closed. He'd request Ashok do an extensive background check on Kevin. Something was wrong with him. Perhaps he was part of the leaks.

Was this place secure?

"Have you swept for bugs today, Jackson?"

"Every day, Ed. And Ashok has verified with his own sweep."

The aroma of fresh coffee filled the air as the four-minute timer went off. "More coffee?" Jackson sprang from his chair and popped over to his eight-cup Cafetière with freshly brewed Moonson Malabar coffee.

Ed and Ashok sat at Jackson's worn cherrywood kitchen table. Ed admired again Jackson's extensive array of cookbooks. Ed was amazed that, despite the fact Jackson was a foodie, loved to cook, barely exercised, and seemed to always be eating, he was fit and trim.

Jackson was not a handsome man, with a slightly hooked nose and acne scars, but he made up for his lack of looks with a brilliant mind. Jackson, a professor at Harvard, had been tapped by Ed to be his analyst for Operation Bittman. Jackson's analysis had been invaluable, and with Elda gone, Ed required that skill on his team. Ed had used a lot of persuasion before Jackson agreed to come to DC and to radically cut back his lecture hours at Harvard to only a few a year. Jackson had done his time in the military and the CIA and had expressed a desire to live more freely. He'd resisted being in a government-related institution again. Ed, securing Jackson a part-time position at Georgetown University, had helped clinch the deal.

"Thanks for having us here, Jackson. Are you sure your wife doesn't mind?"

"No, Ed. In fact she loves it. My work night *in* is her girl's night *out*. She's off taking to a movie with her girlfriends. Now that the kids are grown and out of the house, she's loving her freedom. She figures that I'm here enjoying my time with my guy friends."

Ed analyzed Ashok's and Jackson's behaviors. Perhaps he was getting paranoid, but the leaks had to be coming from *somewhere*. He was running out of possibilities.

Jackson strolled back with the coffeepot. Ashok held out his cup. Ed covered his with his hand, to signify he had enough for now.

"I had an interesting visit from my accountant, Kevin Ball, today." Ed studied their reactions. They seemed genuine. He wished that Elda was here to help him suss things out. Until he was sure of Ashok, he would have to do his own deeper background checks on spouses and friends of his employees.

"He's the one that is always annoying you, right? What was different about today's visit?" Jackson asked.

"He asked me if Elda Ainsworth worked for me."

"That sounds rather specific, Ed. Why would he want to know that?"

"You're the analyst, Jackson. You tell me."

"I don't know what it could be, unless someone is trying to trace her organizational connections."

"That's a possible angle. Ashok, can you dig deeper into who Kevin Ball is and what he's doing?" It would be a positive indicator for Ashok if he finds Kevin was dirty. Of course, Kevin might be clean. Then what? Ed found himself spiraling with these thoughts. He missed Elda's clarity.

"Most definitely, Mister Ed."

Ed nodded at Ashok. "Thanks, Ashok. You mentioned you found some interesting intelligence?"

Ashok beamed. "Yes. Yes. You will find this most interesting."

Jackson leaned in, and Ed took a deep breath, knowing from experience it would take Ashok a while to get to the point.

Ashok kept going. "I have been most diligent in my searches and following the disinformation, but I think we're well aware of that area, and it is most easy to follow and stop these happenings."

Not impressed with this info, Ed leaned in. "Yes, Ashok, I agree. We understand it will increase as we head toward elections and that there are many eyes watching it."

Ashok shook his head and nodded. "Yes, yes, Mister Ed, you're most right in that, but I think you will find this other data much more to your interest."

Sitting back in his chair, Ed waited patiently for the story to unfold.

Ashok pressed on, smiling as he rattled off his accomplishments. "You see, first I have found a number of Chinese companies here in America who are using their companies as fronts to bring over Chinese citizens to America."

"But, Ashok, that is nothing new," Jackson said. "They've been doing that for years."

"Yes, yes, they have, Mister Jackson. And they're obtaining permits for these people to work in different high-tech companies and give the IP they discover to China. They're also spying on a variety of well-connected American citizens."

Ed frowned and put in his two cents. "But, Ashok, that is not our problem. That is something the FBI needs to handle. Our area of expertise is Russia."

"Yes, yes, you're so correct, Mister Ed. I will transfer this material to the FBI," Ashok consented.

"Sooooo?" Ed's eyebrows threatened to disappear into his hairline, his wide eyes begging Ashok to make his point.

"The real discovery are some interesting transactions in real estate and art," Ashok revealed, with a lilt in his voice.

Both Jackson and Ed leaned forward. The meat was forthcoming.

"As you know, the United States is a tax haven for oligarchs. I have learned much from you, Mister Jackson, about this and have used those facts to direct my searches."

"We, the US, have levied sanctions on many of the Russian oligarchs," Jackson piped in. "But there are many other oligarchs, including those who are United States citizens. These folks have bought up vast quantities of United States properties, including massive portions of waterfront and island communities. They've also been trading in the arts to both launder and hide money."

Ed cleared his throat but restrained himself from speaking. He didn't want to send the duo down the information rabbit hole.

Nodding and pointing, Ashok went on, "Yes, yes, exactly, as Mister Jackson stated. And I, Ashok, have noticed these are encrypted messages talking about these territories of real estate here in the United States, as well as properties in the United Kingdom."

Unable to stop himself any longer, Ed probed, "And who are they traced to and what are they up to?"

"Exactly, Mister Ed! That is what we wish to know!" Ashok lightly pounded a fist on the table.

Ed held his fist up to his mouth, inhaled, and blinked at Ashok, unable to say anything kind at that moment.

"But these messages carry traces that imply they may be instigated by Russia," Ashok asserted.

Ed tilted his head and moved his eyes from one side to the other and back again. "Ah, so it *would* be in our bailiwick to follow this trail."

"Yes, Mister Ed. That is exactly what I have been saying," Ashok said.

A knock sounded on Jackson's door, and Charlie strode in. "Sorry I'm late, all, but I was busy slipping a tail. Not to worry—it was Frank, I believe."

She snagged a kitchen towel and rubbed the sweat off her neck. Jackson took the towel from her with two fingers and dropped it onto the floor.

Charlie smiled at him. "Thanks, Jackson. Anyway, I also gathered some intelligence by talking to others in Frank's cyber group. Frank is insisting his crew focuses on disinformation and the old politics angle and stays away from infrastructure cyberterrorism. They're culling out a lot of instances where Russians are attacking our electrical hubs, hospitals, and the like, but Frank appears to be squashing it."

"Ah, Miss Charlie, ma'am," Ashok cut in, "that would make most sense."

Charlie swiveled toward him. "Why, Ashok? Did you find something out from the details I gave you?"

"Yes, I most definitely did." Ashok sat back with a smug look on his face.

Charlie stared at Ed and Jackson, who shook with unexpressed laughter. "What?" she queried.

Ashok reminded her, "Do you remember, Miss Charlie, I told you one of the contacts you gave me traced back to Alexei Alexeev's cell phone?"

Now Ed and Jackson showed their confusion as they chimed in with, "What?"

Ed shook his head. He was in charge, and half the time he didn't know what was going on. "But Alexei is long gone. The intel we got informed us he was strangled in his apartment in Moscow. We've always suspected Tosh, but that's not his MO for eliminating someone."

"I managed to pull some data from Frank's cell phone,"

Charlie spelled out, "and I gave it to Ashok to analyze. He came right back with Alexei's number."

"Yes, yes. Most definitely," Ashok tacked on. "I did some research into who replaced Alexei, and it is a man called Adrik Lebedev. His mission is cyberterrorism. What if it is he who now owns Alexei's cell and is controlling Frank?"

Jackson scowled. "Could Adrik be running the real estate scam too?"

"Sorry, what real estate scam?" Charlie lifted a brow.

They filled her in.

Charlie raised her hand. "Ed, can I go to the UK? It would beat being thrown down the stairs by Frank."

"What?" the three men blurted out in unison.

"Never mind. Just fly me over the pond," Charlie insisted.

Chapter Ten

Maxim Komarov glowered at Alwyn Griffiths, who stood outlined on the hill, hands on hips, glaring at the man in front of him. The stiff breeze fluffed his hair. The rolling expanse of green fields and intersecting winding roads with hedgerows behind him gave a grandness to his already tall figure.

"Who do you think you are, Alwyn? Just give up and sell if you know what's good for you and your family."

Alwyn spat at the man in front of him. "You're fucking crackers if you think I'm going to sell my land to *you*. This has been in my family for generations. I'll go under with the farm before I'll let you *sglyfath* developers steal it."

"You may very well go under—six feet under," Max retorted.

"This is Welsh soil. It's been in my family for generations, and I will *never* give it over to foreigners. Now sod off." Alwyn strode away across the rolling Pembrokeshire turf.

Max stormed back to his rental car. He was very used

to doing land deals for the Kremlin, but this one was especially problematic.

"He is still refusing to sell." Max stood leaning on his car in the parking lot of the Premier Inn in St. Davids, Wales.

He noticed the cobblestone parking spaces were barely large enough for the bigger vehicles in the lot. One car was parked over the yellow line, which irritated him. Many things annoyed him lately, especially this project he was on.

He returned his focus to his phone and Boris. "There's talk he's going to gather a bunch of locals together to stop the land sales here. What would you like me to do next?"

Despite the wind crossing the speaker, Boris's voice came clearly over the phone. "Keep an eye on things and update me on how they progress. I will send someone to help you handle the situation there."

Boris marched into the laboratory. Gorky Krovopuskov was working under a hood with the air blower sucking any fumes up and out. Boris cleared his throat and waited. He was always respectful to anyone who could kill him.

Gorky was a wizened man with a slender bent-over body, wrinkled face, and beaked nose. He wrung his hands together as he spoke in a crackling voice, "You're lucky nothing in here is terribly poisonous today." Gorky chuckled, ending in a high pitch.

Boris slowed his breathing and tried to not inhale deeply. He laughed with gritted teeth at Gorky's old joke. "Would it be possible for you to make something to convey a clear message? Something that would demonstrate to others they should not follow in someone's footsteps?"

Gorky's eyes lit up, and he rattled off the choices. "Novichok is tried and true and easy to deliver, but is not always fatal. It *would* point to Russia, since we've used it before on Navalny. Ricin is also a good alternative, but death may take a few days. That one got a lot of press with the murder of Georgi Markov with a poisoned umbrella. It would also point back to most likely being done by a Russian. It has great flair. If you want it to appear as a drug overdose, you could use Carfentanyl. Yet that could cause harm to whomever is delivering it. Gelsemium is highly toxic and easily delivered in food. You could use Polonium-210, but that takes longer, and the radiation could be an issue to whomever is delivering it. I rather like the natural toxins, such as Batrachotoxin. It causes heart failure, so displays the drama of someone clutching their chest. Always a good touch. But we could go with Maititixin or Botulinum toxin. Both are deadly."

Boris worked to control the horror welling up inside him. *This man is Dr. Death.* He took a few shallow breaths. "I would go with your recommendation. I do like the chest-clutching bit though. How would the Batrachotoxin be delivered?"

Gorky wrung his hands again, smiled, and trotted to a cabinet. "Ah, that's the fun part. The Columbian Indians use blow darts. We can deliver via an automated form of it. See? This gadget straps onto your wrist, pops out with a button, delivers the stinger with another, and retracts before anyone is aware of what happened. Or we have the ring, which pops open to display a poisoned needle. Stick someone and cover the mechanism back up. And there's a delightful choice from the old Cold War days. The poisoned spike in the shoe. Click your heels to pop it out, a slight kick, a small puncture, and *click*, it's retracted. None the wiser."

Boris's eyes watered from his attempts to control his breathing. He had to get out of there. "*Khorosho.* I will send an agent to you, and he can select what works best for him. *Spasibo*."

Boris backed out, watching Gorky lovingly stroke one of the shoes.

———

Maxim crouched at his table to make himself small and unnoticed. He stared up at Alwyn Griffiths standing on a sturdy dark-oak chair in The Bishops pub, his head nearly hitting one of the old wooden beams, his voice echoing off the stone walls. This man didn't know when to shut up. Maxim had warned him to keep his mouth closed.

"All right, friends and neighbors," Alwyn started. "You all know me, and I know you, I do. We've been childhood friends and worked together to till and maintain this land of ours. My farm's been in my family for generations. We all stand proudly on Welsh soil, we do."

"Hear, hear . . ."

"And now, what it is," Alwyn shouted, "these fucking foreigners swoop in to steal our land from us. I'm not being funny. The money they offer is far less than it's worth, it is. That's buzzing, it is. Just not fair, see. I'm tamping, fuming, raging, I am. And one of those foreigners sits over by there." He drew attention to Maxim, who sank lower in his chair.

"But it's real money. And these are hard times," whined a man from the audience.

Alwyn countered. "How long will that money last you, Rhys? And what will you have when it's gone? Where will you live? What will your children do? Do you know what I mean though? I'm only saying, I am."

The tone in the room shifted from one of debate to one of consensus. Maxim glanced toward the door. It was time to leave. He was a loyal servant of the Kremlin, but violence was not his cup of tea. He did the verbal intimidation and transactions. Others took care of anything that needed to be emphasized.

"Fuck the fucking developers!" one attendee cried out, to a chorus of cheers.

Alwyn indicated Maxim. "He calls himself Max, but what is his real name, right? Who does he work for? We don't know him, no. We don't know his family, we don't. His speech is foreign. He does *not* have our interests in mind. He wants to profit off our hard work. He wants to stand on our shoulders and drive us into the ground. Bastard. Thief!"

A growl rose from the crowd. One man took off his boots and lobbed them at Maxim, hitting him on his shoulder. Max rose and made a beeline for the door. Shoes, boots, and jeers followed him.

Chapter Eleven

"**S**TAS!" ELATED TO SEE HIM, SNEZHANA TOOK her feet off her desk and trotted over to give him a hug. "What brings you here? Are you going to quit that Kremlin crap and join us?" He looked paler than usual, if that was at all possible.

"I need your advice, Snez. Where's Anatoly?" Stas swiveled to look around.

She hoped it wasn't something that needed to be man to man, although she couldn't imagine what that was. Both guys were celibate. Or perhaps better termed, asexual? "Oh, he stormed over to the gym to destroy a punching bag or two. He pays to replace them, so they continue to let him use the facilities. You know how tense he gets when he hasn't killed for a while. He's even off his pastries. I fear he's also depressed about losing Tosh. But enough on all that. What's up?" Snezhana eyed Stas expectantly.

"Boris took me from Adrik's bunch and ordered me to build a team for him. That's not my expertise. I need help." His voice held an anxious note.

"And . . ."

Stas took a big breath. "And I fear Boris will never let

me leave, even if I manage to do this successfully."

Snezhana patted him on the shoulder. "Tell me what he said."

Stas recited the events from Boris's office. "He said, 'Well, Stas, I understand you've been doing an excellent job for Adrik. However, you're necessary for another project.'"

"How did you respond?"

"I thought I'd throw up, but I told him I was *very* much looking forward to working on his project, but I wondered if I could let go after that. I let him know that I only came on board to work on one project here, but Adrik threatened me, so I stayed. But I want to go back to my life."

"And what did he say?"

"He said he'd make me a deal. If I started his project and staffed it with excellent developers, we could discuss this again. I'm not a manager, Snezhana. I've never hired anyone. I need your help. If I fail at this, he will eliminate me."

Snezhana sat back down and wheeled in her chair, twirling her hair, mulling on Stas's problem. She stopped. "Do you have any spare time to help me in return?"

"Of course I can. This work is tedious and boring."

Snezhana smiled. "Great. Although I despise Boris and hate helping him, for you, I will source and vet the people for this project. All you'll need to do is to judge they're technically sound."

Stas snickered. "I can do that in my sleep."

Snezhana chuckled. "*Khorosho.* In return, I need your help on a personal project Anatoly and I have been working on. Do you have your computer with you now?" Snezhana directed his attention to his backpack.

Stas whipped out his T-Platforms rugged laptop machine containing the Elbrus-8S chip and running the ultra-secure Astra Linux Operating System and situated it on one corner of Snezhana's desk. "At your service."

Of course he carried his laptop with him. "Sophia gave us a lead on a man who could potentially give us info on the remaining moles in the US, UK, and the Kremlin. He was working as a mercenary for Ukraine but actually spied on their military and passed secrets back to Russia. The photo Anatoly snapped of this corpse matches the one Sophia gave us, but we don't have the access anymore to go into the government databases to run his fingerprints."

"Is that all?" Stas's fingers flew on his keyboard. "Who needs access. Give me those prints . . . *Pozhaluysta.*"

Snezhana handed Stas a thumb drive. "*Vot.* And, Stas . . ."

"*Da?*"

"Anatoly and I are going to go after whoever planted the informers and extract revenge for Elda and Tosh. We'd like your help."

Stas smiled broadly. "Count me in."

———

Goddamn asshole.

Charlie sneered as Frank paraded through the work area. He was definitely full of himself, which wasn't a crime, but she sensed something else was going on with him. Could he be a foreign agent? If so, which country was running him? He isn't well trained, which suggested he has been recruited as a mole and not a professional agent. How did he even get this job?

One of her coworkers called out to him. "Hey, Frank! There's a lot of chatter about real estate transactions in the United States and Wales. Possibly of Russian origin. Shall we dig in more?"

Charlie perked up. Now this could be of interest.

"Ignore it," Frank bellowed back. "We've got bigger fish to fry. Stay with the social media disinformation."

"Shall we at least tell the spooks handling the Russian office about it?" the man asked.

Frank shut him down. "Certainly not. They have more important things to dig in to. Focus on our mission."

Interesting. He was hiding information about Russian activity, which could bolster her theory that he was working for them. *Uh-oh, here he comes.*

Frank stopped in front of Charlie's desk. "Don't you have anything better to do than to listen in on others' conversations?"

Charlie smiled at him, replying coyly, "Actually, no. And it's quite informative."

"You better finish up and get out of here. Your days are limited," Frank said in his snarkiest tone.

"Really, Frank, from the way you drive, I'd say *your* days are limited." Charlie countered.

It was long shot, but it hit home. Frank stuttered, turned, and stomped off to his office.

So it was Frank . . .

Chapter Twelve

THE THRUM OF KEYBOARD CLATTER SPILLED OUT into the hallway. Glancing around to ascertain no one was paying attention to her, Sophia trotted into MI6's message center. All eyes were on their individual monitors and did not notice her arrival. Sophia inhaled the comforting aroma of plastic and electronics. She searched for her friend Heather Lewis and, locating her, popped over to her cubicle. She stuck her head through the opening and whispered, "Hi, Heather, got time for lunch?"

Heather nodded. "It is that time, isn't it. I'm a bit peckish. How about if we meet in a half hour at the regular place?"

"Bob's your uncle." Sophia turned and sneaked out. She didn't want to call attention to her intel gathering. Her new bosses had her sorting through boring cold cases. She swung by her desk to pick up her purse. As she unlocked her desk drawer to access it, Treacher Walker sauntered up and stood close to her. Too close, in Sophia's opinion.

"What do *you* want?" she demanded.

He leaned in. She could feel his breath on her neck,

and she inhaled the stench of stale cigarettes as he exhaled.

"Lunch?" he proposed with a smile, displaying his coffee-stained teeth.

"What? Did you lose your badge again and need help getting into the cafeteria?" Sophia mocked.

His smile disappeared, and he clenched his fists.

There's the real Treacher.

He recovered and leered. "I'll make it worth your while."

"In your dreams, Treacle. I'm a married woman." She slung her purse over her shoulder and waved him to one side.

He took a half step so she would be forced to brush by him. Sophia elbowed him aside on her way by.

"It's Treacher, you twit," he called after her.

⁓

Did I see that man before? Sophia glared at a man who bumped into her. "Sorry, luv," he apologized as he paraded by. Sophia glanced over her shoulder to assure he kept on moving and they were not being followed.

Heather and Sophia strolled side by side along the south bank of the Thames. The river was low, with birds pecking at the gravelly sand along its banks. The laughter from playing children floated over to them, combining with the rhythm of the motors and wash from passing boats. A dog barked in the distance. Sophia could not shake the feeling she was being tailed.

Thick gray and white clouds gathered overhead. Sophia pulled her coat closed to keep the wind chill out. She tossed a crinkled white paper sack to Heather, apologizing. "It's a jam butty—sorry, but they were all out of tuna. I know this disgusting thing is your second favorite. It's on squishy white, as you like it." The two sat on the concrete embankment near Riverside Park to eat.

Heather chuckled as she reached into the bag and rustled out her sandwich. Crinkling her mouth, she spit out, "Yuck. Pickle." She discarded the offending fruit over the side and into the river.

"Hey, that's green. It's gotta be health food," Sophia quipped.

Heather chuckled and unwrapped the wax paper covering the sandwich, using it as a plate on her lap.

Sophia glanced up and down the road, then turned to business. "I'm sorry to bother you, but except for you, I seem to be shut off from the information flow. As we just said, I think there's something rotten somewhere in our organization."

"I am suspicious too and more than willing to help you in any way that I can," Heather mumbled between mouthfuls. "Not much time today, sorry, but I've some interesting chatter going on in the Russian sector."

Sophia reached into her lunch bag and pulled out an avocado-and-cheese sandwich on wheat bread. She took a substantial bite, and with a mouth too full to speak, nodded for Heather to continue.

Heather leaned in and whispered, "I think there is a Russian asset in Wales. And a not-too-smart one either. He has not changed phones and called the same number numerous times. The phone routes through a few switches before it connects, but it's not an encrypted line. They must be pretty secure about this man's cover."

Sophia swallowed her mouthful before asking, "So where does it terminate?"

Heather smiled knowingly and flicked her forefinger in the air, "That's the juicy part! It's a number at the Kremlin. The caller is complaining about someone who will not sell his land to him. His Kremlin contact told him to stay put and they would deliver assistance. It sounds like something is going down."

Sophia brightened. "Where's the developer?"

Heather gestured with her half-eaten sandwich. "Interestingly enough, in Pembrokeshire, Wales. At an inn in St. Davids. I can text you the address once I'm back at my desk."

Finally, something to act on. "Excellent! Pembrokeshire, Wales, hey? That's an area Elda knew well. I wish she were alive and I could have her support there. I learned so much from her. I'm not supposed to be a field operative at the moment, but it wouldn't harm anyone if I took a couple of days off and sussed this out."

Excited, Sophia crammed the remainder of her lunch into the bag and rose. "Thanks, Heather." She squinted up river. Did something move when she did? She must be imagining things.

She plopped back onto the embankment when Heather mentioned, "Oh, and there was an interesting find in the Ukraine."

Sophia frowned. "Ukraine? What would interest us there?"

Heather glanced around furtively. "Apparently a Ukrainian soldier blew away a Russian mercenary."

"*Really*," Sophia retorted, with dripping sarcasm. "And so . . ."

"Well, the mercenary's name is Joseph White. He was ex-CIA and may also have been dealing with James during Operation Bittman. He matches that man you showed interest in." Heather grinned.

Sophia leaned in. "Do we have a definite ID on the body?"

Heather nodded. "Yes, but of greatest interest is that something is off about the incident. The bullet wound appears as if two bullets were fired through him at the same entry point but different exits. One casing matches the Ukrainian soldier's weapon, but we haven't found the other.

With the condition of the building, it may never be found. We suspect, however, that a third person may have been involved."

Sophia let out a breath she didn't know she had been holding. "Interesting . . . Please keep me posted on anything that comes in."

"Of course. And thanks for the sandwich."

Sophia, up and on her way, waved in acknowledgment. Heather's last words reached her. "Be careful."

Boris thumped his fist on his desk. He did not have the right people. He had to send someone to Maxim to eliminate the Welshman. This deal had been delayed too long. It was time to bulldoze through these roadblocks. Boris was not a fan of diplomacy.

He paced his office. Aha. *Emil owes me a favor.* He and Emil had never been friends, but he couldn't ignore paying Boris back. Boris knew Emil had had resources to spare and knew the penalty his family would pay for ignoring Boris.

Boris picked up his phone and made the call. A short time after he hung up, a woman stood tall in the entryway frame. Good, Emil had come through.

Nyoka Morozov stood silent and still as Boris circled her, as if establishing a horse's pedigree. His nostrils flared at a somewhat metallic scent emanating from her. *That reminds me of something.* "Your résumé is impressive. It claims one hundred kills."

Silence.

"You may speak at any time, you know."

Nyoka nodded.

Boris liked that she was sparing in words. Now to see if she could act. Boris filled in the conversational gaps. "If you wanted to murder me, how many ways could you do it?"

"If I wanted to eliminate you, you would already be dead," Nyoka hissed.

Unfazed, Boris went on. "By what means?"

"Pick one. The heels of my stilettos are spikes. My watch contains a wire noose. This ring can deliver poison. My hands can snap your neck." She smiled, and her penetrating canine teeth glittered. "To distract you, I could bite your neck, or"—she displayed red-polished nails, filed to points—"or scratch your eyes out. Shall I go on?" She raised one perfect eyebrow and stood silently.

Boris got an image of a coiled snake waiting to strike. He waved a hand. "*Net*. That is sufficient. You will do." Finally he had a real killer on his assassin staff. He relished a moment of picturing his enemies slayed by her.

Nyoka smiled again, displaying her canines. The smile stopped there. Her dark, lifeless eyes stared at Boris.

He identified the smell. Dried blood.

He motioned for her to exit the room.

What could be wrong with her? Emil had said Boris could keep her as long as he needed. Boris didn't trust Emil. What was the catch here?

Boris read through Nyoka's CV again. He looked at her reviews and past assignments. All excellent. From the reports, her most recent mission to remove a traitor in the Ukraine went well. She covered up her involvement nicely, and the man was dead.

Well, he needed a killer, and this woman was definitely one. He'd send her to Wales. If she succeeded, he'd keep her. And if Emil had double-crossed Boris, he would have her dispatch Emil.

What could go wrong?

Chapter Thirteen

T HE BRAKES SQUEALED THE TRAIN to a stop. Hot air puffed from the engine. Nyoka stepped onto the gray concrete platform at the brick train station in Haverfordwest. A discarded metal milk jug lay across the way, and a stray chicken ran down the tracks. She sneered in disdain. This should be an easy kill. Plebeians.

She strode to the Station Self Drive rental office to pick up a car. Her lip curled, and she spit on the ground when she spotted the place. It looked like a gas station with two repair bays and no pumps. The man behind the desk was out of shape, soft, and overly chatty. If he didn't have a contract here, she'd eradicate him. Perhaps when she returned the van, if no one was about. His existence was annoying.

"So just you for the camper van?" He rubbed the stubble on his chin and glanced at the window.

"Yes." Nyoka felt her chest constrict with the need to snuff out this gnat. She caressed her canines with her tongue to calm herself.

"Do you have an itinerary? I'll be glad to suggest places for you to see." His smile displayed yellowed, poorly maintained teeth.

"No need." Nyoka rubbed her wristwatch, envisioning the wire noose around his neck, his eyes bulging as he kicked in his final death throes.

"Here's a map and also a brochure of places of interest in Wales." He consulted the paperwork in front of him. "Only a week. Oh, too bad. You could easily spend a month exploring here." He presented her with the brochure, map, and a copy of her paperwork.

Taking the offered papers, Nyoka drawled, "My boss is a hard taskmaster." She studied the jugular vein in his neck, visualizing it spurting blood, and smiled thinly at him.

"Oh, isn't that always the case, hey? Well, enjoy! I will bring the van around front." He popped through the back door to the garage.

Nyoka breathed in a lungful of air and sauntered out to take control of the van.

"See you in a week! Call if you need to extend your stay." He stood in the parking lot, waving at her.

Nyoka waved one perfectly manicured red-polished hand and sped away, heading northwest toward St. Davids.

<center>~~~~~</center>

The views were spectacular. Too bad Oliver wasn't there with her. Sophia gazed out the kitchen window of Point Cottage in Little Haven, Wales. The late-morning sun sparkled on the water of St. Brides Bay. She reminded herself to focus and get out of vacation mode. There was no way of knowing how dangerous the people she was hunting would be.

Sophia dropped her duffel in the bedroom. She checked her phone for messages and saw one from an unknown contact.

RGNT ND FOR A VACA IN WALES. WD XXX TO PK UR BRAIN. CHARLIE

Charlie! What a flash from the past. She texted back, GUD. WHR R U?

LONDON

London?! Sophia texted, M IN WALES. PK U UP AT HWEST TRN STA. HV COTTAGE N LOVELY SPOT.

HV CAR. C U IN 4+ HRS.

Interesting . . . Why was Charlie here? Sophia supposed she'd find out soon enough. She did welcome the extra manpower. She thought back to when she first met Charlie. Elda and Oliver's friend Emily had both been alive then. Elda had believed in Sophia and empowered her to operate and set up James. Sophia's knowledge of spy craft and disguises were mainly from working closely with Elda. Sophia drew power from that time to this situation. She would find out who was operating in Wales and shut them down.

Sophia grabbed her phone again to look at the message. How did she know for sure it was from Charlie? She texted, HOW DID EMILY DIE?

The reply was: SINGLE SHOT BETWEEN THE EYES. CLOSE RANGE. WHAT WAS MY DISGUISE WHEN I WAS TAILING YOU?

POSTAL CARRIER.

GOOD ONE. AND WHAT COMPANY'S TRUCK DID WE USE TO BRING SNEZHANA IN?

CEX.

VERIFIED. GOOD CATCH. ELDA TRAINED US BETTER THAN THAT SLIP.

Whew. It was Charlie all right. That could have been catastrophic.

The lack of action was irritating, the silence annoying. Maxim paced back and forth by the foot of the unmade bed in his room at the St. Davids Hotel. This was the part he didn't like. He was a real estate developer, not a murderer. He stopped, sat in the desk chair, and rolled it back and forth while scrolling on his phone.

Nothing.

Where was the assassin? Maxim checked to ensure he was e-ticketed on the train to London. It would be good to get out for a few days while the killer did his work, then Max could return to a cowed population and get the deal inked. He was looking forward to being back in Moscow. This damp, dreary weather with all the green pastures irritated him. He far preferred the concrete and cold of Moscow. The rules were clear to him. He scanned his room and felt as bleakly empty as the lack of decorations on the walls.

A rap on the door startled him. He sprang up and peered out the spy hole. A tall woman with pale skin and jet-black hair stood examining her red-polished nails. *Kakogo cherta? What the fuck?*

She knocked again. He opened the door, and she strode in.

"Excuse me?" Maxim kept the door open, expecting she would leave.

"Why? What have you done?" the woman queried, in a throaty voice with a Russian accent.

"This is my room. I must ask that you leave. I'm waiting for someone." He gestured for her to go.

"You are waiting for *me, ty pridurok.*" She reached across him and closed the door. "Now, give me all the facts about the man who is holding this project up."

"You can't be . . ." Maxim stammered, "I'm waiting for a man."

Nyoka narrowed her eyes. She smiled, displaying canines to Maxim, and hissed, "And why would *that* be?"

"The job we need done is man's work. It's not suitable for a woman." Maxim backed up a step. The force field of her angry energy was palpable.

She glared at him. "Your job is to give me all the information you have. I will decide the rest."

Maxim evaluated the woman. She stood about six feet tall. Her hands were large with V-shaped red nails. Her yellow eyes were devoid of warmth. She appeared coiled to strike. Perhaps this woman was capable of killing a man. He decided to give her what she wanted now and hoped she left quickly.

"His name is Alwyn Griffiths. He lives on one of the farms we're trying to buy. He is the center of the resistance. I do believe if he is removed that the sale will go through." He indicated the pile of paperwork on the desk. "See there? Everything is ready to go. All it needs is a signature."

"So you've done your work here?" Nyoka summarized.

Maxim puffed up, pleased that she recognized his accomplishment. "Yes, I have. Please let Boris know how organized everything is. I will return to Moscow with the signed papers once Alwyn is gone and his son signs."

"Yes," she hissed. "Your work is done."

<hr>

Slamming the door behind her, and carrying a stack of papers, Nyoka stalked into the inn's office. "Hello? Is anyone here? I need to use a copier."

An overweight, unshaven man made an appearance in the doorway. "Through that door. I'm going out for a *mwg*." He held up his pack of Marlboros and lumbered out the door.

Nyoka sent daggers with her eyes to his back. Fat pig. She could skewer him. But she best get this done and scram.

Nyoka nipped behind the desk and located the DVR for the camera equipment. She used the side of her fingernail to unscrew it and extract the internal drive. Pocketing the drive, she put the system back together. Reaching next to the DVR, she turned on the copier. Lifting the flatbed cover, she scratched the glass with her diamond ring. Take that, fat bastard. She admired the three letters she had carved and made a copy of a blank sheet of paper.

Nyoka giggled as she sauntered to her camper van. The piece of paper fell from her hand when she hopped into the driver's seat. It floated and landed in front of her left rear tire. The tire marks almost obscured the *D* in *DIE*.

Chapter Fourteen

ABSORBED WITH THOUGHTS OF WORK, Charlie registered the view, without fully appreciating it. On one side were the green and brown undulating fields, dotted with sheep, and on the other, the depth of St. Brides Bay beckoning as the tide rolled in against the cliffs.

Sophia and Charlie had popped onto the nearby Pembrokeshire Coast Path. The wind threatened to blow them over the cliff.

Aware that she had missed something Sophia had said, Charlie looked at Sophia. "I'm sorry. What did you ask?"

Frowning, Sophia repeated, "What brings you here, Charlie? You're not the type to take a vacation."

Unsure if she should tell Sophia everything, Charlie hesitated. "I don't have the full picture yet, Sophia. And I'm not sure where to start."

"How about at the beginning?" Sophia's grin contradicted the concerned look in her blue eyes.

"Funny," Charlie deadpanned. "Well, you possess the right clearance level, and I'm going to assume you also have the need to know." She struggled with her official ethics before spilling. "I guess the start of the whole thing is back in the Ukraine, where I tracked a man who was a double agent and may have been a mole during Operation Bittman. Unfortunately, I killed him before I got him to spill his guts."

"The Ukraine?!" Sophia gasped. "Was it this man?" She held up her phone for Charlie to view.

The man in the image was younger, had longer hair, and looked less threatening than the one she had met in Ukraine, but it was definitely him. "That's the one. Where did that picture come from?" Charlie gawked at the image.

"I received intel on this man and researched him more. This was his school photo, one of the last pictures he allowed to be taken. I sent Anatoly to find him in the Ukraine, but someone arrived there first. Now I see it was you."

Charlie wondered if she had heard Sophia correctly. Her eyebrows leapt for her hairline. "Anatoly, the Russian assassin?"

"Yes," Sophia affirmed. "He and Snezhana are no longer associated with the Kremlin. They're now running a private investigation company. I required some boots on the ground, so I hired them."

"Small world." Charlie shook her head in amazement. It was apparent that Sophia knew more than Charlie did on this man so she should share her information. "Well, all I got from the traitor was an indication there is a more extensive network of moles than we suspected. I hoped I might pick up a tidbit that could tell us more where Elda is."

"But, Charlie, she's dead."

"Do you *really* believe that?" Charlie snapped.

"We have *no* reason to believe she's alive, Charlie."

Charlie stopped short and faced Sophia. Her eyes narrowed. She shook her finger at Sophia. "Elda *is* alive. I know it in my heart." First Ed, now Sophia. Elda was alive, but Charlie's statement was received with disbelief and an implication that Charlie was irrational.

Sophia gazed at Charlie with sad eyes and a downcast mouth. She started to open her mouth to speak.

Charlie held up her hand to stop her. "This is not an emotional reaction, Sophia. *Think* about it. Elda orchestrated the final standoff and the removal of James. She led Tosh to the warehouse. She sent us all out while they talked. Two gunshots and then *nothing*. We entered and saw a huge amount of blood and followed a trail leading to the river. It was all much too pat. We searched everywhere, and no trace of either of them was found."

"But, Charlie, that's the point. The bodies could have floated off and will never be discovered." Sophia laid her hand on Charlie's arm.

Frustrated that she was not heard, Charlie shook off Sophia's hand. "They would have surfaced somewhere. Again, too convenient. And if they're truly dead, we will find their remains somewhere. Or we will find them alive. We did not look deeply enough. We need to channel both of their minds to discover what they did. And why did they not trust anyone enough to disclose their plan."

"If there was in fact a plan."

Charlie bristled at Sophia's statement. "We need to know."

Sophia affirmed and redirected. "I hear you, Charlie, and we can discuss it more later. Now is not the time. There's an immediate problem to solve here, right? What do you know?"

Charlie rubbed her forehead and resumed their hike. "There's a real estate scam going on involving both the United States and United Kingdom, managed out of Russia, most likely by our old friend Adrik. The intent of the operation is to disrupt the economies on both sides of the pond.

Frank Garcia's US intelligence team is reluctant to follow the trail, and we traced a call from Frank to Alexei's phone."

"Alexei Alexeev? Tosh's old boss? But he's dead."

"That's the one. It implies that Frank is being run by the Russians."

"Is this a continuation of Operation Bittman, where Russia was actively working on disinformation to derail the political structures of the democracies?"

"I personally think this misinformation may be part of a larger scheme to sow discord in nations that Russia considers foes. My opinion is that the Russians set the infrastructure and had a degree of success in Operation Bittman and are expanding into more aggressively disrupting infrastructures—physical, economic, political, any way they can weaken us. Ed suspects there are more moles on both sides of the pond. I'm not sure who is trustworthy."

Sophia gave Charlie a thumbs-up. "Well, you're in the right place, Charlie. You can rely on me. I think there's a Russian agent here in the UK running things, but my organization is also not hot to trot to follow up on this. Officially, I'm here on *vacation*."

"You haven't proven yourself untrustworthy yet. So what leads do you have?" Some actionable intel would be great.

Sophia filled her in. "There's a man called Max staying at a inn in St. Davids. He is the developer on this real estate project. We traced a call from him to the Kremlin."

"Well, it appears we need to visit him and also the man opposing the deal," Charlie said, with a bounce in her step. "What's his name?"

"Alwyn Griffiths."

Charlie squinted. "Alwyn Griffiths, hey? A native from this section of Wales?"

Sophia nodded. "Yes. His family's owned the land for generations."

"Interesting. I wouldn't think he'd want to sell then."

"Exactly. You're spot on."

Charlie stopped. She had drifted perilously close to the edge of the cliff, and it was a *long* way down. She edged in and turned around. "Shall we head back and divide and conquer?"

Sophia grinned. "Definitely. You take the Russian and I'll take the Welshman. He'll probably be more prone to chat with me, since I have a distant cousin from Pembrokeshire. The Welsh tend to like their own."

Charlie flashed an okay. "You're on. Text or call if you need me. Whoever is done first should meet the other."

"Bob's your uncle." Sophia's face fell.

"Speaking of which, how is Oliver? He always said that."

"Oliver's okay." Sophia looked down, her lips quivering.

Charlie reached out and touched Sophia's arm. "Just okay? What's up, Sophia?"

Sophia shook Charlie's hand away and strode on. She took a long breath and, without looking at Charlie, stated, "Nothing big, Charlie. He's only a touch depressed right now. You remember how excited he was about being a dad and decorated the nursery and built a crib?"

"Yes. What happened?" Charlie wondered, afraid of the answer.

"Our surrogate miscarried," Sophia shared in a matter-of-fact tone.

"Oh fuck. I'm so sorry, Sophia." Feeling helpless, she clenched and unclenched her fists at her side.

"No worries." Sophia brushed it off. "We're going to try again with another surrogate once Oliver feels up to it. Not a big deal, really."

"And you?" Charlie knew Sophia couldn't mean it, when she insisted it wasn't a big deal. It had to have some impact on her feelings.

Sophia shrugged and kept on walking.

"And . . ." Charlie pushed, hoping to help Sophia work it through.

"I'm fine." Sophia glossed it over in an emotionless tone.

"You know, Sophia, it'll be a lot easier for you in the end if you talk about your feelings and stop pushing people away. This all can't be easy on you."

Sophia chuckled. "'Ah, Grasshopper. You have learned well,' as your mentor, Elda, used to say."

"And . . ." Charlie insisted.

Sophia rolled her eyes. "Okay. You win. I'm not fine. The IVF wasn't a party. I'm not looking forward to going through that again. Having a depressed husband is not fun either. But I adore Oliver, and I'll try again when Oliver's ready. For now I focus on work."

Charlie backed off. She stopped, waved to her left, and pointed out, "Speaking of which, we're back to the cottage and the cars."

"Let's go."

〜

Fuck. Charlie slammed the door behind her and inspected the nearly decapitated man lying on the floor at the foot of the bed. Although he hadn't been long dead, opportunistic flies already gathered. Charlie studied the body and the area around it. It was always interesting how different a dead body was from a live one. Even if it had no markings on it, something had left the body that made it alive. *Fuck, Charlie, stop theorizing. Get out of your head and find as much evidence as you can.*

Being careful not to put her knee in the pool of blood, she knelt next to the corpse and frisked him. An international driver's permit identified him as Maxim Komarov.

Avoiding disturbing the crime scene, she photographed the body and scanned the room for any evidence. She spied a single piece of paper on the desk, which had scrawled on it, LEAVE NOW OR REGRET STAYING. An envelope next to it was addressed to *THE FRIGGIN' DEVELOPER*. She photographed both and backed out the door.

Charlie looked around again. There was nothing that could help identify the killer. *Gads! Sophia may be in danger. What if the murderer went there?* She grabbed her phone and texted Sophia. BE CAREFUL. THE DEVELOPER IS DEAD.

Smashing camper van. Sophia pulled into the gravel driveway in front of Alwyn's farmhouse. She saw the front door was ajar and eased it open. "Hello?"

No answer. The essence of generations of living, old wood, dust, and coffee hung in the air.

She tiptoed through the carpeted living room and to the kitchen in the back. She spied a cup of cold coffee by the sink and a dish soaking in the basin. Definitely a bachelor pad. Her phone vibrated, but she ignored it. Now was not the time to be distracted. She didn't know who had left the front door open.

Above her she heard a floorboard creak. *Perhaps I woke him?* She turned to return to the front hallway to meet him coming down the stairs. Instead she saw a tall woman with long black hair descending the steps.

Who was she? "Hello. I'm sorry to have barged in like this, but the door was open."

The woman reached the hallway and stood mute, staring at Sophia.

Unnerved by the yellow eyes boring into her, Sophia stammered, "Is Alwyn at home? We had a meeting."

The woman spoke in a tone so low that Sophia moved

in to catch her words. "He is upstairs."

Sophia moved in front of the woman and put one foot on the first riser. "Thank . . ." Her words were cut off by the noose tightening around her neck.

Damn! I don't have a weapon. Charlie spied Sophia struggling to extricate herself from a noose around her neck. She glanced around the entryway and spotted a metal-and-wood Rounders bat in the cane holder. Grabbing it, she swung with all her force, aiming at the tall woman's head. The metal of the bat connected with bone with a satisfying thwack. The woman collapsed at Charlie's feet. Without the noose holding her up, Sophia fell forward onto the carpeted stairs with a thud.

Charlie hopped over the body. Sophia was bleeding from her neck. Charlie triaged her and was satisfied nothing was fatal. She went to lift Sophia up when, coughing, Sophia gasped, "Did you kill the bitch?"

Charlie glanced over her shoulder at the body behind her, "Yes. We need to get *you* to medical care. Can you stand and walk? My car is outside."

Sophia nodded and winced.

"Hurts, hey?" Charlie took out a handkerchief and tenderly blotted the cut around Sophia's neck. "Yeah, that's nasty. Wait. Don't move. I'll help you up, but first we need to identify this body."

"You carry handkerchiefs?" Sophia croaked.

"Sure, you never know when someone will try to cut off your friend's head." Charlie took a snapshot of the woman on the ground and went into the kitchen for a sharp knife. Returning with a cleaver, she spread out the digits of the woman's right hand and severed the index finger.

Sophia gagged and threw up on the woman. "My God,

Charlie, was that necessary?"

"Quickest way to obtain a print without a fingerprint kit," Charlie shot back. She put her arm around Sophia to help support her and escorted her to the car, depositing her in the passenger seat. While stepping around to the driver's side, Charlie googled doctors and found a St. Davids Surgery nearby.

"I'll return to search the body for ID. No time now. We need to get you looked at."

Charlie zoomed away from the doctor's office, over the winding Welsh roads. Part of her brain admired the rugged coastline and the green rolling hills, while the other worked through the logistics of removing the body from the farmhouse. Plus, she worried about Sophia. She wondered if she should call Oliver. She answered herself. She would wait for an update from the doctor first.

Charlie had stressed with the doctor that Sophia was a vacationing MI6 agent and he would need to sign an official Secrets Act form and to not tell others she was there. She'd made up that load of crap, but he'd believed it, and the story bought them more time to figure next steps.

Charlie put the car into park in front of Alwyn's house. She noted the camper was missing and another car was in its place. *Strange* . . . The front door was still ajar. She gripped the bat she had taken with her and slowly entered.

Damn—the body was gone.

She heard a noise from the kitchen and approached cautiously. Rounding the corner, she was surprised to spot a new player hoisting himself up and onto a kitchen chair. Friend or foe? She hefted the bat and jumped into the kitchen to create the element of surprise. The man fell off the chair, his leg remaining on the table.

"Who are you?" Charlie noted a false leg on the table, with a dart sticking out of it. The man had deep, bloody scratches on his face.

He raised his hand in front of his face in a defensive position. Charlie lowered the bat, inquiring more gently, "What happened here?"

"Hal-lo. I am Rhys. Alwyn's me butty." He shook his head and rubbed a hand over his eyes. "Could you please 'elp me up? I'm in a bet of a pickle here. Me leg's on the ta-able."

"I rather noticed that. I'll help you up, but please do *not* touch the dart. Where did it come from?"

"I came over to talk with Alwyn about the developer, you see. The door was open, as it is now, isn't it. There was a noise from the kitchen, so I went to see, right? And I thought I'd spew chunks. It wasn't normal, you see. 'Orrible, that."

"What was horrible?"

"She stood with her finger on the gas stove. I could smell the burning flesh, I could. I rushed to help her, but she didn't take kindly to that. Next thing I know, I'm down on the ground with a scratched face and the dart in me leg. *Diawl*, that woman is a real devil. A *Brych*, that she is." He took a breath before finishing up. "So I stayed down, 'oping she'd think she took me out with the dart. And she left." He reached for his leg.

Charlie cried out "Wait" and gingerly extracted the dart, being careful not to touch the tip. "This is most likely poisonous." She rustled in the kitchen drawers until she came up with a piece of parchment paper and plastic wrap and secured the dart, surrounded first by the paper and then in the wrap. "Done. Be cautious with your leg. There may be residual poison in it too."

"Devil woman. Don't worry. I'll throw it in the washer, 'ey."

Charlie raised her eyebrows at the thought of someone

washing his leg in the washing machine.

"Gentle cycle, of course, right?"

"Of course. So where did the woman go to?"

"I 'eard her go upstairs and then back down and out the door. A car drove off."

"Where's Alwyn?"

Rhys knitted his eyebrows. "I 'aven't seen 'im. 'E could be upstairs, 'ey?"

Charlie felt her neck tense. This couldn't be good. "You're right. Bitch lady told Sophia he was upstairs. I'll go look. You stay here and put ice on your face." Charlie stepped over the remnants of Sophia's puke in the entryway and padded up the stairs, careful to make no noise. She stepped into the dimly lit hallway and toward a door open on the right. She peeked around the corner. Alwyn's dead eyes stared back at her, his body lying at a strange angle on the floor, as if he had fallen while in the death throes. A slight dab of foam gathered at both corners of his mouth.

"Damn."

<hr>

"Bloody hell."

The shout reached Charlie as she made sandwiches in the kitchen in the Little Haven cottage. Alarmed, she dropped the bread on the counter, where it fell off onto the floor. *Damn.* Grabbing a carving knife, she rushed into the cottage bedroom to see Sophia sitting up in bed holding her neck.

"Cor, that smarts," Sophia complained.

Relieved, but also chagrined at her reaction, Charlie advised, "Don't rub it. It's healing. I don't want to have to take you back to the doctor."

Sophia waved her hand. "He was pleasant enough, but I do think he was glad to be rid of the sneaky beakies when you picked me up. So now we're no longer rushing about and I'll live, I'd welcome another pain pill. Are there any more details on the bitch who did this?"

Charlie reached into her pocket and took out Sophia's pill bottle. She shook one out and handed it to her, setting the bottle on the bedside table. "I don't think you're a suicide risk, so I'll let you manage your pills. As to the woman, I don't know. She was tall, with black hair and long, sharp-pointed red nails. And apparently an extremely hard head. I smacked her with enough force to kill her."

"She was also a coward who attacked me when my back was turned. I bet her knickers are in a twist over losing her finger." Sophia rubbed her neck again. "Bloody hell that hurts. I wish you had cut off her head."

"You could say she'll be a bit miffed over losing her finger, Sophia," Charlie observed dryly. "Speaking of that, I sent it to the embassy in London to that woman Heather, who you mentioned is on the up and up. She will have some initial analysis done on the QT and forward the results to Ashok so he can try to track this woman down. What do you want to do next, Sophia?" Charlie perched on the edge of the bed. She was all out of plans.

"Can you please pass me my phone."

Charlie reached for Sophia's phone and froze when Sophia said, "I think we need to call Anatoly and Snezhana."

"Are you sure that's advisable? You do know the Russians are behind all this. What if they're still in cahoots with the Kremlin?" Charlie countered.

Sophia stopped a headshake partway and grimaced. "Trust me. Not these Russians."

CHAPTER FIFTEEN

"**B**LYAD'! I WILL PUT AN END TO whoever did this to me. They will die a slow and painful death." Nyoka cursed whoever had cut her finger off. She paced in front of Boris's desk, whirled, and spat into his trash can at the side of the desk. Static electricity from the office rug caused her long black hair to fly outward, creating a mantle, giving the impression of a bird of prey.

Disgusting woman. Boris cleaned his nails with his five-inch letter opener. "You were supposed to kill the Welshman, not my developer, Maxim. I am now going to have to replace him. Why on earth did you eliminate him?"

"His work was done there," Nyoka hissed. "He was not a team player. You can do better." Her yellow eyes dared Boris to respond.

Boris decided it was better to let that issue go for now. At least Nyoka had lost a finger as a small penance for what she had done. He could easily replace Maxim. He mentally noted that he may need to get rid of Nyoka if she continued to be a loose cannon. "Tell me again what the woman you killed looked like." He fingered the point of his letter opener, testing the sharpness. *I can always stab her with this if she gets out of control.*

"Why does she matter? She was dying. She didn't do this." Nyoka stopped short and dug her nails into Boris's desk.

Damn her. That was mahogany. Why were all these assassins so stupid? *Glupyy. They don't think these things through.* Sighing, he paced his words. "If this woman was a friend of the Welshman, she could be collateral damage. Meanwhile, we cannot ignore the fact whoever came in behind you may have been working with her."

"She was blond and English. Probably in her thirties," Nyoka spat out.

Oh, that rules out a lot, Boris internally quipped, willing himself not to roll his eyes. "Good observation. I will ask Stas to initiate a search on the database we have on British intelligence agents. Will you be available to look at whatever pictures he comes up with?"

"Yesssss." Nyoka's tongue slithered out and licked her lips, caressing her right canine on the way back into her mouth.

Boris shuddered.

The essence of earth, fertilizer, and male perspiration filled the dimly lit room in The Bishops pub. "We're bloody well tamping and we're not going to stand for these foreigners trying to run us off our land. In Alwyn's memory we will fight on." Rhys stood on the same chair from which Alwyn had commanded the crowd.

"But how?" queried one from the group, in a faint voice.

Charlie spoke up. "You let us handle that. You be our eyes and ears."

"But you're just two women, you are," announced

another man. Rumblings of discontent could be heard throughout the gathering.

Sophia turned to Charlie and whispered, "This could get ugly."

Charlie muttered back, "Do they still tar and feather here?" She started scribbling on a small piece of paper.

Sophia shook her head and replied, "We have to get them on our side. This is a tight town. We need to make this crowd into a first alert system for us."

Charlie folded the piece of paper and handed it to Rhys, who nodded and handed it back. Charlie crumpled it up, shoved it in her mouth and started chewing. She followed it with a swig of beer.

"What flavor was that, Charlie?"

"Berry. It goes well with the brew. Let's see how much of a leader Rhys is and if he can stem the tide before we get run out of town."

"Stop this, right?" Rhys defended Charlie and Sophia. "Stop your chopsing. I'm not being funny. These are government agents, right. And this one 'ere"—he indicated Sophia—"is related to Alwyn's third cousin twice removed. Now we keep an eye out for any foreigners and let these ladies know immediately, right?"

Rhys signaled for Sophia to stand on a chair next to him. She stepped up, and Charlie pushed a chair to his other side and stood there. She addressed the crowd. "*Haia. O America dw i.*" There was a smattering of applause in response to Charlie's use of their language. "Sophia here and I are well trained to fight and defeat these people who are trying to steal your land from you. We are working for you. Your job is to help us by telling us, or Rhys, if you see anyone out of place. *Ti'n iawn?*"

Rhys gave her a thumbs-up and agreed, "All right!"

Sophia spoke, "We are going to make this right, 'ey. My blood is in this land too. We have a responsibility to carry on for Alwyn."

A grumble went through the assembly. "For Alwyn," Rhys shouted.

The crowd cheered back, stamping their feet in unison. "For Alwyn."

———

There's a strange odor in here. Yaromir's nose twitched as he stood at attention in Boris's office. He inhaled deeply to steady his nerves. He missed Tosh's steady hand on his shoulder, and he distrusted Boris. *This* man would not give him a second chance, as Tosh had. He noted fresh scratches in Boris's desk and imagined what happened, but said nothing.

Boris looked Yaromir up and down and lifted his gaze to lock eyes.

Yaromir stood rock still.

Boris broke eye contact and referred to his screen. "Your record indicates you were successful in all your past missions."

Yaromir kept his face impassive and nodded. Tosh must have left out what really happened.

"There is nothing in here about your most recent trip to America, however," Boris commented.

Silence. Yaromir wondered how Boris knew of his mission in America.

"Have you finished that job?" Boris asked.

"*Net, ser.*"

"Well, put it on hold for now," Boris directed "I will follow up with the accountant. I need you to work for me. You will go to Wales and transmit a clear message to the people who are holding up my land deal. I would think some accidents, perhaps some painful beatings, should do the trick, now that we took the wind out of their sails by removing the ringleader."

Yaromir nodded again. *Khorosho. I can do this.*

"Your instructions and tickets will be emailed to you via your secure account."

Yaromir stood silently. Best not to say anything.

"Dismissed," Boris barked.

Yaromir spun on his heel and left the office.

———

Boris dialed and waited for the connection. "I understand that you have met Yaromir."

Kevin's breathing came through the line, a cough, and then, "Yes, I have. Who might you be?"

"That is of no matter to you. You may call me your handler. I own you. If you ever doubt that, Yaromir can set you straight. Do you understand?"

"No, not really."

"You must remember your parents telling you that you owe the motherland and it was up to *you* to pay back the gift we have given to you and your parents?" There was silence on the other end of the line. Boris continued. "I can only assume that you are listening to my every word. It would not behoove you to have the truth of your origins come out to your employers. Nor would they appreciate the favor that you did for Doug Clark."

"How do you know all this?"

"You are our creation, Kevin. You now work for me. Understand?"

The tinny sound of a wastebasket hitting an object came over the receiver and then sounds of Kevin puking. Boris waited until he heard silence. "Don't worry, Kevin. It will be easy. I have need for someone to help me settle a few real estate transactions in the United States. You will be perfect for it."

"I am an accountant, not a real estate agent. What about my assignment here?"

"You will be what we want you to be. I am sure you are a fast learner. Stand by for further instructions. And for now, drop the other mission." Boris hung up. He was grateful for his predecessors who had so wisely thought of this scheme with Kevin's parents. He would return the favor by planting some flowers for his successors to pick.

Out of a deeply ingrained habit, Charlie looked around to ensure the area was clear. She automatically scanned for snipers and landmines. She laughed at herself. A *bit extreme for a mission in Wales, Charlie.* Still, there had been a number of bodies already, and a killer was out there. One could never be too careful in her occupation. Expect the unexpected. Plan for what you didn't know. All good mantras given to her by her mentor, Elda. If she followed that line of thinking, why stop at only one assassin? Surely the Russians would send another out as backup. Perhaps he or she was here already. She spied Rhys in the Park and jogged over to meet him.

The strong wind buffeted Rhys and Charlie as they met in the park across from The Bishops pub. They shook hands.

"Thanks so much, Rhys, for bringing everyone in line to help us." Charlie nodded and gave him a thumbs-up to convey the meaning in case any words were lost to the wind.

Rhys yelled, "I 'ad to, right. It is our land, and we need to work together to defend it. But we need your 'elp, 'ey."

"Well, thanks again. Do we have any new information?"

"I have it that a stranger has rented a room at the St. Davids hotel," Rhys reported to Charlie, shouting over the wind.

"What's he look like?" Charlie yelled back, circling her face with her forefinger and middle finger to emphasize her words.

Rhys held out his arms as far as they would go. His answer was succinct. "Big."

Charlie trotted back to her car and headed out. *Big* described a lot of Russians. From Sophia's info she ruled out Anatoly.

She parked, then hugged her body against the exterior wall of the St. Davids Inn. She slipped into the management office, and the reek of unwashed male and dirty ashtray assailed her nostrils. As she rounded the corner, she discovered a disheveled, unshaven, portly character exiting.

Charlie held out her hand with two ten-pound notes in it. "Got a minute?"

The notes vanished into his pocket. "Just a minute, right?"

Charlie doubted she could stand his stench for more than that. "Did a stranger check in recently? A large man?"

He smiled, displaying tobacco- and coffee-stained teeth. "Ah, you're the copper, right?"

"Right." She rubbed her hand below her nose for a whiff of hand lotion to cut the stink from his breath.

He turned around and selected a key from its hook. "You'll probably want the spare key. Number's on it. Room's across the way. I'm going out for a fag. I never saw you take the key, right?"

"Right." Charlie slipped the key into her pocket to keep both hands free. She realized she could not keep out of the line of sight of her destination, so she decided to march up to her target's door and confront him. She would use the key only if no one answered the door. She felt in her jacket pocket for the filled hypodermics the doctor had given her.

She knocked on the door. It opened.

"*Ty!*"

"You!"

Charlie popped back into the manager's office. "What do you have for alcohol here? The stronger the better."

He jumped at her entrance. "What? Nothing, right? Go to the pub." He scowled.

Charlie held out three more ten-pound notes. His eyes widened. He snatched the money and reached down under the counter, coming up with an opened half-pint of Paddy's Irish Whiskey.

"That will do." Charlie returned to Yaromir's room. She looked down at him, knocked out by the drugs she had injected into him. She had last seen him in a park in DC when he was involved in an operation to turn a United States senator. She had stabbed him in the neck with a hypodermic full of knockout drugs then and discovered the hard way that one syringe was not enough for his body weight. Luckily, Elda took him down with a second jab. Elda would be proud of her this time. Charlie used two syringes to topple him.

She took the unconscious body by his feet and dragged him out and over to the dumpster and propped him up against the side. She removed his shoes, socks, belt, wallet, and cell phone. Next, she poured the Irish whiskey into his mouth and down the front of his shirt. The smell of alcohol permeated the air. She took the almost empty bottle and put it into his hand and wrapped his fingers around it. She stepped back to admire her work.

"Sleep well, Yaromir."

Ed jumped as Kevin barged into his office, slamming open the door. "What on earth do you want? Have you heard of knocking? It's all the rage now."

Kevin smirked and wandered around Ed's office. He fingered a check on Ed's desk. "David Miller? Why are you paying this man fifty thousand dollars?"

Ed snatched the check out of Kevin's sweaty hand. The accountant seemed to be nervous. "Who I pay money to is none of your business, Kevin. Do you have a reason for being here?"

Kevin tapped Ed's keyboard, awaking his computer. "You forget, Ed. I approve your budgets." An email was displayed on the screen. The FROM, TO, and SUBJECT fields were blank. The body of the email was unfinished. It read: DAVID, I AM IN DESPERATE NEED OF A COMPUTER EXPERT. I AM MAILING YOU A RETAINER TO START A SEARCH FOR ONE. EVEN A PART-TIME HIRE WOULD HELP.

Kevin snickered. "So that's it, hey, Ed. You have finally decided to get into the high-tech world? You can't do much spying nowadays without a computer whizz on your staff."

Ed grabbed Kevin's collar and then put his hands on Kevin's shoulders and spun him around, facing the door. "Get out."

Kevin laughed and left Ed's office.

Good. The seeds were planted. Now to see what Kevin did with them.

———

Kevin's cell startled him. He whipped it off his desk and ran into the stairwell, adjacent to his DC office, to answer it.

"You *will* do a job for me," Boris instructed him, without preamble.

Kevin's heart pounded in his chest. He found it hard to breathe. He held on to the railing and coughed.

"Is that a yes?" Boris snarled.

"Yes," Kevin choked out.

"Yes, what?" Boris demanded, his voice dripping knives.

"Yes, sir," Kevin rasped.

"There will be a substantial amount of money produced for various holders from real estate sales in the United States."

Kevin stood in the metal and concrete stairway and nodded at his phone. Realizing Boris couldn't see his answer, he articulated, "Yes."

"What . . ." Boris prompted.

"Yes, *sir*," Kevin wheezed.

"I will need for you to make certain it is deposited in untraceable and nontaxable accounts outside the United States."

Kevin sighed a breath of relief. Moving money around was in his bailiwick. "Yes, sir."

"Did you find out the information Yaromir wanted you to find out about Elda?" Boris rasped.

He had forgotten to finish that. He needed to get Boris off his back. "She is most definitely dead."

"You're sure?" Boris uttered in a steely tone.

"Yes," Kevin lied. "I talked to everyone. There is no trace of her." He hoped that was right or he was probably a dead man.

"Good. We can proceed."

"I have some information you may find interesting." And hopefully get him some relief from his handler.

"What?"

"I was just in Ed Wilson's office and learned he does not have any computer expertise on his staff."

"Excellent. Well done." Boris hung up without waiting for an answer.

Kevin stared at his phone and wiped the sweat off his brow.

Ed took off his headphones. Kevin was dirty and working for someone with a Russian accent. Now what to do with that information? He wasn't sure who to trust in his own organization. Elda was the only one he'd felt secure about. She would have loved that he used one of her microtransmitters and deftly secreted it under Kevin's collar. There was zero chance that Kevin would find out that David Miller was dead. That information had most likely died with Alexei Alexeev.

Ed checked his computer for the transcript of Kevin's conversation and copied it off onto two different thumb drives. He would take the copies off site and lock them up in his home office safe. If Ashok turned out to be 100 percent trustworthy, then Ed would give him one to run voice recognition on.

Ed laughed at his situation. Right now he didn't have computer expertise in his organization for the most sensitive information. He'd use Ashok enough so that no one would suspect Ed was checking each person out as a potential leak.

If Ashok came up with something meaningful on Kevin that helped prove Kevin was spying for the Russians, then that would count in Ashok's favor and Ed could lengthen the leash he had him on.

Setting up tests for each person to pass was tedious. He missed Elda's spidey sense, as she called it. She could evaluate a person in such a short time. Damn her for dying. He missed his friend.

Could Charlie be right that Elda was still alive? *No.* That line of thinking went down the wishful-thinking route, which *never* leads to anything good. He needed to move on, as did Charlie. The past was gone. Elda was dead.

CHAPTER SIXTEEN

ELDA PACED BACK AND FORTH in the living room. "I wonder what Olga is doing. She's been gone all morning. Did she say anything to you, Tosh? I'd like to get us working on our next steps."

Tosh, feet up, engrossed in a book, just shook his head.

Elda walked over and glanced at the title, *The Art of War*, by Sun Zi. "All warfare is based on deception." She laughed at his look. "Don't be surprised, Tosh. I read too."

"By the way, Elda, how is Sophia doing?"

"How did you guess I disappeared to London last week?"

"For one, we live in the same house, and you weren't gone long enough to make it to the States."

"I had a walk around London. Seems that Sophia has been sidelined and is using a woman named Heather Lewis to get her information. I wasn't able to locate a good position to read their lips, but there's something going on in Wales that they were both interested in. It would be great if we could enlist Sophia as part of our team."

Olga flung open the door and strode in.

"Doesn't that woman ever knock?" Tosh snapped and slammed his book closed.

Elda ignored him. "Hello, Olga. How are things at the other villa?"

"Very good," Olga announced with a mischievous smile.

"Uh-oh. What did Olga do?" Elda pried.

"Olga work out Jim and Yuri. Now they sit on the couch, with feet up, watching TV, complaining they can't move. Winky men." Olga turned to Tosh, who stood straight and glared at her. She clapped him on the back. Tosh stifled a cough.

"This one Olga likes. He looks like a twig, but he doesn't break."

Elda sat with her eyes twinkling and a hand over her mouth to hide her grin. She startled. A bark outside reminded her so much of Vee's.

"Oh yeah. Olga forgot something on Vespa." Olga stomped out.

Elda dabbed at her eyes. She observed Tosh watching her. Elda jumped down his throat. "What?"

"Nothing . . ."

"Allergies."

"Right."

Olga jogged back in, followed by Vee, who wore *doggles* and a little white scarf. Vee ran at Elda and bounded onto her with such force Elda nearly toppled over. Elda lifted Vee and hugged and kissed her. "Vee! Oh, Olga, how can I thank you?"

"Enough of that mushy stuff. Olga go make tea and biscuits." Olga marched off into the kitchen. "Her bed and crate are in the sidecar, along with food and dishes," she bellowed back,

"Olga, I love you." Elda set Vee on the floor.

A snort came out of the kitchen in response.

"Good." Tosh stood. "Now maybe you'll stop moping for that little animal and we can get some work done." Vee ran over to him, wagging her tail. He stooped to pet her, and she licked his nose. "*Chert!*"

Olga handed Tosh a cup of hot tea with two chocolate bourbon creams on the side. He grunted his appreciation. She made Vee sit and awarded her a dog biscuit. Vee trotted off to bury it in her bed for later and wiggled her way back to lie on Elda's feet.

Elda clapped her hands. Vee sat expectantly. Olga plopped onto the couch with her tea. Tosh dipped a bourbon cream into his tea.

"Okay, guys. Now that our main operative is back with us"—Elda paused to scratch Vee behind the ears—"let's figure out how to snag either Stas or Ashok. We must enlist someone to help us gather more intel and write a program to sort through the data we're obtaining from Ed's machine. There's too much there to eyeball."

"I want Adrik's hide," Tosh snapped.

Elda nodded her agreement. She needed to balance Tosh's and, to a lesser extent, her own, desire for revenge, with the operational need to eliminate the opposition. "Although I want vengeance for all the shit they put us through during Operation Bittman, and how they continuously tore us apart, we need to focus. Our primary objective must be to find and remove the moles we never found and those double agents who were blocking our organizations from going after them. By doing this, hopefully we will plug the remaining leaks in Ed's department and MI6. And if we remove whoever ran James and Alexie, we will extract our revenge for losing Dave, Oliver's injuries, and the harm done to Tosh's team. Perhaps we can establish a situation where Tosh and I can become undead again. So as I see it . . ." Elda pushed over a whiteboard and wrote:

1. FINISH PULLING OUR TEAM TOGETHER
2. FILTER THE DATA FROM ED'S OFFICE TO DETERMINE THE LEAK THERE.
3. IDENTIFY THE MOLES AND THE HIERARCHY SO WE'RE NOT ONLY PRUNING THE LEAVES BUT DESTROYING THE ROOT.

"Is that all?" Tosh commented dryly.

Chapter Seventeen

THE SCREEN IN FRONT OF HER was a blur. Elda's fingers hurt. She sat with her Apple MacBook Pro laptop propped on a small table in her jury-rigged office on one side of the villa's living room. She was writing the logical flow for a program to sift through the transcripts from the bug under Ed's desk. They also needed a program to sort through the information captured from his computer. Her eyes were sore from hours of manually scanning it. Elda felt her impatience disturbing her concentration. She needed to identify the moles more quickly. This was taking too long. She wished Ashok were here. He could automate this in a few minutes. Suddenly a message appeared on her screen.

WHO ARE YOU? —A

Where did that come from? Had her wishing conjured up Ashok?

She called to Tosh. "Tosh, I think someone discovered our tap in Ed's office, and I think it may be Ashok."

Tosh strode over and peered over Elda's shoulder. "What makes you think it's Ashok?"

Elda pointed to her screen. "This message is incoming on a program Ashok wrote for us so we could communicate anonymously and securely outside official channels."

"What if it's not him? Can you answer him without being detected?"

"It could be a her, you know."

Tosh sighed. "Yes, I know. Now can you answer them or not?"

Elda smiled. She still enjoyed the small victories with Tosh. "Yes. I can try something that only Ashok or a few of the team would recognize."

She spun up the full application and typed: A friend. —Vee and pressed Send.

They waited.

One keystroke at a time, a message returned: Elda?

Elda sent: Who are you?

Ashok!

Tosh looked at Elda. "How do we know it's really Ashok?"

What computers do you have?

ASUS, Samsung, Dell Ultrasharp, and BenQ Zowie XL2546 monitors, two Dell PowerEdge servers, a DigitalStorm Aventum custom tower, and a T-Platforms rugged laptop containing the Elbrus-8S chip and running the ultra-secure Astra Linux Operating System.

Elda glanced up at Tosh. "Do you still doubt that's Ashok?"

Tosh narrowed his eyes, reached over Elda, and typed, How did you find us?

I analyzed the packets being transferred from Mister Ed's machine over the ethernet cable to the company server, and compared side by side what was being sent and what was being received. They were identical, but the transmission speed was too slow. Something was slowing it down. It was non-destructive and clever. It had to be an inside job. Who would be able to do this type of thing?

Elda stared at Tosh. When he was done reading, she asked, "Do you *now* see that it's Ashok?"

"It certainly sounds like him."

Elda typed: Shhh. Tell no one. But we need you. Wait for our instructions.

I will do so immediately. You will be delighted.

Elda sat back in her chair and smiled at Tosh. "That's Ashok all right."

Nyoka sauntered into Stas's cubicle and towered above him. Stas swirled his chair around and froze, seemingly mesmerized by her Goth look and beautiful pale skin, highlighted by the blue glow of the monitors.

She scrutinized him and slithered her tongue around her index fingertip and one perfectly polished fingernail.

Stas smiled at her.

"Did you find the blond woman?" she hissed.

"Oh, Boris sent you? Not yet. Do you know how many blond women there are in the United Kingdom?"

"Not as many as in Scandinavia," she quipped.

Stas laughed. Nyoka raised an eyebrow.

"Do you have any other identifying information on her?" Stas asked.

She motioned to her own left-hand ring finger with her bandaged right hand. "She had a wedding ring. I would think that would indicate she isn't an active field agent."

"And you have no ring. Is that because you are an agent?" Stas observed.

Nyoka was enjoying Stas's admiration and obvious ploy to see if she was single. She winked at him and moved back to business. "How can you find her?"

"We can do the process of elimination of those who don't fit. I can devise a program to filter out all the active UK agents, which would be a smaller set to review. Do you have a few minutes now?" He indicated she could sit in the guest chair.

"I'll stand."

Stas's keyboard clattered without pause as he typed in the commands to sort out the married blond agents from the UK databases. He narrowed the results down to only those who were currently office based. He soon came up with a small collection of pictures. She leaned in over his shoulder as he scrolled through them one by one.

"*Prekrashchat'sya!* That one." She zeroed in on the likeness on the screen.

Stas stiffened in his chair. "May I print it for you?"

Nyoka shook her head. Stas's eyes followed her black hair swirling around her shoulders. "No need. I will never forget her face. Just tell me where she lives."

"*Der'mo.* What is wrong, Stas?" Anatoly grunted.

Stas, standing in the doorway of Toshchiy Chastnyye Detektivy, bent over, gasping for breath. Anatoly went to him, pulled off his worn canvas backpack, and led him to one of the spare chairs in the office. Snezhana took a bottle of Volzhanka water from the small office fridge and handed it to Stas.

Trying to lighten the moment, Anatoly joked, "New exercise program, Stas?" Anatoly whapped Stas's back, which sent Stas into a coughing spasm. "If you want, I can take you shopping for more suitable clothing."

Snezhana glowered at Anatoly. She looked at Stas with concern. "What's wrong, Stas? It's unlike you to exert yourself in this way."

Stas slugged down half the bottle of water and wheezed. "I came as quickly as I could. We need to warn Sophia. But she may already be dead. Can you send her a message?"

"Probably not if she's dead," Snezhana let slip and clapped her hand over her mouth.

"Why?" Anatoly demanded, his fists clenched. "What happened, Stas?"

"I'm sorry. I didn't want to give her the information, but she was there when I found it." Stas's lower lip quivered, and his eyes filled with tears.

"Who? What did you give her?" Anatoly growled.

"She asked so nicely and is so beautiful," Stas blubbered.

"Who!" Anatoly bellowed.

Stas fell out of his chair and curled up in a ball on the wooden floor. The remains of his bottle rolled to one side, spilling water as it went.

"*Der'mo*." Anatoly slammed his fist down on the nearby desk, causing a pen to roll onto the floor. "I am sorry, Stas."

Snezhana glared at Anatoly. "*Shtopat*. See what you've done, Anatoly. Let me handle this. Clean up that water and let me deal with Stas."

Anatoly secured a towel and swabbed the floor with one hand, crumpling the plastic water bottle in his other hand. Stas flinched from the crunching sound. Snezhana's eyes sent daggers Anatoly's way.

Snezhana knelt down next to Stas. "Who is so beautiful, Stas?"

He sniffled. "Nyoka. So beautiful. Such a haunting metallic bouquet. She was so close to me."

"Nyoka," Snezhana whispered. "A lovely name. And who does Nyoka work for?"

Wiping his nose on his sleeve, Stas uncurled. "Boris."

Anatoly gave a low growl. Snezhana held up her fist, and Anatoly quieted. He rocked back and forth on his feet.

"Boris . . ." Snezhana murmured. "So of course you had no choice and had to help her."

Stas nodded. "I never thought Sophia's picture would

come up as a match."

"*Tam, tam,*" Snezhana consoled, and dug more. "So what else did Nyoka want on Sophia?"

"Her home address," Stas muttered.

"*Der'mo!*" Anatoly heaved a wooden chair across the room, where it bounced off the wall and landed, one leg askew. Wood chips scattered about. "Enough of babying this man, Snezhana. Sophia may be in danger."

Anatoly grabbed the end table. Snezhana's stare froze him in place. Knowing she was not to be disobeyed, he retrieved the chair and sat down. "You are like Tosh, you know, Snezhana?" With that thought expressed, his anger and loss bubbled up. He clenched his fists and pounded his thighs. "*Der'mo!*" He popped up and started pacing back and forth, like a caged lion deprived of his meat.

Snezhana glanced Anatoly's way, while continuing to pry the situation out of Stas. "Why did Nyoka want Sophia's home address?"

Stas shook his head. "I don't know. She only said she would never forget her face, but she spoke as if Sophia was no longer alive."

Snezhana looked kindly at Stas and said softly, "Can you describe Nyoka?"

Stas brightened. "Oh, she is so beautiful. Her skin is the palest of white colors. Her hair is gorgeous, shimmering, long, and jet black. Her nails are painted red. She always dresses in black. The Goth look of it all is stunning. Even the bandage on her hand adds to her look."

Anatoly perked up. "Are those nails filed into points?"

"Yes."

Snezhana helped Stas up and back into his chair. She turned to Anatoly. "Recognize her?"

He mulled. "Perhaps. Let me make a few inquiries. I think she's a new up-and-coming assassin. If I'm right, and if Sophia is alive, she is in big trouble."

Chapter Eighteen

Olga's Vespa GTS spun into the Tuscany villa's driveway and stopped in a cloud of dust. The day was dry and warm, with the faint perfume of olives in the breeze.

A small man with a black leather jacket, mirrored sunglasses, short black hair, black slacks, and black leather Harley boots popped out of the sidecar. He stood in the sun and sniffed the air, then followed Olga to the house.

Olga swung open the front door. "Hi, honeys! I'm home."

Yuri and Jim groggily looked up from the cloth couch, where they had fallen asleep in front of the television. Yuri cleaned the drool off his mouth, peered around, and leapt up. "Where's Vee?"

Olga chuckled. "Don't worry. Olga delivered Vee to Elda."

"*Chto?*" Yuri exclaimed.

"What? Did you say Eldah?" Jim blurted out.

The small man standing behind Olga stepped to her side. "And don't worry. Elda will take excellent care of her dog."

Olga tapped her nose and smiled.

"Eldah? Is that you?" Jim stood and shook his head, as if to clear it.

"Elda!" Yuri hopped up and ran to give her a bear hug. "You're alive." His face fell, and his arms dropped to his sides. "And Tosh . . ."

Smiling, Elda gave Yuri a pat on his upper arm to console him. "Don't worry, Yuri. He's alive as well. We both need you two to join our team. We're going after the rest of the moles."

"Damn. They won't sell." Kevin stood by his rental car in the parking lot of the Residence Inn in Charleston, SC. A sea breeze brought the sound of gulls and the threat of rain. He looked up as a great blue flew over. He was totally sick of seeing beach and birds.

He had visited the developers on Johns Island, Seabrook Island, and Kiawah Island and had a few more to visit along the coast, before he flew back to DC. He didn't get the attraction of this locale. Beaches bored him, as did shopping, and he couldn't understand the attraction of some huge old oak tree. People regaled him with stories about how friendly people were and how wonderful the slower pace of life was down here, but city life and fast-paced action were more his scene.

He decided to call Boris for advice before he kept at his wild-goose chase. Hopefully, Boris would let him off the hook and let him go back to DC.

He dialed and updated Boris. "I created the offshore accounts and have systems in place to launder the sales proceeds through Bitcoin conversion and back to the owners to deposit in those accounts. But none of them are willing to play along. They perceive the profit we're offering them but want to know what else they can buy and where."

"Why is it so important for them to know now?" Boris sputtered in a frustrated tone. "Their money will be safely stored and *tax-free*, since we will manipulate the market figures to show them losing money on their deals. They can invest it again later. We must prod them to move so we impact the real estate market *now* in that ritzy area of America. The more we can affect the economy and make wealthy communities implode, the better."

Kevin translated the different worlds for Boris. "These guys like to own land. It's what they do. They buy cheap and sell high. They're already antsy that they're not selling high, but they understand that with the tax breaks and the lack of agent costs, the money in their pockets will be the same as if they did. Plus, they realize the value of their properties will soon plummet if they don't play along with us. We only need to give them a little extra persuasion."

"Find out," Boris ordered, "if throwing more money their way will be sufficient *persuasion*. Report back to me when you have that answer. There are many ways we can persuade them."

<hr>

Why hasn't Yaromir reported in yet? Boris thought. He would like to use him in South Carolina to nudge the developers along. Nothing fatal, but painful. Boris's groin tingled at the thought. He could use Nyoka, but she was experienced with the Welsh part of this operation, and it might be necessary to send her there again.

Once they did this land deal, the developers would be compromised and he could use them again in the future. The seeds he was planting in the Western worlds took many forms. Disinformation molded unwitting believers to Russia's agenda. Spies planted within government and businesses helped disseminate Russia's message while passing back valuable information and blocking initiatives that might thwart Russia's progress.

It was death by a thousand cuts. Bit by bit he was undermining democracy. His hidden moles were making their ways up their respective hierarchies to be well positioned by the time they were activated. Others in important areas were easy to buy. Greed for money and power. People were so easily manipulated.

Of course other organizations in Russia were helping to achieve the same goals. Slowly they sliced off pieces and destroyed their enemies.

Operation Bittman appeared to have failed, but under the cover of its losses, his agents high in the United States and British governments and intelligence organizations were more firmly in place. He doubted that anyone would be able to connect Operation Bittman, the real estate losses, slowdowns, and leaks in various intelligence organizations, and a dead body in the Ukraine.

There would be many others dead before it was all over.

Boris's hands waved like a conductor as he thought of all the chaos he would sow. Electrical outages in the severe heat of cold, key individuals dying suddenly of strokes, supply chain slowdowns, protests and riots, assassination attempts, . . .

He laughed as his invisible baton struck another fatal chord.

What was missing to accomplish his goals? Boris surveyed a printout of his organizational chart. "*Net.* It's not right yet."

Boris secretly admired Nikita Khrushchev. He loved Krushchev's statement: "We will take America without firing a single shot. We do not have to invade the US. We will destroy you from within." He admired Krushchev's balls to tell Kennedy that "we voted for you." Boris believed there were times to still use the Cold War techniques, which was one of the reasons he wanted to affirm the US agent Elda was dead and out of his way. She was too skilled an opponent to let live. He would have liked to have kept Tosh and his crew intact, but it ended up being out of his hands when Tosh had died and Adrik had split the team up. He needed to recruit more smart strategists like Tosh.

From his predecessor, Boris had inherited a database of who and where the Russian plants were in the Western countries. He devised a system to ensure the knowledge would be passed down and not die with him. His original set of double agents and moles had been run by Adrik. That org had been decimated: Arabella, Robert, James, Madison, Henry, Nigel . . . all dead. He had only a few active agents left.

Adrik's methods were proving unsustainable. Boris no longer trusted Adrik to manage that part of his division. Boris would be happy if Adrik choked on his chocolate. For now, he would let him live. He needed a manager in place. It wouldn't hurt to have more leverage over Adrik. He typed a confidential text to Stas. FIND ALL THAT YOU CAN ABOUT ADRIK'S BACKGROUND AND CONTACTS.

Boris himself had activated a new selection of informers with Maxim Lomorov, now dead, Kevin Ball, Frank Garcia, Joseph White, and Treacher Walker. Nigel Davies had used Kevin Ball as a patsy to launder money for Operation Bittman. Boris needed to rebuild his network of spies and hidden moles.

It was time to assign a new handler for that group and to awake more of the sleepers, as well as hand over the running of the real estate project to a new manager. Another one to interview and hire.

Scanning his org chart again, Boris determined it was light in agents who could act as tails, since Grisha had been eliminated. Timur and Konstantin were efficient, but there were times when one lead and two followers were useful. Perhaps he should enlist another manager to head that team? Did he need to have it as a separate functioning section, or should he combine them with the assassins?

Speaking of the assassins, he was low on resources. Losing Borya and Angelina, as well as others in Canada, the United States, and Russia, was a big hit to that outfit. Nyoka was an excellent addition, but many more like her, or better than her, would be necessary to accomplish his various initiatives. Also, Nyoka was hard to control. He desperately needed a handler, now that Tosh was gone. He picked up his phone and dialed his secretary.

"I would like to schedule some interviews immediately."

Charlie trod into Ed's office without knocking.

Ed sighed. What ever happened to knocking before entering? His office was getting a lot of traffic lately, and his routines were all off. He realized Charlie had been through a lot too and still was a young operative, so she deserved some slack. He motioned for her to close the door.

The unmistakable smell of a fresh pot of coffee wafted through the office. "Coffee?" He walked to pour them each a cup, adding cream to hers.

He handed Charlie her coffee, took a gulp from his cup, and started the debrief. "Is Sophia okay?"

Charlie took a sip of coffee before answering Ed. She spilled out the words. "She will be. That assassin is nasty. She took Sophia down like she was a rag doll. An innocent bystander, Rhys, would have been dead had it not been for his fake leg. Maxim was professionally killed. And the killer is now in the wind. I think I should be over there, not back here, Ed." Charlie stood with her jaw locked and her hands clenched at her sides.

"I hear you, Charlie, but we never finished with Frank. If he's the traitor we think he is, we need to remove him sooner rather than later."

"I hear you, Ed," Charlie spat back, "but you don't need me for that. Elda trained me well. I can go after this killer." Her eyes bored into Ed's.

He stepped back from her force field and held up one hand, palm forward, toward her. "We'll see. Spend a few more days working with Frank, and try to come up with something we can use to put him out of the way."

Charlie unclenched her teeth long enough to ask, "Do I have your permission to remove him if necessary?"

Ed scratched his head. "Pergra. Obtain the incriminating evidence first though."

"Damn it, Ed! I thought you believed the Ukrainian op failure wasn't my fault."

"Wait, wait, wait . . ." Ed implored. "Calm down, Charlie. That wasn't a backhanded comment. I do believe you did everything you could have in Ukraine, and I trust you will handle this op as well as you did the other operation."

Charlie took one long look at Ed, spun on her toe, about faced, and marched out of the office.

Ed rubbed his chin. *Gads, she reminds me so much of Elda.*

———

Charlie jogged up the stairs to work and wandered to the break room for a cup of something dark colored that passed as coffee. Frank cornered her in the doorway. Charlie's nose twitched at the smell of his sweat wafting toward her.

"You don't value your life, do you?" Frank sneered at Charlie.

"I think, Frank, you're projecting. The real question is,

do you value yours?" She tapped her nose with her finger and pointed at his.

Veins stuck out on Frank's neck. His eyes narrowed. "You may have bested me in the gym, but watch your back when you're alone in the dark. You'll see who's boss." Frank grabbed his crotch and leered at Charlie.

She laughed and, forgoing her coffee, strolled away, her relaxed body posture demonstrating to Frank she was not bothered by him.

Once back at her desk, Charlie dropped her casual air and texted Ed. Do we have enough to arrest Frank on yet?

The response came, short and sweet. No. arrest may not be solution. Get More Info. Consider midnight rail party.

CHAPTER NINETEEN

ASHOK WONDERED WHATEVER EVER HAPPENED to good IT support? He slipped into the janitorial closet and pushed the door shut behind him. To prevent anyone from unlocking the door from the other side, he inserted a device into the lock. It would also trigger an alarm on his Apple Watch. He removed the grate and stuck his head into the vent. He saw the cut out in the metal, just as Elda had informed him. He crawled in father and gasped. Elda was fortunate this did not cause a fire! He pressed electrical tape over the exposed wired and connected his own tap to the small server Elda had left.

Now to write a program to filter out the good bits.

Bang!

A loose shutter flew backward in the wind. Yuri ran out to secure it and scuttled back to his seat.

The sun shone in through the windows at Elda's villa, but clouds formed near the horizon, in advance of the upcoming storm. Olga, Tosh, Jim, and Yuri sat around the whiteboard in the living room

"The past is becoming clearer." Elda briefed the group. "Ashok managed to ferret out some good facts from the data feeds from Ed's office." She tapped the photo from Sophia's office. "His name was Joseph White. He served as an enlisted man in the army and, after that, in the CIA, gathering intel with boots on the ground. We don't when or how the Russians turned him, but he was an active mole by the time Operation Bittman commenced. He passed materials on to James, helping to set up Tosh and me and our team. We theorize that when we neutralized James, Joseph joined in with the mercenaries in the Ukraine, fighting for the Russians. Part of his role was to gather intel about the Ukrainian defenses and pass it on to the Russian military leaders."

"So, Eldah, why is this man so impohtant? Why ahn't we focusing on the present?" Jim questioned.

Tosh jumped in to answer. "Although the spies are pretty compartmentalized, we think Mr. White had other contacts in DC and that he reported to someone other than Alexei when he passed his stolen data to the Kremlin. We want to find *that* man."

"The Russians would not remove him from the CIA without ensuring a replacement," Olga announced.

"Yes. We suspect that replacement may be Frank Garcia," Elda added. "From what Ashok has said, he's been anxious to get rid of Charlie's oversight. Plus Charlie caught him squashing intel about the Russians that we would find valuable. She also has spotted him tailing her and going through her desk. He's dirty in some way and it fits that he may be working for the Russians."

"We *have* to start moving on this now. We need Charlie," Tosh ordered.

"I told you that," Elda reprimanded Tosh.

"First, we run," Olga proclaimed. "Too much sitting."

She herded them out the door.

"I can't breathe!" The dry Tuscan air brought on an asthma attack for Elda, who'd just run up a large hill ahead of the others.

Olga stopped at the top of the hill and viewed the rest of her troops, in a drawn-out line down the hill, struggling to catch up. "What wussies," she declared in a voice loud enough to reach Elda.

Determined not to be one of those wussies, Elda took a hit of her inhaler and jogged the rest of the way up to stand by Olga. She stood panting and blowing her nose. "Before the rest catch up to us, Olga, I need to know if in addition to whipping this team into shape, you'd like to help me with the logistical side of things, like you have done for me in the past."

"Olga be happy to do that. Olga can do more too, you know." Olga pointed her finger like a gun.

"Yes, you make a good on the ground spy too. Thanks. I'll let you know if I need more from you. You know where the spare weapons are, right?"

"*Da.*"

They strode along the crest of the hill overlooking their villa below them. Elda mapped out escape routes in her brain.

Olga shocked Elda out of her thoughts by asking, "So are you and Tosh . . ."

"Good *god*, no!" Elda coughed out,

Olga shrugged. "Well, you never know. You two do act like an old married couple."

Elda laughed. "Tosh and I are old spies. We understand each other. We also have mutual love for the arts and nature. But we still have our guard up. We understand someday we may be on opposite sides of the fence again."

Olga persisted in probing. "So what about Dawn? You asserted you only ached for Vee."

Elda narrowed her eyes. Through clenched teeth, she spit out, "That carpetbagger? She used me for years. And the moment I was declared dead, she put the house in Maine up for sale and beat feet."

An out-of-breath Tosh and a worried-looking Yuri crested the hill. Yuri beckoned Elda and Olga back.

Elda frowned. "Something's wrong, Olga." They both ran toward the men.

A few minutes later, when Elda and Olga reached him, Tosh filled them in. "It's Jim. I think we need someone with more medical knowledge than I have to evaluate him."

"Where is he?" Elda asked.

"What about Jim? He okay?" Olga demanded.

Tosh held out his hands. "I'm not sure. I think he turned an ankle on a stone. I'm not sure if it's broken."

"Damn," Elda swore.

"Olga see."

Olga took off down the hill, with the others in tow. When they joined her, Jim was sitting on the ground.

Olga had wrapped his ankle with tape from her side pack. She looked at Yuri. "You carry? Olga can help."

Yuri slung Jim over his shoulder.

Jim held his hand over his mouth and burped. "Cahful there, Yuri. Lunch is still digesting."

Elda watched Yuri and Olga jog down the hill, passing Jim between them. When Elda reached the villa, Jim was settled on the couch, with ice on his ankle.

"What's the status?" Elda requested.

"Ah may puke." Jim looked green.

"Just a slight sprain," Olga decided. "Ice and a day off it, and he'll be fine."

"Are you sure?" Tosh nudged Jim's leg, making him yelp. "We can't very well take him to a hospital."

Olga squared off with Tosh and glared at him. "Olga no lie. Olga an EMT. You an EMT, skinny man?"

Elda stepped between them and changed the subject. "I'm relieved he'll be okay. There are not enough operatives on this mission as it is. We can't afford to lose anyone at this point. We will need all hands on deck. We don't know who is going to come after us."

Chapter Twenty

A SHOK SLID TO A STOP IN THE DOORWAY of Ed's office. "Mister Ed, sir, may I please have a minute?"

Ed took his gaze from his computer and focused on Ashok, motioning him in. Ashok did not usually move that fast. "Is something wrong, Ashok?"

Ashok entered. "Can we also call in Mister Jackson? I think he would find this most interesting."

Ed texted Jackson, asking him to join in. He furrowed his brow at Ashok. "What is it?"

Ashok waved his hands. "We must wait until Mister Jackson arrives, Mister Ed. I wish to hear his findings on Kevin Ball before I give my news."

"I think after he arrives, we all should take a walk, don't you?" Ed stood.

Ashok shook his head, set down a device on Ed's desk, and switched it on. The device beeped, cycled through a series of lights, and finally settled on a steady green.

Ed sat again and squinted at the lights. "What do you have there?"

"Ah, Mister Ed, it is most brilliant. I have taken a scrambler and signal blocker, and I modified both the hardware and the software to make it state of the art. While it's on, you could say we're in a cone of silence as far as anyone else is concerned." Ashok patted his latest invention.

"Much better than the one on the old *Get Smart* reruns, hey?" Ed quipped.

Ashok appeared puzzled.

Ed waved his hand. "Never mind. We'll stay here then."

Jackson wandered in, sat down, and took off his glasses, cleaning them on his shirt. "Interesting device."

"Yes, Mister Jackson. It is now called the smart device. Mister Ed named it."

"As in the old spy television show *Get Smart*. It's the Cone of Silence. Please tell me you've heard of it, Jackson."

Jackson frowned. "So sorry, Ed. I don't watch much TV. What's the lowdown?"

Ed rolled his eyes and shook his head. "Over to you, Ashok. It's your show."

"But, Mister Ed, I thought it was your show you were telling us about."

Ed put his head down on his arms on top of his desk. "I give up."

Ashok looked at Ed, then at Jackson, who shook with laughter, and shrugged. "Ah, Mister Jackson, first, what did you discover on Kevin Ball?"

Jackson returned his glasses to his face. "Not much more, unfortunately. But there is one point of interest. I ran his picture through facial recognition, on feeds from different locations in the DC area, and found a match. May I use your laptop, Ed?"

Ed moved to one side and let Jackson sit at his desk. His computer was getting more use than when he was alone.

Jackson pulled up an image, and Ed, Ashok, and Jackson stared at it.

Finally Ed queried, "Who is that man he's meeting

with? He looks a lot like the Russian characters we've tangled with in the past."

"I don't know," Jackson said. "Elda, if she were here, probably could tell us."

Ashok moved in and sent the jpg photo to his secure email. "I will try."

Ed eyed Ashok. "So does this have anything to do with why you called us together?"

Ashok nodded, then shook his head. "Most certainly, Mister Ed. In my research I discovered that Kevin Ball was born in Russia to American parents. They lived overseas long enough that no one could verify if she was, or was not, pregnant when they left the United States. Kevin could be a Russian plant from birth onward. I also have other information on his recent activities. May I?" He moved in and took control of Ed's keyboard.

A notated call log popped up, listing Kevin's calls to the Kremlin number, as well as calls to various people in South Carolina and one call to a location in Wales. Next to that, Ashok opened another window, displaying a flight plan for a private jet from Ronald Reagan Washington National Airport to Charleston International Airport with one passenger, Kevin Ball.

"That bastard." Ed glared at the screen. "He's been sneaking around peppering me with questions and now he's connected to the Kremlin. That's no coincidence. Jackson, you're my analyst. What's this all mean? How dirty is he?"

Jackson took the keyboard, scrolling back and forth through the information. He turned to Ashok. "Do you think this is tied to those real estate emails we have been following?"

"Exactly, Mister Jackson. You are displaying such cleverness. This will have to be examined more closely, but perhaps it is time to send Miss Charlie back over the pond, as you say."

CHAPTER TWENTY-ONE

THE WASHINGTON MONUMENT STOOD TALL against the blue sky and reflected off the Lincoln Memorial Reflecting Pool. Ed, Ashok, and Charlie walked around the National Mall. To any observer, they were tourists, eating sandwiches and taking in the sights on a nice spring day in Washington, DC.

Wiping his mouth with his napkin, obscuring his lips from any lip readers, Ed told Charlie, "Ashok developed a program that needs to be downloaded onto Frank's laptop and also onto Frank's phone. With that installed, we can monitor what he's doing at all times. That should also help free you up."

"Cookie?" Ashok passed Charlie a lumpy object, wrapped in aluminum foil.

"Thanks, Ashok. I'll save it for later." Charlie stowed the foil-covered cookie and thumb drive into her jeans pocket.

Holding his hand over his lips, Ed muttered, "So do you have a plan, Charlie?"

Charlie looked down at her feet. "Yes. I plan on arranging another match with him at the gym." She looked up, sneezed, and held a handkerchief over her mouth and nose. "If all goes as before, he'll be slow in returning to his office. I'll insert the program before he returns." She sneezed loudly and blew her nose with a honk. She glanced at Ed and Ashok, who viewed her with amazed looks on their faces. "I do hope I'm not coming down with anything. I would hate to give it to my new coworker," she deadpanned.

"I'm baaaack," Charlie drawled, using her best Schwarzenegger imitation. Entering Frank's office, the smell of a locker room assaulted her nostrils.

Frank looked up from his computer and growled at her.

My god! He actually growled. How quaint. "Glad to see me?"

"I thought I had seen the last of you. What the fuck are you doing back here?" Frank grumbled, glowering.

Bouncing from foot to foot, Charlie beamed at Frank. "Ah, and I thought you'd be happy to see me. In case you've forgotten, Frank, I'm here to liaison between our two departments, so I'll be in and out as I desire. The more you cooperate, the quicker this all can be."

Frank's neck and face turned red. He slammed his fist on his desk and winced from the pain.

Hummm, if I coded that color, I'd probably say it's a #d66666. Let's see if I can amp it up more. She smirked. "Awwww, can I bring you some ice for that boo-boo?"

"Rematch. Gym. Now."

Oh good, his face is redder. I'd say approaching #be3e3e. Perhaps he'll keel over from a heart attack. He's got to have high cholesterol from all that junk food. Out loud, Charlie consented. "You're on." She held out her hand.

He turned his back and stalked away.

Charlie and Frank squared off at opposite ends of the black mat in the workplace gym.

"I hope you've reviewed your insurance policy." Frank sneered.

"It's the same government policy as you have, Frank, so don't worry—your hospitalization will be covered."

Frank's skin color became three shades of red darker. He rushed at Charlie. She sidestepped him and bashed him with both arms on the back, contributing to his forward motion. He slammed against the concrete wall. His knees buckled, and he put out both hands to assist his slide down the wall. He sat dazed.

"Enough, Frank? Shall I call 911?"

Frank shook his head and winced at the movement. He put one hand up to his head, and it came away bloody. Using the wall, he slowly pulled himself upright.

"Really, Frank, we don't need to finish this," Charlie offered, annoyed he wouldn't give up.

His eyes focused on her, and he snarled and rushed at her again, only to find himself facedown on the mat. He flipped over, sat, and rose.

Charlie held her hand out with a towel. "I'm going to hurt you badly, Frank. Is that what you want? Are you a masochist? Here, wipe yourself off and let's call it a draw."

He attacked again.

"Your choice." Charlie landed a well-placed kick to his groin and, as he doubled over, fisted her hands together and gave him an uppercut to the jaw.

He flew backward and crashed down, his head bouncing off the mat and crashing onto the hard floor. He was out cold.

Charlie walked over and took his pulse. It was somewhat ragged, but there. He was alive. She turned him onto his side in case he threw up when he came to.

Charlie looked at the door. A crowd had gathered for the rematch, and they clapped.

"A man is down. Have some decorum." She selected one man. "You, call 911. Another, . . . you"—she indicated a second man—"monitor Frank. I'm going to change. He needs to go to the hospital."

The crowd parted, giving way for her to walk out the door.

With her back to Frank's office door, Charlie sensed the footsteps before she heard them.

"What are you doing?" a voice called out from the hallway,

Charlie turned and looked at Joe, who stood scowling in Frank's office door, with his hands on his hips. She resisted her instinct to tell the man it was none of his business and remembered Elda's advice that sometimes being nice would get her further.

She took in a long breath. "I'm gathering items to take to Frank at the hospital. I think he'll be there for a while. You know him well. Could you help me?" She was glad she'd installed Ashok's monitoring software before this guy showed up. She held up Frank's phone. "I figure he'll need his cell phone, but I don't have a clue what else I can take to him."

Joe snatched the phone out of Charlie's hand. "I'll take that to him. You clear out. You've done enough to him."

Even better! Charlie held up both hands. "I didn't know you two were friends." She focused on opening her body language, relaxing her stance, keeping her arms loose and hands palm forward, down by her sides. She cocked her head and furrowed her brow.

Joe's face softened. "He can be an asshole, but our paths

have crossed since childhood. He's always had a chip on his shoulder about being adopted, and he feels different from everyone else."

Charlie nodded. "I can see that. You would think he would be more accepting of differences himself." She allowed Joe to take the lead. The lessons from Elda were coming in handy.

"You would think that, but my theory is it's driven him the other way. He's become a loner who dislikes most people. He and I aren't best buds, but he doesn't attack me, and I get him. And I also understand why you had to teach him a lesson."

Charlie held out her hand, and Joe shook it. "Appreciated, Joe. Well, I'll let you select things to bring to him. I'm betting he'll want his cell." She indicated the phone in Joe's other hand.

He looked down at it, as if at a foreign object he had forgotten he held. "Yes. We can't be without these things anymore, can we?"

Charlie turned to leave.

"Oh and Charlie . . ." Joe called out.

She swung back. "Yes?"

"Watch your back once he's up and about," Joe warned her. "I know him well enough to be able to say with confidence he'll kill you if he can."

Charlie smiled. "Just let him try."

Chapter Twenty-Two

SOPHIA'S EYES DARTED BACK AND FORTH. She glanced at the board announcing the flight arrivals from Sheremetyevo International Airport, Russia to Heathrow, United Kingdom. Anatoly and Snezhana's flight had landed. People swirled around, heading in all directions, assorted perfumes, colognes, deodorants, and aftershaves mingling. Conversations in multiple languages assaulted Sophia's ears. She flinched when a man brushed by her shoulder and jumped at a hand touching her back.

"Whoa. Down, Nelly. You're safe here. I have your back."

Sophia winced as she felt Charlie pat her back.

"We'll pick up Snezhana and Anatoly at baggage claim and be out of here in a jiffy." Charlie frowned and stared at Sophia's face. "Are you sure you don't want to take some time off though? You're still healing."

Sophia touched the red scar around the front of her neck and stepped away from Charlie. "*No.* Oliver pleaded with me to quit and stay home with him, but this is my world, and I will work through the jumpies."

"The *jumpies*, hey? Apt. Oh, there they are!"

Sophia watched Charlie wave at a large squarely built man with a blond buzz cut and a svelte, fashionably dressed woman walking beside him. "That's Anatoly. If that's Snezhana, she cleans up well."

Anatoly touched a man standing by the luggage carousel, on his back. When the man turned to look at Anatoly, Anatoly growled at him. Anatoly reached toward a woman's arm, and Snezhana slapped his hand. Anatoly laughed. They collected their luggage and strolled over to meet Charlie and Sophia.

"What was that about?" Charlie puzzled out loud.

"Oh, man-child here is playing an old game of his. He wears a ring that can emit poison and counts how many people he can take out in a short time frame. He reloads the ring from a vial up his sleeve. Right now they both contain water." Snezhana rolled her eyes.

"Thirty-two kills." Anatoly gave huge grin.

"Disgusting," Charlie whispered to Sophia.

Sophia noted Anatoly had a partial hard on. Yes. Disgusting. Elda had mentioned Anatoly was asexual and got his rocks off through killing. Clearly true.

Anatoly walked to Sophia and traced the scar around her neck lightly. "Wire . . . nice . . . A bit longer and you wouldn't have your head, Sophia."

Sophia pushed his hand away. "Don't remind me, Anatoly. Let's get the car. We're heading to the apartment. We turned the nursery into a second spare room for now, so there's ample place to put everyone, if you count the couch in the living room. The apartment will be a more secure place to talk."

⁓

"Nothing. *Damn.*"

Sitting in Sophia and Oliver's London flat, Charlie

pitched her phone down beside her on the couch. Anatoly sat on the floor, busily unpacking his go-bag and checking his weapons. Oliver sauntered in from the kitchen, wiping his wet hands on a black-and-white striped Hedley & Bennet apron.

"Cor! Smashing assortment, Anatoly." He turned to Charlie. "*Nothing* what?"

Charlie took a deep breath and rubbed the sides of her head, where her hair was shaved short. "We sent the finger I chopped off that weird assassin—"

"What? You did what?" Oliver stared at her open mouthed.

Charlie glared at him. "If you keep interrupting me, you'll never hear the whole story. I chopped her finger off to gather DNA and fingerprints, okay?"

"Blimey. You have big goolies." Oliver covered the front of his pants with his hand and moved it upward to emphasize his admiration for her actions.

Charlie smiled with gritted teeth. *Men . . .* "So Sophia's contact, Heather in MI6, is poking around to see what she can find, and Ashok is also poking around on the sly. *Nothing* is turning up in *any* database. It's like this woman is newly hatched. We're now looking at any cold cases that have fingernail scratch marks, or wire noose marks, or teeth marks, as part of the murder. But we have nothing to go on yet." She sat back and sighed.

"WWED? Or WWTD?" Oliver remarked with a wink.

A confused chorus followed his statement.

"Bloody hell?" Sophia sputtered.

"Huh?" Charlie let out.

"*Chto?*" came from Anatoly.

"What would Elda do? Or what would Tosh do," Oliver spelled out.

"We need to find them." Charlie glared at the others.

"Charlie, they are *dead*," Sophia announced.

"*No*. I don't believe so." Charlie scowled at the group. "They're probably hiding in plain sight. We have the brains in this room to find them. They *are* alive."

"*Der'mo!* They are *dead!*" Anatoly slammed his fist on the wooden coffee table, shaking the teacups. A crack slowly appeared where his fist had landed, and spread across the table. The team grabbed their cups and watched in fascination as the coffee table slowly collapsed.

"Bloody hell, Anatoly!" Sophia barked.

Oliver covered his mouth so his wife couldn't see him laughing.

Charlie frowned and repeated to herself, *Men . . .*

Anatoly winced and shrugged his shoulders. "*Mne zhal'*, Sophia and Oliver. I will buy you a new table." Anatoly reached into his pocket and tossed onto the floor more than enough pounds to cover the expense.

"Anatoly. Remember what Tosh told you about wrecking things?" Snezhana reprimanded.

"Tosh is dead." Anatoly growled. The clicks of magazines being removed filled the room.

"Bollocks! They're burning." The bouquet of blueberry scones in the oven wafted from the kitchen. Oliver bolted off to save them.

He returned, smiling, with a plate of hot scones accompanied by clotted cream and triple-berry jam. He offered them to Anatoly, who shook his head.

Oliver's mouth dropped open, and his eyebrows threatened to leave his forehead. "Is he okay?" he whispered to Snezhana,

"I can hear you. Let's get to business," Anatoly groused, sitting on the carpet next to Sophia's chair.

"Snezhana and Anatoly, why did you agree to come?" Sophia asked in a stern tone. "You maintained, over the phone, that I was in trouble and you would tell me more when you arrived, but somehow I doubt you'd fly all this way just to save me."

"You *are* in trouble and you're also correct," Snezhana confessed. "Although we find you a helpful asset at times, saving your life and risking ours hasn't been a top priority . . . until now."

"What changed?" Charlie demanded, not yet willing to trust the Russians.

"This." Anatoly reached up and flipped a snap of Nyoka onto Sophia's lap.

Sophia's eyes widened, and her hand went to her neck. She gasped. "Her! What do you know of her?"

Charlie picked the picture up from Sophia's lap. "Is this the bitch who tried to kill you, Sophia?"

"Yes. Who is she, Anatoly?"

"Nyoka Morozov is a relatively new player for the Kremlin, but she owns a solid reputation as an assassin. She is lethal and has no scruples and no real allegiances. I want to remove her from the game. She makes the rest of us look bad." He selected his squat silver MSS Vul silent pistol and verified the magazine was fully loaded.

Sophia looked at him. "I wasn't aware you possessed such ethics."

"There is a code of honor among thieves," Anatoly grumbled "Why not among assassins, hey? It's a business. We cannot have a loose cannon such as her operating at this level. Even the Mafia won't use her."

Charlie wished Elda was there to help clarify what made each player tick. For now, she sat back and watched.

Oliver, after popping into the kitchen, walked around lobbing bottles of Evian water at each person.

Sophia caught her bottle one handed and batted her eyelashes at him. "Any chance of tea, dear?"

Oliver responded with a leer. "Your tab will need to be paid soon."

"My pleasure." Sophia winked.

Charlie rolled her eyes. Snezhana stuck her finger in her mouth and gagged.

Sophia stuck her tongue out.

"I'll take that, my love." Oliver then got back to business. "So why are you here? Isn't the assassin in Moscow?"

Snezhana shook her head. "We think she's still in the UK, and we *know* she's coming here."

"Bollocks." Oliver grimaced.

Sophia put a hand on his arm. "Now, Oliver, you will *not* play hero in this one. I can protect myself."

"Obviously not." Oliver pointed at her neck. "I need to be back in the game."

"We'll talk later, honey. But remember the last few times you were an operative? I would like to have a husband to come home to. Can you make us all some tea?" Sweetness and promises dripped from her voice.

"Bollocks." Oliver stormed off into the kitchen. The sound of pots and pans clanging rang out.

"How *is* he doing?" Snezhana nodded in the direction of Oliver's exit.

Sophia sighed. "Physically he's all healed. However, this baby thing messed him up. And he's far too protective of me. I can't have him in the field. Perhaps he can be our support person at home?"

"Good idea," Snezhana championed. "It will be your job to sell him on that."

"Bloody hell. I thought you'd say that." Sophia frowned. "What do you propose we do about Nyoka?"

"Kill the bitch." Charlie drew her knife from its sheath and made a stabbing motion.

Anatoly looked up from his weapons. "We wait."

"*That's it?*" Sophia exploded. "We frickin' *wait?*"

What is that noise?

Anatoly sat sentry in a chair next to the front door of Sophia and Oliver's flat. Snezhana slept stretched out on the couch. Oliver and Sophia slept in their bedroom. Charlie, sick of bunking in the nursery turned spare room slash study, had rented a hotel room for the night.

Anatoly tiptoed to Snezhana and put a hand over her mouth, awakening her. She bolted up and grabbed her piece. He motioned for her to wake Sophia. Before Snezhana could act on awakening the other two, Sophia emerged dressed and armed in her bedroom doorway, with Oliver behind her. They fanned out to hide behind the furniture and in the kitchen.

Anatoly watched as someone expertly jimmied the lock, and the door opened slightly. He moved in behind the door, ready to pounce.

The long barrel of the PB/629 silenced pistol entered, attached to the well-manicured hand of a tall, long-haired woman.

Excellent choice of gun. With its PB fixed sights with luminous inserts, it was great for use during low-light conditions. *I may add that to my collection!* With that, Anatoly reached out, grabbing her arm and twisting until she dropped the weapon She butted him with her head, and he swung her around and slammed her against the wall and scratched her face with his ring. Within seconds she dropped like a rock.

Snezhana popped up from behind the couch. "I thought you told me that contained water."

Anatoly grinned sheepishly. "It *did*, Snez, but I replaced the water with my knockout liquid once we got here. I figured it might come in handy."

Sophia glanced down at the body and kicked it, hearing a rib crack. "That will pay you back for the pain I'm in right now."

"*Lisus*, Sophia. I think perhaps cutting off her finger was enough retribution," Snezhana pointed out. "I'm not one to shoot someone lying on the floor. Should we give her to MI6?"

Anatoly snorted. "Let me take care of it. Sophia. Can I borrow that rug?" He lifted the furniture from the nine-by-twelve brightly patterned oriental.

Sophia looked downcast. "Aw, that one, Anatoly? I smuggled it back from India, and I like it a lot."

"It's the right size. I'll bring it back."

———

These do not fit well. Oliver needs to work out. The pair of overalls Anatoly had borrowed from Oliver's disguise kit stretched across his chest, with one shoulder strap unhooked and *Hello Movers* boldly displayed, stenciled on the back. Anatoly trotted out of Sophia's flat carrying a large rolled-up rug over his shoulder.

An elderly lady was leaving her apartment next door. "Oh dear, are the nice couple moving?"

Anatoly affected his best British accent. "No, ma'am. They're merely giving away some things to friends."

"How generous of them. That is a beautiful rug."

Anatoly carried it down the stairs instead of waiting for the elevator with that woman. He was somewhat out of breath by the time he reached the exit. He nabbed a shopping cart left outside, slung his package over it, and jogged around the corner, where he had seen a garbage truck parked for the night.

"*Aga.*" There it was. He looked around to make sure he wasn't being watched, then twirled the body out of the rug and into the back of the truck. Injecting her with a syringe, he reached in and tossed garbage over the assassin to keep her hidden. She should either be dead or out for another twelve hours. Either way, she was a goner. The truck mechanism would crush her to bits.

He rolled the rug back up.

The next morning, dressed in bright-yellow reflective raincoats and orange pants, one man hopped into the cab of the Lambert trash truck, and the other two grabbed the handholds. They stepped onto the back as the driver pulled away from the curb.

One man on the back peered into the trash. "Ey, 'arry, did something move back there?"

"What?" Harry called out, over the sound of the road noise.

"Did you see movement?"

"Probably rats again, Rog," Harry answered, dismissing Roger's concern.

Roger scrunched up his face. "Bloody hell. No, no, I think I see a 'and." He pounded on the side of the truck for the driver to pull over.

The driver stopped the truck and marched to the rear.

"I think Rog went to the pub this morning," Harry said.

At that moment, a hand moved out from under the trash. The three men jumped back.

"Who do you think 'as been 'itting the sauce now, mates?"

A garbage-covered apparition leapt from the truck, goo oozing down her long black tresses. Bits of half-eaten trash speckled her clothing. She hissed at the men, who each took a step away from her. Her yellow eyes glowed in the morning light as she inspected each one of them.

"Run," she spit at them.

They did without question.

Like an animal recovering from its wounds, she shook herself off and climbed into the cab.

Charlie rapped on the door. She could see an eyeball peering at her through the door's spy hole but could not identify the owner. The clicks of multiple locks being undone seemed new for this apartment.

"What the fuck?" Charlie blurted at the occupants.

"We had a nocturnal visitor," Snezhana explained.

Sophia put her hand to her neck.

"Oh no. Tell all." Charlie sank onto the sofa.

The four occupants of the flat took turns filling Charlie in.

"Are you sure she's dead?" Charlie asked.

Anatoly shrugged and grimaced. "*Net*. I used a paralyzing agent on her. I didn't have anything stronger in my kit. But they'll activate the crusher before picking up more garbage, so she's most likely rat bait by now. I did snag a nice addition to my weapons bag." He held up the gun he had taken from Nyoka. "Which reminds me. Is there any way I can get access to MI6's toy room, Sophia?"

Sophia rolled her eyes but nodded. "I don't have direct access anymore, but I'm pretty sure Heather does. Let me check with her. Keep your fingers crossed."

Snezhana pointed out, looking at Anatoly. "We need to look into the landfill and verify that insane woman is dead."

Anatoly backed up and held his two forefingers up in the shape of a cross. "Who's we?"

"Well, actually, it's you, Anatoly. You'll be able to pass for a sanitation engineer a lot better than I would." Snezhana grinned huge.

"*Der'mo.*" Anatoly snorted.

Still learning about each individual in this assembly, Charlie observed the exchange, then leaned forward and inserted herself into the conversation. "Okay, now that we settled that, how do we find Elda and Tosh?"

"They . . . are . . . *dead!*" Anatoly hit his fist on a nearby chair, cracking it. "*Chert*, Sophia and Oliver. Where did you buy this cheap furniture?" He strewed more money onto the couch. "At least upgrade to something that doesn't break when you breathe on it."

"We didn't know it would be undergoing such rigorous quality control," Oliver deadpanned.

Sophia pocketed the money. "You can go furniture shopping, Oliver, after we stop being a B and B."

Anatoly brightened. "Does that mean we get breakfast in the morning?"

"If you cook," Sophia said. "I remember you made a mean breakfast when we hid out in the Colonial Village West safe house in DC."

Anatoly readily agreed. "*Da.* Got bacon?" He loped off to inventory the fridge.

Charlie cleared her throat. "I'm afraid to ask again, but despite what Anatoly believes, we need to find Elda and Tosh—"

Snezhana interjected. "Or at least verify their deaths. With Stas under so much scrutiny in the Kremlin, I don't dare ask him, but we need to tap a geek to do a deeper dive on rentals and house purchases in the regions we think they would have gone to."

Charlie shook her head and sighed. "I already did that, Snez."

"So did we, Charlie, but we had limited knowledge of Elda, although we did have good firsthand experience with Tosh, as you did with Elda. You, Charlie, and your US contacts can provide the other half of the equation to us, and us to you."

"But how do we find them even with our increased insights?"

"There is AI now that we didn't have access to earlier. What if we feed Elda's and Tosh's characteristics, likes, dislikes, skills, aliases, etcetera, into some sort of AI search program and see if we can generate any hits?" Snezhana suggested.

"Great idea," Oliver chimed. "Charlie, you've mentioned problems with Ed's organization, but can you ask Ashok to write such a program without specifically saying why you need it? Have him create enough match variables so that we can fill in what we know and see what the program spits out. You've implied he's bored and looking for more challenging projects."

Charlie gave her approval with a vigorous nod. "He could probably write this in his sleep. It's a good idea. I'll reach out to him."

Anatoly returned from rummaging in the kitchen and reported, "No bacon. Give me some pounds and I'll go buy some." He held out his hand toward Sophia.

Sophia passed him some of his own money back. "It's a short walk to Sainsbury's. Take a right out of here and then another right on Wyvil Road. It's across the A3036. They're open until eleven p.m."

"Watch your six, Anatoly," Charlie warned. "She could still be out there."

Anatoly snorted again. "Just let her try something."

It was dark out when Anatoly left Sophia's flat at Keybridge Apartments. He had turned onto S. Lambert Rd., when he heard footsteps behind, keeping cadence with his own. He sped up to take the right onto Wyvil Road and heard the person behind him do the same. He spied a

Honda CB125 outside the Griffin Belle and sized up if he had time to hot-wire it. Just then a man drove up on a GTS 125 Vespa Super Sport. He shut it off and pushed down the kickstand. Anatoly shoved him from behind, snagged his keys, hopped on, and roared away.

A few seconds later, he heard the sound of a Honda starting up behind him. The Honda sputtered, obviously suffering under the ministrations of someone with little or no experience on motorized bikes. This made up for the Honda's superior turning radius, and Anatoly was able to keep the Vespa in front. The two riders sped the wrong direction down Luscombe Way, swerving around the oncoming traffic. They careened around the loop, cut through the alleys to Hartington Road, and merged right onto A3036.

Anatoly leaned into the left onto Hermans Street, feeling his running board scrape the road. "*Der'mo.*" He slammed on his brakes and pulled up with all his might while keeping one steel-soled boot on the ground as a pivot point, popping a wheelie and completing a turnaround at Opel Links Insurance Company. He headed right toward the other driver.

Neither one flinched, and Anatoly dove off his bike before the impact. The other man skidded with his bike to the side of the road.

Anatoly dragged the occupant off the bike. "*Yaromir?*"

The door to Sophia and Oliver's flat swung open.

Charlie popped up from the couch, drew her weapon, and stood ready to take out the intruders.

Two large men entered, the second one's face obscured by the man he pushed in front of him.

"What the bloody hell?" Sophia burst out.

"Stand down," Anatoly yelled from the rear. "It's me,

and I brought Yaromir." He pushed Yaromir into a sitting position on Charlie's spot on the couch.

Charlie tracked the intruder with her gun. "What are *you* doing *here*?" She elevated her pistol and aimed it at his head.

Wide eyed, Yaromir focused on the barrel of Charlie's pistol. "I-I-I was looking for Sophia."

Sophia startled, pointed to herself, and burst out, "Me? How do you know of me? And how do you know where I live?"

"I asked Stas to find me a friendly who would help me get out of the UK and avoid being sent back to Moscow. Are you Sophia?" Yaromir raised an eyebrow.

Sophia stood in attack mode. "Obviously, dimwit. And who are you?"

Charlie, glaring, answered for Yaromir. "He's Yaromir, an assassin who used to work for Tosh. I left him by a dumpster in Wales. Why are you here, Yaromir, and why did you say you can't go back to Russia? Is that road rash on your face?"

Yaromir wiped his hand on his face, and blood transferred to his palm. He hung his head. "I failed. Boris will have me terminated. He doesn't give second chances."

Snezhana went into the bathroom and came back with a wet facecloth. She put it in Yaromir's hand and clamped his hand to his face. "Hold that there."

Charlie looked Anatoly up and down. "Anatoly . . . you look, shall we say, disheveled. What happened?"

Anatoly grinned. "Vespas are better than motorcycles."

Snezhana slapped him up the side of the head. "Not again. My demented younger brother. *Cosa sie pazzo?* Did anyone see you?"

Sophia doubled over laughing. Charlie looked puzzled.

"Anatoly has a history of stealing Vespas," Sophia explained.

"No one saw me," Anatoly informed them, "and I sanitized both bikes. This one was much nicer than that *kusok der'ma* I stole in Florence."

Oliver strolled out of the kitchen, wiping his hands on a dishcloth. "Anatoly, *you* stole something?" He stopped short and indicated Yaromir. "Friend or foe?"

Yaromir scratched his head. "Neither?"

"What if we sent him to a resort in the Bahamas?" Charlie suggested, frowning.

"Where?" Sophia tilted her head at an angle.

Charlie looked over at Sophia. She brightened. "Elda told me this story about when she and Yuri were on opposite sides, she decided to not kill him but to remove him from the action. He arrived in a wooden crate to this amazing place in the Bahamas."

Anatoly chuckled. "I remember Yuri telling me how much fun he had at that place. He was considered quite the catch, according to his stories."

"The resort is all inclusive and run by friends of the agency," Charlie said. "We get a discount on any of the *customers* we send their way. They keep an eye on them and take care they're happy, but also that they don't contact anyone or leave."

"And it's a step up from the *durdom*, where Elda sent that guy from the Russian embassy in our joint op," Snezhana further elucidated. "You'll love it, Yaromir. Yuri insisted he'd willingly go back there."

"And it will give us time to figure out what to do with you, Yaromir," Charlie admitted. She sat down on a chair.

Sophia plopped down on the floor beside her.

Anatoly paced back and forth. "*Net.* That's too good for Yaromir. I have a better idea."

Yaromir looked at Anatoly with fear in his eyes.

"What?" Charlie narrowed her eyes.

"What was the name of that Welsh guy with the fake leg?" Anatoly asked.

"Rhys," Sophia answered.

The smell of hot pastry blew into the room with Oliver, who held a tray of mixed berry scones. Charlie took a scone from Oliver, who always doled out the food, and took a big bite while waiting for Anatoly's answer.

Sophia grabbed one too. "Dear, the way you're cooking, I'll need a gym membership."

Oliver scanned her body with his eyes and leered his appreciation.

Snezhana gagged.

Anatoly waved Oliver away. "First Rhys agrees to have a picture of him taken, in which he's dead. You know the drill. Fake blood, and we can have him remove the leg and put blood all over his stump. Maybe stage it on the train tracks."

"And . . ." Charlie took another bite from her scone.

"Yaromir transmits the image to Boris and beats feet back to Moscow. He is victorious, and we're not paying for his luxurious vacation. *Pobeda-Pobeda*, or win-win, as you would say," Anatoly concluded.

Oliver came by with the scones again, but Anatoly refused.

Charlie narrowed her eyes. "What do we get in return?" She took another chomp from her scone.

Anatoly tore a loose scrap of skin from his finger. "*Prostoy*, very simple. Information. Yaromir tells us the names of everyone who works for Boris."

"You're getting to be quite the strategist, Anatoly," Snezhana admired, adding, "I think you'll need a Band-Aid for that," pointing to Anatoly's dripping finger.

Oliver lunged to place a towel on the white rug beneath Anatoly's hand and ran to the bathroom for a piece of plastic and antibiotic cream.

"Thanks, Snez." Anatoly held his hand to Oliver to be tended to and turned to Yaromir. "Deal?"

Yaromir nodded.

Anatoly put his face close to Yaromir and growled. "If you fail us, I will kill you. And you *know* I am better than you."

Yaromir's head was now as far back into the couch as it would go. Sweat broke out on his forehead. He shook his head up and down vigorously. "*Da.* I will do as you say. *Pozhaluysta*, help me."

Anatoly gave everyone the double thumbs-up and flopped onto the couch. "My job is done."

"Did you bring the bacon, Anatoly?" Oliver asked. "We need eggs too. While you're at it, you can take the broken bits of chair to the dumpster."

"*Chert.*" Anatoly jumped up, snapped up the chair pieces, and stomped back out.

***

"*Der'mo.*"

The next morning dawned with Anatoly on top of a trash heap. Flies buzzing around his head, he tossed trash over to one side. He picked up a sharp piece of metal and decapitated a rat sniffing around him, throwing the carcass after the rest of the garbage. The stench of rotting food and other matter assaulted his nostrils.

After two hours of digging through the recently dumped refuse, he pitched his rubber gloves onto the pile and stomped back to Sophia's flat. The stink of garbage wafted in with him.

"Take off your shoes, Anatoly!" Oliver cried out.

"Bloody hell, Anatoly. You stink. Go take a shower and change your clothes," Sophia commanded, then held up her hand. "But first, what did you find?"

"There were no human remains there."

CHAPTER TWENTY-THREE

"**C**RAWL!"

Elda winced as she saw Olga fling herself onto Tosh's back, driving his chest into the Tuscan dirt below. She hoped nothing was broken.

"Umph. *Chert.*" He gasped under her weight and sneezed as he snaked his body through the dust.

Olga chortled. "Look, skinny man. What if you had a huge pack on your back? Olga light."

Tosh grunted at Olga. "You are *not* light. And I don't do packs." He crawled forward and did a shimmy and bucked. Olga held on, and laughing, she popped up and over and slammed onto Elda's back, flattening her.

"Oh my god, Olga! No more biscuits." Elda panted as she rose to her hands and knees and clawed her way forward. She was not in agreement about this part of Olga's training. It did make them a lot stronger, but perhaps using packs would be a good alternative.

Ahead of them, Yuri chuckled. Hearing that, Olga lurched off Elda and ran to his crawling form.

Yuri heard her approach. "No, please, Olga, not again."

Olga patted him on the back. "Okay, Yuri. You be good and do everything Olga asks, right?" Why did Yuri get a pass on the Olga squish?

He reached the end and lay there, head in the dirt, spent. "*Da*. Olga. *Da*."

Elda came in side by side with Tosh and collapsed. Jim finished soon after them and dropped to his belly. Olga stopped her timer and grinned broadly. "Yeah. Olga likes. Much better this time. We break for tea and then we start training again."

Groans emanated from the prone bodies.

"No? You want to do more now?" Olga wore a huge smile on her face.

Elda leapt up. "I'll make tea!"

"Don't forget Olga's biscuits . . ." Olga shook her finger at Elda.

Tosh limped after Elda into the kitchen. "I think every muscle in my body hurts."

"What, you have muscles?" Elda grabbed a bottle of Tylenol from the junk drawer.

Tosh swatted Elda with a soggy dish towel. She was too exhausted to dodge it. "Before we are too tired to think, perhaps we can figure out how to bring Charlie here? And, hand over a couple of those painkillers."

Yuri and Olga wandered into the kitchen. They talked simultaneously, "Charlie's in London with Snezhana, Anatoly, and Sophia. Shall we bring her here?"

"Better yet, let's go there," Tosh and Elda cried out, in unison. Elda high-fived Tosh. It would be great to get back into the field.

Yuri held out his hand for a Tylenol, swigged it down with water, then volunteered, "I'll arrange travel."

"I'll find a place for you two to stay," Olga, monitoring the ceramic teapot, chimed.

"Yuri, can the travel not be in coffins this time?" Elda begged.

Yuri chuckled.

Olga looked puzzled. "Coffins?" She checked her watch and poured Tosh a cup of tea.

Tosh accepted his tea. "Longer story, Olga. I'll let Yuri fill you in."

"Argh, that's hot!" Tosh spit his tea back into the cup, missing splattering the living room floor.

"Blow on it," Elda advised from her perch on the comfy overstuffed chair.

The team regrouped in the villa. Jim lay supine on the couch, with pillows propping up his foot and another two under his head and back. Olga and Yuri, having called in favors for travel arrangements, planned meals in the kitchen.

Tosh took his Earl Grey tea and dragged a chair over to sit down next to Jim. "How's your ankle feeling?"

Jim wiggled his foot. "All good, Tosh. It's happiah than a clam in high tide."

A scowling Tosh peered at Jim as he tried to figure out if that was a good thing. The silence floated between them.

"That's a good thing, Tosh, wicked good," Elda interjected.

Tosh snorted.

Jim laughed. "Ah keep fohgetting that you're a flatlandah, Tosh."

Tosh crinkled his brow. "You speak an entirely different language, Jim. Where do you live?"

"Down East."

"Is that Maine?"

"Ayuh. 'Tis."

"Do you live near Elda?"

Elda raised an eyebrow.

"Looks like Eldah's living in Tuscany," Jim drawled. "And I'm in a villa here, so I guess you might say that."

Tosh sighed. He wasn't going to obtain any background on Elda from Jim.

As if mind reading, Elda affirmed his thought. "Good try, Tosh, but Jim's a tight-lipped Mainer."

Tosh snorted. "I'll learn where you live yet, Elda."

Elda chuckled. "Keep trying. I'm a nomad. Speaking of which, let's change and pack. It's showtime!"

Wearing a limo driver's uniform, Yuri drove up to the drop-off zone at British Airway at the Florence Airport. He came around to the passenger side of the black sedan and opened the back door. An old woman wearing a gray shawl and holding a cane shakily scurried out of the car, with the chauffeur's assistance.

Yuri helped her to the sidewalk, pulled a walker from the trunk, and waited as an elderly man scooted across the backseat. Yuri reached in and helped the frail man stand and grasp his walker. When the man's battered taupe fedora fell off, Yuri picked it up, dusted it off, and settled it on the man's head.

"Hurry along, Frederick. We'll miss our plane," the woman called from the walkway.

The bent-over old man coughed and spit on the ground. "Stop nagging me, Bertha. You've been nagging me for sixty years now." He pushed the rollator slowly in front of him, parallel to the sidewalk, until he reached a ramp for the curb. Yuri, rolling their single piece of luggage, followed him, eyes darting from one to the other.

Yuri stopped next to Bertha and whispered, "Should I come all the way in with you?"

To ensure he would pass facial recognition while in the terminal, Bertha inspected his face. He had a short beard and mustache, and his cheeks puffed with internal prosthetics. His nose was lengthened, as were his ears. He wore a black cap down low on his forehead and mirrored sunglasses.

"Well, there is no way we can carry that luggage, young man," Bertha asserted. "Of course we need you to accompany us."

Frederick's rollator swayed precariously with the weight of Frederick's canvas backpack perched on the front of it. Yuri reached out to grab the pack. Frederick slapped his hand. "Hands off that bag, young whippersnapper. I can carry it."

"Sorry, sir." Yuri stepped back but kept close by both of them.

"Oh hush, Frederick," the old woman called out from the sidewalk in a quivering voice. "The nice young man was just trying to help you."

"I can do it myself, Bertha."

Yuri flagged down a porter who was handling curbside check-in for British Air. The old couple displayed their tickets and gave the porter their luggage.

Yuri held the door open while they shuffled into the terminal. He followed the bickering couple to the counter, where they both acquired wheelchairs to take them to the gate. Yuri and the British Air assistant rolled their eyes as they wheeled the two squabbling elders away.

At the gate, Bertha thanked the driver and assistant, slipping each a one-pound coin. "There, youngsters. You did well. Bless your hearts."

Yuri smiled wryly, tipped his hat, and pocketed the money. He handed Bertha a card. "Call when you return, and I'll pick you both up."

"Well, it better be both of us," Frederick snapped. He

turned to Bertha. "What's he thinking? That we're so old, one of us will die over there?"

"Hush, Frederick," Bertha admonished, then turned to Yuri. "Thank you again. Frederick always gets a bit testy when he's flying."

"Testy? Who's testy?"

Bertha patted Frederick's hand. Yuri walked away, admiring their role-playing but knowing they had been out of the field for a while. He hoped they were on their game. *Bog s toboy* . . . He translated in his head. *God be with you.*

Is he getting frustrated by the wait?

Elda was afraid Tosh would make a scene. Or worse yet, drop his cover and race off the plane. She was praying that their new identities, disguises, and the matching biometric data entered in the immigration database would hold up.

"When are they going to get us?" he whined, in a loud, crotchety voice.

She patted his hand. "Hush, Frederick. They will be here soon. We mustn't overact." She coughed and *corrected* herself. "Overreact, that is. I forgot my B12 and Lion's Mane this morning. It's hard to find the right word sometimes."

"Don't hush me, Bertha. My claustrophobia is kicking in." He wheezed and grabbed his inhaler and took a noisy puff.

Elda heard a flight attendant tell another, "He's starting to panic. I'm going to wheel them off myself. I'll be back in a flash. I'll grab Hank to help me."

Tosh winked at Elda as they were wheeled from the plane.

Elda tried to keep her face impassive. Inside she was

elated. Heathrow was like coming home, as she had flown in and out of it so many times. She longed to leap out of the wheelchair and twirl around, absorbing the sights and sounds. She breathed deeply, sucking in the smell of Heathrow, the essence of duty-free, the whiff of jet fuel, the international combinations of various perfumes, soaps and aftershaves, bad coffee and good tea. She wallowed in the bustle around her as thousands of people passed through the airport. She looked over at the wheelchair next to her and saw Tosh observing her. She winked at him.

The attendants wheeled them to baggage claim and over to the taxi stand, where they helped them into a cab.

"Keybridge Apartments, 1 Exchange Gardens, London," Elda directed the driver.

"*Interesnyy . . .*" Tosh mused.

"Time to visit the grandchildren, Frederick."

My god, we're on the wrong side of the road! Elda took a long breath and struggled to orient herself to driving on the left again. She glanced at Tosh and saw his fingers on his pulse. *Oh good, I'm not the only one struggling.*

"It's been a while since we've traveled, wouldn't you say, Frederick?" she said in a thin, scratchy voice,

He grunted an affirmative.

The driver swung onto the M4. They sped past the sporting grounds of Imperial College and soon were viewing row houses on their left. Elda always found the mixture of rundown houses, with plots of green, sepia, and tan mingled within, a tribute to England's conservation of land. At the Hogarth roundabout they swung onto A4. Elda enjoyed the A routes. They were a tad slower, and you could see more. Most of all, she loved the names. Chiswick, Hogarth, Brompton, Hammersmith, Cromwell Road. She repeated the words in her head with an assumed British accent. Italy was gorgeous, but the UK was home.

"Are we there *yet*?" Tosh, a.k.a. Frederick, complained.

Elda patted his hand. "Oh hush, Frederick. We have only about four to five more miles to go."

Once on the A3212, Elda could see the river Thames on her right. They crossed over the Vauxhall Bridge and passed the MI6 building, turned right onto South Lambert Road, and far too soon for Elda's tourist brain, pulled up in front of the flats at 1 Exchange Gardens.

Elda paid the driver and gave him his one-pound tip with a flourish. "There you go, my good man." She backed out of the car and stood, wobbling with her cane, waiting for Tosh to come around, pushing his walker. The driver gave Elda the handle of the suitcase.

They inched their way into the lobby. Olga had supplied them with the keys and the flat number. They elevatored up and entered the flat through the living room/kitchen area.

"*Chert!*" Tosh blurted out.

"Damn. How much does this thing cost a week?" Elda echoed.

Elda and Tosh wandered over to the doors leading to the balcony and took in the view of the city. The apartment had two good sized bedrooms, two bathrooms, a spacious living room with a full-sized couch, coffee table, side chair, and a breakfast bar with stools, leading into the kitchen. The kitchen had stainless-steel appliances. The overhead lights were recessed in the ceiling, and the walls were freshly painted a pinkish off white. The entire color scheme screamed clean, minimalistic, and money.

"Wow," Elda blurted.

"You can tell we're not working for the government anymore. But where did the money come from?"

Elda shrugged. "Olga said to ask no questions but did mention someone owed her a favor."

"Some favor. I'll have to ask her about *that* one," Tosh declared with a laugh.

"I'd be interested in that story myself." She turned away. "Let's remove these outfits and pop over to Sophia's, hey?"

"*Da.* I recognize the old-people getup is a good disguise. Younger people often don't give a second look at the oldsters, plus they do not see them as threats. Despite that, I'm sick of being so elderly."

"Oh hush, Frederick," Elda teased.

Tosh threw a couch pillow at Elda. She ran and beat him into the corner bedroom. "Dibs on this one!"

"*Chert.*"

———

Elda took in the view of Anatoly holding an open hardbound book with one hand. She assumed the other hand held his Magnum. Charlie stood poised to spring on the other side of the door. Sophia hid around the corner in the kitchen, but her toe poked out the doorway.

"May we interest you in some Girlguiding cookies?" Elda posited with a lilt in her voice, her hazel eyes set off by her dark-green cap. Her spiked blond hair stuck out at angles beneath the cap. A waist-length black leather coat, washed-out blue jeans, and green suede sneakers, with internal lifts and a thick sole, completed her outfit.

Next to her, Tosh stood looking dapper in a russet leather flat cap, blue-and-white striped shirt, sepia leather flight jacket, and dark-blue jeans. His outfit was topped off, so to speak, with a pair of steel-toed Harley boots. Inserted lifts gave him additional height. Old scars left from chicken pox, a slightly hooked nose, and patchy beard growth diminished the handsomeness of his face. Mirrored sunglasses hid his dark-brown, almost black eyes.

Anatoly growled. "We aren't buying anything." He started to shut the door in their faces.

"Wait!" Charlie shouted.

⁓

I knew it! Charlie ran past Anatoly and knocked him to one side in her rush to get to the door.

Anatoly cursed her. "*Der'mo.* What is wrong with you, Charlie?"

Charlie skidded to a stop inches away from the two salespeople.

The woman held out a box of Classic Chocolate Girl-guiding cookies. "You must really like these cookies."

"It is you! I knew it! You're alive!" Charlie turned to the rest of the team. "They're alive!"

Still holding his revolver inside the book, Anatoly squinted at the two strangers at the door and shook his head. "Charlie, you're imagining things."

"Damn it! No I am not." Charlie stomped her foot. "Come off it, guys. Tell them," she implored the two at the door,

Sophia came out of the kitchen and peered at them. The man took off his sunglasses and stared back. "Nah. Too different."

Snezhana, who had been quietly studying the two people, suddenly burst into tears. "*Dyadya!*" She wrapped her arms around him in a bear hug.

He hugged her back.

Finally vindicated, Charlie thought.

Elda grinned ear to ear. "Well done, Grasshopper."

CHAPTER TWENTY-FOUR

ANATOLY SAT ON THE FLOOR TO THE **SIDE** of the stuffed cloth chair, munching on a scone, silently staring at Tosh and Elda, while Snezhana and Sophia filled them in on all the happenings to date. Anatoly interrupted with, "I need to kill that bitch. How do we find her?"

Elda held up her hand. "Patience, Anatoly. The fight is coming. First, let's summarize. Second, strategize. Last, act."

Anatoly snorted. "*Der'mo*, Elda. This planning takes too long. I think I liked it better when you were dead."

Elda lofted a couch pillow at Anatoly, who fielded it and placed it behind his back. She turned to Tosh. "Will you summarize for us?"

Tosh stood. "*Da. Spasibo*, Elda. This is what I know so far, from everything Elda and I gathered, and from the findings you all gave us."

Sophia supplied him with a large pad of flipchart paper and a couple of markers. Oliver set up the easel.

Tosh wrote on the whiteboard as he summarized.

"Killed in Ukraine: Joseph White, ex-CIA, mole for James. But we have a lot of players running around still. Nyoka, a new assassin, probably sent by Boris, the new Kremlin bigwig—"

Elda cut in. "And we have no idea how complicit he was with Operation Bittman."

Tosh continued. "Nyoka killed Alwyn, an innocent, in Wales. Adrik works for Boris and is using Alexie's phone to run Frank—"

"That bastard." Charlie snarled.

"Well done, Charlie, for beating the crap out of him," Elda said.

Tosh glared at them. "We suspect both Adrik and Frank are dirty from Operation Bittman. We know Ed's organization is still leaky, and Kevin Ball, Ed's accountant, is most likely run by the Russians. To complicate things, we are not yet fully staffed. Ashok wants to work with us. Stas is a bit stuck right now. We have Yuri, Olga, and Jim in Italy. And we're using Yaromir as our double agent."

"And we're not sure how this land deal in the US and Wales fits in with everything," Elda added.

Tosh jotted

ACTION PLAN: GET ASHOK

on the board and turned to the gathering. "Did I get it all?"

"Enough for now. We can add to it as we get more data," Elda commented. "Let's act on what we can. Charlie, please text Ashok now and give him the heads-up we will need him."

Fingers flying, Charlie typed to Ashok. "Done. He's in."

"Well done." Tosh returned to his list.

- FIND REST OF MOLES

"Well, that covers it." Anatoly sneered.

Elda drilled down. "It's asking a lot, but I'd like Ashok

to research which American couples had children while in Russia and possibly who in the United States adopted Russian orphan children, like Arabella and Kevin."

"Is that doable, Elda?" Tosh asked. "Do you know how many children were adopted from Russia by Americans? It was a twenty-two-year program that ended in 2013. Every flight back from Russia to America, during that time, had crying babies for the entire time the plane was in the air."

"True, Tosh," Elda agreed. "So we limit the age range. I'm guessing the operatives are in their thirties now. Those born in 1991, at the beginning of the program, would be thirty-three. We look at adoptions from 1984, when there are fewer to sort through, to 1998. Charlie, can you pass that task to Ashok? I'm sure he can write some sort of search and filter program. Something that is extensible so we can add parameters and screen out more."

"Roger that, Elda." Charlie started typing to Ashok. "What about initially narrowing it further to those in the military or with government jobs?"

"Excellent, Charlie! I was right to pick you as my successor. I think you, and Snezhana as Tosh's next in line, will go far."

Snezhana and Charlie beamed at Elda.

Anatoly raised his hand.

Tosh recognized him. "Yes, Anatoly?"

"I would like to add another action item." He walked up to the easel and wrote,

\- ELIMINATE FRANK, KEVIN, ADRIK, BORIS, AND REST OF MOLES

Tosh slapped him on the back. "Don't you worry, Anatoly. You will get your chance. We will rid the systems of these traitors to the UK and America, and these disgraces to our Mother Russia. Most of all, we will enact revenge for the harm they did to us. They took away our jobs, hurt my grandniece, injured and killed our teammates, all for their own profit and advancement, not for the good of Mother Russia. They lied to us and have been unethical. There are rules to what we do. That is why it all works. They stepped outside the lines one too many times. I mean to teach them a lesson and get our honor back."

Chapter Twenty-Five

CRASH. SHARDS OF CERAMIC, MIXED with a dark liquid, splattered across the floor. Boris had flung his coffee cup against the wall. He slowly made himself a new cup of coffee while listening to Kevin's message again.

"It's me, Kevin. They won't budge at the price we're offering them, but one hinted that, with another half million US dollars, he'd sell." Kevin paused, then continued. "I think if we have another twenty mil to play with, I can get them to sell."

Boris did his own calculations. There were six developers. Kevin could buy them off for five hundred thousand dollars to maybe two million, tops. He asked for twenty million from Boris, figuring Boris would probably cut that back to ten, which would mean Kevin could clear around a half a million. That was on top of the 10 percent commission that Boris promised him.

Boris tapped on his desk, considering the next steps. That little bastard Kevin was trying to skim off the top of this deal. Perhaps he needed to be shown a lesson.

Thud! The side table toppled over, and the man's meaty fist seized the water glass before it went with the table. *Good reflexes, but clumsy,* Boris thought.

The brutish man dribbled water down his chin and chest as he drank. He plunked the empty glass down on the floor, next to the upended table, and looked expectantly at Boris.

Did any of these assassins possess a grain of couth? Boris stood to dismiss the interviewee, when a shot rang out and his door opened by the weight of a body falling into the office.

Pridurki! Boris stormed out of his office into the waiting room, where two men tussled on the floor. One man sat on a chair reloading his gun. Boris's secretary relaxed at her desk, having a cup of tea. Boris kicked at the two men on the floor with his steel-toed boots. The struggling stopped.

A rugged, athletic-looking man, who seemed to be in his late twenties, trotted into the waiting room, stopping short at the disarray. He looked at Boris. "Would you like for me to get this cleaned up, *ser?*" He strode to the man with the recently discharged weapon, ripped it out of his hand, and turned it on him. "Leave!"

The man rose up to attack, then toppled, with a neat bullet hole in his head.

The young man turned to the secretary. "We'll need a cart."

She nodded and dialed.

"Who are you?" Boris asked.

"Dmitri, *ser,* your two p.m. interview." He stepped over to the body blocking Boris's office door, slung it up and over his shoulder, and plopped it on top of the man he'd just killed. He checked the pulses of the men on the floor.

"They're still alive, *ser*."

"Fix that, then come in and see me." Boris marched into his office and shut the door.

Two more shots rang out.

Interesting. Where was his folder? Aha! Dmitri Smirnov, twenty-right years old, ex-military, a boxer, currently working at a security firm. Boris reread the note he'd made on Dmitri's file. *Is he capable of killing?* It appeared as if that question had been answered. He would hire him on the spot.

Boris's receptionist knocked on his door, "Your next candidate is ready for you, *ser*."

Boris peered into the reception area and was almost disappointed at the lack of chaos. A woman, neatly attired, with shoulder-length blond hair and stunning deep-blue eyes, rose and held out her hand. She introduced herself in a throaty contralto. "Murka Mikhailov at your service, *ser*."

Her résumé had impressed Boris. Only thirty years old and five verified kills while on projects for the Kremlin. She served in the army and had swiftly risen through the ranks to senior lieutenant. Those who served with her said she didn't tolerate ignorance or disobedience, and her treatment of the enemy was far from the Geneva convention rules, but she got the mission done. Most of all, she was loyal to her higher-ups.

"Come in. Take a chair." Boris waved her over to the chair on the side of his desk. She waited until he sat, to sit down herself.

So far she was impressive. "Tell me, Murka Mikhailov, why should I hire *you* over all these candidates?" He patted the stack of folders on his desk.

She looked him in the eyes. "Because, *ser*, I will follow your orders. I will never disgrace you or this office. I will get the job done, no matter how distasteful others may think it is. When I say I can do something, I can. If I can't, I will tell you what I need to be successful. I will not fail. I think my record speaks for itself."

Boris put his hand on his chin and stared at her for a full minute. She waited without fidgeting. "*Khorosho.* I would like to hire you with a three-month probationary period. If I'm satisfied with your performance during that time, I will give you a raise and the probation ends."

She raised one eyebrow. "And if you're not satisfied?"

Boris shrugged. "Your successor will eliminate you."

She looked at him for a beat. "Fair enough."

Boris stood to dismiss her. He shook her hand and opened the door to the waiting room, "Good. Come back tomorrow at 0800. My receptionist will direct you to the conference room. Your first mission starts then."

A body flew into the room from reception.

"Your next interviewee is here," his receptionist commented.

A second man stood in the waiting room, panting, with fists clenched. Murka gave him a steely gaze and ordered, in a voice that dripped with threat, "Sit down." He held up his hands, backed up, and plopped into a chair.

Murka stepped over the groaning prone man and sashayed out the door.

***

The anticipation and suspicion in the air were palpable.

Nyoka, Yaromir, Dmitri, and Murka sat around the oval-shaped conference room table, warily eyeing each other.

Nyoka was a bit worse for wear, with a bandage on her face and on her right hand. She hissed when Dmitri tried to talk to her. She held her ribs with her good hand and winced when she moved.

Yaromir breathed rapidly and repeatedly glanced at the door to the room. Would Boris accept his story, or would he make an example of him in front of everyone? Perhaps shoot him? He wiped his brow with his hand.

Dmitri perched at the edge of his chair, rocking back and forth.

Yaromir entertained the thought Dmitri had the urge to go to the bathroom.

The newest member of the unit, Murka, sat rock still at attention. Her eyes darted from one player to the next. Her hand twitched at her belt.

So that's where your weapon is, Yaromir assessed.

The door slammed open. Yaromir and Murka bounded up. The rest stayed seated.

Boris nodded his approval at Yaromir.

Yaromir relaxed. He wasn't dead yet.

Boris started without preamble. "It's time to get to work. Yaromir, congratulations on your work in Wales and the United States. Since you're familiar with the United States and met Kevin Ball, I'm sending you back there. You'll take Dmitri with you. I wish to give a strong message to Kevin, and also to Frank Garcia. I need them in place, so do *not* kill either of them. Yaromir, you will show Dmitri around DC and also South Carolina. We have subtle warnings to give to a few developers there. There is more in the folders in front of each of you. *Khorosho?*"

"*Da, ser*," Yaromir assented.

Dmitri nodded.

Boris slapped Dmitri on the head. "You will treat me with respect. *Ponimat?*"

Dmitri started to reach into his blazer but was stopped cold by the sight of Yaromir leveling a SR-1 Vektor sidearm at his forehead. He withdrew his hand. "*Da, ser.*"

Boris glared at him and roared, "What? I can't hear you."

"*Da, ser*," Dmitri roared back.

"Now that's *much* better," Boris remarked in a soft voice.

"Thank you, Yaromir." He picked up where he left off. "Now, Nyoka . . ."

"*Da, ser?*"

"I need you to take Murka back to Wales and finish up the business there. Ensure the paperwork for the land sales is properly filed and all resistance is gone. I'm also sending, separately, Konstantin and Timur, from my Location division, to help you ferret out any hostiles. These two men are experienced at tailing but will need you to remove any they find. They will contact you if, and only if, they discover an issue. More documentation is in your folder. *Khorosho?*"

"*Da. YA ponimayu*," Nyoka hissed.

Boris stood in dismissal. "All of you, stop by the lab and get kitted out. And while you're at it, stop by Adrik's office and tell him I'd like to see him immediately."

"All of us, *ser?*" Yaromir queried.

Boris smirked. "*Da.* That should make him piss his pants."

CHAPTER TWENTY-SIX

"**A**SHOK IS ON THE SECURE VIDEO CHAT,**"** Sophia yelled to the others, who crowded around her computer. "Go ahead, Ashok."

"Miss Charlie gave me some search parameters as well as some names of people about whom we are suspicious. The search is still ongoing, but I do have a match."

Elda leaned forward. "And who matches, Ashok?"

"Hello, Miss Elda. How nice to see you again."

"And you too, Ashok. What are the wonderful tidbits you've discovered?"

"Yes, it is delightful information. Miss Sophia will be most interested in this. Is she there?"

"Here, Ashok. What do you have?" Sophia inquired.

"Treacher Walker fits the search criteria," Ashok informed her. "I will forward you the data. However, I need some time to gather additional facts on him."

Sophia smashed a fist into her palm. "Bloody hell. I knew he was slime."

Charlie, who had been working in the nursery-turned-study, ran into the living room. "They're on the move."

Snezhana, who'd been working with Charlie in the study, wandered out behind her.

"Huh? Who's on the move, Charlie?" Tosh queried.

Sitting side by side on the couch, far into helping analyze the data from Ashok, Elda and Tosh looked up from their screens and simultaneously shook their heads, to focus on Charlie. Anatoly woke up from his nap on the floor and rolled over, propping his head on his arm to listen.

Charlie held up her phone. "Olga texted me. She's received intel a private plane landed at Dulles International Airport and one of the men that deboarded is Yaromir Kozlov."

"*Interesnyy*," Tosh remarked. "What business would Yaromir have in DC? And who is with him? We need to pull information from Yaromir. Snezhana and Anatoly, you're to hop on a flight to DC. Locate these two and find out what they're doing in America."

Elda cleared her throat.

Tosh turned to her. "I will be the handler for the team. Sophia will stay here and assist me. You and Charlie will be operatives together."

Elda nodded and smiled, happy to be going into the field again. "One addition. Anatoly and Snezhana should use disguises."

Charlie typed a few lines on her phone. "Olga gave us a second lead. Another private plane landed in Heathrow, and guess who's on it?"

"No guessing games. *Who?*" Tosh barked.

Charlie glared at him but answered politely. "Sophia's gal pal, Nyoka. Confirmed by facial recognition."

Elda ran her fingers through her hair as she puzzled it all through. "Well, they're not taking any pains to hide their whereabouts. They must be pretty confident they won't encounter any resistance. Anyone riding shotgun with her?"

Charlie sent them all a text with a photograph she received from Olga. "This woman. Recognize her?"

All heads shook.

"No one, hey?" Sophia said. "I'll send it on to Ashok to see what he can ferret out on her."

"While you're at it, there were two additional men on another private plane." Charlie sent around another picture.

Elda identified them. "Konstantin and Timur."

"They were used as tails by the Kremlin. They now work for Boris," Anatoly clarified.

"Why on earth are they in the UK?" Elda tapped a picture to her chin. "I wonder if they're going to Wales."

Charlie grinned and bounced on her toes. She clapped Elda on her shoulder. "Looks like we're on, teammate."

Elda rolled her eyes. "Remember this mission is to, if possible, capture and discover who they are working for and what they are assigned to do. Charlie and I will go in without disguises and use ourselves as bait to draw them out."

Charlie winced. "Oh. Suddenly this mission took a downer twist."

Elda winked at her.

Oliver, followed by Sophia, wandered out of the kitchen with four paper lunch bags and doled them out to Snezhana, Anatoly, Elda, and Charlie. "There's some extra scones in yours Anatoly. I figured you all would be grabbing your go bags and running off again, so I made these lunches."

Elda looked at Sophia. "That man is pure gold. I'd keep him if I were you."

Sophia planted a long kiss on Oliver. "I plan on it."

Snezhana shook her head. "*Blyad'*. They're at it again."

Oliver flicked his dish towel at her.

Sophia returned to her cell phone, then looked up from her typing. "Anatoly and Snezhana, look at your email. You're e-ticketed to Dulles. Yuri obtained hotel rooms for you at the Capital Hilton in downtown DC. Charlie and Elda, Yuri's got you on the train to Wales, but you're going to have to move it to make it on time. Info about your accommodations will be emailed to you both."

Charlie and Elda grabbed their go bags, tucked their lunches in to them, and ran out the door.

Tosh looked at Snezhana and Anatoly. He clapped his hands to rush them along. "*Idti, idti, idti.*"

Chapter Twenty-Seven

DIMITRI AND YAROMIR STRODE INTO CUSTOMS and immigration. Yaromir presented his British passport to the immigration officer handling the private plane arrivals.

The officer glanced at Yaromir's face and placed the passport on the scanner. "Business or pleasure, Mr. Richards?"

Ignoring the sweat gathering beneath his armpits, Yaromir grinned at the man. "Pleasure. I have always wanted to see the capital of the United States of America."

The officer typed on his keyboard. "What do you do for work, Mr. Richards?"

"Construction."

The light on the passport reader turned green.

I am so grateful for Stas's skills, Yaromir thought.

The officer stamped and handed the passport to Yaromir. "Enjoy your stay, Mr. Richards. Seeing DC at night is always a treat."

"Thank you, sir." With relief, Yaromir swung his carry-on bag over his shoulder and strolled outside to wait for Dmitri, who soon joined him. "Any problems, Mr. James?"

"None at all, Mr. Richards."

Yaromir hailed a cab. "Let's go crack some skulls."

Yaromir and Dmitri faced off in their deluxe double hotel room in the DC Beacon Hotel. Their luggage was strewn across two beds. Dmitri played with a switchblade he had bought from a local arms source.

Dmitri clenched his jaw. "I will take care of the accountant."

Yaromir scowled. "That doesn't make sense. I am his handler. We work together."

Dmitri put his foot down. "No. I work alone. And apparently, as his handler, you did not impress him enough." He snapped open the knife.

Fists clenched, Yaromir took a step forward.

Dmitri closed his blade and held up his hand. "Listen to me. That was not a statement about your abilities. I know these accountants. They are not scared by physical size, but they are frightened to lose money. Let me handle Kevin Ball. You take care of the man called Frank. His profile says he's a bully, which means he's also a coward and will readily cave to your methods."

Yaromir punched one fist into the other hand. "Yes, I will take care of Frank."

The cameras swiveled, following him in. Wearing a suitcoat and tie, Yaromir marched into the lobby of Frank's office. "I have an appointment with Mr. Frank Garcia." Aware he was being recorded, he kept on his mirrored sunglasses and pulled his hat low on his brow.

"I'm afraid not, dear," the woman behind the desk said. "He's in the hospital. Is there someone else who can help you?"

"Oh my, will he be out soon?" Yaromir hoped to be able to leave the lobby before he matched in someone's database.

"I don't have that information. I can page someone who works in his area." She reached for her desk phone.

Yaromir waved his hand at her. "No, no. That won't be necessary. I'll call to reschedule with him. Do you know what hospital he's at? I'd love to gift him a food basket or flowers."

The secretary withdrew her hand from the phone. "George Washington University Hospital. It's quite good. I understand he's out of critical care and has been moved to a private room. That's wonderful progress."

"Thank goodness. I appreciate you letting me know." Yaromir swiveled and strolled out. *Get away from the cameras*, the voice in his head screamed.

Yaromir goggled at the rounded facade of the George Washington University Hospital building. He'd act as a concerned relative of Frank's.

Whoop, whoop, whoop.

Yaromir ducked at the sound of a low-flying helicopter. He glanced up to see a red craft heading for the trauma-center roof. He marched inside and to the gift shop, where he bought a bouquet of large colored balloons, and strode over to the information desk. "Excuse me, but can you tell me what room Frank Garcia is in?"

The information aide consulted her list. "He's on a restricted-visitor's list."

Yaromir gave her his best smile. "We figured he would be, so the office sent me to represent everyone. We're hoping to lift his spirits and have him back to work soon." He held out an ID he'd pinched from a man whom he'd passed at Frank's business site. The image wasn't a great match, so Yaromir was banking on the balloons to hide his face and on her not looking too closely.

A couple walked up behind Yaromir. The man impatiently tapped his foot and cleared his throat.

"He's on the fourth floor in the Acute Rehabilitation Unit," the aide in the information booth told Yaromir. "Use those elevators over there and press four. Once there they will direct you to his room."

"Thank you so much, ma'am." Yaromir strolled to the elevators. He was conscious of the round black cameras in the ceilings. He pulled his hat lower on his forehead. Once in the elevator, he held the bouquet on the side toward the camera, effectively blocking their view of his face. The elevator rose with seemingly glacial speed.

Disembarking on the fourth floor, Yaromir approached an aide, who directed him to Frank's room. "Only five minutes. He's very weak."

"That's all I need."

<hr>

Yaromir jogged away from the hospital. He let go of the balloons, and they rode off on the wind. He turned his jacket inside out and dumped his hat in a waste receptacle, replacing it with a Washington Nationals baseball cap. He hadn't mean to kill him—only to scare him. Who knew Frank would have a heart attack? Luckily the staff was so busy attending to the code blue they didn't notice him. But man, he was fucked. He couldn't go back to Boris. Or could he spin this somehow? Maybe Sophia and that crew could help him again?

Anatoly, wearing a Boston Red Sox cap over his jet-black buzz cut, a neatly trimmed mustache and beard, and extra clothing, complete with lifts in his shoes and a long topcoat, to make himself appear larger, strolled out of Immigration and Customs. He chewed gum, with spare amounts stuck in his cheeks, to distort his face. He walked up to Snezhana, who sported long blond hair, acne, and wore two-inch square-heeled knee-high boots over black tights. On top she draped a cape, covering her shape. She also chewed gum, but hers was bubble gum, and she made large bubbles and popped them.

"I rather like you with blond hair, Snez," Anatoly complimented.

Snezhana returned the flattery. "I think that mustache and beard becomes you, Anatoly."

Her phone buzzed. "It's a message from Stas."

Anatoly read it over her shoulder, barely finishing, when he dialed Tosh. "We have something from Stas."

"What is it?" Tosh prodded from the command center in the Tuscan villa.

"There's an agent from the Kremlin, Dmitri Smirnov, in DC, looking for Kevin Ball's address," Snezhana said.

"*Interesnyy*. Can you arrive there first?" Tosh asked.

Snezhana shook her head and then shrugged. She verbalized her answer so Tosh could hear it. "I don't know. I'll ask Stas to give us a five-minute head start once he locates Kevin."

Chapter Twenty-Eight

KNOCK. **K**NOCK. **P**OUND. **W**HAM. The pounding shook the door.

Kevin swore. *Who the fuck is that? Don't they know I have a doorbell?*

Kevin was sitting in his boxer shorts and T-shirt, streaming the movie *American Gangster*. He stopped in the bathroom on his way to the door and pulled on an old pair of jeans he had left hanging on the back of the door. He sauntered to his door and flung it open.

"I'm not buying anything," he snapped.

Kevin started to shut the door, but the man pushed it open and walked in. "What the fuck?" Kevin sputtered.

"Are you Kevin Ball?" the intruder asked in a polite tone.

"None of your beeswax who I am. Who the fuck are you?" Kevin snarled at him.

The man smiled. "I'm someone who is going to give you some friendly advice."

Kevin pointed to the front door. "I don't need no friendly advice. Now get the fuck out of my house."

The stranger reached out, captured Kevin's hand, and snapped his little finger. Kevin screamed. "What the fuck?" He couldn't believe the pain that burned up his arm from his hand.

"I advise you to listen to me," the man said softly.

Kevin held his injured hand in the other and screamed, "Get the fuck out of my house. I'm calling the police." He turned to reach the phone.

The man grabbed Kevin's hand again and pulled back a second finger until he heard it pop.

"Fuck!" Kevin stamped his foot, bouncing up and down from the pain.

The man patted his hand. "That one's probably only dislocated. I don't advise you call the police if you want to keep your fingers on your hands."

Kevin plopped onto his couch and looked wide eyed at the stranger. His mouth moved, but nothing came out. He rocked back and forth in pain.

"No need to speak. Just listen." The man sat on the table in front of Kevin. "You will tell no one of this visit, understand?"

Kevin glared at him.

The intruder took a pair of pliers out of his jacket pocket, clutched Kevin's wounded hand, and ripped a fingernail off his third digit.

Kevin felt like he would throw up. The pain engulfed his entire hand and arm, and his head started to throb in time with his heartbeat.

"Understand?" the vicious man inquired.

"Yes, please god, yes. What else do you want? I can make you rich." He clutched his arm to his body and held it with his other arm while he shook with pain and shock.

The man chuckled. "Ah, money. You weak Americans always think that's the solution to everything. Not now, Kevin. Nonetheless, money is the topic at hand."

"I don't have a fucking clue what you are talking about,"

Kevin screamed through his tears.

"I did ask you to not talk but to listen." The Russian extracted Kevin's hurt hand, applied the pliers to the knuckle of Kevin's fourth finger, and pressed as hard as he could until he heard a crunch. He moved to one side of Kevin.

Kevin threw up. He was engulfed by pain.

The attacker laid out on the table in front of Kevin a list of all of Kevin's hidden offshore assets. "I will be monitoring the amounts in these accounts. And if you try and hide your money elsewhere, I will find it." He reached inside his inside pocket and took out a switchblade.

Kevin shrank back on the couch.

The man popped the blade open, lifted a paper from the table, and sliced it in two equal pieces.

Kevin stared, mesmerized, as each half floated back down to the table in front of him.

His torturer pointed the knife at him. "And for every dollar you steal from Boris, I will extract a body part from you. Understand?"

Kevin nodded yes, and his body trembled.

His tormentor finished up. "Here's the last of the message. You will give back one percent of your commission to Boris as an apology for trying to fleece him. And you will stop trying to pocket money off the real estate deal. You are being paid well. Understand?" Dmitri held up the pliers.

Hoping this wasn't a trick to make him speak when he wasn't supposed to, Kevin nodded.

"I need a verbal response."

"Yes," Kevin choked out. "Tell Boris I am very sorry I ever thought of making more than my due."

"Good boy." The Russian rose and walked out.

There was a violent pounding at Kevin's front door. *No,*

no, I can't take any more. The door buckled inward as it was forced from the lock. A huge bearded stranger stood outlined in the doorway, with a slender blond woman behind him.

"I can't believe how poorly they are making things in America now," the man commented to the woman.

Kevin dropped the ice pack he had been holding on his hand and rose from the couch. "W-w-w-who are you?" He could hardly breathe. His heart pounded in his chest.

The man took in the scene and turned to the blond. "It appears as if Dmitri was here first."

The woman agreed. "I'll leave you to find out the information, and I'll hunt down Dmitri."

"Save him for me, Snez. I haven't had a good kill in far too long."

"*Khorosho*, Anatoly." She turned and jogged out the door, pulling it shut behind her.

Anatoly turned to Kevin. "You might want to sit down before you fall. We know you had a friendly chat with Dmitri Smirnov. You will now tell me all about it and what you are up to for the Russians."

Kevin shook his head. Tears filled his eyes. "I can't. He will kill me."

Anatoly displayed a frightening grin. "You don't get it, do you, fat boy? I will kill you if you don't tell me."

Sweat broke out on Kevin's forehead. What an impossible situation.

Anatoly picked up Kevin's damaged hand, examined it, and put the ice pack back on it. He held Kevin's good hand firmly in his. "You see, Kevin, I am an assassin. I don't like to torture people. I love to feel and watch the body as the life drains from a person."

Oh my god. This one's worse than the other one.

"Furthermore, sometimes information is useful. Let's start with what mission you are doing for the Kremlin."

Kevin hesitated. Anatoly took the pinky on Frank's good hand and snapped it. Kevin screamed.

Anatoly patted Kevin's arm. "There, there, my good man. We can prevent any further damage to your hands if you tell me what I wish to know. I assume your hands are necessary in your livelihood. Although speech recognition software is getting very good, I hear."

"I'm an accountant for the CIA," Kevin blurted out.

"Yes, yes. We know that. What job are you doing for the Kremlin?"

"Real estate. I am handling the money for large real estate transactions," Kevin sputtered.

"Ah, good. And what are you doing for them?"

"I am helping launder money from sales in America and purchases in Wales," Kevin said through tears.

Anatoly smiled. "Excellent! Now do you have any paperwork on these transactions?"

"Yes, in my study. In the safe." Kevin indicated with his head.

"Let's go open the safe." Anatoly gripped Kevin by an arm and helped him stand.

On wobbly legs Kevin led Anatoly to his safe in his study and with his good fingers opened it. He drew out the paperwork and turned it over to Anatoly, who verified it.

"Now give me the account numbers," Anatoly demanded.

Kevin complied. *It doesn't matter . . . My life is over.*

***

Anatoly swung Kevin around. "You were good. I will make this quick." With a swift motion, he snapped Kevin's neck. He lowered the body gently to the floor and closed the corpse's eyes.

Anatoly noted his partial erection was ebbing. This assassination was not as satisfying as when he could hold them close and feel the struggle as the life ebbed from the body. *Now that's a kill.*

Anatoly took a cloth from a small packet in his pocket and applied disinfectant from a tiny bottle. He washed areas on Kevin that might hold Anatoly's DNA. He picked up the papers and took the money and gun from the safe. He pointed and repeated, *"Proveryat', khorosho, ochistite,"* the mantra of "Check, okay, clear," his routine before leaving any room. No trace of him remained.

He returned to the living room and did the same mantra. Finally he went to the front door and cleaned off the mark his boot had made. Satisfied, he left the scene.

While jogging down the street to the metro, his phone buzzed.

Found him.

———

Snezhana ran down the stairs as if she were late for her train. She spotted Dmitri on the escalator heading to the red-line trains. She reminded herself to remember her training from Tosh. Switch from front to rear tails. Expect the unexpected. Once on the platform, she looked at the metro map on her phone and up at the announcements of arriving trains. If he finished his job here, he would head back to a hotel to grab his gear and dash to the airport. The Kremlin probably advised he stay at the Washington Downtown Hilton, so that would mean the red line. That train arrival was in two minutes. She moved to the line to board the incoming train.

She gazed at her phone, holding it eye level so she could still see over it. He had not lined up at the door down the track from her. She streamed onto the train with the others. She boarded so she could see out the windows and observe if he boarded. If he did, it would be a last-minute hop into the car, to lose any tails.

Sure enough, the doors started to close. Dmitri leapt into the car behind Snezhana. She texted Anatoly. ON RED LINE 2 DUPONT CIRCLE C U THERE.

Anatoly texted back. K.

She glanced at the metro map on the wall above her, and when gazing back and forth, checked to affirm he was still there. Two more stops before it . . . One more stop . . . The hotel stop. She flowed with the rest of the car onto the platform and moved over to one side, where she stopped to tie her shoe. The doors closed. He stayed on the train.

Blyad'!

———

Bzzzzz. Anatoly felt his phone vibrate. A message from Snezhana.

LOST HIM.

He texted back. DER'MO. K WILL GO 2 HOSPITL 2 SHK DWN FRANK.

With a scowl on his face, he put his phone in his pocket and sprinted to flag down a taxi. "George Washington University Hospital please."

At the hospital, Anatoly tossed the fare, plus a good, but not too good (which would flag him as someone to remember), tip into the plexiglass cash drawer and hopped out of the cab.

He stopped at the gift shop and bought a small floral arrangement, marched up to the volunteer with the patient room list, and presented the plant to her. "Any chance you know what room Frank Garcia is in, honey?"

The middle-aged volunteer blushed. "He's a popular patient today. Someone from his office just left here."

Anatoly surveyed her with big blue eyes, contrasting

sexily with his black hair. "Oh really? I was supposed to be the office representative. I bet you know what he looked like. I think you're an excellent judge of character."

She leaned forward and said in a low voice, "He was a big man, but not at all as well built as you are. Brown hair and eyes. And I detected a slight accent."

Anatoly beamed at her. "You're good. I know who he is. And what floor did you say he was on?"

"Fourth. You have a slight accent too. What is it?" The volunteer woman fanned herself with a piece of paper.

Anatoly gave her a conspiratorial look, "Oh, you are *very* good. Nice ear." He laid on the accent thicker. "British. I'm an ex-pat."

"Oh, I so love the British accent," she gushed.

"Thanks, luv." Anatoly strolled to the elevators. He disembarked at the fourth floor. The hallway swirled with controlled chaos as the intercom repeatedly emitted "code blue."

An aide stood to one side, staying out of the way of the response team. Anatoly sidled up to him and whispered, "Code blue. That's a heart attack, isn't it?"

The aide, clearly eager to reveal his knowledge, replied, "Yes. It's this man, Frank Garcia. He came into trauma from a severe accident at work. I imagine he took a bad turn. They're trying to save him now."

"Ugly, that," Anatoly commented in his British accent, and swiftly left the floor. He wound his way down to the basement level, where he calculated the feed for the security cameras would be. Once there, he dialed Ashok. "Ashok, I'm at George Washington University Hospital. In the basement. Can you walk me through what the wires from the cameras look like and how to put a tap on so you can access the cameras and attached recording devices?"

Hysterical laughter and snorting came over Anatoly's line.

In the Capital Hilton hotel, Snezhana stomped into Anatoly's hotel room, slamming the door behind her. "I can't friggin' believe I lost him. *Blayd'*. Tell me you had better luck."

Anatoly, sitting at the desk, glanced at her from his laptop and motioned for her to join him. "Ashok helped me get this data. He accessed the security servers remotely, so I didn't need to do anything. In fact, he laughed at me when I asked him how to tap into the lines for footage. What should I know? I'm not a *komp'yuternyy gik*."

Snezhana leaned in over his shoulder, and he pointed at the frozen frame on his screen. "Look at who this is."

"Yaromir. Stupid bastard doesn't even disguise himself well."

"*Da*," Anatoly agreed. "It's time we gave him a . . . how did Elda put it?" He paused and looked with raised eyebrows at Snezhana.

"Come to Jesus."

"*Da*. It's time he either worked with us or got removed from the picture." Anatoly struck his thigh with his fist, emphasizing the point.

Chapter Twenty-Nine

"**This is not at all like the Russian** stations." Timur gazed up at the bright vaulted ceilings and then the people milling around the electronic departure boards and politely queuing to board the trains. He pointed. "Why is there a bear in a raincoat? I thought Smokey the Bear was American, not British."

Konstantin chuckled. "You have not worked outside of Russia, have you?"

"*Net.*" Timur wandered about with his mouth gaping.

"*Dozhidat'sya!*" Konstantin put his hand out to keep Timur from advancing any farther. "In this car, quick."

"*Zachem?*" a bewildered Timur asked.

Konstatin shoved Timur into car, climbed into the seat across from him, and put down the window, to see down the train more clearly. "I thought she was American. Why is *she* here?"

Timur cocked his head. "Who? Why are we hiding?"

"Do you remember the American woman we tailed for days in Moscow a couple of years ago?"

"I can barely remember today's mission, Konstantin.

Are you sure this is the same woman?"

"Perhaps not, but if it is, it would be quite the coincidence that she is now in Wales." Konstantin frowned.

"What do you want to do?"

"Boris told me we had free rein to track down anyone we may be suspicious, and if, and only if, we feel they're a threat to this expedition, we will call in for reinforcements."

Timur frowned and scratched his head. "But the others from Russia are just women."

Konstantin patted his pocket. "Exactly. This is why I arranged to purchase weapons for ourselves. We may be the only ones able to protect this mission."

Timur's eyes went wide. His hands shook. "S-s-so, w-w-what do you w-w-want to do?"

"We follow them."

❀

With a metallic screech of the brakes and a whoosh of escaping steam, the train pulled into the station at Haverfordwest. The bitter burning smell from the brakes hung in the air. Elda closed her eyes for a moment, overwhelmed by memories of when she'd been stationed nearby. She took an expanded breath and shook away the demons. She opened her eyes to see Charlie frowning at her with concern. "No worries, Charlie. Just some old shit floating by. All's good. Let's go rent a car."

They grabbed their gear and jogged over to the Station Self Drive rental office.

A chatty man greeted them and explained about the two lines of cars available on site. "You gals will probably want the Yaris, you will."

Elda detected Charlie's fists were clenched, which mirrored the feeling she had in her own jaw. "Actually, I was thinking of the Octavia. It's nice to have the power if you need to move out of the way quickly. I don't know if the traffic laws are the same, but it used to be if you hit a sheep, you paid for four generations of animals. I'd rather be able to scoot out of the way." Elda gave the man her most endearing smile.

"Well, ladies, if it's too much power for you, you can always come back and swap it out." He grabbed a set of keys and motioned to the door. "I'll meet you in the parking lot."

Elda winked at Charlie and turned to leave. She suddenly stopped and gazed out the window.

"What is it, Elda?" Charlie squinted one eye, as if sighting her gun.

Elda rubbed her neck and chewed on the side of her fingers. She scowled and scratched her ear. She shook like a dog coming out of the pool. "Could be nothing, Charlie. Just keep an eye out. My spidey sense is on overdrive."

<hr>

Thud. Charlie dumped her gear in the bedroom at Point Cottage in Little Haven, Wales. "I'm glad Yuri rented this cottage for us. I'm familiar with it, and being right on the coastal path, it has good escape routes."

"Plus, I think if we stayed in St. Davids, we'd be far too noticeable," Elda added. "Yuri told us there is food in the fridge. Let's rustle something up and, after eating, go out scouting for our friends." Elda looked at Charlie, who stood there rubbing the buzz-cut side of her head. "What?"

Charlie pleaded with soulful eyes. "Can you cook? I'm rather abysmal at it."

Elda laughed and patted Charlie on the back on their way to the kitchen. "Don't you worry—I can . . ." Her voice trailed off as she stuck her head in the open fridge. "I can make a mean bacon, eggs, and toast. Gads, don't those guys know how to cook anything else. At least there's milk and orange juice, and, please god, let there be coffee."

Charlie held a pound of coffee aloft. Elda snatched the bag. "Big Dog Coffee! Okay, Yuri redeemed himself."

Soon the aroma of coffee brewing and bacon frying filled the kitchen. Elda called into the living room, "Eggs over easy?"

"I will be grateful for any way you cook them," Charlie said.

Elda laughed.

Charlie glanced down at her phone. "Ashok reached out to Stas and found out Boris hired a new assassin, Murka Mikhailov. From his description, she fits the picture of Nyoka's sidekick."

"Come sit here while I cook, and we can strategize about this evening." Using two forks, she fished the bacon out onto a paper towel, then with one hand expertly cracked an egg into the hot pan.

Charlie sat on a kitchen stool.

"Once it gets dark," Elda outlined, "I was thinking we'd drive to St. Davids and have a look around. My money is on a rental car being in the Premier Inn parking lot."

"I'm good with that," Charlie allowed. "Do you want to drive, since you're more familiar with the area?"

Elda rubbed her left pectoral muscle. "Certainly."

Charlie noticed Elda's gesture. "Is there a problem, Elda?"

"Driving on wet, narrow dark roads on the *wrong* side of the street isn't my cup of tea, but you're right. I *am* more experienced at driving on the left, as well as more knowledgeable of this section of the country. I just remember many close calls on these roads."

"Ah, did you say *over easy*?" Charlie grimaced at a hard blob in the pan.

"That one can be mine." Elda flipped it off onto her

plate, buttered the pan, and started a second egg. "Let's chow down and get going."

The night was pitch dark, the clouds masking any illumination from the moon or stars. Rain pelted down steadily. The headlights lit up small sections at a time as Charlie and Elda drove north.

"Charlie, look behind us. That car has been following us for a while. I'm going to speed up. See if he matches my acceleration." Elda pressed the gas pedal down, and the car leapt forward.

"He's still the same distance back, Elda," Charlie reported.

Elda's stomach soured, and her mouth went dry as she pressed down harder on the accelerator, going far faster than the conditions allowed. "Now?"

Charlie counted out the time and the distance and did a quick calculation. "Same speed, Elda."

"Crap." Elda squinted at the road ahead. *Is that an object?* "Damn! It's a truck!" In the distance in front of them loomed the outline a dark truck jackknifed across the road.

"Hang on!"

She slammed on the brakes and spun the wheel to send the car into a controlled 180 degree skid, turning inches from the truck's side. When the front whipped around to the direction they had come from, Elda hit the power and gave the wheel a turn to torque the car back to driving a straight line. The car that had been following Elda sped by, the driver inattentive to the road and peering to see who drove past him.

Timur?

Crash. The sound of metal and plastic disintegrating reached their ears, and the sight of flames shot up behind them.

Elda kept on driving. Ten minutes later, shaking, Elda stopped in a layby. "Can you drive for a while, Charlie? This incident activated too many memory-lane buttons for me. I need a break."

"Sure." Charlie popped out and ran around to the driver's side.

Elda slid over to the passenger side. She closed her eyes until Charlie announced, "There's a car heading our way."

Elda sat up and peered through the night. A car drove slowly by them. "That's Konstantin."

Konstantin looked at them as he passed. He screeched to a halt and pulled off the side of the road.

Elda was amused when she noted he put on his blinker before making a U-turn to head in their direction. Her amusement dissipated, and her brain switched to ways to evade him. She envisioned a map of the area, praying her memory of the roads still held true.

"Quick, Charlie, turn left here."

Charlie threw the steering wheel over to make the sudden turn. They skidded off onto a narrow side road with hedgerows on either side. The road curved, with no lights and miles of fields behind the hedgerows.

After Charlie rounded a curve, Elda cried out, "Slow to a crawl at the break in the hedgerow on the right. I'm going to jump out there."

Charlie downshifted and slammed on her brakes right before the opening and crept past it.

At the break, Elda dove out and vaulted behind the wall. Charlie pressed the accelerator and sped away. Elda stood on a rock and braced her M&P 380 SHIELD EZ pistol on top of wall, slowing her breathing. Waiting.

Headlights approached. Konstantin drove slowly, hunched over his steering wheel, squinting in the darkness. He came close enough for Elda to recognize his outline.

He spotted her and fired out the driver's window. The bullet went wide.

"Stand down, Konstantin. I don't want to kill you." She discharged a warning shot.

He stopped the car, rolled down the passenger window, and blasted three rounds back.

How many cartridges did that handgun hold? "Throw out your weapon and put your hands up," she shouted, then fired a round that crumbled his windshield. She saw the muzzle flash as he fired again. The bullet chipped the stone wall forming the structure for the hedgerow she was using as a shield. His shots were coming closer. Elda could wait until he was out of ammunition, but she had no way of knowing if he had another magazine or not. It was time to end this before he got lucky and killed her. Aiming carefully, she put a bullet in his head. Released from being braked, his car meandered into the hedgerow and stopped again.

Elda ran to the car and saw she could not open the doors on either side, due to the narrowness of the road and height of the hedgerows. She arranged her coat over the remains of the front windshield and climbed through the broken glass.

Konstantin was dead.

Elda picked up a large, pointy piece of glass and used it to pick the bullet out of his head. Then she drove the glass shard in, to replace the casing. Not an exact match, but she doubted the police here were going to be suspicious after his car crash. Tourists had many accidents here. They drove too fast for these roads, often drunk.

She sent a text to Charlie. KONSTANTIN GONE. FOLLOW ME.

Puffing from the exertion of moving a dead body in a small space, she hauled his corpse into the passenger seat and searched the car, finding a bottle of unopened vodka in the backseat. *Perfect.*

She backed down the road to a turnaround, where she met Charlie. Elda filled her in. "I'm going to throw the body off a cliff. Follow me and give me a ride back to the cottage."

"What about the car?"

"I'll sanitize it as much as possible, making sure there's no DNA matter, prints, or shells, then I'll ditch it with him in it. Hopefully, it will crash badly enough to obscure the previous damage."

At the cliff, Elda cleaned the car and took her coat. She moved his body back into the driver's seat, opened his mouth, and poured vodka into it, then poured more out on the ground, capped the bottle, and left it on the passenger seat. She'd had the foresight to grab a stick from the field she had been in, and she now used it to jam the accelerator down. She rolled down the driver's side window and closed the door.

All set. She leaned inside, almost doubled over the window jamb, reached the key, and started the car. The acceleration flung her back and outward. The car ripped away and flew over the cliff with the body.

"Two down. I wonder how many are here?"

Chapter Thirty

THE WAVES CRASHED AGAINST THE CLIFFS as the tide rolled in. Elda sat across from Charlie at the kitchen table, looking out over the bay, each deep in their own thoughts.

Charlie brushed both sides of her head with her fingers and cleared her throat. "Can we talk?"

Elda frowned. "Sure." She hoped Charlie wasn't feeling insecure. Now was not the time to hesitate.

Charlie bit her bottom lip and raised her eyebrows. "I mean, really talk? I need to understand what I'm seeing."

Elda chewed the side of her forefinger, looked at Charlie sideways, and furrowed her forehead. She trusted Charlie would be mission focused and not get all emotional on her. Elda did not want to share her own demons with Charlie. "Okay, Charlie, shoot. What's on your mind?"

"What happened to you when we arrived in Haverfordwest?" Charlie put her hands together and held the tips of her forefingers against her front upper teeth. She breathed shallowly.

Elda sighed. She was so used to operating on her own.

But transparency was important in leadership. She'd have to share enough to ensure Charlie had trust in Elda's abilities. "Oh, pulling no punches, I see." Elda held up a hand, taking a moment to center herself. "Wales and I have history. Being here was a dark time in my life. I carried that blackness around in the center of my chest for years. When I arrived at the Haverfordwest train station, it was as if I'd never left. It all came flooding back, threatening to paralyze me."

Charlie looked concerned. "How did you move on?"

Elda gave a weak grin. "I embraced the darkness and told myself I was no longer in it. I oriented my mind to the here and now, and on the whole, it worked."

"On the whole?"

Elda scratched by the side of her eye, wiping away an invisible tear. "Yes. When I was here the first time, I was driving aimlessly around one dark, wet night, contemplating driving off a cliff."

Charlie's eyes threatened to pop out of her head, but she said nothing.

Elda shrugged. "As you can see, I didn't drive off that cliff. But I was driving too fast on a road not too far from here, when I almost crashed into a truck stopped across the intersection. There were no lights on the truck. No reflectors. It blended perfectly into the black of the night, which at that moment, mirrored the darkness of my being. In a split second I had to decide whether to live or die. I'm not sure I consciously did, but my foot hit the brakes hard, and the car stopped inches away from the side of the truck." She breathed in and nodded. "It reassured me that my instincts and training will kick in and I will prevail."

Charlie, perched on the edge of her seat, leaned toward Elda. "What happened next?"

Elda held her hands palm up and shrugged again. "I turned the car around and went back to the house I lived in. I never mentioned the incident to anyone."

Charlie furrowed her brow. "So tonight brought all that back?"

Elda relaxed her body language. "Yes, it did. Nevertheless, I'm surprised to feel it's gone for good now. Sending that car off the cliff was so freeing and therapeutic. Konstantin carried past-life Elda and all her baggage with him. Of course, I wouldn't ever advise that to a client."

"Wow. Excellent. Thanks, Elda. As Piglet said, 'I just wanted to be sure of you.' I needed to know you're at the top of your form and able to have my back."

"Ah, Grasshopper, you have learned well."

They both laughed.

"But, Master, I cannot yet grab the pebble from your hand."

Elda studied her and winked. "I bet you can. In any event, for now we will work together and have each other's back. I think something to eat and some strategizing is in order. Then a quick nap before tonight's battle."

"Please, not bouncy eggs again," Charlie pleaded.

"Bacon, toast, and marmalade?" Elda offered, after peeking inside the fridge.

"Only if you drive to St. Davids tonight." Charlie shook out her hands and stretched her fingers.

Elda nodded. "Deal. Now let's figure out what we're going to do if we meet Nyoka. I am not looking to add another scar, especially on my neck. So let's role play and try to anticipate every move she could make. I get to play Nyoka."

"Aw. I was ready to file my nails too."

Charlie jumped off the couch into a crouch, her side-arm pointing at the threat. Who was there?

"Whoa, Grasshopper. It's only me. Don't shoot." Elda flicked the light on and held her hands up.

Damn PTSD. "Sorry, Elda. Sophia calls them 'The Jumpies.'"

"No worries, Charlie." Elda studied Charlie. "In our profession, I call it good reflexes. Get ready. It's time to hit the road. We have a couple of hours before sunrise. We should be able to make it to St. Davids in a half hour."

Elda slid her Smith & Wesson revolver into her underarm holster. She confirmed the magazine for her Smith & Wesson M&P 380 SHIELD EZ pistol was full and stuck the 9mm in her waistband holster, slipping extra bullets and filled cartridges into her pockets. She inserted a sharp knife into an ankle sheath and stowed two filled syringes into her inside jacket pocket. She glanced over at Charlie and stopped everything to exclaim, "Wow. That's sweet. Is that an MP7A2 submachine gun?"

Of course she knew her weapons. Charlie had slung over her shoulder a two-foot-long black weapon. She held it in front of her with two hands so Elda could view it.

Elda stroked it. "Aimpoint red-dot sight, forty-round magazine with armor-iercing high-velocity rounds, and a tailor-made suppressor. Personally, I like the look of the weapon without the suppressor. Short and lethal, like us."

She approves. Awesome. "I figured we may need some extra fire power."

Elda chuckled. "I'm hoping we don't need that beauty, but it's good to have you on my side. Let's do a comm check. No talking. All clicks and arm signals."

Charlie saluted.

Elda snorted. She pushed a button on what appeared to be a wristwatch while pressing her earpiece in.

Charlie gave her a thumbs-up.

Elda returned the gesture. "Comms are good. Okay, let's go."

They bustled into the car, with Elda at the wheel. She kept the speed within reason, but soon they pulled into St. Davids. She doused the lights as they crept by the Premier Inn.

"There's the camper van she used last time," Charlie whispered. "Do you think they'd be stupid enough to rent the same vehicle?"

"Assassins aren't always PhD candidates, but we shouldn't underestimate her because she's a creature of habit," Elda replied in a normal-level voice. "It could be a ruse to lure us in, or maybe she just likes it. It *is* a good disguise. By the way, we don't have to whisper, Charlie."

Charlie blushed. Damn.

"And if you'd like, Grasshopper, I can teach you some techniques to help you control that blush."

Damn. It's that obvious. Charlie sighed, "Please, Master."

"We can't park in the parking lot, in case they're light sleepers. I'll motor us to the plastic plant down the road, and we can jog back here." She glanced around. "There's not much cover, so we'll have to shimmy across the last hundred yards or so."

Elda cut the engine and drifted into the St. Davids Assemblies parking lot. She pulled the car well over to one side and set the parking brake. She and Charlie slipped out and ran bent over until they had to body crawl to the hotel. Elda blessed Olga's training, which allowed Elda to keep up with someone much younger and not be out of breath.

Once there they located the office and sidled against the wall to the door. Elda took out a lockpick set and opened the door in a matter of seconds.

"Damn, it's all paper registrations. Shield me. I need to use a penlight." Elda held a penlight in her mouth while rustling through the registration log. She shut off the light and turned to Charlie. "I think we have it. Two women signed in yesterday. I'll grab the spare key to their room so we can check it out."

Suddenly the door slammed open.

Nyoka and Murka arrived in the doorway, outlined by the moonlight.

Shit. We can't use our guns in this tight space. Elda clicked her watch once and nodded to the right, signifying Charlie was to take Murka. Elda would take Nyoka, who stood in front of Elda. Elda was glad they had rehearsed. Hopefully, Nyoka would act as Elda anticipated. First she needed to remove that poison ring.

Nyoka lunged at Elda. Elda drew her knife and clutched Nyoka's arm. Ignoring Nyoka's canines sinking into her bicep, Elda slid the blade's point behind Nyoka's ring and carved the ring off her finger, along with bits of skin, tendon, and muscle. Nyoka's teeth lost their grip as she screamed.

Elda twisted Nyoka's arm, swinging her around and slamming her face forward into the wall, hearing the satisfying sound of Nyoka's nose breaking.

Nyoka twisted to release herself, but Elda wrenched Nyoka's arm higher, letting go when she heard the pop of a dislocated shoulder. Nyoka reached out with her other hand to rake Elda's face with her nails.

Palm forward, Elda brought up her hand to protect her face, and felt Nyoka's nails dig into her hand.

Elda wrenched Nyoka's bad shoulder, throwing her off balance. With her steel-toed boots, Elda kicked Nyoka in the side of her knee. Nyoka toppled, hitting her head on the counter on the way down.

Now that was a lucky break. Elda felt for a pulse. Alive. She zip-tied Nyoka's arms behind her back and, using a knife, pared off the sharp points of Nyoka's nails. She looked around and saw Charlie was holding her own, so scanned the room for a toolbox. Finding one, she rummaged through it until she came up with a pair of pliers. *This will teach you not to bite.* She imagined performing a bloody dentistry on Nyoka's canines. No, she couldn't do that. She dropped the pliers back in, dug deeper into the box, and came up with a metal file. But she could blunt those damn weapons. Turning to the unconscious Nyoka, she rolled her over onto her back and carefully dulled the points of the two teeth. She tipped Nyoka onto her side so she wouldn't asphyxiate if she vomited.

She then turned to Charlie, who was still in her battle with the second woman. "Need any help, Grasshopper?"

"No. She's mine."

Charlie braced herself and glared at the assassin, who planted her feet shoulder length apart and leaned forward on her toes. Damn. This wouldn't be a pushover.

The woman lashed out with a high kick, causing Charlie to jump backward.

Oh, she's got moves too. Charlie parried with a kick that grazed the woman's knees.

She acknowledged Charlie with a nod and a faint smile. "Murka, and you are?" she said in a soft, sexy contralto,

"Charlie." She saw that as an attempt to throw her off.

They circled each other warily. Murka was right handed and right footed. Being ambidextrous, Charlie had an advantage.

Murka's fist shot out in a jab, catching Charlie on the shoulder. Charlie responded with an uppercut, catching Murka's chin. The two warriors danced away and came back together as Murka lunged at Charlie.

Charlie swiveled and with her momentum and body

weight, hip checked Murka to one side.

Murka's back caught the counter. She winced.

Oh good. This one's human. Charlie followed up on her advantage with a quick kick to Murka's abdomen.

Murka lunged and grasped Charlie's foot and twisted, throwing her off balance and to the ground. Murka propelled herself on top of Charlie, only to be met by the soles of Charlie's feet and bent knees. Charlie accelerated Murka's trajectory, tossing Murka over her head. Murka bounced off the doorframe and landed on her back.

Charlie heard Elda ask if she needed help.

"No. She's mine."

Charlie rolled and rose to a crouch. Murka managed to pop back up and attacked again, this time with a stiletto in her hand.

Charlie parried Murka's slash with her arm and delivered an uppercut with her other fist, which connected soundly with Murka's jaw. Charlie could hear Murka's teeth slam together. Charlie followed that by slamming her forearm against the side of Murka's head and a kick to her knees, which toppled her.

Charlie kicked Murka's dropped knife aside. Pushing her knee into Murka's back, she grabbed her hands and zip-tied them behind her.

Dripping blood from her arm, Charlie stood to see Elda had vanquished Nyoka and was now removing the hard drive from the security system.

Elda pocketed the drive. "Well done, Grasshopper. We have hostages to bring back and interrogate."

Charlie looked down at the two captives. "What shall we do with them?"

Elda eyed Charlie's arm. "Let's throw this garbage in the trunk of the car, stop you from losing more blood, sanitize this place, and get to the doctor."

"Where are we going?" Elda started the car. She and Charlie had cleaned up in the small office bathroom, located a bucket and mop, and scoured away all traces of the fight. Elda had found a towel and electrical tape and had fashioned temporary bandages for her arm and hand, and Charlie's arm.

Charlie directed down the road. "St. Davids Surgery. The doctor won't be pleased to see his sneaky beakies back."

"I thought we were just birdwatchers," Elda snarked.

They pulled into the small car park in front of the surgery and popped in to see if the doctor was free. To their good fortune, he was.

He looked at Charlie. "Not you again, hey?"

Charlie gave an endearing smile. "Afraid so, Doc. I'm addicted to your white walls and the smell of antiseptic."

The doctor rolled his eyes but struggled to hide a grin. "Still the Secret Services Act bit?"

"Yup," Elda chimed. "We've been out birdwatching and had a slight mishap."

"Slight mishap?" The doctor examined Elda's bicep. "These look like teeth marks."

He looked at Charlie's arm. "If I hadn't heard you tell me differently, I'd bet this came from a knife fight."

"You know how vicious those birds can be, Doc," Elda retorted. "Can you patch us up?"

"When were you last inoculated for tetanus?" he asked. "You'll both need stitches and a tetanus injection. And the tasty one will need antibiotics."

Elda chuckled and pulled out her tetanus card from her wallet. "You're right, Doc. It looks like I'm due."

Charlie's mouth fell open. "You carry your tetanus shot card with you?"

"Sure do," Elda replied, nonplussed. "And the rest of my vaccinations and medications. You best start doing that too, Grasshopper. When was your last tetanus revaccination?"

Charlie scratched her head and grimaced. "I'm not sure."

The doctor finished sewing up Elda. He moved over to Charlie and put antiseptic on her wound. She flinched but stayed silent. The doctor reached into his cabinet and selected two syringes and a small bottle.

Elda withdrew her arm from her shirtsleeve, exposing her deltoid. The doctor administered her booster.

She exhaled. "Not quite as bad as the typhoid shot is, but it carries a kick nevertheless."

Charlie grimaced and closed her eyes. "*Wow.* That packs a punch."

The doctor shook his head. "You say nothing through stitches but whine at a little jab. What type of agents are you?"

"Wimpy ones," Elda snarked.

"Well, wimpy one, I don't suppose you have access to a pharmacy? Or a UK medical card?"

"Nope. Sorry." Elda slid her arm back into her shirtsleeve.

The doctor reached back into the cabinet and took out an empty pill bottle. He unlocked another cabinet and counted out fourteen pills into the first container. "Right. Two pills a day, twelve hours apart, for seven days. Do *not* stop until they are *all* gone." He handed the bottle to Elda. He reached in again and counted out four pills. "Painkillers, if you need them. They will cause drowsiness, so please only take them if you're safe."

"We're in your debt, Doctor. We'll be out of your hair now." Elda pocketed the stash of antibiotics and painkillers.

She rose and left a good amount of pounds on the table. "I hope this covers everything."

"Don't worry. Just save our country," he directed.

The front door slammed open. An older man and woman ran in, stopped, and panted while they worked to catch their breath. They both spoke at the same time, finishing each other's sentences. "Thank goodness someone is here. We just had the strangest experience. I think we need the police."

Who were these people? Elda squeezed her arm to her side to reassure herself that her gun was tucked in its holster. "We're with the British government. What happened."

The woman sized Elda up.

Elda flashed her a badge, as well as opened her jacket to let them see the holster under her shoulder.

"Oh my," the woman declared. "Well, you look capable of handling this matter. Arthur and I were taking a stroll by the office, and we heard the strangest noises coming from the trunk of the car in the carpark."

Elda swiveled and pointed to Charlie, who ran out the door. Elda encouraged the woman to continue.

The woman was more than glad to oblige. "Well, dear, Arti cannot leave well enough alone. He found the car was unlocked and popped the trunk. You won't believe what jumped out at us!" She fanned herself with her hand.

The dolts had popped the trunk? Damn. Elda resisted the urge to scream at the couple.

The doctor pushed a chair to the woman. "Perhaps you should sit, Catrin?"

Apparently the doctor knows this birdbrain. Elda ran her hands through her hair, her curls flying in every direction. She tensed her toes in her shoes, holding herself in place, willing herself to hear what happened.

The woman plopped down. "These two women rose up, as if out of the dead! One had this huge mane of black hair and yellow eyes. She actually hissed at us. Hisssss." Catrin fanned herself again.

Arthur picked up the story. "Their hands were tied behind their backs, but one knelt and pulled a knife out of the snake woman's sock and then stood. They managed to stand back to back and cut their ties. It was a bit bloody a deal there, it was."

"And then," Catrin interrupted, "once they were both free, the evil one hissed at us again. We were frozen in place, we were. It was lucky they ran away, it was."

Charlie trudged back, shaking her head.

"Gone?" Elda asked.

"No trace."

"We had a bit of a mess here." Elda held her phone away from her ear in preparation for Tosh's response.

Instead, a big sigh came over the airwaves. "Is everyone okay?"

"Charlie and I have a few bites and cuts, but we've been patched up. The unfortunate part is we captured Nyoka and Murka and had them in the trunk of the car. However, when we were in the surgery, some well-meaning civilians let them out. We have no clue where they went."

"What about Konstantin and Timur?" Tosh wondered.

Elda was surprised Tosh took everything so calmly. "They required driving lessons. Timur crashed his car and went up in a ball of flame. Konstantin flew over the cliff in his."

Tosh chuckled. "Fell or was pushed?"

Elda shrugged but remembered Tosh couldn't see her. "He somehow ended up with a piece of windshield in his head."

"*Khorosho.* I can't wait to hear the full story," Tosh said in a dry tone. "I'll have Ashok search the video feeds from the trains and airlines to see if Nyoka and Murka show up."

Curious as to why Tosh was so unruffled, Elda probed. "How's it going on the other side of the pond?"

"A similar mess." Tosh's voice was flat. "Dmitri's in the wind. Kevin has been taken care of. Anatoly is going to chat with Yaromir. We don't know Frank's status yet."

Elda frowned. "Damn. We should be better than this."

"*Da.*"

***

"Ready to rock and roll?"

Elda gazed out over St. Bride's Bay in Little Haven. Charlie's question cut through her rumination. "Yes."

Charlie gave Elda a hard look. "Do you need a few more minutes?"

Elda glanced once more at the water and the cliffs. "I probably won't see this view again, but that will be okay. The shadows of Wales are gone from my soul. I'm left with the beauty of this landscape to remember." She turned to Charlie. "Let's go." She looked Charlie up and down. "Oh, I like your outfit."

Charlie wore a waist-length black leather jacket that zipped down one side of her torso. The large side zipper pockets, leather epaulets, and silver buttons enhanced the tough-girl look. Her black jeans were formfitting, with a rip in one knee. Her short hair was colored pink. She completed the outfit with mirrored sunglasses and two-inch square-heeled side-buckle black boots.

"Do you need me to sew your pants though?" Elda pointed at Charlie's knee.

"It's the style," Charlie retorted, and then saw Elda was laughing. "Oh, you've got a look too."

Elda had colored her hair black and spiked it, adding blond highlights at the tips. She'd changed the shape of her face with inserts in her cheeks. Her eyes were a deep blue, and she had a pair of mirrored sunglasses hanging in her outside pocket. Her jacket was russet-colored leather and Italian made, with padded shoulders and a collection of snaps and zippers. Stitching outlined the pockets of her navy-blue jeans. Her Harley-Davison boots gave her additional height, finishing off her disguise.

Elda handed Charlie a falsified passport and pocketed her own. "Let's get going then."

They dropped the car and the keys off at the station and boarded. Elda loved riding on trains, especially the old-style ones. She sat on the bench, listening to the mesmerizing sound of the wheels on the track. It was hard to keep focused on her surroundings, as the clickety-clack threatened to lull her asleep.

Elda shook her head to focus. She scanned the car. She noticed Charlie, sitting across from her, was doing the same, and nodded her approval. Charlie gave her a thumbs-up to indicate all was clear. Elda returned the gesture.

Elda gazed out the window, returning her view to inside the car, whenever passengers boarded. The dark greens and light browns of the patchworked countryside gave way to rows of brick houses and finally to the clutter of houses and businesses that preceded any major airport.

Elda stepped off the train, leaving her past behind.

Chapter Thirty-One

"**W**E GOT HIM," ANATOLY SHOUTED.

Snezhana ran to peer over Anatoly's shoulder. Anatoly sat at the table in his DC hotel room, on a secure chat with Ashok in one laptop window and scrolling through video feeds in the other. Anatoly froze the screen at a frame of Yaromir walking into the Beacon Hotel. "There he is."

"Is this a real-time feed?" Snezhana inquired.

"*Da.*"

"That's only about five minutes away by taxi. Let's go pay him a visit," Snezhana ordered. "I'll be back here in a couple of minutes. We can jog over."

Dressed in baggy jogging gear, Snezhana popped into Anatoly's hotel room. She had thick-sole joggers on, which increased her height, and a black curly wig. Her eyes were now hazel.

Anatoly met her at the door. He had a five o'clock shadow, and his blond hair was now chocolate brown. His running shoes were a size larger and padded inside to make them comfortable. He wore a gray-and-black Washington, DC, baseball cap and mirrored sunglasses. His running clothes were also a size too large, which helped conceal Anatoly's true dimensions.

Snezhana held up her cell phone. "I got his room number from Ashok. He's on the fifth floor."

"Time to teach him a lesson."

"When did you decide we clamored to inhale exhaust fumes?" Anatoly coughed. He and Snezhana ran side by side north along Sixteenth Street Northwest.

"You're lucky the traffic is moving smoothly here. I can only imagine it during rush hour," Snezhana commented.

They ran with ease together, dodging a few people here and there without having to step into the road.

"*Fu.* Give me the wide streets of Moscow anytime. Hey, isn't the White House around here somewhere? I remember going by it when we were working with Elda."

Snezhana chuckled. "It's in the opposite direction. But yes, Anatoly, good memory. It is nearby."

Anatoly brightened. "How about that spy museum where I got those great brass knuckles? Do you think we can swing by there again?"

Snezhana slapped him on his arm. "*Net.* Elda's not here to bail you out from a smash and grab. No unauthorized shopping on this trip, Anatoly."

They jogged right on Bataan Street Northwest and fell into a cool-down walk.

Anatoly stretched his back, his pecs straining at his shirt. "So what's the plan here?"

"I thought we'd barge in unannounced," Snezhana replied with a shrug.

Anatoly snorted. "*Khorosho.* I can work with that. I'll lift us a room key. Stay tuned. You may have to bail out your mentally deficient brother."

They strolled into the lobby and beelined for the service elevator. Anatoly stumbled into a maid, who waited there for the next car.

"I'm so sorry," Anatoly said, twitching and flailing.

Snezhana held out an arm to steady him. "Forgive us. My father has Parkinson's." She used her forefinger to clear away a tear forming at the corner of her eye. They all stepped into the lift. The maid pressed five and backed away from the other two.

The car stopped at their floor, and they departed in opposite directions.

Anatoly flashed the universal access key and winked at Snezhana. "I'll use the key, and you'll drop it back where the maid will find it. And oh, by the way, your *father*?"

Snezhana grinned. Anatoly growled. They padded in silence to the room. Anatoly badged himself in and handed the key to Snezhana. He burst in on a surprised Yaromir, who held his hands up. Anatoly inserted a facecloth into the doorjamb, to keep it open for Snezhana.

Anatoly growled. "You didn't fulfill your end of the bargain, Yaromir."

Much to Anatoly's surprise, Yaromir started blubbering. "*YA znayu.* I know. I have failed time and time again as a spy and as an assassin. I let you, Snezhana, and Sophia down when you saved me the last time."

"*Bozhe moy.*" Anatoly looked at Yaromir in disgust. "Man up."

Yaromir plopped down on the desk chair and put his head in his hands.

"So make it right now, Yaromir. Who are the people in the Kremlin?" Anatoly demanded.

Yaromir looked up. "*YA ne znayu.* I *really* don't know, Anatoly."

Anatoly backhanded him, "Don't give me that *der'mo.*

Who?"

Snezhana walked in behind Anatoly, closed the door, and stood observing.

Yaromir spilled. "I used to work for Tosh, as you did. When they broke up his organization, they moved me away from that side of the house. Adrik took Stas to round out his cyber orgs, and Boris Siderov took over as Adrik's boss."

"Did Adrik betray us?" Anatoly demanded.

"I don't have access to that level of information," Yaromir whimpered, "but he was the man in charge before Boris re-organized."

"Boris is building an assassin contingent that includes me, Dmitri Smirnov, Nyoka Morozov, and Murka Mikhailov. He has a poison lab headed up by Gorky Krovopuskov. And of course, Adrik and his cyber geeks. That's all I know. It's very compartmentalized."

"Where are the moles?" Anatoly trained his gun at Yaromir's head.

Yaromir stared down the barrel. "I only had information on the ones we were sent after, Kevin Ball and Frank Garcia, here in DC. Nyoka and Murka were sent to Wales, but I don't have access to their contacts."

Anatoly's eyes swept the hotel room. He could not see any sign of a second occupant. "And where was Dmitri staying?"

Yaromir looked around, as if seeing the room for the first time. "He was staying here. But his gear is gone."

Anatoly lowered his weapon. "I don't know what to do with you, Yaromir. We trained together, but you are not operating well."

Pop. Yaromir fell off the chair.

Snezhana holstered her noise-suppressed pistol, sashayed over, and put a bath towel under Yaromir's head to catch the blood. "He was a fuckup, Anatoly. He lost his mojo and anything that made him useful to us. He was a liability."

"The next one is mine, Snezhana."

Chapter Thirty-Two

CHARLIE FELT NERVOUS. SHE WAS HANGING OUT there undisguised and alone as bait to flush out Murka.

She walked into the Los Milagros Hotel in Columbus, New Mexico. Ashok had found evidence that Nyoka had crossed the border into Mexico at the Columbus New Mexico Port of Entry a few days before but had yet to find any trace of Murka. Elda had diverted to New Mexico from their trip back to Italy.

"Any messages for Charlie Burlamachi?"

The desk clerk reached behind him and handed Charlie an envelope. Inside was a small dark-blue piece of paper, on it written, *Here. Cameras in room. Blueberry. Yum.*

"Do you have any water?"

The clerk handed Charlie a small bottle of water. She crumpled the note up and chewed it, following it with half the bottle. No matter what Elda claimed, these notes were never digestible. How did Elda arrive before her? Elda had dropped her off at the airport. Charlie had examined every other passenger on her plane, and Elda was not one of them. She shouldered her bag and trudged up to her room on the second floor.

Showtime.

Good. The bait was set.

From her seat at a table outside the front door of the café, Elda had a good view up and down Taft Street and Route 9. In the distance she could see Charlie's hotel. Elda had no need to eliminate Murka, but she would like to know why she was in Wales and where she was going now.

As instructed, Charlie had dropped into a number of places on her way to her hotel and mentioned where she was staying. Down the road at the Borderland Café, Elda watched on her phone as Charlie settled in. Elda had flown in a military plane to the old runway in Camp Furlong, a stone's throw down the road. She clicked her heels together to shake some of the road dust off her boots.

Elda's steak quesadilla arrived just as an old truck, driven by a stunning blond, motored across the intersection of Taft and Lima, heading in Charlie's direction. Elda flagged down the waiter and asked for the check and her food to go.

She texted Charlie, SHE'S HEADING UR WAY. Elda paid her bill, grabbed the wrapped food, and threw money onto the table. She jogged over to her loaner, an old Ford beater with a souped-up engine and new Michelin tires.

Charlie jumped at the knock on her door. She took a deep breath and opened it. Murka stood there and leaned against the doorjamb.

Charlie cleared her throat. "We meet again." *Oh my god, Charlie, what a lame line*, she chastised herself.

Murka emitted a low, sexy chuckle. "Yes we do. And are you going to invite me in?" she replied in her contralto voice.

"Only if you promise not to kill me."

"Perhaps just this once." Murka brushed past Charlie, leaving a scent of cologne in her wake.

Charlie reminded herself to get a grip. This was a Russian assassin. "So you work for Boris Sidorov?"

"Ah, you are very well informed. And I assume you work for the CIA?"

"That would be a fair assumption. What were you doing in Wales?"

"Boris needed to ensure a land deal went through. But I am sure you know all this already."

"And why are you in New Mexico?"

Murka stepped forward until she was inches away from Charlie. "I'm thinking of taking a vacation in Mexico to let things cool off. Would you like to come with me?"

"I can't."

"Aha, but you would like to, *da?*"

Charlie took a step backward. "You need to leave. *Now.*"

"And why would that be?" Murka stepped in again.

"I don't want to kill you."

Murka laughed. She leaned forward and gave Charlie a gentle kiss on her lips, then stepped out onto the balcony, affixed a small wire from a wrist device onto the railing, and rappelled down, just as Elda drove up. Murka waved and ran to her truck.

Elda revved her engine.

Murka spun out and headed north on Main Street.

Elda headed south on Main and West on Lima, then south on 11 and waited at the intersection of Routes 9 and

11.

Murka's truck came motoring down Route 11 South. She spotted Elda. and as she passed, she slowed down, shrugged, and mouthed, *Worth a try.*

Elda could see why Charlie was taken with this woman. However, when she met up with Charlie, it was time she and Charlie had a come-to-Jesus discussion about relationships with foreign agents. Trust no one. In the end it always boiled down to kill or be killed.

Chapter Thirty-Three

"**B**OZHE MOY!" OLGA STOOD WITH HER HANDS on her hips and yelled at the morose bunch. "My god, group! You would think one of us died. You all need to get your blood pumping. Put on your running shoes— we're going jogging."

A few minutes later the team straggled out the door. Tosh encouraged them with his usual *Idti, idti, idti.*

"Go, go, go, yourself, Tosh." Smiling, Elda trotted by Tosh's side. "You don't know how much I missed this."

"Do we need to call one of your friends to examine you, Elda?" Tosh ribbed. "In case you haven't noticed, it's hot and dusty, and we haven't eaten yet."

She swatted his arm and increased the pace.

"Damn it, Elda." He accelerated.

They ran neck and neck up the hill, leaving the others behind. Once at the top, they paused to catch their breath and let their heart rates slow down. The two looked out over the Tuscany landscape and breathed in the unique smells of that region.

Elda spoke first. "I'll miss this when we have to leave."

"What do you think about keeping the villa?" Tosh proposed. "You never know when we'll need a safe house or a break from it all."

Elda inspected his face, trying to read his intention. "Can I have your word this would be a safe house and *never* a place we lure the other to torture or kill them? When I was a kid, we used to define an area as *gools*. When you reached gools, you couldn't be made *it*—as in tag, you're it—tackled, hit, stolen from, or touched at all. It was a safe space. This would have to be gools in every sense of the term."

Tosh held out his hand, "*Da*. Gools it is."

Elda shook with him, then they jogged down the hill.

"Oh by the way . . ." Tosh stopped for her attention.

"Yes?" Elda turned to him with a smile. Tosh was getting predictable.

"Where was this magical place of childhood gools?" He winked.

Elda chuckled. "Beat you to the villa." She took off ahead of him.

"Damn you, Elda!" Tosh raced to catch her.

Back at the house, they raided the refrigerator for sparkling water, while Olga, humming, put on a pot of water for tea.

"Tea and biscuits, Olga?"

"Of course, Elda. Olga needs her energy, as do you and also the skinny one here."

Tosh growled at her. She growled back, causing the three of them to convulse with laughter.

Elda clapped her hands. "Okay, team, let's regroup in the living room with the rest."

"Time to get rid of some of the baggage." Elda pointed at the wall charts and wrote on the whiteboard as she spoke. "In the United States we have, as known moles, Kevin Ball, whom Anatoly killed, and Frank Garcia, who may or may not be dead. Ashok said he was making good progress on that list of potentials and would have it to us within the hour. Until we have more data, I'd like Charlie to go to DC to ensure Frank is dead. Do you agree, Tosh?"

"*Da.* Good call."

"Great. Two assassins were sent by the Kremlin to the United States, Yaromir Kozlov and Dmitri Smirnov. Yaromir is dead. Dmitri is in the wind." She scribbled on the whiteboard.

"I want Charlie to see if she can find out where Dmitri went while she's in the United States," Tosh said.

"Good idea." Elda aimed her dry marker at Charlie. "Charlie, use Ashok to pull traffic and airline feeds."

Charlie saluted.

"The Kremlin sent the near-indestructible Nyoka Morozov to assassinate Maxim Komarov, in the UK. She is in Mexico somewhere. What does it take to kill this woman? We chased Murka Mikhailov to the Mexican border, so I am now assuming all three new assassins are now there together." Elda tapped the marker end to her chin. "Two others the Kremlin dispatched, Timur and Konstatin, are dead. Sophia suspects Treacher Walker as a mole, and we should soon have confirmation on that one from Ashok. If he is, I would like someone not employed by MI6 to question him."

Anatoly raised his hand, "Pick me, teacher. Pick me."

The room broke up. Through a few snorts, Elda managed to cough out, "Yes, Anatoly. Please see what he knows. If need be, you may use your *toys* and remove him. Speaking of which, I heard Sophia got you into MI6's toy room. What did you lift this time?"

Anatoly reached into his bag and showed Elda his 1P63 Obzor sight. "I can't believe they had this." He also held up an Aimpoint T2 red-dot sight. "What great add-ons these are to the AK-103 assault rifle that Tosh got me last year."

"Well chosen, Anatoly," Elda praised.

Anatoly sat back with a satisfied smile and a pastry.

"Where did you get that, Anatoly?" Tosh asked. "It looks like a *sochniki*."

"It is. Olga got it," Anatoly said,

Tosh looked at Olga, who tapped the side of her nose and winked at him.

Charlie spoke up. "Before we go on, I have always been bothered by the note in Maxim's hotel room. Who wrote that?"

"I can answer that," Elda replied. "When we used Rhys to bail out Yaromir, he admitted to writing the note to the developer. He was trying to help his friend."

"Thanks, Elda." Charlie sat back in her chair.

"And there's the Kremlin . . ." Elda prompted.

Tosh took over. "We only wish to remove those that plotted against us during Operation Bittman. Yes, America, the United Kingdom, and Russia are at odds, but this is not to make one side's intelligence agency weaker. It is to get rid of those who work against others within their agency."

Elda raised her eyebrow at him.

Tosh held up his hand to her. "Boris is new. He did nothing except reorganize his department on Adrik's recommendations. Adrik is our target. I will handle Boris."

Snezhana piped up. "May I please rid the agency of that fat-slob traitor Adrik?"

Tosh lit up. "It will be fun to see how you do it, niece. *Da.* Okay with you, Elda?"

"Yes, Tosh, definitely. Snezhana needs the experience.

You and Anatoly can be over there for backup."

Elda's phone dinged. She read the text out loud. "Ah, Ashok has news for us."

<hr>

"I have a partial list for you, Miss Elda and Mister Tosh. It's only indicative these people may be long planted and not definitive that they are active spies. I think, though, you will be most pleased at the thoroughness and accuracy of the information." Ashok's face looked out at them from the video chat screen.

Elda sensed Ashok's mood. "You look worried, Ashok. Is there an issue with the search?"

"Oh no, Miss Elda, the search is working quite well. Most excellent."

"Do we have any that are definitive and still alive?" Elda grilled.

"Yes, we do, Miss Elda. However, I want to research a touch more before I give out the list of names. I ran a statistical probability analysis on what we have using for search criteria and moles that we know. The results should be more."

"We probably won't find all the plants, Ashok," Tosh reassured. "Not only have we limited this search, but there are many other ways the Russians use to turn people. They have well-trained swallows and ravens who use sex to entrap. They exploit greed or weaknesses, such as avarice, addictions, extremism, living falsely, to name a few common ones."

"We are aware there are informers in Congress and other sectors of the government," Elda added. "Not all have been planted since birth. Also, I would suspect there are many who haven't been activated yet, and some who may never be."

"Thank you, Miss Elda and Mister Tosh," Ashok said. "Well then, as I have said before, Treacher Walker is one who definitely fits the bill. And now I have gathered the incriminating data on him. He was working in the background for the Kremlin on Operation Bittman." He hesitated, then resumed. "As for some others, well, Ashok is expert at computers and not what you do with the wonderful findings he gives you."

Elda tilted her head and squinted at the video screen.

Tosh frowned and rubbed his chin. "Yes, Ashok. You are quite good. Who else do you have?"

Ashok stalled. "I research everything very well before giving it to you. But still, this may not be what you want."

"Yes, Ashok. That's okay," Elda encouraged, thinking, *It's not like Ashok to downgrade his work.*

"There were many parameters. I have verified the results multiple times," Ashok justified.

"Ashok, you always give us the most wonderful information. What is it about this one?" Elda prodded.

Silence.

"Ashok?" Tosh prompted.

Ashok eyed the screen and spilled. "It's Mister Ed. I fear he matches the parameters."

～

Slam. The door swung shut behind Elda. She ran up the dirt road, the dust from the road mingling with the tears running down her face. *Not Ed, no. He is my friend. I confided in him. I trusted him.* She ran blindly, not caring where she was going.

～

Oh no. Chert. Tosh spotted two orange running shoes poking out of the shrubbery by the side of the road. He came close. Elda lay prone in the grasses. He padded up to her.

A muffled, teary voice reached him. "You're slipping, old man. I can hear you."

Tosh's heart leapt. She was alive. "Fuck you, Elda."

"*Khuy tebe*, Tosh," Elda cursed back at him.

He sat down in the grass next to her. "You know, Elda, Ashok's data is probably correct, but that doesn't mean Ed has turned."

She hoisted herself up on one arm. "What?"

"There are many moles the Kremlin planted in different countries. But they wait until they need them to activate them. Ashok's list may help us stop the ones we suspect from being activated."

Elda sat up and dried her eyes on her sleeve, leaving bits of dirt and grass on her face. She offered with a weak smile. "*Interesnyy . . .*"

"*Da, Interesnyy . . .*" Tosh offered her a handkerchief.

Elda blew her nose. "I trusted him."

Tosh patted her arm. "You know the old rule of trust no one—betrayal may come from within?"

"Moscow Rules. Yes, I know them." Elda folded her arms across her chest.

"And you once asked Ed if you could trust him. He answered, 'Trust no one.'"

"Yes. But he proved himself trustworthy again and again," Elda countered.

Tosh nodded. "Yes, he did. Your instincts are most often spot on, Elda. I don't think Ed has been turned yet. At any rate, we need to verify that and to see what they have on him. Also, we have to see if he can be turned."

Elda scowled. "Why can I trust you, Tosh?" She stuck out her bottom lip.

Tosh grinned. "You and I are old spies. We know and obey the Moscow Rules, but we also have honor among thieves."

Elda's shoulders dropped, and she unfolded her arms. "Plato. One of my favorites. Yes we do. We do our jobs and play that game and would kill each other, if necessary, to achieve the objective, but we respect each other and know when we have to lie to each other."

"So when we're at gools, you can trust me. When we are playing our individual games for our countries, you can't. Right now we're operating on the same side for the same goals. Because of that, *for this mission*, you can trust me."

Elda gave him a faint smile. "Damn. Some days it sucks being a spy."

"*Da.* Let's go back and dream up a sting to pull on Ed. That will prove it one way or the other." Tosh stood and held out his hand to Elda.

She accepted it.

"Get Ashok on video," Elda demanded. She set her jaw firm and allowed anger to flash in her eyes.

Ashok pulled back from the camera. "You wish to discuss the data, Miss Elda."

"Yes, Ashok. The parameters were to look at adoptions from 1984 to 1998, in the military or with government jobs," Elda reminded.

"Yes, Miss Elda. You are most correct."

"That would make the majority of the candidates in ages ranging from in their twenties to in their forties, assuming they were adopted shortly after birth," Elda snapped. "A few may have been as old as teenagers when adopted, but that would have been rare. Ed is in his fifties. And I have never heard him say he was adopted. As a teenager, he would have remembered it."

"You are very right, Miss Elda."

"And I met Ed when he was a teenager, working for his father on an undercover CIA venture in the UK. He's the reason I'm in the business. His father hired me after I left the military. How did his name come up?" Elda demanded.

"Well you see, Miss Elda, I was looking further into Kevin Ball. From the data, John Clark, using his influence as chair of the Senate Intelligence Committee, helped Kevin obtain his current job."

Elda exhaled loudly, her brow furrowed. "Damn. John Clark was an old friend of Ed's. But John helped us by playing double agent in a sting the Russians were playing and led us to shutting it down. Ed revealed the old connection and acted as John's handler in that case."

"*Interesnyy*," Tosh said.

"The connections go deeper, Miss Elda," Ashok proposed. "I learned the arrangements for the trip to Moscow for Kevin's parents were paid for by Robert Clark."

"John Clark's father?" Elda sucked in a breath. She hadn't seen that coming.

"Yes, Miss Elda. You once told me to follow the money, so I proceeded to do so."

"And . . ."

"Kevin's school tuition was paid for via scholarship from a small nonprofit. John Clark and Ed Wilson both have donated to this nonprofit."

"So in essence they paid for Kevin's schooling?" Elda clarified. Could Ed have really been that dense?

"Yes, Miss Elda."

Elda rubbed her eyes under her glasses and drew her hand across her forehead, willing it to relax. "Where did that money come from?"

Ashok looked down at his notes. "Ed Wilson earned that money via dividends and stock options from investing in an offshore company."

Elda questioned, in rapid-fire mode, "Where is the company located?"

"It claims to be located in Bulgaria, but I am suspicious it is a shell cooperation. I have also traced the payouts to find only a percentage of them went into Ed's United States account—the majority was funneled into an offshore account." Ashok looked at Elda with large mocha-brown eyes.

Elda stopped, took a deep breath. "Whose shell company is it?"

Ashok shrugged. "I don't know yet, Miss Elda, but so far the lines are leading to the Kremlin."

"What is the social security number associated with Ed Wilson's accounts?"

Ashok displayed it on the screen.

"That's it!" Elda pumped her fist in the air.

Tosh looked at her in surprise. "What?"

"Ed's not necessarily off the hook, but Ed's father is also Ed Wilson, and neither of them like using Senior or Junior with their names. That number is *not* Ed Wilson Junior's SSN. Pull Ed Wilson Senior's SSN. We'll wait." Elda held her breath.

Small coughs, throat clearing, and feet shuffling disturbed the silence in the living room. Anatoly rhythmically pounded his fist into his thigh. Snezhana played with an invisible ponytail. Elda bit at the sides of her fingers. Tosh checked his pulse. Olga did bicep curls. Jim twiddled his thumbs. Sophia stared at the ceiling. Oliver passed out water.

Ashok came back online. All eyes snapped to the screen.

"Yes, Ashok?" Elda demanded.

"You are right, Miss Elda. That is Ed Wilson the senior's SSN," Ashok confirmed. "I am most sorry I missed that."

"Excellent!" Elda beamed. "No worries, Ashok. All's well that ends well. Let's hope this is one that ends well. Now, let's set the bait and see if Ed Wilson the junior is complicit in any of this."

Tosh looked at Elda with a boyish grin. "How do you plan on doing that?"

"Gather round and I'll map it out."

Tosh selected Anatoly and Sophia. "You two need to get Treacher."

<hr>

"Tosh, I need to speak with you alone." Elda stood.

Tosh narrowed his eyes. "*Da?* What is it Elda?"

"Outside." Elda whirled and headed to the door.

Tosh and Elda stepped out into the backyard and stood, arms crossed, facing each other.

"You don't seem upset we don't have all the moles," Elda started.

"I'm not that worried, Elda." He uncrossed his arms.

"Why?" Elda gave him the evil eye.

"It's simple. Our current mission is to ferret out all who worked against us in Operation Bittman, destroy them, and hopefully, return to our jobs. When we do, I will be working for Russia again and you for America." He held his hands at his sides, palms up.

Elda nodded. It was now so obvious. "Ah, I see. Having agents we aren't aware of may be an advantage to you, then."

Tosh looked at Elda with a sheepish grin. "Exactly. My goal for this mission is *not* to dig out *all* the moles but to remove all the traitors. Except, of course, if we find spies that America planted in Russia, but that isn't what your country does, is it? Your government prefers the John Wayne style of riding in and confronting your enemy face to face."

Elda relaxed her stance and snorted. "Good characterization. It's good to be clear about where each of us stand. I know I said I only wanted revenge. And that's the way I started. But I *now* want to find every last mole Russia planted in the United States and our allied countries. In all good faith as an operative for the United States, I can't let them remain."

Tosh gave a thumbs-down signal. "*Net*. We are not together on that one. I am in my heart loyal to Mother Russia."

Elda inhaled and exhaled to collect herself. After taking a beat to think it through, she came out with, "I understand."

Tosh's gray eyes bored into Elda's brown ones, studying her. She stared back without flinching.

"Where does that leave us, Elda?"

Elda stood tall. "We continue to work together and see if we can suss out all that happened in Operation Bittman. We work together to destroy them and get our revenge. This started out as something you and I planned together. I would like to finish it that way. As you said, we will soon enough be on opposite sides again. Let's hold it off for as long as we are here. Does that work for you, Tosh?"

"*Khorosho*, Elda." Tosh's eyes wore a hint of sadness.

They shook on it. Elda looked at her hand and chuckled.

"*Chto?*" Tosh frowned.

Elda smiled. "It's just that, in the future, I will have to scan for micro transmitters."

Tosh laughed. "And I will have to chase down alligators."

Chapter Thirty-Four

"**G**ET YOUR SKANKY PAWS OFF ME." Sophia slapped at Treacher's hands. The two of them stood in the hallway in MI6.

Treacher leered at Sophia but removed his hands from her waist. "You know you want it, babe." He cupped himself with his hand.

Sophia rolled her eyes. "Treacle, if you were the last man alive, I'd turn into a lesbian before bedding you."

"Into girls, hey?" Treacher drooled. "That can be arranged. I'd love a threesome."

They both stood quietly as a colleague strode past them. Sophia's phone rang. "Saved by the bell." She put the call on speaker.

Oliver's voice boomed out. "Hey, hon, got a minute?"

"For you, always. What's up?"

"I have to go out of town tonight. I left a casserole in the fridge for you. Will you be okay?"

Sophia smiled at his thoughtfulness. "Perfectly, my love. See you tomorrow?"

"Not till late," he informed her and cut the connection.

Treacher leaned in toward Sophia. "I know where you live. I'll be by around eight p.m." He licked his lips.

Sophia shuddered and pushed him away from her. She could feel Treacher's eyes following her hips as she sauntered away.

"I'll take your lack of answer as a yes," he called after her.

───

The hallway was dark as a night without moon or stars. *The damn light must have burned out.* Treacher stepped out of the elevator and felt his way along the wall to Sophia's flat. He reached up to knock on her door, when a large man grasped him from behind. His mouth was covered by a hand before he could yell. He felt the man's body against his back and grunted for help.

The flat door swung open, and he was manhandled into the living room. He sensed someone leaving the flat and heard the door close behind that person. *What the fuck?*

───

With his arm under Treacher's arm and shoulder and over his mouth, Anatoly lifted him by his belt and muscled him into the apartment. He noticed the furniture had been moved off the large rug he had used to move Nyoka's body from this same location. He seized a conveniently placed hand towel and shoved it into Treacher's mouth. He picked up a roll of Gafffa tape and tore off a generous piece, which he used to seal the towel in place.

Treacher bleeped and struggled to free himself. Anatoly turned him around and, with his body, pressed Treacher against the wall. He felt with his gloved hands for the hyoid bone under Treacher's neck and slipped a garrot on over Treacher's head. While putting pressure on the hyoid bone with one hand and twisting the garrot with the other, he gazed into Treacher's eyes. Fear stared back at him, and Treacher kicked ineffectually at Anatoly.

Anatoly watched as the fear in Treacher's eyes turned into recognition and then resignation. Anatoly heard the snap of the hyoid bone and could tell, from the sounds Treacher was making, that his tongue had fallen back into blocking off his airway. Treacher's eyes were wide; his struggles ceased. He slumped down, the garrot and Anatoly's hand being the only things holding him off the ground.

Anatoly kept the pressure on for a few more minutes and tested Treacher's pulse.

Gone.

Anatoly rolled Treacher up in the rug and sat on the couch, waiting for his erection to go down, before slinging the carpet over his shoulder and heading out.

A good kill.

Harry and Roger grabbed onto the handholds and stepped on the back of the Lambert trash truck as the driver pulled away from the curb. They hopped on and off, throwing bins of trash into the back. Roger thumped the side of the truck to indicate they should compress the load before their next stop. The compactor moved down and pushed into the trash. When it rose back into place, there was a bloody piece of clothing caught on it.

"Bloody hell. What's got caught in there now, Rog?"

"I'm not up for the third degree by the coppers again, 'arry. Let's finish our run and leave the lot in the dump."

"Okay. I see nothing, Rog." Harry thumped the side of the truck twice to signify they could move on.

The sound of a magazine being slammed into a semi-automatic weapon turned heads. Olga and Yuri appeared in the kitchen doorway with weapons drawn. Elda and Tosh flew off their chairs, kneeling and pointing their pistols in the direction of the sound. Charlie lay prone with her MP7A2 submachine gun at the ready. Snezhana readied her weapon on the top of the couch.

Having returned from London, Anatoly sprawled on the floor in the living room of the villa, checking his weapons. "*Der'mo*, does everyone have Sophia's jumpies?"

Olga and Yuri holstered their weapons and went back inside the kitchen to make tea. Elda and Tosh resumed their conversation. Snezhana spun in her chair and played with her hair. Charlie continued doing pushups on the rug in the middle of the room. Jim was outside gardening. Sophia was still at her flat in London.

Tosh clapped his hands. "Everyone. Come here. We have work to do."

Elda called Jim in. Olga and Yuri came in from the kitchen, carrying their tea and biscuits.

Olga was covered in dirt. She mopped the sweat off her face with a kitchen towel.

"What? Nothing for the rest of us?" Anatoly groused.

Olga tossed a paper bag to him. He caught it, reached inside, and with a huge smile, pulled out a *sochniki*. He took a huge bite and mumbled, "Thank you, Olga."

"Don't you talk with your mouth full," Olga reprimanded.

Jim hobbled inside in stocking feet.

Olga looked at him with a cocked head and raised eyebrows.

"Muddy boots," Jim explained. "Ah watahed the gahdan."

Elda looked over at her team, noticing Olga's unusually disheveled condition. "My god, Olga. What have you been doing?"

Olga held up her arms to display her popping biceps. "Olga fixing the patio bricks. They are crooked. I dig them out and put them back."

"Focus, people." Tosh clapped his hands for everyone's attention. "It's time to get moving again."

The spies sat in a circle, with Elda and Tosh sitting side by side.

Tosh started. "We need to verify Ed's position. He can identify most of us, but he's never met Olga or Jim. So you two are going to DC to pull a sting on him. If he plays along, then we have a problem to deal with. If he reports the contact, he's most likely innocent and the Ed we know and love. We'll run it a few times to see if he's consistent or if he can be bought. Elda will give you two the details. No need to disguise yourselves. Ashok will ensure you're not reported and wipe any personal info from the database."

Elda spoke up. "I will be running operations from here, with Yuri handling the logistics. Once we are sure Jim and Olga don't need backup, Tosh will head off to Moscow to have a tête-à-tête with Boris. Snezhana will go to Moscow to handle Adrik. Anatoly will go with her as backup."

Charlie raised her hand. "And me?"

"You'll go to DC to work with Ashok to try and find Dmitri, Nyoka, and Murka, and you can coordinate with Stas. You could do this remotely, but we also need you to see if Frank is dead, and if he isn't, to eliminate him."

She turned to Tosh. "Can you please ensure Olga and Jim are prepared for their mission? I want to run Charlie through a few martial arts moves before she goes."

"*Da.* No problem. Olga, Jim, come over here and let's huddle."

"Oh, you are getting touchy feely," Elda teased.

"*Poshel na khuy*, Elda."
"Fuck you back, Tosh."

In the backyard, Elda and Charlie faced off. Elda waited to see if Charlie would fill the gap, and sure enough, Charlie moved in first. She swung her leg up to flatten Elda.

Elda recoiled a few inches, and the kick went wide. "That was close, but not good enough. Plus, you wobbled and would have been easy to topple."

Charlie regained her balance. "But you didn't bring me out here to have a boxing match, did you?"

Elda grinned. "Well intuited, Grasshopper. No, I needed to be alone with you and give you a message to pass to Ashok."

Charlie stood and cocked her head. "*Interesnyy*, as Tosh would say. What is it?"

Elda fell into her professorial stance. "The time will come soon when we have done all that we can and the team will split up, going their separate ways. Tosh and his crew will go back to Russia, and we will go back to DC. I feel Tosh distancing already."

"And what do you want me to do?"

Elda held her forefinger up in the air. "I want you to tell Ashok to hide the list of moles from this group and give us *only* those who were complicit in Operation Bittman."

Charlie rubbed her hands along the sides of her head, as if her head hurt. "But don't we want to find all the moles, Elda?"

Elda took up her training,. "Yes, Charlie, we do, but Tosh doesn't. Tell me why."

Charlie stayed silent for a few minutes.

Elda waited.

Holding the sides of her head and looking down at her

feet, Charlie came out with, "If we discover all that Russia planted and Tosh goes back to work for Russia, then he won't have as many tools to attack us with. It's still Russia versus the United States in the end." She looked back up at Elda with a worried look.

"Exactly, Grasshopper. Well thought out. Now you must work to theorize these things on your own and run them by me, instead of the other way around."

"Yes, Master. So we are going to continue to find the moles but not disclose we are doing so?"

"Yes. The line is being drawn in the sand. Détente is coming to an end."

Chapter Thirty-Five

FOOTSTEPS FELL SOFTLY IN THE DARK NIGHT. Ed changed the rhythm of his footfall and could hear the faint cadence of another person behind him. He switched to the curb side of the sidewalk to keep away from the shadowy entrances to the buildings around him.

Someone is following me. I think he limps.

Ed picked up the pace and swiveled around the corner. He skidded to a stop inches away from mowing down a solidly built woman. "Excuse me, ma'am." He moved to go around her but was stopped by her arm swinging out, making an effective barrier. Whoever was behind him caught up and stood by his side, leveling a gun at him.

Ed held up his hands.

The woman reached into his overcoat and extracted his piece. She knelt and plucked out his knife from his ankle sheath.

The nearest streetlight was not functioning, and Ed found it difficult to see their faces. "Who are you and what do you want?"

The woman spoke. "Olga. You will remember Olga, hey?"

"I certainly will," Ed said primly. "And what does Olga want?"

The man next to Ed spoke up. "Ah'm, Jim. Ah can make you a lot of money."

Ed noticed they both had different accents. Interesting.

"How?" He'd keep them talking. Perhaps someone would come along and they'd scurry off.

"You give us info. We give you money," Olga stated.

Ah, that old game. Who did they work for? She could be Russian. She must think he's with the CIA. He'd play along. "What information?"

The woman clapped him on the back, nearly toppling him. "We let you know."

The two disappeared with surprising speed. Ed glanced at the ground behind him and there lay his handgun and his knife.

Tosh slammed the palm of his hand down on the desk. "Stop that damn habit. It's a tell that you're nervous. We can't afford showing our emotions."

Elda was biting the sides of her fingers. She sat with Tosh at her makeshift office desk, waiting for the real-time feed from Ed's office to begin.

"Much appreciated, Tosh. I'll try. By the way, I think your pulse is fine." Elda indicated Tosh's wrist, where he held two fingers on the artery.

"Touché, Elda. I will remember that."

Elda pointed at her screen. "There! He's sending something with an attachment." She messaged Ashok to forward the attachment over, since the feed only contained the message envelope.

She moved her hand to her mouth and put it back down. Glancing over, she saw Tosh grinning.

The wait seemed forever.

"You know, Elda, syncing for an email feed every two seconds won't make it come any faster," Tosh snarked.

Elda glared at him. Just then, an email from Ashok with the attachment arrived in her inbox. She hastened to open it. "Excellent! He's filled out a contact report by two possibly foreign agents trying to set him up to exchange money for information."

Tosh glanced at the report and looked at Elda. "*Khoro-sho*. So what do you want to do now?"

Elda rapidly typed an email to thank Ashok and instructing him to forward any future attached reports from Ed. "Knowing Ed, he will try to reverse the sting. Let's see how many secrets he's willing to compromise to do so and what happens to the money he gets."

Elda texted Olga, PROCEED TO PART 2 OF PLAN.

<hr>

"Fuck. You again?" Frank sneered at Charlie, standing in his office doorway.

Charlie held up her hands in mock surrender. "Careful, Frank. From what I hear, you just got a pacemaker installed. You don't want to it to push off rhythm."

Frank paused, clenched and unclenched his fists. "What are you doing here?" He took his cell phone out of his shirt pocket and deposited it on his desk.

Charlie moved closer to Frank's desk, where his cell phone lay. "Just finishing up, Frank. You'll be glad I found the information I required and should be able to go back to my own department after today."

"By the way, which department was that? You never told me," Frank responded with disdain.

Charlie cut off further conversation. "No, I didn't." She turned and marched out of Frank's office. Once near her desk, she texted Ashok. Did u get it?

Y - Rdy in an hr

An hour later Charlie picked up a cloned cell phone, identical to Frank's. "Thanks much, Ashok."

Ashok, already deep into the next project, waved good-bye.

Charlie jogged over to her office and went looking for Frank. She was informed he was out for lunch. She swung by his office. *Great! He left his cell. Typical careless Frank.* She performed the swap in seconds. She sauntered over to her desk and started to clean it out, ensuring she could make a fast exit.

She wandered by Frank's office once more and saw he had returned and was eating lunch, so she went to grab a cup of coffee. From the break room, she heard a shout, "Frank's down."

Charlie ran to Frank's office to see Joe doing CPR on Frank. She dialed 911. "I have 911 on the line. What's the status?" she yelled to Joe.

"I found him this way. . ."—Joe gasped between com-pressions—"on the ground, unresponsive, not breathing, no pulse."

She relayed the statistics to 911. She texted Ashok, Done. erase app. The text sent and then disappeared from her phone. "EMTs are on the way. I will meet them at the door and escort them up," she called to Joe.

Charlie ran down the stairs and skidded to a stop at the door as the EMTs arrived. She waved to them. "Over here! I'll escort you up."

Once at Frank's office, Charlie stood out of the way and was soon joined by Joe.

He shook his head. "Damn, it looked as if he would make it after they implanted the pacemaker. But I don't think they can turn this around."

The EMTs put leads on Frank from a portable defibrillator and continued CPR. The defibrillator instructed, "Shock advised." The EMTs took their hands off the body and called out, "Shock advised. Stand clear." They administered the shock and followed the defibrillator's instructions.

"How long was he down before we got here?" an EMT called out to Joe.

"I'm not sure. I found him like that. I worked on him for at least fifteen minutes, maybe more, before you arrived."

"So he could have been down for ten minutes before you saw him?" the EMTs queried.

"Easily."

Charlie chimed in. "I called 911 at twelve forty-five, and Joe was doing CPR already. It took me five minutes to trot to the front door and another five to get back here with the EMTs. So that's over ten minutes."

One EMT made the calculations. "And we've been doing CPR on him for twenty minutes. Conservatively, it totals to forty-five minutes." He nodded at the other man. They stopped CPR. The first EMT looked at his watch. "Time of death one eighteen p.m."

Someone in the hallway started humming, and another whispered to the tune *Ding dong the witch is dead.*

Charlie looked at Joe. "Sorry, Joe."

Joe shrugged. "No worries. He was a bastard."

"It worked well, Ashok."

Charlie stood outside the building, slightly away from others, watching as the EMTs loaded the body into their car and drove off. She held her phone close to her ear to be able to hear Ashok over the hubbub of the curious crowd.

"Thank you, Miss Charlie. Yes, I knew it would be effective. Pacemakers tend not to like the combination of magnetic pulses and enhanced cell phone signals. Combined with his elevated blood pressure from seeing you, it was a pretty sure bet his heart would fail totally and not be able to be revived. Although it was lucky for us he was stupid enough to carry his cell phone in his shirt pocket." He paused.

Charlie praised him again. She was learning it made him work harder. "Very good research, Ashok. Now have you found any information on where Dmitri may be?"

"I am still working on that, Miss Charlie. I think I may have found some film of him entering Mexico. I sent it to Stas to see if it matches what he has. I'm also waiting for the details on this person from immigration there. Ashok leaves no stone unturned."

Charlie grinned at her phone. "You do miracle work, Ashok. Despite that, it'll be damn hard to locate him in Mexico. I'll get your info to Tosh. The Russians may have to handle him when he surfaces in Russia again. Who knows, perhaps he can be turned into an asset."

"So true, Miss Charlie. I will tell Stas to be on the lookout for him still."

"Did either of you find a trace of Murka or Nyoka in Mexico?"

"Not yet, Miss Charlie. We are most diligently looking, however."

"I trust that you are, Ashok."

◦───◦

"Stand down for now, Charlie." Elda's order came clearly over Charlie's cell phone, despite the hubbub surrounding Charlie on the DC streets.

"I'm willing to go after him," Charlie pleaded, anxious to be of service and prove to Elda what she could do.

"Let's find out if Murka and Nyoka are with him first.

We know Murka also went to Mexico. The Mexican government is very accommodating to Russian spies. It's a haven for them and a great place to use to immigrate to the United States. We should research it more as we hunt for moles. But I can't let you go there alone. The largest portion of GRU operatives in the world are in Mexico right now."

Damn. "All right, Elda. I hear you." Charlie shuffled her feet, her lips drawn into a pout. Aside from taking Dmitri down, she was hoping to have a rematch with Murka. She wanted to show Elda that she could overcome her attraction and take Murka down too.

Elda's kind laugh echoed in Charlie's ears. "Ah, Grasshopper, Ed once told me you reminded him of me when I was younger. I can see why. Don't worry. You *will* get your chance."

Charlie sighed. "Now what?" She glanced around her to establish no one could overhear her side of the conversation.

"Come back to the villa. We'll regroup."

"Will we go after Dmitri and the rest?" Charlie asked eagerly. A horn blasted. She swirled to look. Nothing. She brought her focus back to her phone conversation. "I'm ready, willing, and able."

Elda shut her down. "Not at this time. They were not part of Operation Bittman. We'll wait until we stop working with Tosh and his team."

She'd need to follow up with Elda on that comment. "When will that be?"

"Soon." Elda hung up.

The warm tropical breeze caressed his pasty white legs. His toes played in the soft white sand. Dmitri took another sip of his vodka and iced-tea drink and slathered more

SPF 50 sunscreen on the exposed parts of his body. Cancun was treating him well. He appreciated Boris's advice to lay low for a few months.

A sexy contralto voice whispered in his ear, and he could feel the barrel of a gun at the back of his head. "You really should stay alert at all times." The pressure on his head disappeared, and Murka dropped into the chair beside him. She put her Modelo Negra beer into the chair pouch, dropped her sleek Stechkin APS automatic back into her pocket, and settled in next to Dmitri.

"How did you find me?" Dmitri inquired in a bored tone.

Murka shrugged. "It wasn't hard. I just thought, where would a man who thought he was god's gift go to unwind?"

Dmitri laughed. "Is Nyoka here?"

"Not that I can see, and she would be a hard person to hide." Murka took off her shoes and socks and buried her toes into the warm sand.

Dmitri tossed her the sunscreen, then looked her up and down. "Would you be interested in spending some quality time together while we're here?"

Murka put her hand on his arm. "If I swung that way, I would *do* you, but you would do far better picking up a local who could enjoy it. Men do nothing for me."

"You never know until you've tried me."

Murka smiled. "I am sure you are very proficient, but it's a solid no."

"What's your type?"

Murka closed her eyes and inhaled, as if remembering someone special. "I have not found many who interest me. Surprisingly, I recently did, but there were too many obstacles in the way."

Dmitri leered. "Interesting. If you meet her again, can I watch?"

Murka opened her eyes and glared at him. "Certainly

not. And anyway, if I meet her again, she may try to kill me."

The full moon shone over the ruins of Calakmul, Mexico, far into the jungles of the greater Petén Basin region, near the Guatemalan border. The huge stone ruins grew out of the surrounding green lushness. A bat flew over the heads of the assemblage crouched nearby.

A woman wore a headdress of snakeskins, woven into her black hair tresses, that stood out from her head, as if electrified. As she stood and stated "*Q'alajinik*," the crossed bones woven into her long skirt clattered. She ran out into the clearing. The gathering, chanting "*Ixchel*," danced around her. She held her hands up to the sky, the moonlight shining off her long, pointed nails.

Nyoka was well hidden and enjoying her time as a Mayan goddess.

CHAPTER THIRTY-SIX

THE KNOCK ON HIS OFFICE DOOR STARTLED Adrik. He wasn't expecting anyone. He wondered why his secretary hadn't sent whoever it was away.

He groaned as he lifted his bulk from his chair and waddled over to open the door. There stood Anatoly and Snezhana. Anatoly wore a black suit and tie, and Snezhana wore a short formfitting dress with nylons and heels.

Adrik drew back his head and looked at them wide eyed. "Anatoly. Snezhana. This is a surprise. I'm not taking any meetings today though. Talk with my secretary to make an appointment." He peeked around the corner and was surprised to find his secretary wasn't at her desk. "Where did she go? Well, I'm sure she'll be right back. You can have a seat and wait for her in the waiting area."

He turned around to find Snezhana and Anatoly in his office, motioning for him to come in and shut the door. "I must ask for you to leave."

Snezhana sat down in a chair. As she crossed her legs, her skirt hiked up to reveal a length of thigh. She smiled at Adrik. "We'd like to have this conversation *today*, Adrik. So please come in. Anatoly will shut the door behind you."

Adrik backed away from them and around his desk. He plopped onto his chair and opened the bottom drawer to grab a candy bar. As he unwrapped it and shoved it into his mouth, Snezhana observed, "Quite a stash you have there, Adrik. Do you buy them from different places or have them delivered?"

Through a mouthful of candy bar, Adrik mumbled, "Delivered every Monday morning."

"How convenient." Snezhana uncrossed and crossed her legs.

Adrik's eyes tracked her leg movements with interest. Perhaps he'd talk to them for a bit. He swallowed. "Why are you here? Are you looking for business?"

Snezhana winked at him. "Do you remember Operation Bittman, Adrik? Anatoly and I were sorting through and throwing out Tosh's files, when we came across that one. What we never understood in it was, why it was necessary to attack the Russian contingency? We can understand taking out the American and British spies, but couldn't you accomplish your objectives without endangering us? I know this was a long time ago and water under the bridge, but we want to close it out, and understanding everything will help us do that. So we came to the source. I understand you had good reason for all that you did." She smiled sweetly.

Adrik puffed up. "I can help you with that. My apologies for putting the two of you in any danger, but I had confidence our operatives were superior to theirs so that you would survive. My motivation was twofold."

Anatoly and Snezhana leaned in with interested looks on their faces.

Adrik pulled out and unwrapped another candy bar. He took a bite and spoke, with bits of chocolate falling from his mouth. "Tosh threatened my position and advancement. His Cold War ways were old world and no longer relevant. But he had built up a lot of political currency. He didn't see the need to be subservient to me or change his methods. So I decided to discredit him by having him fail on the mission."

Snezhana nodded. "But what about his team?"

Adrik shrugged. "Collateral damage. It was the easiest way to go. Targeting one person, Tosh, would have looked suspicious, and I didn't have enough resources to protect everyone else. There was no one person on the team I desired to help me in my own goals, so it was cleaner just to order getting rid of everyone."

Snezhana shook her head in what Adrik interpreted as amazement and admiration. "And you did *all* that on your own, without orders from above? What initiative."

Adrik straightened his shoulders, which had the unfortunate effect of sticking his stomach farther out. "Yes. It was all my doing."

Snezhana blinked her eyelashes at him and exhaled a breathy, "Wow. You thought it out, Adrik. Thank you so much for letting us know. We'll be able to close the case now."

She stood and signaled to Anatoly they were leaving. Adrik stayed seated.

"We'll leave you to the rest of your day, Adrik. Our apologies for the interruption."

A small lorry pulled up to Adrik's office building in the Kremlin. The driver was a tall woman with long dark hair and a white coverall uniform that declared she worked for Russian Candies.

Snezhana opened the back of the lorry, noted the real

delivery woman was still unconscious and that her zip-ties were holding. She took out a cardboard box the size of a shoebox and closed and locked the van. She pranced up toward Adrik's office to deliver the box.

She looked pointedly at the secretary. "These are the special-of-the-week chocolates. Mr. Lebedev is such a steady customer that we are giving him these at no charge. Can you ensure he, and only he, gets them?"

The secretary pulled her hands away from the box. "Of course. I understand completely."

Snezhana patted the secretary on her arm. "Perhaps you could be so kind as to open the box and pour the individually wrapped candies into his candy drawer?"

Snezhana watched as the secretary walked the box into Adrik's office, opened the bottom drawer of his desk, and dumped the contents in.

"Thank you so much." Snezhana pivoted on her toe and strode away.

———

Adrik wandered back into his lobby from picking up an early lunch. *Today is a good day.* On his way into his office, his secretary flagged him down. "*Ser*, the candy woman made a special delivery today. They are expressing their appreciation for you being such a good customer."

Adrik beamed. Today was getting better.

"*Ser?*" the secretary asked.

Adrik turned at his door, anxious to get to his candy drawer. "*Da?*"

"May I take an early lunch? I have a friend in town." She held an overstuffed purse in one hand and a bag of personal items in the other.

"*Da.*" Adrik felt magnanimous and added, "In fact, take the afternoon off."

"Spasibo, ser."

Adrik watched her grab her nameplate and shove it into her purse and scurry out. Strange. Perhaps she wished to show her friend what a great job she had.

He turned and lumbered to his desk, plopped onto his chair, and pulled open the drawer. What a great collection of candy. He brushed away the drool that had started at the corner of his mouth and selected a bar with a red-and-black-colored wrapper. He savored the chocolate and started coughing. It was difficult to breathe. He reached for his water bottle and collapsed onto his desk.

A few floors up from Adrik's office, Boris looked down at the résumé in front of him. Impressive but somewhat older than was needed in the assassin group.

He opened the door, and the candidates sitting in the waiting room fidgeted and looked at him expectantly. One sat still and analyzed him through steel-gray eyes. Boris hadn't spotted him when he'd first glanced around the room. The man blended in and had cropped up from nowhere. He was dressed in gray, with a long greatcoat and bowler hat, and was almost ghostlike. *If I believed in ghosts . . .*

"Artyom Glazatov?" Boris called out.

The ghost stood and slipped behind Boris into his office. Boris turned, and the man was already seated. Unnerved, Boris hurried for the security of his office chair behind his desk.

His interviewee moved the office chair diagonally, so Boris shifted his chair in order to better face the man. He noted he now could see out his office window. Perhaps he should rearrange his office. It was a much better view.

Boris cleared his throat, but before he could speak, the ghost asked, "I need to know some particulars, to see if I want to work for you."

Boris's neck veins stood out, and he could feel his face blotching. "*Kakogo cherta!* I am the hiring manager here."

The man in front of him did not move or blink. His words floated across to Boris. "Yes, you are, but that doesn't mean you have control." Artyom smiled, offsetting the sting of his words.

I may like this one . . . "What do you want to know?" He glowered at Artyom.

"There was a mission against the Americans and the British, as well as some of the operatives here in the Kremlin. It was called Operation Bittman. Were you involved in that?" His tone was nonthreatening.

Boris wondered if this man was a real candidate or if he was an undercover auditor. Either way, that operation had been a disaster. He had vowed to distance himself and erase all traces of any connection he had to it. He decided to stick to that story line. "I am aware of Operation Bittman, but it was not my call. Adrik, who is on probation working for me, was the architect of that fiasco."

Artyom nodded at Boris. "Have you heard of Tosh Chelovek and his team?" His gray eyes continued to bore into Boris's.

"Yes, that was a great loss. Tosh was a superior operator and handler. Unlike Adrik, I am a big believer in Cold War techniques being used in random with more modern techniques." Boris felt as if this man could read his mind and was staring into his soul.

Artyom raised an eyebrow. "If Tosh were alive today, would you hire him and give him free rein over his people and their actions?"

"This is a strange line of questioning. Can you tell me why you're asking so much about Tosh?" Boris slapped his hand down on his desk. He felt his face sprouting blotches.

Artyom's answer came to him on a calming breeze.

"Yes, once you've answered my question."

Boris felt he was being hypnotized and compelled to answer. He looked down at a red dot that had become apparent on his hand. *Kakogo cherta?* What was that? Did something bite him? His eyes widened. The dot traveled up his arm and out of sight. He nervously swatted the side of his head, where he assumed the dot landed. *Blyad'. He's got a sniper.*

Beads of sweat formed on Boris's forehead. He decided he no longer had the upper hand and that it behooved him to be honest. "In a heartbeat. I need professionals to work with. I am having difficulty beefing up my team. Most of the recent candidates are boorish morons."

"Then let's discuss the terms of my employment." Tosh presented Boris with a card and his real résumé.

<hr>

Der'mo. Tosh signaled for Anatoly to stand down. Anatoly packed up his Vintornez silent sniper rifle. He was disappointed he hadn't had a chance to fire his weapon. It was fun watching the man sweat and try to swat away the laser dot.

With gloved hands, Anatoly replaced the brick he had chiseled out of the outside wall, and then the inner concrete block he had chiseled out. He smoothed wall compound over that and rehung a portrait of Putin. He looked around the small, unused dusty room. "*Proveryat', khorosho, ochistite.*" He backed out, sweeping away his footsteps. Soon the dust would fall again and erase any sign of human presence.

Chapter Thirty-Seven

THE HAIRS ON THE BACK OF ED'S NECK stood up as he reached out to put his key into his apartment doorknob. Something felt off. He scanned the doorjamb. Intact. No sign of a forced entry. His alarms hadn't gone off either. He drew his gun and inserted the key. Slowly he opened the door to find the barrel of a pistol pressed against his head, and he was relieved of his weapon.

"You won't need this winky weapon. Olga not here to harm you." Olga put her arm around his back and steered him to his kitchen table, where Jim was already seated, with a cup of tea.

"Tea or coffee?" Olga offered. The smell of coffee brewing filled the air.

This was worse than his office. Didn't anyone have boundaries anymore? "Coffee, please. Black." He looked at them with an eyebrow raised.

"You are wondering what we want, hey? Olga tell you." She set a cup of coffee in front of him and plopped down with her cup of tea. "Before we do that, do you have biscuits?"

Ed shook his head.

"Too bad. I bring biscuits next time," Olga declared. "Now, we need you to give us some scoop. We make it worth your while."

Jim took a small money-deposit bag and placed it on the table in front of Ed.

Ed unzipped the bag and peeked in. There must be over ten thousand dollars in there.

As if reading his mind, Olga announced, "There is fifteen thousand dollars in there."

Ed zipped the bag, placed it on the table, and slid it toward Jim. "What do you want?"

Jim pushed the money closer to Ed. "Tell us the name of the agent who replaced Eldah aftah she died."

Ed frowned and tilted his head. He leaned forward. "That's all?"

Olga shrugged. "For now."

Ed's eyes narrowed. "For now?"

"*Da*. For now." Olga smiled.

Ed scratched his head. It was suddenly very hot in the room. He imagined his head would explode. He craved things to slow down. He hadn't been an active agent for years. "Do I have time to consider this?"

"No." Jim displayed his automatic, which had apparently been resting on his lap under the table.

"Frank Garcia," Ed spit out.

"Final ansah?" Jim probed.

Ed looked at him with surprise. He might be American or at least have lived in the United States for a while. "Final answer."

Olga took the cups and washed them and also wiped down the tea and coffeepots and stove. Jim rose to his feet and limped to the door.

Olga took the bullets out of Ed's gun and returned the weapon to him. She shook her finger at him. "Remember, you tell no one about this. We have another request that may take you longer to research." She positioned an envelope in front of him.

Ed was disappointed to see that both Jim and Olga wore latex gloves. They'd made sure to not leave traces of their DNA, and no prints. Jim and Olga probably weren't even their real names either.

"What a Boy Scout," Tosh declared.

In the Tuscany villa, Elda trotted over to look over Tosh's computer. There was another file sent from Ed's machine via Ashok's magic.

"Exactly fifteen thousand dollars reported and turned into the government, along with the details of the encounter. Good boy, my Ed," Elda said with a big smile. "He gave us the name of the Russian mole and didn't give us an active American agent's name, especially Charlie's. I would guess that's because he suspects Frank. Let's see what happens on the next ask, and if he passes that one, I'd say he's on the up and up. Do you agree, Tosh?"

"*Da*. Let's see how it goes, but so far he's proving our theory correct, and I seriously doubt he's a mole."

"Good." Elda sat so she could see Tosh's face as she opened up the next line of conversation. "So on another subject. How did it go in Moscow?"

Tosh looked back at Elda without expression. "I suspect Boris was more complicit in Operation Bittman than he is admitting. He's letting Adrik take the fall. That's okay, since Adrik *was* guilty as all hell."

Elda raised an eyebrow. "*Was?*"

Tosh shrugged and turned the corners of his mouth down. "His doctor warned him about eating all that chocolate."

Elda noted Tosh's eyes were unexpressive and there was

no accompanying smile. "Okay. What's *your* plan?"

Tosh turned away from Elda so she couldn't read his face. "You know that saying about keeping your friends close and your enemies closer? I will watch and learn and bide my time. I believe Boris has information about the remaining moles. If we kill him, we lose that lead."

Elda snorted. "Did you get a good deal?"

"*Da.*"

Elda waited. Tosh resumed typing on his computer. Their professional barriers were reforming.

Ed selected his burner phone and dialed Ashok. "Can you please come to my office now, and bring the Cone of Silence?"

He pelted crumbled-up pieces of paper at the hoop over his wastebasket while waiting for Ashok. Within minutes, Ashok, holding his invention, skidded to a stop in Ed's office door. The Cone of Silence cloaking machine was soon sitting on Ed's desk and blinking green.

Ed waved Ashok to a chair. "Ashok, I need your help with this, but no one must know."

"I will most willingly help you, Mister Ed. And my lips are sealed." Ashok drew his pinched-together thumb and forefinger over his mouth.

Ed sighed in relief. "This will take a while, but a foreign agent requested the names, addresses, birthdays and social security numbers of everyone in this organization. I want to give them bad but realistic data. Can you create a database with this information in it?" Ed passed Ashok two pieces of paper with a filled spreadsheet on them. "Here is the falsified data. Can you create it and place an electronic version of it on a thumb drive for me? Again, no one must know of this, except you and me."

Ashok beamed. "Yes sir, Mister Ed. I will do this most promptly and have it back to you today."

"Perfect."

"Thanks, Ashok." Elda signed off the video chat with Ashok. She strolled into the kitchen, where Tosh was sitting, having tea and biscuits. "He's clean!" Elda did a little dance around the kitchen.

Tosh spit his beverage out through his nose and grabbed a pile of napkins to clean up. "*Lisus*, Elda. Not while I'm drinking."

"So he created a parallel database with false information in it. He's got the info on the thumb drive, and the database will be identical, in the case of someone hacking in to validate it."

"*Fantastika*. So what's next?"

"Time to go over the pond and accompany Olga and Jim to get the material."

Damn. Not again.

Ed stood by his front door and rubbed the back of his neck. He hesitated before drawing his weapon. It might not be them. He inserted his key, unlocked, and slowly opened the door. Again his gun was taken from him. *Damn, I need to be better at this.*

Ed looked around his living room and saw only Olga holding his pistol.

"Coffee's ready," she pronounced. "And we have biscuits."

With a sigh, he led her into his kitchen. There, he saw Jim sitting drinking tea, along with another man, who looked vaguely familiar. He was small and neatly dressed with a bowler hat, beard, and mustache. British? "And, who's the new addition to the party?"

The man stood. "I'm here to tell you you're off the hook. You have passed our tests," he said in a contralto voice.

Ed shook his head in confusion. "Tests? What tests?" Who were these people?

"Did you know, Ed, that your father was dirty?" the small man explained. "That he was an adopted Russian orphan who, in his later years, worked for the Kremlin to launder money for them?"

His eyes wide, Ed took a step backward. "What? No! I am of English descent. My father was an outstanding operative for the CIA." What type of game were they playing?

"That's true too, Ed. Your father was a complex person. But the Russians had their hooks in him. You're aware how these things go. They start with small requests, and before you know it, you're in too deep. Look, I printed it all out for you so you can see the data behind our accusations." The man dropped the papers onto the table.

Ed looked down and lifted up the pile. He started shuffling through it and scanning the incriminating evidence. As he turned each piece, he shook his head and exclaimed, "No, no, no . . . This isn't real. How do I know you haven't fabricated this evidence?"

"Log in to the databases yourself. You have access. Look at the date-time stamps on the associated files."

Ed looked up with tears in his eyes. "How did you find all this?"

The man put a hand on Ed's arm. "We were looking for the traitors who betrayed us in Operation Bittman and the leaks in your organization. Since one way of finding a portion of these people was to look at those who were of Russian parentage, we decided to pull records on any orphans who were adopted and now were in government service. The name *Ed Wilson* came up."

Ed, taking a Kleenex from a nearby box, dried his eyes and blew his nose. He scratched his head and leaned forward, peering at this stranger. "Did you pull off this sting because you thought it was me?"

"We narrowed it down further to your father, but I had to be sure of you, Ed."

"Wait . . . Betrayed *us*? Operation Bittman? Who are you?" Ed stared at the man, came closer, and peered into the man's hazel eyes. He shook his head. "It can't be. You can't be. We looked everywhere for you."

Chapter Thirty-Eight

"**Certamente, Lorenzo. Grazie mille.** I look forward to our meeting in Florence." Snezhana, sitting in a hotel in Moscow, ended her call and dialed Yuri in Italy.

Yuri picked up on the other end. "*Privet?*"

She twirled her hair with one hand. "Good news, Yuri. I know you were puzzling on how to get a large group of people undetected to our secret villa in Italy. I have a way to get everyone from the United States back to Italy. And we can even pick up our MI6 friends along the way."

"That is good news, since I was going to have to use coffins again, and Elda would be pissed at that." Yuri laughed at the image of Elda in a pink-lined coffin, sitting up with a submachine gun. "So what do you have?"

"Do you remember the multimillionaire I dated, Lorenzo?"

"Seriously, Snezhana? I can't keep track of your boyfriends."

Snezhana rolled her eyes. "Well, he helped me out before, and now he has a problem. His flight crew got recruited by another millionaire, and his jet is left stranded in DC. So we have a jet!"

Yuri acknowledged her news. "*Khorosho*. How much do we have to pay the crew?"

Snezhana twirled in her chair. "Well, that is a tad tricky. The crew walked off, which is why the jet is stranded in DC."

"*Chto?* Who is going to fly it?" Yuri's voice cracked from the high note of his surprise.

"That's not my problem. You're the logistics guy." Snezhana heard him sigh. "Oh, and, Yuri?"

"*Da?*"

Snezhana could hear the trepidation in his voice. "Tell Elda I will be a tad late in returning to the villa. I need to make a stop in Florence to demonstrate to Lorenzo how grateful I am. Always best to keep him on my good side."

"You have a good side?"

***

The flight crew marched across the tarmac to the white plane that sat poised, shining in the sun. The two of them wore black suits, one with wings, and name tags on the breast pockets and stripes on the arms. Their black leather shoes were well polished and gleaming in the sunlight. Each wore a cover with a gold stripe, but no insignia. They climbed up the stairs of the jet and greeted their flight staff of one.

The four-striped captain went ahead, while the three-striped first officer stopped to chat. "Hello, Olga. Everything set?"

Olga gaped at the uniforms. "Olga want uniform too, Elda."

Elda chuckled and tapped the door of the wardrobe.

"You should find a jacket with your name on it in there."

Olga bounced over to the closet, humming.

Elda strode into the cockpit and took the copilot's seat.

"You know how to fly?" Charlie fiddled with the controls and pop-ups.

Elda shrugged, belying her nerves. "I've picked up a thing here and there. My dad used to take me into the cockpit with him and show me the displays."

"What was that on, a B25 bomber?" Charlie joked.

Elda grimaced. "I also had to take over and land a crippled U-2 when the crew was incapacitated by food poisoning. It's always a waste to jump out of a perfectly good plane."

Charlie chuckled at the old joke.

"And I had an occasion to fly a whirly bird. But I am hoping you have a dab more experience than me." Elda looked at the instrument panel at her side and in front of her. "I heard a rumor that you had your pilot's license, Charlie?"

"Actually no. I did take some lessons, though, and had quite a few rides when overseas."

"Oh, have you flown a Falcon 2000LXS before?"

"No, but a plane is a plane, hey? And this is one of the most advanced man-machine interfaces. It practically flies itself. We're both computer savvy, so it should be easy. Are you a gamer?"

"No, I detest them. A waste of valuable time that could be spent learning something. Like, perhaps, how to fly a plane. The only one I played was *Myst*. Such a civilized game. But I suppose there's no time like the present to become a gamer."

"There are great plane simulation games available. Even one on the Falcon. I did do a few spins on it last night. Plus, I did a lot of searches to find out specs on the plane itself. According to the website, all the checklists are automated and link to a synoptic display system that activates pop-up diagrams of the relevant systems. These two displays stacked vertically in the center of the instrument panel are the inboard multifunction display units."

"Great, so we're flying using Google now?" Elda looked at the T-shaped array of monitors across the dashboard, played with her trackball cursor control device on a joystick between her knees and tightened her harness. "So the MDUs tell us what?"

"They display specifically selected strategic flight information, such as navigational functions, FMS, systems pages, checklists, etcetera."

"It's the etcetera that worries me," Elda quipped.

"And that thing you're playing with between your legs allows you to interact with the controls. The other two displays are dedicated to short-term tactical information. Through these displays we can see all the output from aircraft sensors affecting systems, communications, navigation, and flight management."

Elda clicked around some more. "Ready as I'm going to be."

Charlie's voice came over the speaker. "This is your captain speaking. The seat belt sign is now on. Please ensure your seat belts are buckled. Our cabin crew will be coming around to verify that they are secured."

Elda's voice followed. "This is your copilot speaking. Our flight today will take us from DCA to LHR for a brief stop, refueling, and passenger pickup. We will continue to land at FLR, Florence, for our bus ride to our final destination. Olga, can you please pick up the private line?"

Olga strode over to the interplane phone and picked up the receiver. "Olga here."

Elda's voice came over. "Can you fly a plane?"

"Uh-oh. No, Olga never tried, but do you want me to?" Olga bounced on her toes.

"Ah, that's okay, Olga, not now, but tighten up those seat belts back there." She hung up.

Olga clumped over to Ed, strapped in on the right side of the cabin. She checked his seat belt and that his footrest was down. She secured the small television on his table.

Jim was at the table across the aisle from Ed, nestled into one of the oversized seats with a retractable footrest. "I'm secure, Olger."

Ashok sat sound asleep in his seat, with his head against the window and a neck support holding his head up. Olga slipped a small pillow between his head and the window, tightened his seat belt, and covered his legs with a small blanket.

She examined the galley, to confirm all was stowed, and the bedroom area, to verify the bed was folded up. She did one last walk around the chocolate-and-cream interior, verified all doors were locked, and lifted the phone receiver to call the cockpit.

"All systems go here, Captains."

Elda turned to Charlie. "Ready for final checklist, Captain." Charlie and Elda rapidly ran down the final checks, verifying they were ready for takeoff.

"Fuel check."

"Tanks are full, selector in proper position, boost pumps and mixtures set, auxiliary fuel pump is off."

"Fire check."

"Magnetos and electronic ignition is on, engine at idle, parking brake off."

"Flight controls."

"Instruments and radio operational. Directional gyro good to go. Altimeter set. Flaps and trim set for takeoff. Landing gear position lights working. Flight controls free and correct. All systems ready."

"Passengers."

"All passengers on board and strapped in.

"Doors and windows."

"Locked."

"Taxi lights."

"On."

Charlie looked at Elda, who nodded her head and gave a thumbs-up, adding, "We can do this, Charlie."

Charlie toggled the microphone. "Tower, this is Falcon 209KH. We are ready for takeoff and holding short of runway one for takeoff to LHR."

"Falcon 209KH, you are cleared for takeoff," the tower responded.

"Cleared for takeoff, runway one. Falcon 209KH," Charlie repeated.

Charlie let go the brakes and taxied to the runway. She took off like a rocket.

With her body pressed back against her seat, Elda commented, "Jesus, Charlie. This plane has the same response as a fighter. Can you dial back the Gs?"

"Oh god, we have to land this sucker, hey?" Charlie blotted the sweat on her brow with her handkerchief and looked over at Elda.

Elda gave her two thumbs-up. "We got it up in the air, didn't we?"

Charlie let the breath she had clearly been holding out with a whoosh. She ran her hands down the sides of her face and rubbed her eyes. "Oh yes, that was quite the takeoff, but I think I can do better on the next one."

"I hope so. Let me check in the cabin and ensure everyone is still there. Then why don't you take a break." Elda unbuckled and rose from her seat. She put on her jacket, unlocked the cockpit door, and marched into the cabin.

A white-faced Ed shook his head. "I can't believe you two hijacked this plane."

Elda slapped him on the back. "We didn't hijack it, Ed—we're doing Lorenzo a favor and returning it to him."

"In how many pieces?" Ed asked in a serious tone.

"That remains to be seen." Elda shrugged.

"Can Olga do snacks and drinks now?" Olga tied a bibbed black apron on.

"Go for it, Olga," Elda said. "Everyone relax and watch television or nap. There's a bed in the back. We'll give you plenty of notice before landing. I'm going to hit the head and then let Charlie stretch her legs."

Ed put his head down on his table.

***

"One bounce. Not too shabby, Cap," Elda congratulated Charlie. "We're down in one piece." She smiled to take any sting out of her words.

Charlie shook her head and frowned. "Too much vertical speed. I'll do better in Florence. At least we got the landing gear down." She started scrolling through the downloaded PDF of the Falcon 2000 user manual she had on her iPad.

"Yes, that was helpful," Elda deadpanned.

They followed the tower's instructions and taxied over to refuel. Once topped off, they drove the plane over to their assigned spot to pick up Sophia and Oliver.

Sophia and Oliver, carrying their go bags, marched to the plane. Oliver sported bright orange-and-green-plaid knickers, knee socks with orange, green, and white diamonds on them, black-and-white shoes, a white shirt, and a dark-green vest. On his head perched a flat green tweed cap. He sported a well-trimmed mustache and mirrored sunglasses.

Sophia wore a pink houndstooth golf skirt, topped by a bright-pink long-sleeved polo shirt and crowned with a bright-pink golf visor. Her hair was died a chestnut brown. She had on matching mirrored sunglasses.

Olga lowered the stairs and stood at the top to greet them. She held up her hands to shade her eyes and put on her own pair of mirrored sunglasses. "Olga blinded by you two."

Sophia laughed but sobered up at Olga's question.

"Have you two done your wills recently?"

Chapter Thirty-Nine

Snezhana donned a black wig, a black evening gown, black stiletto heels, and contact lenses that turned her eyes a hickory brown. She swung a long Italian wool coat over her shoulders. She had no need for luggage, since most of her things were at her apartment here in Moscow, and she had enough to get by on at the villa. She left her room and walked down the hotel hallway and knocked on Tosh's door.

Tosh, garbed in a long black suit coat, black slacks, black leather shoes, and a gartel, topped by a flat-brimmed hat perched on his head. His disguise was completed by a short black beard, sidelocks, and thick black-rimmed glasses.

Anatoly stood next to Tosh. The lower part of his face was completely covered by a large, bushy beard that altered the shape of his lips. Prison tats and a skull ring were tattooed on his fingers. His head was shaven to a close black buzz cut, and he wore silver chains around his neck. He wore a Harley-Davidson T-shirt and a studded leather biker jacket. His feet were encased in ten-inch-high harness boots.

Tosh handed Snezhana and Anatoly their paperwork.

"We're flying from Moscow to Milan and taking the train to Florence. The three of us are going to leave the hotel separately, and each is to be responsible for ensuring we are not followed. Do not, under penalty of my wrath, lead anyone to the villa or tell anyone where we are staying."

"*Da, ser.*"

"*Da, dyadya.*"

Tosh pointed at Snezhana. "Be especially careful about what you let slip when you are paying back your rich boy toy. *Vy ponimayete?*"

Snezhana met Tosh eyeball to eyeball. "He is a means to an end. Don't worry. *YA ponimayu.*"

"*Khorosho.* Anatoly, you're first. There's a motorcycle parked in the garage. Here's the slot number and ticket. If you don't crash it, it's yours when you return to Moscow."

Anatoly's eyes lit up. "Excellent!"

Snezhana rolled her eyes and slapped him on the head. "*Sie pazzo.*"

Anatoly laughed at her. "Not that crazy, Snez. Finally, my motorcycle escapades are paying off."

"*Idti,* Anatoly." Tosh threw him the keys to the bike.

Anatoly caught the keys one handed and jogged out the door, closing it behind him.

Tosh looked fondly at Snezhana. "Be careful, *moya ple-myannitsa.*"

"*I will, moy dyadya.*"

"There's a limo arriving for you in ten minutes. Is your room wiped?"

"*Da, dyadya.*"

"Well then, you may wait here with me until they call you."

Snezhana's phone buzzed. She looked at the message. "The car is here."

"*Idti, idti, idti.*" Tosh clapped his hands to spur her on.

She gave him a quick hug and ran out the door.

Tosh closed it, walked around the hotel room, erased any possibility of prints, verified he left nothing behind, and strode out to catch a taxi.

<hr>

The extended team milled about in Elda and Tosh's villa in Tuscany. Ed had recovered from the rocky flight and sipped a cup of coffee. Oliver and Olga prepared snacks in the kitchen. Anatoly cleaned his weapons, which lay carefully organized across the floor. Ashok had positioned his laptop and was typing rapidly. Elda and Sophia updated the charts on the wall. Yuri played with a stray cat on the patio. Tosh stood unmoving, staring out the window.

Elda separated from Sophia and walked to Tosh. "Tosh?"

No answer.

"Tosh?" Elda repeated in a louder tone of voice.

"*Da?*" Tosh shook his head, turned and focused on Elda.

"It's time we finished up this mission."

"*Da.*"

Elda clapped her hands. "Let's get everyone in here for a sitrep and action plan."

"What about Snezhana?"

"She will be here shortly. She can catch up when she arrives."

Oliver and Olga strolled in from the kitchen, with a charcuterie board of salami, prosciutto, pecorino and mozzarella cheeses, sliced Italian bread, kalamata olives, roasted red peppers, basil pesto and garlic, and hot-pepper-infused olive oil in dipping bowls. On another tray lay chocolate biscuits, bombolini and sfogliatella pastry, and a tea and coffee service.

"All right! This is more like it." Anatoly hopped up and seized two pastries. Olga pitched a couple of napkins his way. He fielded them and sat back down on the floor.

Yuri came in through the kitchen and sat next to Anatoly, placing a cat and a small bowl of milk on the floor. Anatoly rolled his eyes.

Still busily typing, Ashok shook his head at the food offerings. "Thank you very kindly, Mister Oliver and Miss Olga, but I need to finish up this list for Miss Elda."

Elda set up a projection screen to one side of the string charts.

Just then Snezhana strolled in wearing a long black evening dress, heels, and a black wig. She kicked off her heels at the door.

"No tails?" Tosh inquired.

"No tails," she answered.

Elda looked at Ashok, who nodded. "It is all ready for you, Miss Elda."

"Thank you, Ashok."

"Okay, gang, we have a list of those we are sure were complicit in Operation Bittman."

The team each leaned forward.

"First, we have a list of the mercenaries that were hired. This is only a partial list. We know there are many more. If we can capture at least one of these men, we may obtain leads to others." Elda brought up pictures, names, and locations, displaying one at a time on the projected screen.

"Then we have a few that are associated with the CIA." She displayed those. "The FBI . . ." Again she projected the images and data.

She continued listing the agencies and displaying the results. "And the Secret Service, MI6, and Congress."

"Do we kill them all?" Anatoly stroked his MP-412 REX .357 Magnum revolver.

Elda and Tosh spoke as one. "No."

"I *do*," Tosh added, "want to eliminate the mercenaries who blew up our last villa."

Oliver chimed in with, "Perhaps we can also kill the bastards that shot me up in Montreal?"

Anatoly spoke up. "Angelina Rodin, the assassin who attacked you and Tosh, has been taken care of."

Elda raised her eyebrows. Anatoly shrugged and went back to cleaning his weapons.

Elda walked over to the white board and wrote, ACTION PLAN.

Anatoly groaned.

Elda scowled at him. "Here's what I propose. The Secret Service one is easy. I have Tom as a contact there, and he is totally trustworthy. We turn the evidence over to him and let him take it from there. Agree?"

A mumbling of "*das*" and "yes" and a "Bob's your uncle" floated up to her.

"Definitely, Elda," Tosh agreed. "We don't want to be caught taking out a Secret Service agent."

"I know a lot of the players in the FBI," Charlie said, "and a few that I trust. Let me reach out and identify the right one to give this information to. The FBI can clean up their own house."

Elda nodded. "CIA?" She looked at Ed.

"Don't worry. I can get the right person from the CIA on these assets. They'll be as dead as if we handled it ourselves," Ed responded.

Elda wrote the assigned names and mole categorizations on the whiteboard: ELDA—SS→TOM; CHARLIE—CIA; ED—FBI

"Now we have Congress . . ." she noted.

"Give that one to me too." Ed tapped his chest.

She modified Ed's list to read: ED—FBI, CONGRESS.

"That leaves the mercenaries." Elda turned to the group for input.

"Even though we've only identified a small subset of all who attacked us, there's a lot of players on the list Ashok gave us," Tosh said. "I vote for all of us working together to take them out."

Elda looked at him in surprise. "You vote now and not order?"

"It has to be a volunteer mission. Whoever feels they have skin in the game of vengeance should step forward. The rest can support us from here and various other locations. The mercenaries on that list are a diverse lot, located in many different places."

Anatoly bounded up. Sophia and Oliver stood. Elda stayed on her feet. Tosh rose to stand by her. Snezhana wandered to be by their side. Yuri joined them.

Charlie cleared her throat. "Although I don't have skin in the game for vengeance, I would like to be in on this."

Ed jumped into the conversation. "As much as I also would like vengeance for Operation Bittman and the harm they did to us, I can't sanction this campaign. Elda's dead, but you, Charlie, are an active agent working for me. I can't let you be in the field on this one."

Elda turned to Ed. "Do you think Charlie needs additional training? Could you somehow spin this as an observing role where she sits out unless she's attacked?"

"I'll consider that angle," Ed responded.

"Consider it quickly," Elda said.

Ed lifted an eyebrow.

She smiled and put her hands out palms up. "Just mirroring my handler."

***

"One, two, three . . ."

Sweat rolled off the end of Elda's nose into the dirt below. She was glad Olga was helping her whip the team into shape, even though it reminded her that she was still out of shape from her self-imposed vacation in Italy. She looked over at Tosh and saw he was also struggling. *Good job, Olga, we need this.*

Jim stood guard while the outfit, led by Olga, did push-ups in the backyard.

". . . sixteen, seventeen, eighteen, nineteen, twenty."

"Up, up, quick." Olga bounded up.

The group obeyed. Elda winced as the group struggled to their feet. They needed to be a team that moves as one.

"Time for Olga's favorite exercise. What is it?"

"Squats." A chorus of groans combined with the answer.

"That's right, sqvats!"

They had already started.

"And what exercise do we love to do?" Olga shouted on the tenth squat.

"Bear crawls," Elda yelled back.

Anatoly growled loudly, and the flock hit the ground for bear crawls.

"Up, up, up, quickly now!" Olga directed.

Everyone sprang up. Elda noted that already the team was quicker in responding.

"What you doing up? Get back down and do mountain climbers!" Olga knelt and touched her fingertips to the ground.

Yuri groaned.

"What's that groan, winky man? Olga make you do two more." After thirty seconds, Olga again ordered, "Up, up, up!"

The group stood, covered in dust, panting and sweating.

Olga grinned and gave them all a thumbs-up. "Good job. Now we can eat!"

Anatoly grabbed a bombolini and a sfogliatella pastry, holding one in each hand. Olga positioned two biscuits on her saucer. The others helped themselves to the charcuterie board. While they chewed and slurped hot beverages, Tosh took over the whiteboard. He erased it and wrote, KREMLIN CONTROLLERS: ALEXEI —DEAD; ADRIK—DEAD.

"Are we sure that's all? What about the people who trained the attack squads?" Elda questioned.

Tosh shook his head. "We'll never be able to determine that. It's enough that we got those who ordered the training." He continued to write. FINANCING: KEVIN BALL— DEAD

Elda interrupted again, "Do we have *any* idea where the money originated from?"

Ashok spoke. "It was laundered through so many channels, it would take forever, if we could find it at all."

Tosh raised an eyebrow and glared at Elda, who bowed and motioned for him to continue. He wrote, OLIVER'S MONTREAL ATTACK: MAN CHASING OLIVER—DEAD; MACHINE GUN SHOOTERS? ONE IDENTIFIED. STILL NEAR MONTREAL.

Elda raised her hand.

Tosh groaned. "Yes, Elda."

"How about if we assign and plan each one as you list it?"

Tosh nodded. "*Da*. Good idea. I propose we use Anatoly to dispense with this man. He lives in a remote territory, so he can be killed and it would take days for the body to be discovered, if done on a Friday after work."

"I would like to question him and see if we can determine the identities of any of the others," Elda argued.

"*Net*," Tosh said. "Remember when we tried to capture some, and all of those we did had suicide capsules under their molars?"

"I'm not pulling teeth again." Anatoly pounded his fist on his thigh.

Elda gave in and signaled her approval with a thumb-up. Charlie fidgeted. Elda turned to Charlie. "If we get to a point where you are required, or can observe, without complicating the operation, I'll push that agenda with Ed."

Tosh jotted, St Petersburg attack: Attacker dead; Tuscany villa attack: Hit squad? One co-conspirator identified in police cover-up. Lives near Montepulciano.

"That's convenient," Elda stated. "I propose Snezhana handle this one. He's unmarried and unattached. With her charms, she can most likely get close to the man. I would doubt that he has a suicide pill, so she might be able to tease intelligence from him."

Snezhana smiled and looked to her uncle for final approval.

"*Da.* Good choice, Elda."

Charlie frowned.

Elda turned to her. "I don't want you or any of my team working in Tuscany. I am trying to preserve it as a safe space."

Tosh continued to work his way through the events and players from Operation Bittman.

Seattle attack and David's death: Suicide bomber—dead

NYC attack: Attackers—dead; Coconspirators?—Man at desk identified. Lives in NYC.

Ed spoke up. "Although I will vow I never heard of this man, this would be on US soil. I propose we have a United States citizen do it."

"Yes, definitely. Ed and I will chat on this later," Elda said.

Tosh went on. Tosh attack in Moscow: Attackers—dead

MI6 Traitors: James, Arabella, Henry—All dead

Newburyport attack: Angelina Rodin—dead; Train Station—One killed and One on the run.

"Clearly United States again, so it's over to you folks," Tosh said.

Chapter Forty

"**P**LEASE, PLEASE, PLEASE, I NEED THE EXPERIENCE of stealth-mode work. I can handle myself in a war, but this job is different. And you know, Ed, I'll be safe with Elda."

Elda chimed in. "Same black-ops rules as always, Ed. No identification. Fingerprints not in any database. Clothing non-US and generic. Same for weapons. And you'll have full deniability of any knowledge, should by some freak chance anything be traced back to you."

Silence.

"Charlie will be on vacation," Elda added. "We'll give you a full itinerary and plane tickets for her trip to Hawaii."

Ed held up his hands. "I know nothing. I will deny any involvement. As far as I know, you are dead, Elda, and you are on vacation, Charlie." He turned to Ashok. "Are you ready to go back to DC?" He then addressed the room. "I was never here."

"Thanks, Ed," Charlie said.

"For what?" Ed eyed Charlie, who mumbled, "Oops."

Elda took Ed's arm. "Let me help you with your disguise." She motioned to Ashok. "You too." She dragged them both into one of the bedrooms.

A short time after, a scruffy-looking workman appeared. He had a few days beard growth, pockmarked skin, and a hooked nose. A disgruntled looking Indian woman in a sari accompanied him.

"Miss Elda, ma'am. Why do I have to be the woman?" Ashok groused.

"Ed's too tall to pull it off. Plus, his voice is far too low. You can reach the higher pitch if you need to."

Ashok pouted.

"Relax, Ashok. It's only for a short time."

Tosh walked over and shook Ashok's and Ed's hands. "We will probably not meet again. Safe travels."

"Eldah?"

Jim had been sitting quietly, chatting with Charlie by the fire. He stood and limped over to Elda.

Elda looked at Jim with warmth and concern. "Yes, Jim."

"Ah think Ah'm done here, right?"

"I would say so, Jim. I am very thankful for all your help. Can you do me one more favor, though?"

"Sure. What is it?"

Elda motioned for Jim to follow her into the yard. Once there she leaned in close to him and whispered, "Can you take Vee back home with you?"

"Be glad to." Jim frowned. "What was all that about Yuri taking her though?"

Elda looked around to ensure they couldn't be overheard. "That was just a way to get everyone here, providing I was alive still. It served its purpose. But now it's time you and Vee got settled in back north again."

They stood silently side by side. The warm Tuscan breeze wafted by. Elda realized how much she would miss this place and the break she'd had while here, but she also knew it was time to return to her life again.

"What . . ." Jim stopped, then restarted. "What if you don't return this time?" His face knotted in worry.

Elda put a hand on his arm to comfort him. "Don't worry. I plan on returning. But in case I don't, she'll be in good hands. Plus, I've stipulated in my real will that you'll have enough money to take care of her."

"I'll open the house for you and get things ready for your homecoming," Jim declared.

"I appreciate that." Elda shook his hand. "Remember, no word of where you're going to anyone here."

"No worries, Eldah. My lips are sealed. I'll gathah Vee's belongings and head ovah to the other villa for mine."

They walked in together. Jim went into Elda's room to pack up Vee's stuff.

Tosh stared steadily at Elda. She strode over to him. "It's time for Jim to leave the group. We don't have use for him in our next round of operations. And I want him to take care of Vee for me, since I'm heading out again."

Tosh agreed. "It does appear as if it's time to weed out the nonoperatives. What about Olga?" He cocked his head in the direction of the thumping and clanging in the kitchen.

"I'd like for her to be here to close up shop."

***

"You're bleeding."

Yuri ran into the villa with a yowling cat carrier. Bloody scratches covered his hands. He looked at where Olga pointed. "Poor *Koshka* didn't like being shoved into a box."

Charlie inspected his hands. "You'll need antibiotic cream. Cat scratches are dirty things."

Olga ran for the first-aid kit.

While Olga applied ointment and Band-Aids to his cuts, Yuri addressed Tosh. "I would like to go back home. You don't need me here in Italy for the remainder of this mission. I can help you with any logistics from my office."

"*Da*, Yuri. It's time for you to go home."

"Thanks, Tosh." Yuri patted the cat carrier. "I'm anxious for Kosha to meet Katya and settle in. I'll go gather my things from the other villa and catch a ride to the airport with Jim."

Tosh motioned Yuri over to him. He typed in notes on his phone. Try to find out where JIM IS GOING. Yuri nodded.

Elda observed the two of them from the other side of the room. She ambled to Yuri, and he hugged her. "Good-bye, Yuri. I have enjoyed working with you again. Good luck with your new cat."

On cue, a hiss and howl came from the crate. Elda and Yuri laughed.

"Olga, I'm leaving," Yuri called into the kitchen, where Olga was cooking.

Olga stomped out. "You are a good man, Yuri. Take care of Koshka." She opened the crate, picked up the now docile cat, who purred loudly, gave it a scrunch pat, and pushed it back into the crate.

"Is she a cat whisperer too?" Tosh asked.

"Apparently so," Elda said.

Yuri gave Olga a bear hug. She shook him off. "Touchy feely. Ugh." As she turned, she wiped her eyes and stamped back into the kitchen.

Jim headed out the door with Vee on lead, and carrying her toys and dog bed. Yuri yelled to him, "Hold on there, Jim. I'll ride to the villa and to the airport with you."

"Ayuh," Jim acknowledged.

Chapter Forty-One

"THANK YOU, MY GOOD MAN."** Anatoly pocketed his passport and went to the baggage claim in Montreal-Pierre Elliot Trudeau International Airport to retrieve his clubs. He was dressed in bright-red, dark-blue, and stark-white diamond-patterned golfing pants and a colorful neon Hreski golf shirt. He had a well-trimmed black mustache, black hair, and umber eyes. He wore a Union Jack British flat golf cap. He had decided Oliver's golf outfit was a great example of how to hide in plain sight and had created his own garish version.

He'd flown one hour and fifteen minutes via air Lufthansa from Amerigo Vespucci Airport in Florence to Munich International Airport in Germany, with a one-hour-and-fifty-five-minute layover. And then from MUC to YUL, an eight-hour-and-fifty-five-minute flight. During the flights, he'd read through the background on the assassin and caught a good six hours sleep. He was ready to roll.

Anatoly learned the man he hunted was originally from Korea but was now a Canadian citizen living outside of Montebello, Canada, a town of over one thousand year-round residents. Kenauk Nature, one of North America's oldest and largest private fish and game reserves, was nearby, so when not working, the killer could enjoy his favorite activities of mountain biking, kayaking, golfing, and hunting. From the photos, Anatoly could see the man worked out.

Anatoly marched over to the car rental place to obtain a vehicle for the approximate ninety-minute drive to Montebello. Yuri had reserved a room at the Fairmont le Château Montebello.

Anatoly made one scheduled stop along the way. On the seat next to him lay a small case enclosing a disassembled sniper rifle. Anatoly wasn't sure how the contact Elda set him up with obtained this Swiss-made rifle, but he itched to put it together and try it out. He deliberated how he could smuggle it out of the country and back home with him. He'd text Yuri and see if he had any contacts who could help with that.

Pulling in front of the hotel, Anatoly gave his keys to the valet, shouldered his clubs, and lifted his satchel of toys and to-go bag. He marched into the lobby and up to the clerk.

"Good day, my man. Storm Chadwick checking in. I believe you have an open-ended reservation for me?"

The clerk typed on his keyboard. "Oh yes, Mr. Chadwick. We have a lovely room for you. Will it be just yourself checking in?"

Anatoly gave the man an engaging smile. "Just me, my good man. I am here on a short vacation, and also want to scope out the neighborhood for a possible hunting trip with my mates. And I can't pass up playing a round or two of golf while I'm here, can I?"

"Please do enjoy your stay, Mr. Chadwick. Your room is on the top floor, with a great view. Let us know if you need anything."

"Brill. Ta." Anatoly slung his bags over his shoulders and headed off, impatient to play with his acquisition. He jogged up the stairs. Once in his room, he sat on the edge of his double bed, laying out the parts of his new toy. At less than ten pounds empty, it was featherweight. Within minutes he assembled the pieces of his B&T SPR300 PRO Integrally Suppressed Bolt Action Pistol. He snapped on the folding stock, a ten-round magazine filled with sub-sonic ammo, a brass catcher, and a Zeiss LRP S3 6-36 scope. He modified the pistol grip with the modules, to best fit his hand size.

He stroked the assembled weapon. *Ah, my black beauty. We will have to give you some action.*

―――――――

"Cheerio!" The brightly dressed Anatoly waved at the clerk at the desk. Carrying his clubs, he strode out to his black 2022 Ford Mustang. He threw his clubs in the back-seat and peeled out.

He drove into town and parked by the side of the road. Anatoly had read in the assassin's file that he stayed mainly in his house but did drive into town once a week for grocery shopping at the Marché Bonichoix–Gestion R & B Cou-ture, cheese at the Fromagerie de Montebello, and a brew at the Bresseurs de Montebello microbrewery. Today was his shopping day. Anatoly expected the man would settle in back home after his morning out on the town. Soon he spotted the assassin in his white 2020 Nissan 370Z. The man *was* a creature of habit.

Anatoly put the Mustang in gear and followed the man, stopping both behind and ahead of him at the various des-tinations. Suddenly the man deviated from the routine on file, and instead of turning into the lot for Marché Bonichoix, he continued east on Route 148, heading out of town. He picked up speed and swung a sharp left into the lot for Mécanique 725. Now facing in the opposite direction from Anatoly, the assassin rolled down his window.

Der'mo! He was made. Anatoly spotted the barrel of a CZ-75 semiautomatic pistol just as his driver's-side window shattered into pieces. The Mustang dug up clumps of dirt as it fishtailed off the road. Anatoly kept his head down and steered the car from memory while stomping hard on the gas pedal. He needed to evade this man and ditch the loaner.

Anatoly swerved left onto Côte Ezilda. He calculated the Mustang could outrun the Nissan on a straight road. The distance between the two cars grew greater as Anatoly pushed his automobile to its limits. He steered left onto Route 50 and hooked another left, speeding down Mount Mjr, swinging right on Rue Henri Bourassa, an immediate left onto Rue Roupe, left on Rue Laval, right onto Rue St. François Xavier, then a sharp left into a driveway near the end of the street, where waited, scanning Route 148 for the Nissan. He was breathing hard and willed his respiration to slow down. He was being chased by a seasoned professional and not one of the dolts he had been used to handling lately. Anatoly's time as a private eye had not enhanced his skills.

He placed his MP-412 REX .357 Magnum revolver by his side. His new toy, the B&T SPR300 PRO Integrally Suppressed Bolt Action Pistol, was not assembled, and he didn't want to take his eyes off the road long enough to put it together. The sharp turns through that small neighborhood should have lost his tail, but he was more of the mindset that the Nissan would have headed directly to Route 148 and turned right, back the way it came. His read of the assassin was that he was egotistical and sure of himself and therefore would still be wary but would think that he had scared off the Mustang's driver.

Anatoly heard the roar of the Nissan coming from the east on Route 148. He spotted it as it sped by Rue St. François Xavier back into town. The driver did not glance up Anatoly's street. Even if he had, Anatoly was far enough back in the driveway to make it difficult to identify his car. Anatoly wiped his hand across his face and noticed it was bloody. He had supplies in the truck he had stashed and would fix that later.

Anatoly waited a few minutes, then turned left, away from town on Route 148 and then right into the Marina Municipale. He parked his car next to a white panel truck with MICHELS stenciled on the doors. He slipped into the front seat and grabbed a first-aid kit from the glove compartment. He picked a shard of glass out of his cheek and applied a bandage to keep the blood from dripping on his clothing. He took a thick pair of gloves out of the toolkit in the backseat and bashed out the remaining glass from the driver's-side window of the Mustang. He picked up the pieces of the glass and put them into a small bag and deposited it in the truck.

He climbed into the enclosed back of the truck, where he changed into a yellow shirt, red hard hat, and gray work pants. Taking care to not drive the pickup fast enough to alert a cop, he sedately motored back onto Rue Notre Dame, Route 148. He caught sight of the assassin pulling into the parking lot for Marché Bonichoix. That fit the guy's MO perfectly. He would finish his rounds and go home.

At the intersection of Routes 323 and 148, Anatoly maneuvered the pickup to the side of the road, and waited for the Nissan to drive by. Once out of sight, Anatoly headed north on Route 323, then left on Chem. Des Golfeurs. He parked, pulled bright golfing clothes on over his dark-green-and-black camouflaged getup, and heaved his bag of clubs over his shoulder. He strode confidently over the course to the fifteenth hole, where he disappeared into the thick forest of trees, where he separated his weapon kit attached to the clubs, removed the golfer's uniform, and shoved it and the clubs well out of sight. Now blending with the scenery, he snuck through the dense grove until he was in line of sight of the target's house.

Carrying his sniper rifle, Anatoly scrambled up a tree to assess the situation. The house was hidden, nestled in the woods near the golf course. In the front of the house was a pool and a concrete patio, with a red grill shining in the late-day sun. Anatoly used his scope to scan the area. The house had obvious alarms on all windows and doors, and the mowed region around the house was encircled by a short fence about a foot inside the perimeter. Anatoly calculated that was probably a pressure-sensitive spot that triggered an alarm, if there was pressure on the outside of the fence, followed by pressure on the inside. He also figured these systems did not wire into the police or any external agency, as an assassin would take care of intruders himself.

He could paralyze the man and drown him in his pool to make it all look like an accident, but that would require getting past the security systems. If he killed the man first, Anatoly could search his house at his leisure. Plus, he couldn't afford to let the man get a second glance at his face and be on the alert.

He patted the case next to him. *Well, my black beauty, I did promise you some action, and at this distance, you will do wonderfully.* The light was waning. Anatoly checked the wind direction and speed and sighted on the grill. He hunkered down in the tree. He saw his target in the kitchen, putting away groceries. He estimated the man would be done in under five minutes. He waited for a clear line of sight for the kill.

Four minutes and thirty seconds later, the patio door swung open and the man stepped out to fire up the grill.

Anatoly reviewed the wind and range. The man pivoted and jogged inside, shutting the door behind him.

Does he suspect I'm here?

The door flew open, and the man sauntered to the now hot grill and tossed on a thick steak. Anatoly lined up his shot. The man turned and scanned the tree line. Pop. The muffled sound of the suppressed round echoed loudly for Anatoly. The man dropped with a hole perfectly centered in his forehead.

Anatoly patted his weapon. *Well done, girl.* He dropped down out of the tree, slipped on a pair of gloves, and pulled covers over his shoes. Carrying his weapon in front of him, he padded to the body. The man was dead.

Anatoly opened the grill and turned the steak. He entered the house and performed a quick search. He took the hard drive from the security system and from the computer. He located a small safe behind a framed artwork and placed a small amount of explosive on the dial, to blow it open. He drew out the papers and stacks of money. He took the man's cell phone and wallet. Satisfied he had enough to sort through, and also to throw suspicion that this was a robbery, he checked each room and retreated to the patio. There, he stabbed the steak with his switchblade, wrapped it in a piece of foil he'd liberated from the kitchen, and turned off the grill. "*Proveryat', khorosho, ochistite.*" He cleared each area.

Anatoly tiptoed back to his tree and ensured he'd leave no trace of a human having been there, repeating to himself, *Proveryat', khorosho, ochistite.* He maneuvered between the trees to his golf bag and stored the SPR300 and steak in it. Switching into his golfing getup, he shouldered his possessions and walked back to the golf clubs, then his truck.

While driving, he unwrapped the steak with one hand, spread out the foil on his lap to catch the juices, and tore off a chunk with his teeth. He licked the bloody juice off his lips. Perfectly done.

At the hotel, he popped up to his room and made sure it was sterilized. "*Proveryat', khorosho, ochistite,*" he confirmed as he scanned each part. Still in his golfing clothes, he ran down the stairs to the front desk.

"There you are, my good man," he told the clerk. "Unfortunately, I must end my vacation and return to work, but I will be back with friends. Your establishment is just crackin'."

The clerk brightened. "We must give you something for your trip." He picked up the phone. As soon as Anatoly finished turning in his key and taking his receipt, a waiter ran up with a paper bag with two maple and cheese-stuffed doughnuts, from the in-house restaurant, Aux Chantignoles.

Anatoly grinned from ear to ear. "I'm *chuffed.* These are my favorites. Thank you." He slung the luggage strap over his shoulder. "Ta-ta."

It was a good mission.

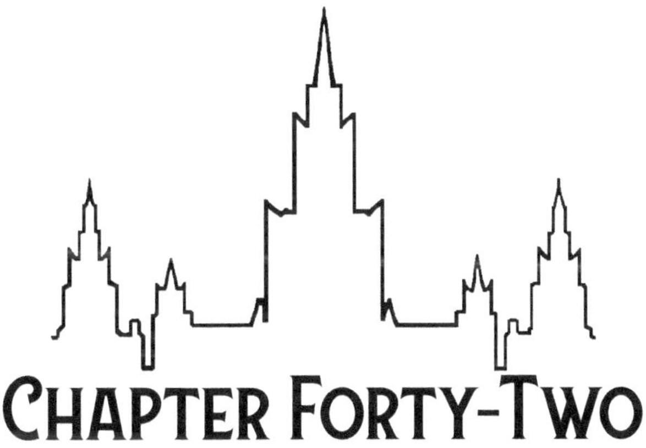

CHAPTER FORTY-TWO

THE TOURISTS AND LOCALS PASSED by the lone woman standing in the middle of the sidewalk. "I can't believe this happened to me." Snezhana stood crying outside the Banca TEMA.

A stout older Italian woman, wearing a flowered button-down dress, pearls, and a gray cardigan, put her hand on Snezhana's arm and asked, "*Cosa c'è che non va, caro?*"

"My money. *I miei soldi.* Gone. *Mi hanno rubato i soldi.* Stolen," Snezhana replied between sobs.

The woman took her arm and led her down the street. "*Polizia. Vai alla polizia.*" She stopped near a nondescript reddish-yellow brick building and pointed at a sign: *POLIZIA STRADALE.*

Snezhana gratefully hugged the woman. "*Gracia mille, signora.*" She dried her tears and walked up the stairs to the door, knocked, and entered the station. Snezhana had been monitoring the station for a few days now and knew that, at this time, only the dispatcher and the captain would be in.

The captain stood as Snezhana entered. He straightened and buttoned his jacket, wiping away the remaining crumbs from his lunch. Snezhana sashayed in, wearing a formfitting black dress hemmed at midthigh and a pair of two-inch black leather heels. She had a gold bracelet clasped on one wrist and gold earrings with tiny diamonds dangling from her ears. Her hands were ring-free.

"*Oh, Capitano, mi hanno rubato i soldi.*" She showed him her empty purse and stifled a sob, delicately patting her nose with a hanky.

"There, there, please sit down. Tell me what happened." The captain patted a chair next to him.

Snezhana sat. She looked up at him with large watery eyes. "I don't quite know. I was in a crowd of tourists and had lost my bearings. When I got on my own again, I wanted to buy a cute hat in one of the stores, and that's when I noticed my cash was gone."

"Do you have other money?" he asked with concern.

Snezhana put her hand to her chest, accentuating her cleavage. "I have my bank card, which is safely hidden, but I was on a budget for this small vacation and had been so looking forward to going out to dinner tonight. Now I must carefully watch what I spend."

"My apologies for the distress you have been through. We will probably never find your money, however. There are bands of roving gypsies who are experts at pickpocketing. They surround their victim and distract them, and by the time it is discovered, they and the valuables are long gone. Where are you from?"

"I am from Rome. It is an amazing city, but Tuscany is so beautiful. I come here to relax. And now this." She looked at him with sad, teary eyes. Her bottom lip quivered.

He patted her arm. "Perhaps I can offer you some solace by taking you to dinner tonight? Where were you planning on going?"

"*Il ristorante Le Logge del Vignola*." She looked up to the ceiling and held her arms wide to illustrate the wonder of that place.

He looked at her chest. "Ah yes, an excellent choice. Please do allow me to treat you to a meal there. You won't regret it."

She looked up at the cop from under her long black lashes. "*Certamente. Con piacere.*"

"The pleasure is *all* mine, my dear."

The restaurant boasted an intimate setting, with candlelit tables, warm beige and brown décor, and efficient staff. The captain was an engaging conversationalist.

"What was the most amazing exploit you ever led?" Snezhana asked as the alcohol flowed.

"There have been so many, my dear." He puffed his chest out and fingered his brass buttons.

Snezhana swooned. "I can only imagine. I would think that men would look up to you and ask you to hold their secrets."

"Not only men, but governments."

"How magnificent. Italy should be proud to have you," she gushed.

"Italy and Russia too." He winked.

"Amazing." She patted her chest and fanned her cheeks. "Do tell more."

"Let me say that no one ever found the bodies or suspected that foreign agents were involved when a villa blew."

"Fascinating . . ." Snezhana gazed, through hooded eyes, at the captain, with her lips slightly apart. She ran her tongue over her bottom lip. She leaned forward, intent on his answers. "And you made sure those secrets were kept.

Did you capture the bad people in the villa?"

The captain smirked. "Whoever was there was of no consequence. My contacts paid handsomely for me to help them. I have enough for many dinners, my dear."

Snezhana buttered him up. "You are amazing." Inside she fumed at the man who enabled the mercenaries to go after her and her coworkers.

The captain leaned in to whisper, "What next, *mia bella*?" The captain wobbled as he stood and held out his arm to Snezhana. "Perhaps I can interest you in a nightcap?"

Snezhana smiled at her capitano. The candle in the center of the table had burned low. The remnants of the strawberries flambé, white chocolate, mascarpone, hibiscus, and vanilla dessert lay on a shared plate between them. The wine bottle was empty, and the bill had been paid. The *cameriere* showed signs of impatience as he hovered near the table.

Snezhana fluttered her eyelashes at the captain. "Clearly this absolutely delicious meal has run its course. I'm having such a wonderful time, however, and I'm reluctant to say good night."

The captain wobbled as he stood and held out his arm to Snezhana. "Perhaps I can interest you in a nightcap?"

"That would be lovely." She took his arm and leaned into him as they strolled to his house. Once there, she excused herself to go to the bathroom while he mixed drinks. She peeked into his bedroom and caught sight of fur-lined cuffs attached to his bedposts. A small whip stuck out from under the bed. *Time to get the upper hand on this one.* She searched his medicine cabinet and noticed prescription heart medication. She flushed the toilet and returned to meet him in the kitchen.

"Let me help you with that." She took the vodka bottle from his hand and applied generous splashes to two glasses he had lined up. She added a spot of cranberry and a small pour of orange juice. She handed it to him. "To the sunrise."

He kissed her, and his hand ran down her back and clamped on her butt as he pulled her close to him. She could feel his erection starting. "Oh, *Capitano*, would you like to go into the bedroom, and I will clean this up and meet you there?"

"*Si, la mia Bellissima donna.*" He leered at her and staggered off in that direction.

Snezhana hunted through the drawers and came up with tape, a clear plastic three-gallon garbage bag, and a handheld vacuum sealer. She treaded into the bedroom to find him naked and strapped into the handcuffs. She held up the bag. "Shall we play?" As she suspected, his erection grew. She unbuttoned her blouse to her bra and bent to secure his feet. She could hear his ragged breath. She sashayed to the head of the bed and checked his cuffs were secure, pulled the bag over his head, secured it to his neck on both sides, and started sucking the air out with the portable device. He breathed in more rapidly in his body's automatic attempt to get more air. He sucked the plastic into his mouth, further inhibiting his airway. His feet drummed on the bed. He thrashed, and his eyes bulged. Snezhana waited until he became still, returned to the kitchen, and put away the vacuum sealer and cleaned any trace of her prints from the kitchen, bathroom, and bedroom.

After twenty minutes she put on plastic gloves and felt for his pulse.

Nothing.

Chapter Forty-Three

"**O**LGA, WHERE'S TOSH?" ELDA YELLED. She wandered into the kitchen and spied Olga pounding dough on the table. The thumping reverberated through the wooden planks. "We usually go jogging at this time."

Olga picked up the dough and slammed it back down, folded it, and pummeled it with her fists. "Winky man left a half hour ago. He was dressed in his running shoes."

"And something else too, I hope," Elda quipped.

Thwack went the dough.

"Ah, there you are. I was just heading out," Elda announced to Tosh, who jogged up the driveway. Tosh looked down at his feet and started to pass Elda. She put out her arm and stopped him. "I get it, Tosh."

He nodded.

"But tell me, what did you do to piss Olga off?"

He looked around. "Is she still angry? Perhaps I better stay out here for a while."

"Yes, perhaps you better . . . What did you say?"

Tosh knitted his eyebrows together. "I would think she'd be flattered, not mad. I asked her if she would join my team."

"And her response was . . ."

"I think it went something along the lines of, 'Have you no ethics, winky man? To try and recruit Olga, a friend of Elda's, right here in gools? And you definitely don't know Olga at all. You think Olga would want to work for anyone, never mind Russia?! Do you use your brain?' And then she slapped me on the side of my head. It still smarts." Tosh rubbed the side of his head.

Elda's let her eyes spit fire. "You know, Tosh, she's right. If I didn't think I might hasten your onsetting dementia, I'd slap you on the other side of the head."

Tosh hung his head. "I know. I know. I'm sorry, Elda. I just didn't think I'd see her again."

"You're leaving soon, aren't you?" Elda's eyes watered.

"*Da*." He turned, obviously so Elda couldn't see his face.

"There's a bench over there. Sit. I'll bring you some water and tell you when it's safe to come in." Elda took a deep breath and marched into the villa.

***

"Tosh, we have a message from Snezhana and another from Anatoly," Elda called out the window to Tosh, still hiding outside. She reminded herself not to tease him when he returned. She recognized that the male ego could get easily wounded and Tosh was no exception.

"Is it safe to come in yet?" he yelled back.

The sounds of pots and pans clanking ceased, and Olga was now humming in the kitchen.

"Yes." From Elda's experience, Olga didn't stay mad long, nor did she hold grudges. She just had a strong sense of what was right and what was wrong.

Tosh cracked opened the front door and peeked in.

They really didn't have time for this today. *Man up, Tosh.* Elda impatiently waved him on. "Come in, winky man." Oops. There she went, teasing him. Mentally she kicked herself. It was okay when it was just the two of them, but she didn't know how Tosh would take it when there was a third person involved.

He squared his shoulders and jogged over to where Elda sat. "What's the status?"

Elda smiled. Olga was amazing. Tosh feared no man but was cowed by this woman. Olga had that effect on her too. If Olga said to jump, Elda would answer, "How high?" Tosh would never admit it, but he needed reassurance and a way to handle this woman.

"Don't worry, Tosh. Just apologize to Olga and everything will be okay."

"Harrumph."

Despite his verbal rejection of her suggestion, Elda could see Tosh had heard her and was thinking on it. Time to get him focused on their operatives. Elda showed him her screen. "It looks like Snezhana verified the captain worked for the Russians and covered up their attack during Operation Bittman. He is still in their pockets and had no qualms about who was being taken out that day. Snezhana terminated him, making it look like a sex-play accident. That should cause the department to bury that incident without hesitation."

Tosh leaned over and read Snezhana's report. "Well done, Snezhana."

Elda popped up a window with Anatoly's report. "Anatoly was a bit more obvious. He made it look like a hit to deliver a message to whoever still worked with the Canadian, but also covered it up as a robbery for the local police. He obtained a lot of material, which he scanned in and then destroyed. I have Ashok and Stas looking through it."

Tosh raised an eyebrow. "Both?"

Elda shrugged. "I figured we'd share the treasure trove." She hoped to send Tosh the message that they were still working together. For now.

"*Spasibo*, Elda."

Good, he got it. They were still in sync.

To acknowledge that these were Tosh's assets, Elda asked, "Where do we tell them to go next, Tosh?" Elda swiveled her chair and cocked her head.

"Moscow. I will bring back their things from the other villa."

It was a sunny day, and the smell of rosemary and thyme drifted through the dry Tuscan air. Tosh stood with a pair of motorcycle saddlebags slung over his shoulder. He dressed in jeans, chaps, a black leather studded jacket, a red-checkered kerchief tied in the back around his head, Harley boots, and a black T-shirt with a skull-and-crossbones design on it. Charlie had bid him adieu and gone to the other villa to pack for her missions with Elda.

Tosh shifted from foot to foot as he spoke. "Yuri arranged transport for me from the Florence airport. He's also arranged for Anatoly's weapons to be shipped back to him from Canada and also from here. And Olga agreed to mail the nonlethal goods to them. She also said she's going to shut down and sell the second villa."

Elda chewed her bottom lip. "Yes, Olga bought it in the first place, so it's hers to dispose of."

Tosh scratched the back of his neck. "Oh, Snezhana and Anatoly said to thank you for teaching them so much about disguises while they were here. Having Stas change the biometrics in the travel databases was an important addition too."

Elda looked past Tosh and then at the ground. She sighed. "I'm sure I'll regret that in the future, but please do tell them that they are welcome."

Tosh started to speak, stopped, and started again. "Thank you, Elda, for what you did here. You are a formidable opponent, but a better friend. I'm sorry we have to return to our old roles."

"Me too, Tosh. I will miss you," Elda confessed.

"And I you, Elda." He hugged her.

Elda stepped back, removed her jacket, and searched it where he had touched it. She held up a microtransmitter. "Touché, Tosh. Well done."

Tosh winked at her.

Olga came out with a foil-wrapped package and delivered it to Tosh. "Here you go, winky man. You need to put meat on your bones."

He held it in one hand and probed the package with the other. "What is it?"

"Secret family recipe for pecan-blueberry roll-ups. You will like," Olga said.

"I'm sure I will. Thank you, Olga." He placed the package in his saddlebag.

Olga shook her finger at Tosh. "Don't kill Elda, Tosh."

"I can't promise that, Olga, but I hope I never have to."

"If you ever do, you will answer to me, winky man." Olga snarled and stomped back into the villa.

Tosh hopped onto the Ducati Scrambler Nextgen Nightshift motorcycle and roared away.

Elda watched until she could no longer see his dust.

"So Olga will take care of things here. You two have work to do." Olga wiped her hands on her bib apron and then ripped it off over her head. She cleared the flour off one boot by wiping it on the back of her pant leg.

Charlie returned from the other villa, with her packed bag. "I gave the place a once-over, to make sure everything was clean and cleared out, Olga."

"You are good person, Charlie. Olga likes you. You need to do more pushups though. And *sqvats*."

Charlie saluted Olga. "Yes, ma'am."

Olga turned to address Elda. "Olga go in search of biscuits. No messy touchy-feely goodbyes. Olga see you again, you know?"

Elda grabbed Olga and gave her a bear hug.

"Ugh. Olga say none of that!" Olga shook like a dog coming out of a pond, but she had a huge grin on her face. "You be good, Elda. Olga knows what you do." She tapped the side of her nose and whirled to the door. "Olga will take care of everything here. You no worry," she yelled over her shoulder.

Elda chuckled as she wiped her eyes. She turned to Charlie. "Well, Grasshopper, it's just you and me now. Next stop New York City."

Chapter Forty-Four

E LDA TESTED THE EDGE OF HER KNIFE. It was sharp enough for the job at hand. Her phone vibrated. She put down the knife and reached for her pocket.

"What is it?" Charlie whispered.

Elda consulted her cell phone. "It's Ashok. He's discovered an address for Grigory, the desk clerk." She paused, thought a minute, and said, "Park Towers South. Ritzy neighborhood for a desk clerk, even one that works at the Crowne Plaza Times Square Hotel."

"So what's the plan?" Charlie asked.

Elda picked up her knife and fork. "We will finish this delicious dinner. I'm not letting this prime rib go to waste. And those scallops look delicious. Can I grab a forkful?" Elda reached out with her fork before Charlie had time to give permission. "Umm, wonderful. The plan, Grasshopper, is to enjoy the ambiance of this amazing place." Elda looked around at the vibrance inside the Russian Tea Room. The gold of the triple-light sconces and large dark-but-colorful Russian paintings popped from the dark-green walls. The red padded booths and chairs contrasted with the spotless white of the tablecloths. The red-and-black-patterned wall to wall was almost lost in the rest of the room's brilliance. "And to sample their wonderful vodka selection. I am torn between the Russian Standard Platinum and the Beluga Gold. Then we get a good night's sleep and start out fresh in the morning. We had a long flight today."

Charlie and Elda dressed as two businessmen, both sporting short, well-groomed dark beards and mustaches, black suits, and red ties. Elda had dark bushy brows and long eyelashes that made her almost black eyes more intense. Charlie wore a pair of black horn-rimmed glasses.

"But what are we going to do tomorrow?" Charlie set her knife across the edge of her plate.

"We follow him. We need to find out the extent of this guy's involvement with the Kremlin and where the rest of his network is. Then we can decide what to do with him."

Charlie nodded. "Do we continue to use disguises, in case we decide to keep him alive?"

Elda gave her the thumbs-up. "You got it, Grasshopper. Basic black is the color scheme. We need to scope out his apartment. Ashok claims he lives alone." She brought her hand up to flag down a waiter. "A shot of Standard Premium with water on the side for me, and a shot of Beluga Gold for my friend here, also with water on the side."

"But, Elda, I don't drink vodka straight up. It's brutal," Charlie protested.

Elda laughed. "You've been drinking the wrong stuff. Someday you may be working in Moscow. You need to prepare for that."

The vodkas and water came.

"Drink up," Elda instructed. "Take a small sip and savor it to taste the flavor, and then down it."

Charlie shuddered.

Charlie jogged by Grigory without a glance in his direction. She knew Elda was relying on her and was glad of all the hours Elda had trained her to avoid detection. Being the front tail was tricky, requiring hypervigilance and the ability to guess what the target might do. Turning around to check where he was would be a novice error.

Grigory was leaving the Crowne Plaza after his night shift and heading north on Seventh Avenue. He carried a small box. Anticipating his return to his apartment, Charlie took a left onto Fifty-Seventh Street. Grigory continued straight up and into Central Park.

Elda, carrying a backpack, and also in jogging clothes, followed. She spoke softly into her comms. "Grigory entering Central Park."

Damn. She was wrong. Charlie veered right onto Ninth Avenue and entered the park by Columbus Circle, running to intercept his path. She came out behind Elda and Grigory. "Behind you," she whispered.

"Right," Elda acknowledged. "You take the tail. I'm going to veer off to the right and come back in." She picked up her pace and ran right toward the Wollman Rink.

Charlie slowed her pace but passed him at the Central Park Carousel. Once clear, she clicked her comms. "Front tail now, near carousel."

Elda emerged behind them, just north of the carousel. "Got you." She slowed to a walk and blew her nose, letting him pull farther away.

The three of them emerged on East Seventy-Second Street and Fifth Avenue. Charlie zigged off onto East Seventy-Third Street and over to Madison Avenue. Elda followed Grigory. "He's taking a right onto Seventy-Fifth Street, Charlie." Elda went straight on Fifth Avenue.

"Roger that." Charlie sped up and came around the corner in time to see him enter a white-stone facade building with a wrought iron black fence and ornate ornamentation over the doorway. "He just entered a building, Elda." She texted the address to Ashok, adding, FIND INFO ON THIS PLACE.

Elda appeared beside Charlie and bent to tie her shoe.

"How do you do that?" Charlie asked, disgruntled. It would take a while before she matched Elda's skills at this game.

"Not now, Grasshopper," Elda whispered. "Back soon." She ran off.

Charlie started stretching. Ten minutes later a pregnant woman with long walnut-brown tresses and a fat-cheeked pimpled-face waddled up to Charlie and paused with her hands on her belly, to catch her breath. Her ankles were swollen and socks rolled down. She wore black stretchy elastic-waist pants and a flowing maternity blouse.

Charlie was shocked when the woman said in a low tone, "My turn. You change."

Just then Grigory stepped out of the building doorway and headed back in the direction he'd come. He no longer had the box.

"No time for you to change. Make sure you weave a lot, but if I had to place money, I would bet he may be returning home," Elda hypothesized.

Charlie took off again to take up the front tail.

***

Elda met Charlie outside Grigory's Park Towers South apartment building.

Elda had on a black turtleneck, black pants, a black watch cap, black mirrored sunglasses, and black running shoes with black socks. She again had a black mustache and a scraggly beard. Her hair was short.

Charlie gazed at her with an open mouth. "How much does that backpack hold?"

Elda chuckled. "Enough." She handed the pack to Charlie. "You'll find an outfit for you, plus facial hair. I don't have a change of shoes for you, but your runners are black, so they'll do nicely. You can change at the Brooklyn Diner employee bathroom. If anyone hassles you, say Elda sent you. We'll head over there after this for breakfast. I love their freshly squeezed orange juice and scrambled eggs with maple smoked bacon. Now go."

Charlie, shaking her head, ran off with the backpack. She returned dressed in garb similar to Elda's.

"While you were gone, I received a briefing from Ashok. That address Grigory visited is on a terrorist watch list. I don't believe in coincidences. I'm betting he's involved." Elda grabbed the backpack and led Charlie into the building.

Locating Grigory's apartment, Charlie stood lookout while Elda broke in.

"Three locks," Elda said. "But no chains. And there doesn't appear to be any alarm systems." She cracked the locks open in minutes. They closed the door gently behind them and tiptoed their way into Grigory's bedroom, where he lay on his back, his arms over his head, peacefully snoring up a storm.

Elda held one latex covered glove over his mouth and the silenced barrel of a Smith & Wesson to his temple. He started to wake and struggle, but Charlie trapped his hands and zip-tied them together. She flung back his covers, thankful he slept in boxer shorts, and also secured his ankles together. He stopped struggling.

"Now be a good boy and no yelling," Elda instructed, "or I'll have to gag you, and that's pretty unpleasant, so it's best if we wait to do that."

"Who are you? And what do you want? I have money. Take it and leave." His face turned red and blotchy.

"We're not here for money, although we'll probably take that anyway. We're here for information."

"I know nothing," he claimed.

"I doubt that," Elda snapped. "Let's start with what you were doing over on Seventy-Fifth Street."

His eyes widened. Beads of sweat grew on his upper lip. "How do you know that? I can't tell you anything. They will kill me."

Elda handed Charlie her gun and flipped open a cloth case containing a series of scalpels, laying it across Grigory's chest. She snapped her latex gloves at the wrists to call his attention to her medical garb. She donned a white bibbed apron. "This can get rather messy."

Charlie watched in fascination, holding the Smith & Wesson steady, aimed at his forehead.

Sweat broke out on Grigory's forehead. "What is all that?"

"I think you're smart enough to figure it out, Grigory." Elda swiped a hand over her apron. "I will take you apart, piece by piece, until you tell me what I want to know." She brought his hands down to where he could see them and pressed a scalpel into the back of one, enough so that a small bead of blood sprouted next to the blade.

He held still, staring at the blade on his hand. "No, no, I will tell you everything. Just don't cut me up."

Elda kept the scalpel in its place. "Answer the question then, and I will back the blade off. Lie to us, and I press on. We know a lot already, so we will recognize when you are not telling the truth."

"I am currently working as a courier to funnel messages, money, and weapons to a Iranian terrorist cell. They're the ones I visited on Seventy-Fifth Street."

"How do you contact them?" Elda pressed the blade edge a touch.

"Oh god, they are going to kill me," he cried.

"You have an immediate chance of being killed slowly now. Their threat might be baseless."

He sobbed. "They contact me through a gaming app on my computer. When I receive a message, I decode it using a code they gave me, and pick up and bring over whatever they need."

"Well done." Elda wiped the blade with alcohol and put away the scalpel. She used tape to adhere a piece of gauze over the small wound. "You may keep your pieces intact *if* you give us some additional information."

"What? I know nothing more. Please."

"There was an operation with the Russians a while back. You were the night clerk in your current job and instructed to look for two large men, Anatoly and Yuri. You sent them to look for a John Smith and Jane Doe in the pool room. Do you remember that?" Elda asked.

Grigory looked at Elda wide eyed. "Yes, but what does that have to do with the terrorists?"

"Who gave you those instructions?"

He coughed up the goods. "Some Russian called Adrak or Adrick. He spoke in a heavy accent. But he paid well to do that simple thing. I have not heard from him since."

"Watch him," Elda told Charlie. She strode over to Grigory's computer, booted it up, ensured it could connect to the internet, and pushed a thumb drive into the USB slot. She typed a few commands, waited a minute, and then pulled out the thumb drive. "There. Ashok will have a clone of his computer."

Elda returned, placed a large piece of gauze over Grigory's mouth, and secured it with tape, ensuring his nose was free. "Okay. Help me bring him into the kitchen."

The two of them half dragged him to the refrigerator, sat him on the floor in front of it, and zipped his bound hands to the bottom freezer door handle. Elda texted

Ashok, Send the clone of the drive I sent you to Ed's contact at the FBI. Include this address.

"The FBI will treat you much better than your friends on Seventy-Fifth Street," Elda whispered into Grigory's ear. "I would advise you to cooperate with them. Otherwise, I will let the cell members know who ratted on them."

CHAPTER FORTY-FIVE

A GAUNT, WRINKLED OLD BIKER, wearing jeans, Harley boots, a black leather jacket with the American flag on her sleeve, with long, scraggly gray hair, walked into the bar in the Sugar Hill Tavern in Sugar Hill, New Hampshire, accompanied by a younger woman. The other woman wore a silver studded black leather jacket and tight leather pants.

The bartender motioned them to a table and jogged over to get their order. "Passing through, ladies?"

The older, in a smoker's voice, answered, "Yes, sir. Name's Blade. This here's Rebel. Thought we'd stay a couple of nights though. Pretty up here."

"If you're thinking of hanging around, this inn is reasonable this time of year and always neat and clean," the bartender recommended.

"Sounds like a plan," Blade rasped.

Rebel studied her nails. She looked at the bartender and put in her order. "Bud Light please."

The bartender nodded and asked Blade, "You?"

She reached into her pocket and briefly displayed a

gold and blue chip with an *X* in the middle on the table, then restored it to her pocket.

"Cranberry juice and water?" he suggested.

"Yes, thanks," Blade said in a throaty voice.

He strolled to the bar to make their drinks.

Rebel raised an eyebrow at Blade. "Why are we here, Elda?" she whispered.

Blade explained in a low voice. "The intelligence says the driver, Karl, stops here for a drink at four p.m. every day. For your info, he likes cars and bikes. He should notice the flat on your bike and offer you a lift to the local gas station. It's about a twelve-minute ride, so pump him quickly, Charlie."

The bartender brought their drinks and plunked them in front of the women, then returned to the bar.

The clock over the bar struck 4:00 p.m. Right on time, behind Elda, the door opened, and a short, swarthy man with a well-groomed beard and mustache stomped in. Elda saw from the look in Charlie's eyes that their target was there.

"Who owns the dark-blue Harley cruiser?" he eyed Elda and Charlie.

"That would be me," Charlie offered in a gruff voice.

"You got a flat."

"Damn." Charlie ran out to check her bike.

The man sat at the bar, and the bartender put a Bud Light in front of him.

"We'll need to get that repaired. Considering the roads we've been on, I'll bet she'll need a new tire. Is there a Harley dealership nearby?" Elda asked.

The man told her. "No, but Nelson's Auto Repair would be the best." He pointed north. "I can give her"—he indicated Charlie—"a lift there when I'm done here. I'm the local taxi driver."

"Well, we picked the right place to break down." Elda chuckled in a gravelly tone.

"So, local taxi driver, what's your name?" Charlie settled into the passenger seat of the taxi. She was surprised to see it was neat and clean inside.

"Karl." He started the engine.

"Do you have a last name, Karl?" Charlie got bad vibes from this character.

"Karl will do. And you?"

"I go by Rebel." Hoping to obtain the information without spooking him, Charlie asked a simple question, "How long have you lived here, Karl?"

"About ten years."

"Driven taxi all that time?"

He shrugged and sidestepped. "I do odd jobs."

"Odd jobs that pay well, I see." Charlie pointed to the Rolex on his arm.

"You ask a lot of questions." He snarled, glancing at her, then returned his eyes to the road.

"Just like to know who I'm riding with," she retorted. "And I might be interested in picking up some side work myself. Is the work all local to here, or can it be shopped out?"

"This watch and taxi came from a job I did a while back down in Newburyport. Hasn't been much like *that* gig lately. I *can* get you some extra money though."

"That would be handy. What would I have to do?" The hairs on the back of Charlie's neck itched.

"Just relax and lie down and spread your legs."

Charlie heard the doors lock and felt the taxi accelerate. They turned onto a dirt road. *Oh crap. Here it goes.* "That's not exactly the type of work I'm looking for." She hoped Elda was following them and could hear the conversation over the noise of her bike.

He adjusted himself. "I have a couple of friends who

would love to fuck you. Can you handle two at once? Do you like it in the ass?"

Charlie glared at him and said in an icy tone, "Not interested. Shouldn't we be at the gas station by now?"

"There's been a change of plans." He took a sharp left up a driveway.

Karl held Charlie's door open. She slowly exited the taxi and sized the man up. He held a Stichkin Russian pistol.

It was a lousy time to be without a weapon.

Hearing the roar of Elda's Harley Sportster in the distance, Charlie decided to delay him outside. "Look, I'm looking for some decent money, not chump change and *not* by screwing. I figured you were connected, not some two-bit punk. Isn't there someone you can set me up with?"

Elda stopped her bike in a spray of gravel and hopped off. She quickly sized up the situation and approached the two of them.

Karl aimed his weapon at Elda and instructed Charlie, "Great, your mom's here. We don't want to screw an old broad. Tell her to leave, or I'll get rid of her another way."

Charlie grinned to herself. This man would eat those words about Elda. *Watch and learn, little man.*

Elda held up her hands and stepped to her left, increasing the distance between her and Charlie and edging closer to Karl. Charlie nodded to show Elda she understood the plan.

Charlie coughed, and Karl swiveled the gun in her direction.

Elda twirled on one leg and connected her other foot right into his groin. He dropped his weapon and doubled over, and Elda's combined fists came down on his back, driving him to the ground.

Charlie picked up his pistol and knelt, with one knee in Karl's back and the gun to his head. "Who was your

Russian contact in Newburyport?"

"It-t-t w-w-was a long time ago. I don't remember," he stuttered, his cheek in the gravel.

Elda tugged on latex gloves, pulled his cell phone from his back pants pocket, and scrolled through his contacts list. She brought up an app on her cell and cloned his contacts list. She went into the kitchen and came back with a sharp carving knife.

She held his hand down and splayed his fingers apart. She toyed with his pinky with the point. "Perhaps I can make you remember?" With slight pressure, she drew the blade across his little finger, and a line of blood arose.

He gulped.

"I'd like your Gmail username and password too, please." She stuck the point of the knife into his hand, and a bead of blood bubbled up aside it.

"W-w-w-wait!" he stuttered. "It was a funny name. Started with an *A*."

Charlie started to open her mouth, when Elda barked, "Don't shoot. Let him tell us."

Charlie frowned and cocked her head at Elda.

Elda pressed the blade farther in. Charlie clicked a new magazine into her gun.

"Don't shoot!" he shouted. "Adrik. His name was Adrik."

"And your Gmail account?" Elda wiggled the knife.

"NHKarl1234 is my username. My password is Karls-password1234."

"Good boy." Elda texted the account information to Ashok, then added, GRAB THIS INFO FOR US TO SORT THROUGH LATER.

"And your friends? What are their names?"

He hesitated, only to be rewarded by a blade at his throat. "Baranan and Kazamir. I don't know their last names. They are visiting from Russia."

"But you do have their numbers, don't you?" Elda intuited.

He gasped out an affirmative.

"Write their names down, complete with telephone numbers." She placed a pen in his hand and helped guide it as he wrote. She took a snap of that and messaged it to Ashok.

"Good boy." Elda captured his wrists and zip-tied them behind his back. To Charlie she directed, "Holster the gun and help me drag him to the bedroom."

They splayed him facedown in the bedroom, with his hands secured to the center rail of the metal headboard and his feet tied apart to either side of the bed.

Elda found a dildo and lube sitting ready next to the bed. "So who was this for?" She bent over and thrust the rubber toy in his face.

He leered. "Girls. It's always good to fuck in the ass and the cunt at the same time and hear the shrill rise of passion in the bitch's voice. You would have loved it, Rebel."

Elda gnashed her teeth and grabbed her knife, cut the back of his pants and underwear, greased up the object, and shoved into his ass.

He screamed.

"You're right. You sound like a satisfied customer." Elda took a picture. "Tell anyone about this, and your ass will be front page on the *Caledonian Record*."

Meanwhile, Charlie located his laptop sitting on the bureau. She stashed it under her arm. "Ready?"

Elda nodded in satisfaction. "Good. Let's take that, plus his cell phone, watch, and his wallet. Always make it look like a robbery."

Elda dropped the paper with the names on it on the table, face up, dropped a fake FBI badge next to it, and snapped a photograph. She pocketed the badge, located his network, and using the same password he had given her for Gmail, logged on and printed both photos, leaving them on the table. "Let's see how loving and close these *friends* of his are."

Chapter Forty-Six

Elda and Charlie barged into Ed's office unannounced.

"Gads, doesn't anyone ever knock?" Ed threw papers into the hoop over his wastebasket, missing half of them. "You're back. Were you successful?"

"Yes. More to do, but that phase is done," Elda informed him as she tidied up the area around his wastebasket, throwing the papers in from different angles.

Ed snorted. "Show-off. Are you still dead, or would you like a job?"

"Depends on what it is." Elda plopped down onto one of the more comfortable office chairs and spun around in it a full 360, stopping to give Ed her focus. Charlie perched on the corner of his desk.

"I have no control anymore," Ed bemoaned.

"Did you ever?" Elda quipped. "So what do you have, Ed?"

"It's come to the president's attention that we need a covert group empowered to go after these threats to the United States, both abroad and within our borders."

"And . . ." Elda prompted,

"I've funding for this team. It will report to me but won't be hampered by the rules that I, and the rest of my organization, have to follow."

Elda encouraged Ed to finish giving the full story. "And . . ."

"You've probably figured this out by now, Elda, but I would like for you to head this up. I will give you Charlie and Ashok and enough money to build a small org and outfit them. I've also located a black site you can use for headquarters here in DC. It will need some renovations."

"Hot damn." Charlie jumped off the desk and pumped her fists in the air.

"Completely black ops, off the books, no records to the president, no congressional oversight," Ed added.

"How long do I have to think about it?" Elda smiled at Ed with sparkling eyes.

Ed looked back at Elda with a huge grin. "I think I know your answer."

Elda popped up and strode to his door. She turned back. "See you in a couple of weeks. You too, Charlie. Take a vacation and come back here ready to rock and roll."

Vee's bark rang out over the water in the small cove. Elda climbed up the hill from the driveway and was nearly bowled over by her small dog. She bent and hefted up the squiggling body and received licks on her hands and her face. She snuggled into the little one and breathed in the Frito smell of her little paws.

Korinna and Egor peeked out the front door. Elda ran to hug them. Vee squirmed and licked faces during the group hug.

"What are you guys doing here?" Elda basked in the

fresh air and friendship that surrounded her.

Korinna wiped her hands on her apron and then removed it. "Jim told us you'd be back today, so we came to finish setting up the house and brought some supper."

Egor held up a clay bottle of Georgian wine in one hand and a prime rib steak in the other.

Elda put Vee down and clapped. "You're speaking my language. Throw that beauty on the grill, and I'll be right back."

Vee followed Elda upstairs. Elda reached into the closet and unlocked the floor safe. She unloaded her weapon and placed it and the ammo into the safe. Standing, she was aware no traces of Dawn remained and the bedroom was rearranged. She jogged back down the stairs and hugged Korinna. "I love you guys."

Korinna winked at her.

Egor put down three shot glasses on the deck table and poured hefty dollops of triple distilled vodka. "To a new future."

"Yes, to a new future." Elda gazed out over the cove, watching the tide come in, and wondered what it was bringing with it.